Scream Blue Murder

Tony J Forder

Also By Tony J Forder

Bad To The Bone

Degrees of Darkness

Praise For Scream Blue Murder

"Forder didn't spare the horses when writing Scream Blue Murder. This book rockets along, a breathless action-packed ride. Perfect reading for fans of Simon Kernick and Jeff Abbott."
Matt Hilton, author of the Joe Hunter thrillers.

"An action packed, twisty thriller. Great stuff."
Mason Cross, author of the Carter Blake series of thrillers.

Praise For Tony J Forder

'The book is well written gripping and gets right into your mind and feelings as you are taken on a fast paced journey through a book it is impossible to put down.'
Jill Burkinshaw - Books n All

'Degrees of Darkness is an engrossing and haunting thriller!'
Caroline Vincent - Bits About Books

'This is an awesome read that for me that put it on a scare factor alongside Stephen King and Thomas Harris. The heart breaking opening will make most readers just stand back and take a breath.'
Susan Hampson - Books From Dusk Till Dawn

'From start to finish I felt I was reading this in the edge of my seat while holding my breath. It really is that kinda read.'
Philomena Callan - Cheekypee Reads And Reviews

'I read the book in one sitting and was completely enthralled in the story!'
Donna Maguire - Donnas Book Blog

For my father

PROLOGUE

The bearded man bound Luna Novak's hands and feet with rough cord, before tearing off a six-inch section of adhesive tape from a roll and placing it over her mouth. The twenty-four-year-old complied meekly and kept still for two reasons while he did this: first, the vicious slap he had planted on her cheek moments before, which had left her face throbbing; the second being the gun he had taken care to show her at the front door when he first revealed himself not to be the plumber she had been expecting. When he was done with her, Luna looked on tearfully as he moved across the room towards Jack, who was sitting on the floor in front of the massive TV screen.

Jack was a typical seven-year-old, and when he was riveted to one of his favourite shows he was oblivious to anything and everything happening around him. Certainly, he had taken little notice of the two men wearing plain blue overalls who had entered his home a few minutes earlier. The bearded man now stood over Jack, whilst the other propped himself up in the doorway and filmed everything on his phone. The bearded man glanced back at Luna, and though she could not talk, her red and swollen eyes pleaded with him for mercy as she started to wriggle and fight against her bonds. He smiled for a moment, shook his head and put a finger to his lips. Then he raised the pistol, aimed it at the back of Jack's head, and squeezed the trigger.

***

Georgina Ferris was immediately drawn to the man who announced himself at her desk as Vincent Riley. His appointment was in her Outlook calendar, but other than the fact that he was looking to rent a safe deposit box, she knew precious little else about the man. Regarding him closely now, she saw that he was tall and slim, immaculately dressed in a three-piece navy-blue suit, beneath which he appeared trim and toned. He looked like the sort of man for whom the term "ruggedly handsome" may have been coined.

Slightly flustered by her reaction to the potential client, the vault manager nonetheless succeeded in remaining a consummate professional. Her smile was formal, eye-contact nothing more than perfunctory.

"Welcome, Mr Riley," Georgina said, shaking the man's hand. His grip – as expected – was both warm and firm. "Have you come far today?"

"Not at all," he replied. His own smile was equally qualified.

"I understand you're wanting to take a look at our safe deposit vault today, with a view to renting out a unit."

"That's correct. I'm thinking of an extra-large, but I want to see for myself how secure it will be."

Georgina nodded. "Absolutely. You understand that we can go only so far, that I can't let you into the main vault itself until you have actually been vetted and rented a box. However, from the outer ring you can see into the area that contains our most secure safes."

"That will be fine," he said.

"Good. In that case, I'll show you down right now."

It was just a single flight down, but Georgina chose to take the lift. Part of her wondered whether she was excited to be in close proximity to the man. In the small enclosure, his scent was light and citrus-based. Her mind unspooled a scenario where she forced him against the door and licked his face. As the door slid open, Georgina felt a flush creep into her cheeks.

The man walked by her side as they moved along a narrow passageway. He said nothing as she let him through the first of two heavy doors, tapping a password into a wall-mounted entry system each time. The second allowed them access into a circular chamber, three sides of which contained steel-rod doors. Georgina walked across to the one on her left, and gestured with her hand.

"Keycodes got me here, but from this point biometric identification is required in order to access the vaults themselves. As you can see, beyond this barrier there is a vault door. That door is 300 centimetres thick, with five securing deadbolts each the size of your fist. Beyond that are the boxes themselves. Honestly, you won't get anything more secure in the whole of London, Mr Riley."

He nodded, seeming to appraise his surroundings. "What about box keys?" he asked.

"Only two are ever made for each box. One of them is a master, the other unique, so both are required in order to open the safes. You would retain one, and we retain the other."

"How secure is your master key?" he asked.

She smiled. "It is also stored in its own safe overnight. When not secured in there, it is on my person at all times."

"Good. That's exactly what I wanted to hear." He dipped a hand inside his jacket and withdrew a slim mobile phone from the pocket. "Mrs Ferris, please take a look at this, would you."

He turned the screen towards her and pressed a large arrow in the centre. As she focussed on it a video began to play. Georgina had heard of blood turning to ice in the veins but had never considered that possible. Right now, it did not seem so far-fetched.

On the man's phone screen was her seven-year-old son, who sat on the floor watching TV in their own living room. The camera swept across the room to reveal her child minder, whose mouth was covered in what looked like grey duct tape, hands fastened together by thick cord. Georgina's eyes shifted from the phone to Vincent Riley, though already she was reasonably certain that would prove not to be his real name.

"Keep watching the phone," he said.

This time the screen revealed a figure, its back to the phone, looming over Georgina's son. She sensed the figure was a man, but could not see his face. Instead, her eyes were locked upon the gun he held in his right hand. Her mouth fell open, her eyes widened and she started to shake. As Georgina started to speak, the figure squeezed the pistol's trigger.

Water squirted from the barrel and sprayed Georgina's son. He jumped up with a howl of anguish, which paled into comparison with Georgina's own.

"Next time it won't be water," the man standing by her side told her. "Do as you're told and he won't be hurt."

Georgina had always known that she would do anything asked of her in order to protect her little boy. She had simply never believed she would ever be put to the test.

ONE

I was a man on a mission: what should have been a simple undertaking to reach home after a long, arduous, and ultimately fruitless journey from one side of the country to the other and back again. It had been one of those days, though. One that starts out bad and slides on downhill from there. At the moment, I saw no way to arrest its decline.

A five-hour drive on a business trip had led to no reward. A stale turkey and ham sandwich my only nourishment all day long. Some mindless prick had keyed my Saab's rear offside door while it was in the car park. Then I discovered a flat tyre, which had me changing it in full view of the glassy offices of the company who had just rejected me. I had the damn wheel off before I discovered that my spare was also flat. It took the RAC almost ninety minutes to reach me, and a further twenty passed before I managed to get back on the road. And then fifteen minutes ago the tailback resulting from an accident on a northbound stretch of the M5 motorway had forced me to divert to unfamiliar roads. If the rules governing the apportioning of luck were holding true, right now some fortunate arsehole was writhing on a bed covered with fifty-pound notes from his lottery win and getting his balls polished by the tongue of a supermodel.

I shook my head at the thought of my misfortune, wearied by it all. Beyond the twin cones of the Saab's headlights, the road ahead was impenetrably black. Lightning flared over the looming ridges of surrounding hillsides, cutting through the dark wall of night. Outside the car, the air was heavy, thick with moisture, swollen clouds a precursor to a fierce summer storm that had been brewing for several days. Inside the Saab, climate control blew a cool breath over my face.

I stretched out a yawn and blinked rapidly. Told myself to stay the hell awake. I had tried the radio, moved on to the CD player. Sound alone wasn't cutting it. I had powered down my window, but the road noise irritated the shit out of me. I'd even tried singing to myself, but my tuneless voice grated.

Nothing worked.

I was starting to feel numb with exhaustion. Although all I really wanted to do right now was keep on going until I reached home, pulling off the road and taking a break seemed like a better idea than falling asleep at the wheel.

A couple of minutes later, a sign showing a white P on a blue background told me the next lay-by was half a mile in the distance. Almost immediately, drops of rain squelched against the Saab's windscreen. Thin at first, getting thicker and heavier within seconds. From spit to splat in the blink of an eye.

"Damn it!" I said, slamming my palm against the black leather steering wheel.

Slowing to a crawl, I eased the car off the road and into the lay-by, tyres crunching and jolting over a gravelled, uneven surface. A small pothole tested the Saab's suspension. I parked up by an overflowing green waste bin and killed the engine and lights, letting go a long sigh of relief and frustration. I rolled my shoulders and neck, which were stiff with tension. Flexing my fingers, I reflected that although I enjoy driving, long journeys could be a real chore.

Peering out through the windscreen, I saw only the night lurking close by, with not even the distant sodium glow of a town to offer any comfort. *So, this is where the misshapen freaks come sneaking down from the hillside,* I thought, *and either hack me to pieces or feast on my bones. Or both, if they are in a bad mood.* By pulling over I had perhaps saved myself from pulping my flesh and bones in a car wreck, but the soul-sucking Reaper would probably only consider that a postponement of the inevitable.

"Jesus, Mike" I muttered to myself. "You're such a cheery soul. Are you available for children's parties, too?"

I dismissed the negative imagery from that train of thought. Without the Saab's muscular growl in the background, I listened to the rain hammer down on the roof, and lash in slanting sheets against the windscreen. Ordinarily it was a sound I enjoyed. Not this time, however. This time it was yet another in a long stream of annoyances.

I am an angry man. Or at least, had become so of late. I knew why. Drinking was a hard way to live a life, but not drinking was so much harder still. Alcohol wasn't the illness, rather the cure for one.

Or so I had thought at the time.

And a drink was what I wanted more than anything else in the world right now. There was nothing available in the car, and I hoped I would not have touched it even if there were. To help me remain that way I whispered some of the positive thoughts I had been taught: *You are not perfect. You must take one day at a time. You need to do the next right thing.*

It helped. Most of the time.

Lightning speared down from a crack in the sky once more. There seemed little chance of my getting any sleep, but I figured maybe just resting up for an hour or so would be enough respite to enable me to continue in a more positive frame of mind. I checked the dash clock. It was 1.23 am and I still had a three-hour drive or more ahead of me.

No way was I spending the whole night here in the middle of nowhere.

No way would I make it home without rest, either.

Lose–lose.

Typical.

I snapped off my seatbelt, powered back the grey leather seat and settled down into its familiar hollows. I stretched my legs out as far as the footwell would allow. If I had to stop here for a while, I figured I might as well be comfortable. Given all I had endured, I reckon I'd earned it.

My mobile phone was in its docking unit, attached to the dashboard with a rubber suction cup. I reached across to press a speed-dial number. The familiar United States single ringtone sounded three times before the call was connected.

"Hi, Dad."

"Hi, kiddo. What you up to?"

"Not much. Hanging, watching some TV before dinner. You?"

I chuckled mirthlessly. "Wendy, if I told you it had been a shit day, in a week of shit days, in a month of shit weeks, would you believe me?"

"Yes, Dad. Because that's what you always say."

She laughed, which made me smile despite my mood.

The long-haul west had taken me to an initial briefing. This was followed by an anxious four hours waiting for a call-back. And finally, a thirty-minute evening meeting, during which I was made to feel extremely small and even more insignificant by a female personnel director whose demeanour was frigid right from the initial icy handshake. She casually let it be known that one of her peers had coerced her into the meeting, despite her busy schedule and the late hour. Also, that she already had a preference for the contract, and nothing less than an outbreak of plague was going to sway her in a different direction.

I related this entire tale of woe to my daughter.

"What a bitch!" Wendy said.

"I know. Right?"

"Did you hit her, dad?"

"I don't hit women. Ask your mum. No, I simply sat there seething, remaining professional and dignified on the outside."

"Really? You?"

"I did. You would have been proud of me, kiddo. Of course, what I actually wanted to do was reach over the glass table and rip out her tongue."

Again the laughter. "So, you wouldn't hit her, but tearing out her tongue is acceptable behaviour?"

"I said I wanted to. I didn't say I would do it."

What I had done instead was sit and nod and smile and attempt to talk myself up – something I am not big on. It wasn't rocket science – it was a contract to design a whole assortment of packaging, documentation and advertising material connected with a new range of products. A big deal to me and my bank balance, but a drop in the ocean to a chemicals conglomerate.

"So you won't be getting the contract then?" my daughter asked.

"Not a chance. Anyhow, let's talk about something different."

Wendy spent a few minutes telling me all about visiting the beach, shopping trips with her mother, a drive out to check on a new boat her step-father was considering buying. Every second word was "awesome".

When we were done, I thought back to the meeting. Sure, the ice maiden told me she'd consider my proposal and would get back to me by the end of the week, but I knew I wasn't getting the work. So, emerging from the soul-sucking corporate building to find my car vandalised and sitting on a flat had pretty much put the seal on my foul mood for another day. And then the accident diversion, which meant I couldn't pull over into the next rest stop for a meal, a hot drink, and some much-needed downtime.

Instead I was here. In Nowheresville.

I shook my head. All I seemed to do with my life lately was dash from one place to another, without ever seeming to get very far. Now, at last, I was still, going nowhere for the time being, and I felt the tension in my shoulders and neck start to ease. I began to feel comfortable and at peace for the first time in as long as I could remember.

Or at least would have, only now I needed to take a piss.

Right then, as if Mother Nature sensed my sudden discomfort, the rain started to beat down harder still. I swore, but knew right away that I had no option; my bladder would give out on me if I tried to hang on too long.

"Fuck it!" I cried again, then sat up with a jolt and hurled myself out of the car in a flurry of furious movement.

I had no overcoat with me, so I snatched my suit jacket off the back seat and pulled it on, yanking the collar up around my neck and fastening one button. My best Italian-styled suit bore the brunt of the downpour as I dashed up a rise of heaped soil, then down again the other side into a shallow ditch. I tucked myself behind a clutch of wild hedgerow and unzipped. It took several seconds for the first dribble of urine to appear, prolonging my exposure to the elements. Eventually, a steady stream followed like it would never end.

The downpour was so heavy now it hurt my unprotected head and stung my face. Needles of rain jabbed at my skin like wasp stings. I turned slightly so I wouldn't end up pissing against the wind. Regretting the numerous glasses of water I had put away during the day, I mouthed a few more obscenities into the night air and willed my bladder to empty itself before old age simply took away my will to live.

It was as I stood there shaking myself dry that my attention was snagged by lights appearing behind me, rising up from beyond the mound. Moments later, more lights. Barely seconds afterwards I heard what I thought was a sharp snap of thunder way off in the distance. What I saw in the lay-by as I emerged from behind the bushes and climbed back up the dirty embankment, however, caused my flesh to tighten on its framework of bone and muscle.

A silver BMW stood with its exhaust pumping fumes into the moist warm air, the driver's door hanging wide open, pillar lights illuminating the vehicle's interior and adding to the confusion of light and shadow. Several feet away from the car, a man was on his knees by the edge of a pothole, both hands clutching the pit of his back. I could see the man's face only from the side, but it looked blighted by pain as raindrops splashed against the creased folds of flesh.

As I stared at him, unable to truly comprehend what I was seeing, a loud crack shattered the dark night once more. The kneeling man was thrown forward onto his face.

That was when I noticed a second figure.

A man who stood just feet away from the other.

A man who held a gun in both hands.

TWO

The tall and wide figure stood towards the rear of a dark Ford Mondeo saloon. The gun bucked in his outstretched arms, the shot rang out, and the man on the ground twisted sideways and fell still.

I let out a strangled sound that was more yelp than cry, and the gunman snapped his head around in my direction. The man's arms quickly followed, and lightning seemed to erupt from his hands. I felt something whistle past my head at the same time as another gunshot reverberated around the hillside.

There was little time for me to weigh up my options. My eyes captured the entire scene in an instant, and I immediately realised there was no chance that I could run for my own car. The gunman stood closer to it, and would drop me in a heartbeat before I even reached the door.

The thought of another bullet coming my way galvanised both my mind and body, and the next thing I knew my legs and arms were pumping. I sped down the mound of loose soil, raced across to the BMW, dived into the driver's seat, released the handbrake, slipped the automatic gearbox into drive, and then stamped on the accelerator. As the car jerked away, spinning tyres spewing loose gravel in its wake, I glanced into the rear-view mirror and saw the gunman's face bathed in a glow from the BMW's rear lights.

It looked as if he had been dipped in blood.

Only when the car hit the tarmac surface of the road was I able to yank the flapping door shut. As I straightened, a shudder ripped through my entire body. Shock started to numb my system and close it down. At the same time, adrenaline pushed through it. I waited for equilibrium to kick back in. As it always had before.

It felt like only seconds had passed before headlights ensnared me from behind. I knew deep inside the place where dread lives that it was the gunman. I ran a quick calculation through my head. The big German car would probably outrun the Ford, and that could only be a positive thing right now.

As I drove, my eyes continued to flick between the road ahead and the road behind. I felt a prickle slowly crawl across my scalp every time I saw the following headlights.

What the hell had I stumbled into?

Had I actually just witnessed a murder?

It was impossible, yet it had happened.

Right in front of my eyes.

That poor man. Lying back there in the pouring rain, perhaps bleeding to death as I had fled the scene. I felt a rising surge of guilt, lying hot and heavy in my chest. I wasn't sure what else I could have done. I was unarmed. And the shooter, the man now chasing me down, was clearly intent on leaving no witnesses.

I fumbled with the stalks emerging from the steering wheel, unfamiliar with the layout of the BMW's controls. I located the one for the lights, and flicked them on to full beam. I was hammering along at more than eighty now, the car's fat tyres sticking to the slippery road surface even as they hit bends that were too severe for the speed. I checked the door mirror this time. The Mondeo wasn't gaining, but neither was it being left behind. Absurdly, the stark image of a warning sticker that door mirrors used to carry, filled my mind: *Vehicles May Be Closer Than They Appear.*

I put my foot down harder.

At first all I hoped for was to see the lights of other cars travelling on this same stretch of road. Then I gave that some more thought. I couldn't possibly predict what the madman behind me would do even with other people around. The kind of man who could murder someone in cold blood the way he had back there in the lay-by was probably not the kind to leave further witnesses alive, no matter how many bodies ended up in the morgue. I decided that the first chance I got I was going to call the police.

Then it hit me.

I cursed, remembering that I had left my mobile in its docking device on the Saab's dashboard.

I swore again.

Now I couldn't even call for help. Not for myself. Not for anybody else who became involved.

One more glance in the mirror told me the chase wasn't ending any time soon.

I was unfamiliar with the area, though I knew I had long since passed Uffculme. If I could negotiate the twisting road and terrain, I was pretty sure I would ultimately reach the A303, which was a road I at least knew would lead to a larger town. Once I managed to get myself on something other than a serpentine country route, I thought I could probably outrun the twisted killer in the Ford. For now, though, all I could do was hope to maintain or even increase the distance between myself and my pursuer.

I felt myself starting to sweat, beads of perspiration trickling down from my hairline, echoing the runnels of rainwater being constantly batted away from the windscreen by squeaking wipers. I took my eyes off the road long enough to scan the vehicle's interior.

No mobile phone.

Another check behind in the mirror. The Mondeo had dropped back slightly, but even though I felt increasingly uncomfortable driving on a slick road at this kind of speed, the thought of what the man chasing me would do if he managed to catch up and nudge the BMW off the road and down into a ditch, kept my right foot jammed on the accelerator.

"You thought you were having a bad day before, Mike," I muttered to myself. "You never knew what bad luck was until this very moment."

Passing narrow turnings and dirt tracks to my left and right, but having no clue where they led, I was initially reluctant to take any of them in case they petered out or took me in circles. Seeing another side road flash by in a blur gave me an idea, and for the next few minutes I took more notice of signs than I had before, squinting ahead as far as the twin beams would allow. I had gone about another mile when I saw my opportunity.

Rounding a sharp bend, I first killed the lights, then drove my foot down onto the brake, and hurled the car into a turning on the left. The rear end of the long vehicle swung out, and for a moment I thought I had overcooked it. My hands were a flurry of movement on the steering wheel as I imagined the big BMW flipping over. But the SUV righted itself, clipping a hedge as it straightened. Twenty yards or so further off the main road I yanked on the handbrake and sat there watching my mirrors.

Scarcely moments later I saw the Ford flash by.

Immediately, allowing no time to overthink the situation or my decision, I performed a rapid three-point turn, sneaked back to the road and turned right, heading back along the way I had come. The road behind me was now dark. It wouldn't take long for the gunman to realise what had happened, but I was banking on the man turning around and then taking the road I had first driven into.

I throttled back on the engine as much as I dared. If I carried on in this direction, I would go past the scene of the shooting, eventually reaching the motorway again, but I didn't want to get caught in any snarl-ups caused by the accident. The turn I had seen earlier came up on my left and I took it without any hesitation. I was doing less than forty now, finding it impossible to drive faster without lights to guide my way. The road ahead split into a fork, so I took the one on the left and then snapped on the side lights. As a plan to evade capture, it sucked. I simply had no other ideas.

If the man in the Ford had done as I hoped, our two vehicles would now be headed in opposite directions. Every few seconds, my eyes sought comfort in the car's mirrors. Still there was no sign that I was being followed. I pushed the BMW up to fifty and nursed it through unfamiliar curves, figuring if there was anything coming the other way I would see its lights long before any potential collision.

A couple of buildings slipped by. A tiny hamlet of sorts. If they were homes then everyone was no doubt asleep and minding their own business. I guessed these were places that may have found a spot on the map, but their size hardly deserved a name, let alone a mention. Briefly I considered stopping at one of the dwellings and asking to use a phone to contact the police, but that would rely on finding someone not only prepared to open their door to a stranger in the dead of night, but also to allow that stranger to enter their home.

Unlikely, I decided.

Not a chance worth wasting precious time on.

On a fairly straight section of road, with a minor bend ahead in the distance, I glanced in my mirror yet again and saw only darkness. I felt a sharp pain in my chest, so breathed a huge sigh of relief. Attempting to vent everything that had happened in that single breath. But when I switched my eyes back to the road ahead, there were headlights coming straight towards me.

For a second, I was euphoric. I would stop and wave the vehicle down, ask if the driver had a mobile and if so whether they would allow me use of it in such a dire emergency, or at the very least make a call to the police on my behalf. It would all be over soon after that.

But what if it's the gunman?

The last remaining sensible and practical part of me posed the question. And there was no running away from it after that. What if the man in the Ford Mondeo had not done as I had hoped? What if the killer had worked out my hurried and ill-conceived plan, and figured out a way to get ahead and confront me head on?

The car was much closer now. I couldn't risk stopping, but I batted away any other fears. If it was the gunman, he would probably position his car to block the road. I considered what I would do if that occurred. I could ram the Beemer in reverse, but then the advantage would be with the other vehicle. The lights grew bigger and brighter in the windscreen. There was only one thing for it: I had to maintain the advantage at all costs. Rather than slow down in the narrow road, I stood on the accelerator, flicked the headlights on to full beam and gripped the wheel as tight as possible.

As I sped past the other vehicle, the driver leaned on his horn. As we drew alongside each other, I saw an irate face glaring out of the side window of a small truck. It wasn't a Ford, wasn't the gunman, and all I had succeeded in doing was to anger a local by blinding him with my lights. It was a chance lost, but I decided I could live with that. The very worst thing had not happened, and that's all that mattered. For a few seconds, I watched the other car disappearing into the night. I debated turning around and heading after it, try to get the driver to stop, tell him what had happened? It might be the right thing to do, but turning around meant heading back the way I had come.

Back towards the Ford.

Back towards the Ford driver.

I sucked in some oxygen and eased the pressure off the pedal. I felt my heart beating so rapidly I thought I might run out of blood to pump through it. This was crazy. Abso-fucking-lutely insane.

I drove for a further twenty minutes, turning this way and that, a random pattern no one could follow. At least I hoped not.

Finally, I decided I'd had enough. I had no idea where I was or where I was going. I figured the BMW would have an on-board satnav, but had no idea how to bring it up and use it. By now the storm had lessened to a dull roar, rain more of an irritant than a force to be reckoned with. My hands felt slick on the steering wheel. My head ached. My mind was ringing with too many disparate thoughts. I was going into meltdown.

I could drive no further.

Up ahead I saw what appeared to be a more industrial group of buildings. By the time I reached them, I decided this was the place to stop. I slowed down and pulled across the road, bumping onto a forecourt. It was a garage, but one that hadn't sold any petrol for a decade or so if the tattered price stickers were anything to go by. Beyond the immediate building was a narrow, rutted track that led to a hangar-like shed. I bounced the BMW down the track and around the back of the garage. Another, smaller shed stood leaning crookedly, hardly any roof to speak of and no door. I nodded to myself, swung the car around and reversed into the corrugated steel unit. If the murdering bastard found me now then he probably deserved to.

Having killed the engine and lights, I closed my eyes and put my hands down by my sides. I felt a tremor rattle through my body from neck to toes, and for a moment I thought I might vomit. Pain expanded behind my eyes, and a bright light went off inside my head like a distress flare. I heard myself whimpering; a low, childlike noise that sounded like an animal in pain or misery or both. I felt ashamed, and shocked by it.

Only then I realised that the sound was not coming from my own throat at all, but instead from the back of the car.

Inside the back of the car.

Hardly daring to think about what it might mean, I shifted sideways in the seat and looked back over my shoulder, down into the space behind the passenger seat.

A pair of eyes looked back at me.

THREE

It was one of those rare moments in life when the shock is so unrefined, so intense, that I thought I might have literally evacuated my mortal body and was now observing myself from a safe distance. Hearing that terrible sound and turning to see those eyes staring back at me out of the dark had all but stilled my heart. I was caught in the depths of a mute panic that threatened to overwhelm me.

Which then ratcheted up a further notch when a second pair of eyes winked into existence from out of the gloom.

As my vision grew accustomed to the light – what there was of it – I began to assemble shapes out of the dark mass that lay like a nocturnal creature lurking in the stillness. A head swam into view, followed swiftly by another. I hadn't blinked since our eyes first met. Neither had theirs. I couldn't recall having taken a breath since, either. It all felt wedged inside my chest. An expanding balloon on the point of exploding.

"Don't scream," I said. "Please don't scream."

Eyes adjusting all the while, I could now make out a woman and a young girl, both lying sprawled in the footwell between the front and rear seats. The whimpering was coming from the child, the sound stifled by a hand clamped tight across her mouth.

"Did you see what happened back there?" I asked. A trickle of cold sweat leaked from my scalp.

The woman nodded.

"Was that…" my eyes dropped to the little girl, then flicked back up. "Is this your husband's car?"

The woman pulled herself slightly more upright, bringing the child with her. Clutching the girl tight to her chest. This time she shook her head. Slowly. Her eyes still not leaving mine when she spoke.

"No. My boss. Charlie's father."

"Charlie?"

"Charlotte." She pulled the small girl closer – if that were possible – giving her a squeeze. "She didn't see… anything."

I instantly understood. The kid had not witnessed her father being gunned down and I was being told not to talk about it in front of her. I saw it again inside my head, though. A stark re-run every bit as clear and defined as the original.

"Who… who are you?" The woman asked. "What do you want with us?"

For a brief moment, I failed to understand what she meant. Then it occurred to me that she might not have seen everything that had taken place back at the lay-by, and may now be wondering exactly where this man who had raced off with the car fitted in. It was even possible that she believed I was part of it, that I had abducted the two of them.

Again, I glanced at the child. Her eyes were large and round, unblinking, more curious than fearful.

"My name is Lynch," I told them, raising a tentative smile at both. "Mike Lynch. And believe me, I want nothing from either of you. I know as much as you do about what happened back there. Probably less. I'd pulled off the road because I was tired, and honestly I was just minding my own business when it all kicked off."

"Why were you outside in the rain?"

It was a fair question.

"I'd got out of my own motor to take a… I needed to go to the toilet. I heard a sharp crack that even then I think I knew wasn't thunder, came back to the lay-by and…" I finished with a shrug. She knew the rest.

Her eyes bore holes into mine. I saw a deep mistrust there; both suspicion and fear. I could hardly blame her. For a few seconds neither of us spoke, then I asked for her name.

"Melissa," she replied. She offered no surname. "Where are we?"

"I have absolutely no idea. I drove around until I thought I'd lost whoever was behind us."

The woman stared at me for several seconds, and then seemed to come to a decision. She looked down at the girl. "Charlie, when I take my hand away from your mouth I don't want you to scream or cry out. Do you understand me?"

The girl nodded, her gaze never leaving my face.

"I mean it, Charlie. I will be very angry with you if you disobey me." Her accent was northern, I thought. Lancashire, perhaps.

As the sound of her voice died away she removed her hand. I felt tension grip my shoulders, but the kid did as she had been told. "Good girl," Melissa told her. "I'm proud of you." She ran her fingers through the kid's long fair hair.

The child looked up at her. "Where's daddy?" she asked. Her voice was soft and sweet. I still couldn't see her clearly, certainly not enough to appraise her features, but she sounded so much like my own daughter when she was a kid that I felt a swift jab of recognition.

"Daddy had to go somewhere," Melissa said. The casual way she spoke suggested this might be something the kid was used to.

"But why? And why did you pull me out of my seat and keep me on the floor?"

Melissa smiled and rubbed her nose against the girl's. "I was just playing, silly. I'm sorry if I frightened you, Charlie. It was a game, that's all."

I knew children to be a lot smarter than they were given credit for, but at this girl's age they still trust adults implicitly. Her look suggested disapproval, but then she turned her attention to me once again. "Are you my daddy's friend?"

"This is your daddy's new driver," Melissa said quickly, shooting me a look.

"That's me." I flashed the fake grin one more time.

"Where's Roger?"

I looked to Melissa for a way out. She provided it. "Roger is still unwell, sweetheart. That's why Daddy drove today, remember?"

"I like Roger."

Melissa laughed. "And I like him, too."

She glanced at me as if expecting me to join in and inject a little humour for the kid's sake. I wasn't ready for that. I just wanted out of whatever mess I had blundered into.

"I want to go home," the kid said, echoing my own thoughts. She turned to the woman. "I don't like it here." Then she let out a long, wide yawn.

"Me neither." Melissa's eyes found mine. "How about it, Mr Lynch? Shall we get out of here?"

"I'm not at all sure we should be going anywhere right now. There are some dangerous drivers on the road tonight, if you catch my drift."

"I realise that. But I also know that Charlie is very tired and needs her bed, plus looking at this place I'm not sure it would be good to be found here by one of those dangerous drivers you mentioned."

I nodded. Then a thought occurred. "Do you have a phone on you?" I asked her.

Her hand started to reach for her jacket pocket, then jerked back as if something distasteful might be tucked away inside. She shook her head and raised her eyes upward. "No. I left it at home this morning. Forgot it because we were in such a hurry I just snatched up my jacket and left my mobile beside my bed."

I closed my eyes. Of course. There was that Mike Lynch luck again. Usually you'd have to go a long way to find two people who didn't have a single mobile phone between them. Tonight there were two of us in the same vehicle. Then I remembered the kid.

"How about you, Charlie? I don't suppose you have a phone with you?"

The kid giggled as if the question were absurd. She shook her head. "You're funny."

"Yeah. Right." I turned to Melissa again. "Where is home?" I asked her.

"Blackwell. South London."

Impressive. I knew the suburb well. There was some prime real estate in that area. The BMW X3 would fit right in. "So, what are you doing all the way out here?"

"We had to visit someone in Devon. Usually we would stay overnight, but Ray, my boss, also had a meeting close to home first thing this morning."

I blew out my cheeks. I felt exhausted, and the kid's yawn hadn't helped with that. "Look, I think maybe the best thing we can do is find the closest twenty-four-hour service station and have them call the police on our behalf."

Melissa pulled her head back and frowned.

"To report those dangerous drivers," I added quickly.

Melissa looked down at the kid. "Sweetie, do you mind if I have a chat with Mike outside the car. I want to get some fresh air and I think Mike would like that as well before we move on."

"Don't leave me, Mel," the kid said, sinking into her arm.

"I'm not leaving you, silly. I'll be right outside the car. You'll be able to see me all the time. I promise."

Once again, an adult pledge proved good enough.

Melissa opened up her door. "Mike?"

She nodded outside. I took the hint.

The air was a little cooler now, the storm having sucked all the moisture from it before depositing it back all over the countryside. The rain had stopped for the time being, and a light westerly breeze had taken its place. Melissa wore a waist-length denim jacket with button-down pockets, from which she took a pack of cigarettes. With a deft flick, she expertly tapped one out, then lit it with a fluorescent green disposable lighter. She took a long drag and allowed the smoke to filter out of her nostrils. She didn't offer one, which bothered me more than it ought to have done considering smoking wasn't one of my myriad vices.

There wasn't much else to see back here. The ramshackle outbuilding overlooked the rear of what appeared to be a derelict factory, and off to the right there was an area of open land that people had used as a dumping ground for old mattresses, scraps of furniture and the obligatory fridge.

"So, what's this all about?" I asked, keeping my voice low and my head turned away from the kid. "Why the chat out here?"

The only light was whatever was spilling out of the night sky and from the glow of Melissa's cigarette. Even so, I could see she was in her late-twenties – a little younger than my initial estimate. She wore a thin light-coloured sweater beneath the jacket, a patterned skirt down to her ankles, and even in flat shoes she was nearly as tall as me. She took another pull before replying in a hushed voice.

"Listen, Mike, it is way past Charlie's bed time. She is over-tired and extremely confused, and I really don't think I want to tell her that her father is dead right now."

"Fair enough. I can understand that. So let the police tell her. They'll have a trained cop for that sort of thing. You know, some sort of family liaison officer."

"I see. So, you think having a complete stranger tell her is better?" She looked at me with no small measure of contempt.

"She's going to find out sooner or later."

"And I think later is better. I think letting her get some sleep will make it easier on her. There's no good time to tell her, I know that, but to have Charlie find out in the middle of the night, surrounded by strangers in a strange place, followed by all the commotion that will result from it… We can do better than that for her."

I felt my irritation move up a gear. This had nothing to do with me. I had accidentally got caught up in something dreadful, and being a witness I knew I was now inexorably involved with the shooting, but how and when this kid discovered that her father had been murdered was not something I was about to include in my ever-increasing list of concerns. Then something occurred to me.

"What if her father's not dead? We know he was shot, but we don't know he's actually dead."

"I heard two more quick shots just after you jumped into our car and drove off. If someone wanted him dead, I think they would have finished the job before coming after us, don't you?"

I remembered the man lying on the floor, the shot that had forced him down onto his face. The one that then flipped him onto his side. She was probably right. In fact, I had almost certainly seen the shot that killed Charlie's father.

"Okay. You may be right. Fact is, we could probably both do with getting our heads around this shit."

"That we can agree on."

"So, do you know who was doing the shooting?" I asked her.

Melissa shook her head and took a long hard drag on her cigarette before responding. "No. Of course not. No idea."

The response sounded rehearsed. I wanted to ask her more about it, but learning who was responsible did not seem as important as finding a way out of the mess we were in.

"So, who are you to these people?" I asked. "Family? A friend?"

"I'm Charlie's nanny."

I glanced at the BMW. Big car, big money. It figured that the driver would have someone else taking care of his kid.

"I see. And what do you suggest we do right now? What exactly is your plan?"

She sucked on the cigarette a couple of times, one elbow resting on the other arm that seemed to be hugging herself. Then she flicked the stub away, and it fell to the floor in a trail of sparks.

"I think we should just drive on and get as far away from here as possible during the next thirty minutes or so. Then we can find somewhere suitable to pull over and think more about when to go to the police and what to say to them when we do."

"You don't think they might wonder why we didn't report this to them immediately?"

"Actually, I don't really care what they might wonder. Ray is dead, and Charlie isn't. Nothing we do now is going to alter the first part of that statement. I just don't want that poor little girl having to go through all that crap, having to deal with a place as cold and impersonal as a police station. We can let her sleep for a while and make the call later, and then you and I can talk to the police. Is that all right by you, Mike?"

It wasn't. And I didn't see why it should be, either. This was someone else's problem. I was just the poor bastard who happened to see a shooting and then somehow got swept up by the aftermath.

"All I want to do is go home," I told her honestly. "It's all I've wanted to do since last evening. So how about this: why don't I drop you and the kid off somewhere, leave you with my name and address, and then I'll speak to the police when I get home."

"You're forgetting one important thing, Mike."

"And that is?"

"You're driving my boss's car. It goes only as far as we do."

She was right. I had forgotten.

"Then we go straight to a police station."

"You keep coming back to that, and I keep telling you no. I do have another suggestion. How about I drive it and leave you stuck out here on your own. Of the two of us, I am the only one insured to drive this car. Plus, I don't know you, and I may not even want you back in the car with us."

I hadn't thought of it that way, either. In fact, I wasn't thinking clearly at all. "Look, you're right," I admitted. "But let's not be hasty. We should stick together for the time being, but I still think we should go to the police."

"I don't. Charlie is my responsibility and is my only concern right now. But as a compromise, we could stay here for a little while longer if you want. You're not the only one who doesn't want to stray across that man's path again tonight."

It had been one lousy day. But then I thought about the man lying dead in a sodden lay-by, the bullet that had flashed past my own head, the ensuing car chase. All things considered, it could have been a great deal worse. Also, remaining with Melissa and the kid was a whole lot better than being dumped at the roadside like a bag of rubbish.

When my shoulders slumped, I knew I had lost the battle.

"You win," I told her.

The glint in Melissa's eyes told me she had come to that conclusion long before I had.

FOUR

We sat in relative silence for a further half hour. The kid whined for a few minutes about not having her father there, but she soon drifted off the sleep. Other than making soothing noises towards the girl, Melissa did not speak at all. Eventually I grew restless, anxious about the potential for being discovered and hemmed in. The more the notion tumbled around inside my head the more likely and more horrifying it seemed. At a few minutes before three we were back on the road.

I had used some of the time spent waiting to figure out how to get the satnav switched on, but having never used one before I had no idea whether the GPS could tell me exactly where we were. I felt like a Luddite; my daughter Wendy would have figured the thing out in seconds. In the end, I decided to just keep on heading away from the scene of the shooting, because eventually we would come upon a town.

I pushed the BMW as hard as I could on the narrow and twisting roads, and finally came upon a decent surface followed shortly by the main A303 and a set of signposts that allowed me to get my bearings. I hung a left and set off on the road that would eventually lead us in the direction of home. I started to relax now that a few more vehicles were around.

We had travelled less than five more miles when a sign for a Best Inn Town motel came up on the nearside. I decided it was as good a place as any to pull over again to rest up and debate our next move. The car park adjoined a McDonald's and a Shell petrol station, both of which were in darkness, and extended beyond the back of the main hotel building. I tucked the car around there, out of sight of the main road as well as the motel's lobby.

"Can we get a room rather than sit out here?" Melissa asked. "This is no place for me or you to sleep, let alone Charlie. Perhaps this will all seem more manageable once we've had some proper rest."

It wasn't a bad idea. "I can sort that. Shall I pop over and come back for you when I have a door key? Probably better than you hanging around in the reception area."

"Okay. Leave the engine on if there's enough fuel. It's clammy and I'd like to keep the A/C on."

"No problem. There's about half a tank in there." I turned to look back at her. "Don't shoot me down in flames again, Melissa, but are you absolutely sure you want to delay the inevitable? I was thinking that instead of hiding out as if we were guilty of something, there's probably a pay phone I can use right here. The kid's had some sleep."

"Sure. Why not? Let's throw her to the wolves now. In the dead of night."

"All right." I held up my hands, frustrated at the young woman's inability to grasp the reality of our situation. "I was just providing options."

Melissa gave a long sigh, and glanced to her right. The kid was fast asleep in her seat. "Fair enough. I do understand your concerns, Mike. Really, I do. I just want to do whatever's best for Charlie."

Despite the fact that things were not going my way, I admired her taking a stand. Melissa's protective instincts were more like those of a mother than a nanny, always putting the kid first. It had been a long time since I'd had to do anything that wasn't best for Mike Lynch. It didn't come naturally now.

"I'll go and check in, then come and get you. That way you can carry her straight to the room."

"That sounds good." She gave a weak smile. "Maybe you're not quite as superficial as I thought."

"Me?" I touched a hand to my chest. "Shallow as a worm's grave, love. Frankly, I just want to get this over with. But right now, I'm far too tired and way too stressed to think straight or argue with you again."

I got out of the car and walked around to the well-lit entrance which led to the reception area. What I had just told Melissa wasn't exactly true. I did want to get it over with; that much was accurate. But I wasn't looking forward to the moment we had to bring the police into this. It was inevitable, certainly. Just not an experience I was relishing.

Pushing open the glass swing door, I realised that in leaving the air-conditioning on I'd had to leave the car keys in the BMW's ignition. I wondered if it had been Melissa's intention to drive off without me. Thinking about it now, I wasn't sure if I cared either way.

The lobby was making a half-hearted attempt to appear classy, but its ash wood and pastel-coloured walls lacked taste, and reeked of impermanence. There was a vending machine set against one wall, plus a couple of chairs arranged around a table on which someone had splayed a bunch of leaflets. I had to ring for service at the desk. A couple of minutes later an elderly porter pushed through a door marked "Private", tucking his shirt into his trousers. He glanced at the watch on his wrist and muttered to himself. If the man's beauty sleep had been disturbed, I didn't feel at all guilty about it, despite the night porter needing more than his fair share.

"I'd like a room for the night," I said.

"What's left of it," he observed dryly. His voice was cracked, ravaged by smoke and cheap booze, if the yellow stains on his fingers and the sour smell of whisky on his breath were anything to go by. Close up he had the wrinkled skin of a leather wallet, and one eye had a milky glaze over it. A shaving rash ran down one side of his face.

"Single?" he asked, flipping open a book on the reception desk.

I nodded. We were not going to be here long, so what did it matter? Then I thought better of it. When the three of us came through the reception area, we would have to pass right by the porter. I didn't think company rules would allow the three of us to occupy a single room.

"Actually, I've changed my mind," I said hurriedly. "Better make that a double. I might get lucky."

The old guy gave me what he probably imagined was an old-fashioned look, but it came across as more of a scowl. I handed the porter my debit card, which he ran through the scanner. I popped my PIN in and we were good to go. He gave me a key card and told me the room number. "You get your invoice at checkout," he added, giving the computer the same look he had given his early morning intruder.

I took the key from him and shook my head. "I'd get my money back if I were you, mate."

"What?" the man frowned and squinted.

"From the charm school."

I let it sink in before turning away. I couldn't decide if I was more angry with the man for being a miserable old bastard, or the Best Inn Town itself for employing him in the first place.

FIVE

The BMW sat where I had left it, Melissa and the kid still in the back. The young woman hoisted a small leather bag over her shoulder before scooping up the kid and stepping away from the car. We headed across to the main building. When we entered the lobby, the old man was nowhere to be seen. It occurred to me then that the porter had not mentioned where the room was, and for a moment I considered pressing the service bell again. We were in room 213, which I assumed would be on the second floor, so we bundled into a lift that just about held the three of us. The journey up two flights was brief, yet less than smooth. I wondered if the tiny lift felt burdened by the nervous silence. For those few moments, Melissa and I were complete strangers once more.

It was only when we reached the room and I threw open the door that it occurred to me that a gentleman would have at least offered to carry the sleeping child. She wasn't a big kid, but Melissa was obviously struggling with the weight and encumbered by the shoulder bag. I considered apologising, but it was too late now to make any difference. I dismissed the thought. It was far from the worst thing I had ever done.

The accommodation was standard. When I switched on the light, a small room to our left was revealed, containing a shower, sink and toilet. To the right was a small alcove in which an aluminium rail had been hung; a couple of wooden clothes hangers shoved to one side. In the main area stood a small double bed. A long chest of drawers, TV, and a table and two chairs completed the furnishings. Either side of the bed, attached to the headboard, were shelves, one of which held the telephone. I crossed the room to peek through the heavy drawn curtains, and felt relieved to see we were overlooking the rear car park. I began to feel less anxious, my heartbeat steadying for the first time since seeing the gun pointed in my direction back at the lay-by.

Melissa, who had said nothing to me since my return to the car, laid the kid gently down on the bed, her blonde hair splashing across one of two pillows. When Melissa straightened she rolled her shoulders a couple of times and rubbed her neck, causing a momentary resurgence of the guilt I had felt moments earlier. When finally, she turned to me, she took a deep breath before speaking.

"Look at her. Poor thing. I could weep at the thought of what she has to go through. I'm sure you don't still want to wake her up from a nice dream and dump her in the middle of a nightmare."

I switched my attention from her to the kid, seeing the child clearly for the first time. She was about six or seven, I thought, although I was not great with ages. The blonde hair was long and wavy. Her cheeks were rounded and shiny, lips slightly parted as she breathed softly into the pillow. She looked nothing like my daughter, but still I thought of Wendy. Of the times, I had stood over her bed watching her sleep, each breath a tiny miracle. Nothing in life is as pure, as innocent, as a sleeping child.

I considered what Melissa had said to me. What would you want for Wendy? I asked myself. The answer came right away. "Okay. You were right," I admitted. "We did the best thing for her. Let's fix ourselves a drink before we do anything else. Then we can talk about what we both saw and heard, get it right for when we do eventually speak to the police."

Melissa appeared happy enough with that. On the chest of drawers there was a tray with two cups, a kettle and a bowl containing sachets of tea, coffee, hot chocolate and sugar, four small cartons of milk, and a couple of packets of digestive biscuits. Melissa went into the bathroom to fill the kettle. Out of habit more than anything else, I picked up the TV remote and punched the on button, instantly muting the sound even as the set crackled to life.

"Tea or coffee?" Melissa asked when she came back into the room and plugged in the kettle.

"Hot chocolate," I replied, absently eyeing the TV screen.

"I'd like to save them for Charlie if that's all right?"

I glanced at her. Nodded. "Coffee will do. Black, please. No sugar."

Nothing else was said until the hot drinks were ready. I felt edgy being with this woman now, even more so than back in the BMW. We were strangers, thrust together in a moment of terror and tragedy. In the relative darkness of the car, our close proximity had not felt quite so uncomfortable. Now, here in a lit motel room, the abnormality of the situation had a bite to it I could not explain.

I sipped from the mug and let the caffeine do its work. Melissa sat down opposite me at the oval table, stirring her coffee with a plastic spoon. Now that the terror had numbed to a disquieting fear, I thought of a question I really ought to have asked right from the word go.

"So tell me, why would someone want to murder your boss?"

Melissa drank from her cup with its floral motif, added a little more milk and stirred again. Her gaze remained on the table. "I've been asking myself that ever since it happened."

"And you haven't come up with an answer?"

She shook her head.

"Okay, so what happened back there, Melissa? How did you end up in that lay-by?"

She glanced over at the bed. Checking to see if the kid was still asleep, I guessed. "I'm not sure. I was dozing, then all of a sudden we were pulling off the road. We stopped, Ray got out. I was still a bit groggy, the rain was hammering down, lightning flashing all around us, and then I heard the shot. As I said earlier, when I looked out of the back window, I saw Ray on his knees and another man standing by a dark car. The man shot Ray."

"That's precisely the time I stumbled on it," I said. An icy tremor passed along the length of my spine. "At first I couldn't fully comprehend what I was seeing. I must have cried out, because the other guy turned and fired at me."

She nodded. "I heard another shot, but didn't see you until you jumped into our car. By then I'd already dropped down to the floor behind the seats, unbuckling Charlie and pulling her down with me to protect her. At first, I thought you must have been with the man who shot Ray, but after a while I could tell by the way you were driving and looking in your mirrors that we were being chased. I still didn't know what to make of it all, or of you, so I kept Charlie quiet and just stayed still."

"So, you have no idea at all why that man shot your boss?"

"No. I already told you."

I wasn't convinced, but there was nothing to be gained by pushing the issue further. As I pondered my next question, something on the TV screen drew my attention. When I turned to focus on it, I stiffened, as though every muscle in my body had frozen solid. Melissa must have noticed my sudden discomfort, and also turned to look at the TV.

"That's my car." My voice sounded as if it was struggling to fight its way through a dense fog. "That's my bloody car."

I unmuted and then jabbed the volume button on the remote until I could hear the sound clearly. A female voice: "… but as yet police have no clues as to why this shooting took place. A senior officer gave a brief statement a little earlier, confirming that they are looking for Mr Lynch in connection with the murder of Ray Dawson, and the abduction of Mr Dawson's daughter, Charlotte, together with the child's nanny, Melissa Andrews. Given Mr Dawson's connection with organised crime, a gangland slaying cannot be ruled out at this time. Mr Dawson's brother had this to say."

The item cut to a man with a narrow, pock-scarred face. His eyes looked glassy and devoid of emotion. "I can't think of any reason why someone would want to murder my brother," he said. "Nor why they would snatch my niece and her nanny."

"Are the police keeping you informed of progress?" the interviewer probed.

"The police have their own way of working. We have ours. I'm sure they are doing all they can. We'll be doing everything in our power to help them, obviously."

"Are you expecting a ransom demand, Mr Dawson?"

"I very much doubt it. Don't you?"

The man gave a thin smile. It didn't look as if it came naturally. I neither saw nor heard any sincerity, and could only imagine that working with the police was the last thing this man intended. His sort were inclined to resolve issues their own way.

There followed a long shot of the lay-by, emergency vehicles gathered all around it, pulsing lights painting the surrounding area red, white and blue. The female presenter started speaking again, but this time her words made no impression on me. I was too busy glaring at Melissa.

"Organised crime?" I said, trying to keep my voice low so as not to wake the kid. Still, I heard the flint edge to it when I spoke again. "Your boss was Ray Dawson? The Ray Dawson who happens to be a serious villain known to just about everyone in the entire country. That Ray Dawson. Did that slip your mind, Melissa, when I asked you if you knew why someone might want him dead?"

She closed her eyes for a moment. Drank some more coffee. Breathed softly through her nose. Her hands were trembling as she held the cup. "I didn't want to panic you more than you obviously already were."

"Terrific. That's just great. I take it you know the brother? That fucking Rottweiler who was just on TV."

"Yes. That's Chris. But I don't understand. How the hell do the police know who you are?"

"It's not rocket science, Melissa. My bloody car is sitting there in that lay-by. Right where they found the body of a murdered man. A thirty-second check through their PNC system would have given them my name."

"But I still don't see how they pieced it all together so quickly."

I gave that some thought. "Someone obviously found your boss in that lay-by. Police traced him from whatever ID he had on him, made a few calls, someone mentioned you and the kid. My car is found in the same spot. They add two and two together and end up with me."

Melissa ran both hands through her hair. "I'm sorry I misled you, Mike. Really I am. But in truth, what difference would it have made if I had told you?"

"What difference? Are you kidding me? I would have gone to the police there and then and straightened this whole thing out. I would have got myself out of harm's way. It may strike you as odd, but I have no wish to be the prime suspect in the murder of your boss, and I certainly don't want some fucking gangster running around after my blood."

"I said I'm sorry."

I threw up my hands and looked back at the screen. It was damned hard to be quiet when I was so livid. With her, and the situation I found myself in. The feature was still running on the TV. The narrative had cut to a man standing by the side of my Saab. At the bottom of the screen ran a strip naming him as Senior NCA Officer David Hendricks. He was responding to media questions.

"We don't have much more for you at this stage. Obviously, we would ask for the Dawson family to remain calm and let us do our job. The police already have an investigation running, and they are hoping to have some additional news for you shortly."

"Will the National Criminal Agency be assisting in that investigation?" he was asked.

"We will certainly offer them any help they require, yes."

Melissa stood up from the table. "I suppose you are going to call the police now," she said.

"Actually, I don't think I am."

"You're not? How come?" Her gaze narrowed.

Just then, I could not take my eyes off the TV. When I finally turned to her I shook my head slowly.

"You didn't see the gunman clearly, did you?" I asked, my voice breaking on the last word.

"Not really, why?"

I nodded at the flickering screen. "Because that's him. That NCA officer is the man I saw shooting and killing your boss."

SIX

Senior NCA Officer David Hendricks knew when one of his two personal mobile phones rang that the resulting conversation was not going to be a pleasurable experience. He took a few steps away from a group of police officers clustered around the crime scene, to make sure he was out of earshot, then pressed the accept button.

"This is not a good time," he said.

"So I noticed. What the fuck went wrong?" the caller asked. The voice was not loud, but there was a biting edge to it.

"A bit of bad luck. It happens. I'll make it right."

"Oh, you'd better. This could not have gone a lot worse."

"Ray Dawson is dead, isn't he?"

"And that's the only reason we're still talking. Sort it out, Hendricks. And do it quickly."

The connection was cut. Hendricks glared at the phone for a few moments while he gathered his thoughts. Being spoken to in such an aggressive manner was tough to accept, but it went with the territory when you walked the lines in the shadow he had chosen to take. Turning to look back at the scene, Hendricks observed forensic technicians swarming all over it like ants at a picnic. He glanced across at Mike Lynch's Saab and shook his head, kicking out at a pebble and sending it flying across the road.

Once he had accepted that the BMW had got away from him, he'd had to do some rapid thinking. That was the point at which all of his training, experience and reason came into play. It was rational to assume that on a stretch of road like this, Ray Dawson's body might well remain undiscovered until daybreak. Hendricks could not afford to sit around and wait for that to happen; for Dawson's identity to then raise red flags back at NCA headquarters in Westminster, less than half a mile from New Scotland Yard; for the call to eventually land on his plate, and to then have to wait out the requisite time it would take to arrive at the scene if he'd had to travel down from London as expected. Those were hours he could not afford to waste. The gamble he decided to take was a calculated one, worth the slight risk for the sake of an early start in tracking down the owner of the silver Saab.

Decision made, Hendricks had driven back to the scene of the murder and called it in; his own manager first, followed by local CID. National Crime Agency Manager Robin Dwyer had been less than enthusiastic at being woken so early in the morning, and appeared stunned at learning of Dawson's murder.

"I'm not sure if I understand this correctly, David," Dwyer said. Hendricks could imagine his short and stout boss reaching for a cigarette, already planning how best to distance himself from any potential fallout. "You say *you* found him? In the middle of nowhere, and a very long way from either your home or office? Would you care to elaborate?"

"Of course, sir. It sounds worse than it is. I discovered that Dawson was headed down to Exeter yesterday morning, and I thought we might be interested in whatever business he was doing down there – you know, the people he might be meeting. I also thought he might hook up with some faces on the way home, so I followed him back as well. My guess is he spotted the tail at some point, because his motor sped up and unfortunately, I lost him for a while. I wasted a fair bit of time trying to find my way around, and then when I got back on track I chanced upon the scene."

There was a slight pause, and Hendricks wondered if his boss had bought the flimsy story. Or if he even cared about the legitimacy of it. Dawson's death would be mourned only by those who were on the take from him. Dwyer wasn't one of those.

"Did you see any other vehicles tracking Dawson?" his manager asked. "I think we can safely assume that whoever took him out must have been following him. In addition to you, of course."

"I… I can't be certain, sir. Obviously I wasn't expecting something of this nature, so I was probably less aware of my surroundings than I otherwise might have been."

"I see. Best give it some thought then, eh?"

"Yes, sir. I'll do that"

"Okay, David. Tread carefully. Don't piss off the locals. Clearly this will be in their hands once the dust has settled. You must, of course, expect to be questioned, and you will initially be a person of interest to them, I would imagine. Provided you have no smoking gun, nor accompanying gunshot residue on your hands, or blood spatter on your clothing, or any other incriminating evidence for that matter, they will allow you to go about your business. You have no authority in a murder investigation, but you might suggest your intimate knowledge of the man, his family, and their wider business interests, could be a major advantage to their investigation team. I'll contact the area forces myself first thing, just to smooth out the wrinkles."

"Sounds good. I'll crack on then, sir."

"Yes. You do that. And, David… when you get back you can look me in the eye and tell me that story again."

Recalling the awkwardness of the conversation now, Hendricks smiled and shook his head. Dwyer had not been taken in by the story, but would not be overly concerned about the finer details, provided the shit shower didn't touch him. It was Teflon time. Again.

Before calling his boss, he had already dumped the gun he had used to kill Dawson. Alongside the weapon, he had also buried the jacket and gloves he had worn at the time. They would retain the gunshot residue now, not his hands or arms. When firing the shots, Hendricks had made sure not to get close enough to Dawson for any blood or hair or tissue to have settled on his clothing. The only real problem he could think of was the likelihood of trace evidence having been transferred to his vehicle's steering wheel.

Wiping it clean had been an instinctive counter-measure, but these forensics people were good. If they checked, he could be in trouble. He was confident they would not.

Before putting away his personal mobile he replaced the SIM card with one fresh out of its cardboard wrapper, a routine he followed after every single call from certain sources. He was all too aware of just how many criminals were undone by information gleaned from phones. Those who needed to contact him knew his routine, and would simply dial the next number in the sequence he had provided.

Hendricks continued to stand on his own for a few minutes, taking in the crime scene one more time. He thought about all that had taken place since the shooting. Bad luck comes around. It was how you dealt with it that counted. It had been a tough night, but it could have gone worse. The main thing now was to track down Mike Lynch, and hope that he was not alone.

***

Rhino Walsh was 280 pounds of muscle that he wore like an ebony suit of armour. Six-eight, bald as a bowling ball, Walsh was a man with no discernible neck and a chest that looked like the hull of a barge. A proud Yorkshireman, his nickname derived from his love of rugby league, and the Leeds Rhinos in particular. But if you had to say what animal he most resembled, a rhino would not be too far wrong.

The man who sat alongside him was a lot smaller and a lot lighter and, unlike Rhino who pumped iron every day, Keith Breeder, who went by the inappropriate name of Haystacks, had long since allowed his muscles to atrophy. An ex-Hell's Angel, he had not been able to ride a bike since ploughing one into a stationary articulated lorry at more than sixty miles an hour, three years ago. Five months after the accident he emerged from hospital with epilepsy and a steel plate screwed to his skull in order to keep it from falling apart. Scars still littered his face, but he didn't look like the kind of man who spent too much time in front of a mirror.

Chris Dawson reclined in his office armchair and appraised the pair of them. He did not especially enjoy being in their company, despite the two men being his most trusted aides. There was something about Walsh's sheer brute strength, and Breeder's total indifference and attachment to blades, that creeped him out. Dawson was not averse to violence, and enjoyed his own reputation for brutality when it was called for. Yet even he had a healthy fear of both Rhino and Haystacks. Despite these misgivings, he was entirely confident that both men would do absolutely anything he asked of them.

At a fair price, of course. Even the most amenable mule likes a carrot or two.

"I want you to find this Lynch arsehole," Dawson ordered.

The office in which they sat overlooked a glassed-in pool at the rear of his palatial Chigwell home. The night pressed against the windows, which rippled with blue light glancing off the water. Walsh had a glass of fresh orange juice sat on the marble table before him. His colleague chugged on a bottle of Coke, alternately wiping his lips and belching. Dawson sipped iced-tea with a shot of Jameson's. He set his cup down and made slits of his eyes. "Find him and kill him."

Earl Walsh nodded, and shifted in his chair. It was like watching a mountain slough off the inertia of a million years. He had a complicated face, punctuated by a scar on each cheek that looked more like tribal markings than the result of the gangland torture that they were. A similar scar cut a neat slice through his scrotum.

It was his partner who spoke, though. "Are we getting any help on this, boss? Any good intelligence?"

Chris Dawson nodded. "We are, Haystacks, and we will. Early tomorrow, I would hope to have more. Meanwhile, you two can get yourselves down there and start sniffing around. I want you both ready to jump when you have to."

"Just us, or are we taking a team?"

"No, I want you two on this alone. I need this kept in-house, and I don't trust the mouths on any of those other fuckers who work for me."

"Can you keep the authorities at bay?" Walsh asked. He reached out and took a sip from his glass. "Stop them getting to this Lynch character first?"

"It's possible, Rhino, but don't bank on it. I don't know exactly who will be in charge down there just yet, but something like this may be too big to manipulate with the usual ease. If I can buy you a ten-minute head start, you need to make it work for us. If I can't, and they grab him up, well then we'll need to figure out a way of taking him off their hands. I want this bastard dead. No questions."

"Leave it to us, boss. We'll sort it." He turned slightly to look at his partner. "Right, Haystacks?"

The smaller man wiped his lips on his cuff, belched, put down his now empty bottle, and nodded. For him it was almost a speech.

SEVEN

There was not a lot of floor on which to pace, but I made a pretty good fist of it. I usually did my best thinking on my feet, but on this occasion my head was cluttered with loud, wailing voices, each telling me I was in the kind of trouble from which there might be no escape. Hands either spread in confusion, or rubbing my head in anguish, I walked back and forth around the bed, willing myself not to scream.

"I don't believe this," I muttered, head moving as if perched upon a gyroscope. "This can't be happening. It can't be."

Melissa tried her level best to calm me, gently insisting I must be wrong. Her assurances had the opposite effect, irritating me more each time my gaze met hers. Her eyes kept straying across to the little girl sleeping soundly on the bed. I ignored the implied request. There was more to fret about than waking the kid.

"It was him." Finally, I stopped pacing, and instead jabbed a finger at the TV, which had long since moved on to another feature. "That cop was the man I saw in the lay-by."

"You're absolutely certain of that, Mike? No doubt whatsoever?"

"I am, yes. Oddly enough, I never forget the face of anyone who takes a shot at me in the middle of the night."

Her cheeks flushed. "Do you have to be sarcastic?"

"As a matter of fact, I do. Sarcasm, and oceans of it, is sometimes the only thing that gets me through a crisis."

"Look, if you're right, then obviously that changes everything."

"You think?"

"Don't get pissy with me! It's not my fault. I'm as bewildered as you are."

I shook my head at her defiance. "No. Not quite. Not at all in fact. You do have the slight advantage of knowing that you were employed by a fucking psycho-maniac. You must be used to being shit-scared."

Her chin trembled a little, and for a moment I thought she might cry. "Actually, that's not the case at all. Ray never let it touch his home life. And certainly, it never came anywhere near Charlie. But anyway, now you're saying it was the cops who killed Ray. I knew he walked a thin line with other criminals, but I genuinely don't know what this is all about."

She was emotional. I understood why, but was not about to take a step back. "I'll tell you what it's about, sweetheart. It's about us not being able to go to the police now. Neither of us. It's about us being completely fucked, because I have no idea what to do or where we go from here."

My words seemed to register. Concern replaced confusion in her eyes.

"Our faces will be all over the TV news later this morning, Melissa. And on websites and in the newspapers as soon as they can print them."

I thought about how that would play out. We might as well buy ourselves a set of T-shirts with targets printed on the back. I rubbed my mouth and wondered why I had bothered remaining sober these past three months. Then something else occurred to me.

"Oh, shit! Fucking hell! My ex and my daughter. The police will have been touch with them by now, telling them all kinds of shit about me. That I am now wanted for murder. And abduction."

I wrapped both hands around the top of my head, linking the fingers to form a grip. I started to feel physically sick. The thought of my ex-wife and daughter having to sit there while armed cops and probably even FBI agents snapped questions at them, painting lurid pictures of me gunning down a man on the side of the road, and snatching a young woman and child in the dead of night, filled my heart with dread.

"Could you call them?" Melissa suggested. "Tell them your side of things?"

"Not a good idea. By now they'll be recording and tracing every call in or out of the house. I probably wouldn't even get to speak to..."

"What?" she asked me. "What now?"

"My daughter's number is in my mobile phone, which is still in my bloody car. I have no clue what the number is."

"So, what do we do now?"

"We have to split up," I said emphatically. "Go our separate ways."

Melissa scowled at me for a second. Then shook her head and folded her arms. "You're a real hero, aren't you?"

"It's got nothing to do with bravery, and everything to do with practicality. Think about it, Melissa. Everyone will be looking for the three of us together. Agreed?"

"I suppose."

"So, we'll have a better chance if we go in opposite directions."

"And exactly where do you suggest me and Charlie go?"

"Can't you call your boss's brother?" I brightened suddenly. "In fact, yes, call him and make sure he knows I had nothing to do with what happened. I could do without the likes of him on my back. You could even get him to come and collect you, then you can explain it all to him."

Melissa gave a curt, humourless laugh. "I don't have his number; I don't have anyone's number."

"Do you live in?"

She nodded.

"So call the landline. Someone's bound to be there."

"The only people who lived there were me, Charlie and Ray. Besides, I have the same problem as you in that the number's in my mobile and I have no idea what it is."

I looked up at the ceiling. It seemed closer somehow. I felt like punching a wall, and little pinpricks of light danced before my eyes.

"How long have you had the job?" I asked.

"Nine or ten months."

"And you don't know the phone number of the place where you live?"

"No. I told you." Her voice was raised now, and anger flared in her eyes. "I put it in my phone when I first moved in. I've never needed to know it off by heart. Besides, you don't even know your own daughter's number, so don't lecture me. And don't you think that officer you say shot Ray will be tracing calls there as well?"

She was right. I didn't think a NCA agent who was willing to murder someone would be shy about breaking other laws such as phone tapping. That made me think about other things the cop might be doing to track us down. Something was niggling at the back of my mind, but kept swimming out of reach every time I tried to focus on it. I turned back to Melissa.

"Is there no way, no way at all that you can get in touch with the kid's family?" I shot a look at the sleeping child. The rise and fall of her chest was strangely comforting. "Think, Melissa. Think hard, because it may be our only way out of this."

"What do you mean 'we'? Charlie and I have done nothing wrong."

"Neither have I, damnit!" I barely managed not to yell at her.

"What I mean is, in the eyes of the NCA and cops we have done nothing wrong. Me and Charlie. We are the innocent victims of all this as far as they are concerned."

"True enough. So far as it goes. But think it through. That cop has no idea what you saw, either. You reckon he's going to allow you to talk? I guarantee you, Melissa, he'll either weave you into the fabric of his story or he'll make sure you go the same way your boss did. He'll have it down as you and me in it together somehow, or he'll kill you before you get a chance to tell your side."

I let her stew on that for a minute or two. I had been harsh on her, but necessarily so. Melissa might not want to think about such a possibility, and I could tell I had frightened her, but there was no one else around to put her straight. I didn't like doing it, and I really wasn't fond of myself right now. I simply felt that Melissa wasn't fully grasping how serious our situation was.

"So how about it?" I asked again. "Is there anyone you can think of who we can turn to, to contact right now and get ourselves out of this mess?"

"No. I've already said."

"How about the kid's mother?"

"She died a few years ago."

"How about the driver… Roger?"

She shook her head. "Look, I'm Charlie's nanny. I take care of Charlie. I don't have anything to do with anything or anyone else. I know some of their names, but I couldn't even tell you where Roger lives. Nor Chris, other than in Chigwell somewhere. I'm sorry, but that's how it is. Don't you think I'd help if I could?"

I had known Melissa only a short while, and initially she had come across as mature and strong-willed for her age. For the first time, she now looked a little lost and dispirited, her voice resigned. For a moment, I thought about her situation rather than my own, about the years and experience I had on her. She was toughing it out as best she could. Better than me, and I had not seen my boss gunned down.

I was about to try and calm her when the niggle that had been swimming around me reared up like a shark ready to take a huge bite. "Shit!" I put my head back and tried not to hit the panic button. "We have to get out of here. And I mean right now."

Melissa regarded me as if I were crazy. The one thing she clearly did not want to do was move.

"I paid by card," I explained. "If they can trace phone calls, they can also check on my bank and spending. One hit will lead them right to us."

There were no other options available. We had to get away from the motel. I wondered whether we could risk taking the car with us. Eventually I decided we had to take the gamble; I didn't see how else we could get away so quickly.

"Do you know if the car has a GPS tracking system on board? You know, in case it's stolen." I knew that if such a system was on the vehicle I could never find it, let alone deactivate it. Whoever was hunting us would contact the company responsible and have its location within minutes.

Melissa raised her eyebrows. "Can you imagine Ray standing for that? Actually, I overheard him telling Roger that he'd had it removed prior to taking delivery."

That was something at least.

"Good. Let's go," I said, making a snap judgement. "We'll take the car as far as we dare and park up somewhere until morning. Maybe if we both finally get some sleep we can wake up with a clear head and think of a way out of this mess."

Melissa was already on her feet. "They could be on their way here right now."

"All the more reason to get the hell out of here, then. You pick the kid up, I'll carry her to the car."

She nodded. Our eyes met. "Thank you," she said.

"For what?"

"For not just snatching up the keys and leaving us here."

I shrugged and gave half a smile. "For all I know the best thing might still be to get you and the kid to the police, tell them what happened. But I'm weary and afraid and I think we both need a little time to put this together."

She lifted the kid off the bed and laid her in my arms. "Well, thank you anyway," she said. "We both appreciate it."

***

The place was deserted, thankfully. My stomach was roiling when we stepped back outside and started walking around the side of the building, but we were doing the right thing. I swung the BMW out of the car park and headed north back on the A303. Taking the car remained a calculated risk, because at this time of morning there was still so little traffic on the road it would be easier for a police patrol to spot us. I thought it had to be better than sitting back in the motel room and waiting for law enforcement to break down the door. I intended dumping the car as soon as it was convenient, but right now I wanted to put as many miles as possible between myself and the place at which I had stupidly used my bank card.

The kid had hardly stirred during the transfer from motel room to the car. Melissa eased her into the child's car seat, Charlie's head nestling back into the padded rim. The night had turned to shit for all of us, but the kid remained blissfully unaware that her whole life was going to tumble upside down and inside out. Soon enough she would be told. That her father had died, that she was now an orphan. The dirty little matter of how her father had been gunned down would perhaps keep for another day. Not that I wanted to be around when that happened.

"So, what was it like working for someone like Ray Dawson?" I asked, my voice sounding loud inside the car. I glanced at Melissa in the rear-view mirror.

"I told you, he kept all of that away from Charlie. And me. I had no idea who he was when I took the job." Her voice sounded tired and distant. Defensive.

"How did you feel when you did find out?"

"By then I'd grown close to Charlie, and no matter what you think of him or whatever he's done, Ray was a good boss. I didn't believe half the things I heard were true. I still don't."

"Oh, they're true. Believe me. The Dawson family are big time in and around London. Their reach extends far beyond the capital, as well. They are involved in just about every wicked, depraved criminal enterprise you can think of, including people trafficking and prostitution on a grand scale. The Dawsons are responsible for a lot of suffering and misery. And death."

"Like you would know. What do you do, anyway?"

"Me?" I chuckled. What did I do exactly? Nothing worth a damn. "I'm a freelance graphics designer. Boring as fuck, but it pays the bills."

"You swear too much."

"I tend to do that when I'm fleeing from a homicidal maniac."

"It's a sign of weakness."

I nodded. "Oh, I've got a hundred more of those, darling. Anyway, about a million years ago, before I quit the real world and joined the commercial rat race, I was a hard-nosed journalist for a major London-based newspaper. My speciality was crime and criminals. The underworld. The kind of stuff people commonly refer to as 'organised' crime. That's where and when I learned all about Ray Dawson, his family and crew."

"Oh." Melissa didn't sound quite so sure of herself now.

"Yeah. Oh. But like I say, that was in a previous life. A more certain one, oddly enough. Now I am living in a different world entirely, and the only thing I know for sure at this precise moment is that I am shit-scared."

The two of us were silent for a minute or so. Then Melissa said, "I am, too."

I glanced at her once more. Her face was more strained than I had realised. She wasn't what you would call a natural beauty, but there was something soft and gentle about her that could easily draw a man. I hadn't noticed it before, but there was a certain vulnerability about her appearance. Perhaps that was why Melissa disguised it with strength of character.

The world outside the car flashed by in a monochrome blur. I took the A350 and headed north. Some half-remembered map in my mind thought it would eventually take us somewhere close to the M4 motorway. For a time there was only countryside around us, punctuated by the occasional small village. Nothing too built-up or industrial. One stretch took us through what felt like a tunnel of tall hedgerow and small trees, pressed up tight against either side of the road. Eventually we came to a major intersection, and a sign which revealed the name of a town I had actually heard of. I headed that way without a second thought.

I glanced back at Melissa. She had said nothing for quite a while, but she was wide awake. "Do you still think the way forward would be clearer if we grabbed some sleep?" I asked.

She considered the question for a while before answering. "I'm not sure I'll ever be able to sleep again. But no, I don't think anything will be clearer."

I nodded. Truth was, everything was perfectly clear to me: we could not risk going to the police because we wouldn't know who to trust, and in my view the NCA officer who had murdered Ray Dawson could not afford to leave any witnesses alive. Chris Dawson would be hunting me down for what he believed I had done to his brother. The three of us were riding around in a hot car, I couldn't use my credit or debit cards again, and I had perhaps just about enough money to buy us a decent breakfast.

We were screwed.

How much clearer did it need to be?

EIGHT

At some point, we crossed the county border into Wiltshire, and I decided to stop at the first big town we came upon. Chippenham, just south of the M4 motorway, fit the bill; a town big enough to swallow us whole, small enough to be insignificant.

My mind was busy considering where to park up. During the day, there is never a shortage of areas in which you can leave a car without it standing out, but in the early hours of the morning, especially with dawn fast approaching, it's a lot tougher to blend in. As we nosed into the outskirts of Chippenham, however, it occurred to me that, as is often the case, it never does any harm to draw upon a cliché to help you out.

So we hid in plain sight.

Melissa and I sat in silence for what seemed like forever, the BMW's big engine-block ticking away like a Rolex on steroids as it cooled. The kid was stirring a little, but she had plenty of sleep left in her I thought. The street I had chosen to park on was off the main drag, but not so far that we would attract unwanted attention. The only things that might were leaving the engine running – so that had been killed immediately – and the combined exhalations of three people fogging up the glass. There was nothing I could do about the latter, so I decided not to fret about it. My therapist would have been so proud.

Exhausted – both mentally and physically – I yawned so long and hard that I thought my jaw might crack. Both eyes felt gritty, my vision a little blurred around the edges. Another yawn made me feel light-headed.

"Why don't you grab some sleep?" said a voice from the back seat.

I nodded, a third consecutive yawn catching in my throat. "I think I might try. It'll be light soon enough, so it won't amount to anything more than a snooze. You should try grabbing a nap, yourself. When the kid wakes up she'll be an avalanche of questions."

"Speaking of which, would you answer a question for me, Mike?"

"If I can."

"Why can't you bring yourself to call her Charlie?"

I shrugged it off. "Names make it personal."

"That's sad," Melissa said after a while. "I feel sorry for you."

"Join the club."

"You can't be as bad a person as you like to portray. And nowhere near as awful as you think you are."

I laughed. "Don't you believe it."

"If you were, you'd have left us behind."

I looked out at the street while I gave that some thought. It seemed as if we were in an older part of town, the majority of houses wedged close together like novels between two more sizeable book-ends. Simple terraced properties, probably with decent gardens and I could see small blocks of grass to the front. Thin, undernourished trees erupted from the pavements every twenty yards or so, distributed evenly along both sides of the street. A town planner's attempt at convincing the owners they were not living in suburbia. The new and expensive Beemer was a little out of place here, but there was the odd decent set of wheels parked up amongst the neighbourhood dross. We might not be blending in, but we would not be here long enough to matter.

I shifted in my seat, regarding Melissa closely. Her long hair bracketed her face neatly, and in other circumstances I thought I might have been attracted to her. I wanted to say something reassuring, something to alleviate her fears. Instead I asked, "What makes you think I haven't brought you along to act as a shield? You're the only person other than me and that murdering cop who knows what really happened, remember."

This time it was her turn to hike her shoulders. "Maybe you are as big a prick as you say."

"Ouch. That hurt my feelings. And now who's the one using ripe language?"

"Fuck you, Mike." Melissa shook her head, her eyes squeezed almost shut. "Just my luck to be stuck with a low-life, I suppose."

I turned and closed my eyes for a moment. Her luck? If she only knew.

"Sorry," I said. I was, too. "Truce?"

For a second I didn't think Melissa would answer. But she accepted my apology with better grace than I would have.

"Do you have family?" I asked then, something coming to mind. "I mean, I'm assuming parents? Siblings?"

"No. Not really. My only brother left home many years ago, and we have never heard from him since, so I have no idea where he might be now. My parents live in South Africa, but we lost touch years ago. Why do you ask?"

"Thinking is all. We've ruled out contacting either the authorities or Chris Dawson. My daughter lives in California at the moment. So I was wondering if there was someone you could possibly reach out to. I know you don't have your employer's number, but I assumed you would have numbers in your head for family. I guess it doesn't matter either way if they are abroad."

Melissa leaned forward, resting her arms on the back of the passenger seat. "So, how about you, Mike? Your daughter lives in the States, but there must be someone else in your life who you can contact. A woman? Other family members?"

I felt a tug deep in my gut. As I always did whenever anyone mentioned family. A claw hooking my heart. I shook my head. "No, no woman in my life right now. Big surprise there, eh? I never knew my biological parents. I was adopted. They became parents to me. And I couldn't have asked for better, more loving people to take care of me and raise me. Sadly, they are no longer with us."

"I'm sorry. I shouldn't have said anything."

"No, it's fine. I had a wonderful twenty-one years knowing I was chosen. There's no tragedy here, Melissa. They were good and kind, and to me they were my parents."

"So what about friends? Do you not have anyone to turn to?"

I cleared my throat. "I don't think so, no. Choosing someone who would both believe my side of the story and who I would trust enough not to go straight to the police might be a bit difficult. Impossible, even."

She sat back heavily. Shook her head as her tongue snaked out to moisten her lips. "That just about sums you up, I suppose."

She wasn't entirely wrong. There were people in my life who meant a great deal to me, but there were also issues with each of those relationships. My own fault. I am an outspoken man, and that only gets worse when I'm drunk. There was no one, not even my ex-wife, whom I really felt comfortable involving in this. A part of me hoped I was being protective towards them, ensuring their safety by avoiding all contact, but doubt was the real reason I refused to even consider communicating with anyone. Doubt and fear.

Doubt that they would believe me.

Doubt that they would even care.

And fearing both to be true.

NINE

The kid woke up in a bad mood.

I floated up out of my own light sleep, Charlie's whining voice just about the last thing I wanted to hear at that moment. As the words slowly made themselves clear, I heard her asking for her father for about the hundredth time.

I sat upright with a jerk, and rubbed a hand over my face. My neck and shoulders were tight, eyes gluey and sore. I drew saliva into my mouth. It tasted like shit. "Oh, Christ," I moaned. "Does she have to make all that bloody noise?"

That seemed to do the trick, because for a full thirty seconds no one uttered a word. Then the kid said, "He's grouchy."

Melissa laughed. A throaty, dry sound. "Yes. Yes, he is. But Mike is probably very tired still, so we'll make allowances. Okay?"

"Okay." It didn't sound to me as if she meant it.

"Good. Now then, please don't ask about your daddy again, Charlie. In a little while, me and Mike are going to find a place where we can scrub up and eat, then over breakfast we will talk about a few things. Your daddy included."

It went on like that for a few more minutes, the kid never quite letting it go. I checked the clock on the dashboard. It was almost seven-fifteen, and the street had begun to get a lot busier. The sun had been up for a couple of hours, and the heat was already cranking up. We were parked directly outside someone's house, and the three of us were likely to draw some curious glances and unwanted attention if we remained sitting in the car looking as if we had no intention of ever getting out. I told Melissa we were going to have to move on. She shrugged, which I took to be her agreement.

Although we were ultimately heading towards the town centre, the route I took was circuitous. Not entirely aimless, and not lacking direction, either. I was attempting to steer clear of main roads as much as possible. The negative part of me – which in truth is the major part these days – expected to be hemmed in by a dozen police vehicles at any moment. We were exposed in this car. I was beat, feeling sluggish despite my snooze, a dense brain-fog descending on me like a cloud of desperation. I considered pulling over again to wait it out, but right at that very moment I saw exactly what we all needed.

Roadside diners had upped their game since the reign of the Little Chef chain. AJ's was a firm favourite during my travels around the country, and there on the corner of Bath Road and Lowden was one opening its doors to the breakfast customers. I indicated and pulled into the adjacent car park. There was one way in and out of the restaurant, the interior very much in the style of old American diners; plenty of gleaming chrome and red vinyl upholstery. I ordered drinks for each of us, then Melissa and I took turns to visit the restrooms.

The waitress was older than many I had seen in recent years, and she was a damn sight friendlier than most. Moments after taking our order she brought across a pack of crayons and a colouring sheet, set them on the table. Her nametag read Barbara, and she beamed down at the kid and gave a wink.

"Well, aren't you as cute as a button, darling," she said, her accent marking her down as a local. "You got a name or do your parents just call you sunshine?"

Charlie just about jammed all ten fingers and thumbs into her own mouth, giggling behind her hands. I raised an eyebrow – *so now the kid was suddenly shy?*

"That's all right, honey," Barbara said, her smile widening. "If you don't want to tell me your name, you don't have to. It's yours and you get to choose who knows it."

I felt compelled to say something. "This is Charlie," I told the waitress. I looked at the kid and smiled. "Charlie, say hello to Barbara."

But the kid shook her head and played dumb again. I did not want to drag this out any longer than necessary, so I was relieved when the waitress ruffled the kid's hair and threw me a wink this time. "I'll be back with your drinks in a few minutes. Maybe Charlie here will be more talkative when I take your food order."

I hoped not. The less she said right now the better. The kid watched the heavy-set waitress bustle away, then got stuck into the colouring. Every few seconds her attention would skip to me, then the restroom door, before returning to her sheet of paper.

"Melissa will be back before you know it," I told her. "You can stop fretting and just enjoy colouring-in."

The kid considered me for a moment. Then she nodded. "I like bright colours," she told me.

"Me, too. Yellow and orange are good together."

She didn't respond, but immediately put down the green crayon and picked up the yellow one. I smiled. Children bemused me, but to observe them was one of the genuine wonders of life.

Barbara came back to the table and dished out the drinks: black coffee for me, the Earl Grey tea was Melissa's, leaving a glass of orange juice for Charlie.

"Thank you, Barbara," Charlie said, which seemed to just about make the woman's day.

"Oh, you are so welcome, honey." She grinned at me and said, "You have a lovely daughter here."

Precisely the conversation I had hoped to avoid.

"Oh, he's not Charlie's father," Melissa said, stepping in to save the day. I had not seen her return from the toilets, but I could have hugged her right now. Melissa slipped into the booth alongside the girl. "Neither of us are her parents, actually. I take care of her. Mike here gets to drive us around."

Barbara appeared impressed. "Hmm, fancy. Well, no matter. Charlie there is just a sweetheart."

I took the opportunity to excuse myself, thinking I might blow it if I sat there much longer. "It's been a long night and I need to freshen up," I said. "We'll order breakfast when I come back."

Having taken care of my bodily needs, I cupped some running water and splashed it over my face and the back of my neck. I dabbed myself with a paper towel. The man peering back at me from the soap-spotted mirror looked like a much older version of the man who had set out to gain a contract the previous day. My hair, cut pretty close to the scalp, now had unruly clumps sticking up from the crown. My eyes lacked lustre, and were red-rimmed. The virtually permanent five o'clock shadow that usually plagued me was now a growth of stubble. If not for the clothes, it could be an old tramp standing there.

Get a grip, Mike, I told myself. This shit is anything but over.

We ate well. Melissa and I had pooled our cash before entering the diner, and together we had come up with thirty-three pounds plus some change. It was evident to both of us that we were going to have to resolve our situation sooner rather than later. As I pushed my empty plate to one side, Melissa patiently explained to the kid that her father had been called away for a few days on business, and had arranged for Melissa and myself to take care of her until he returned. The kid started to complain, but Melissa pacified her by promising several treats.

"Any suggestions as to where we go from here?" I asked a few minutes later. Charlie was busy drawing on the reverse side of the colouring sheet, alternating between orange and yellow. It seemed as good a time as any to try and make plans.

"Not really. I'm too tired to think clearly. I'm scared, and I'm still very confused about everything."

I felt the same way. I wanted to climb back into the car, drive home and throw myself at the mercy of my local constabulary, hoping to convince them of my innocence. But the nagging thought of what the murdering cop might have said and done to further implicate me in the shooting, made me cautious. Ours was a tough place to be in, tougher still to extricate ourselves from, and our next move had to be the right one for all of us.

"I suppose we could buy ourselves some thinking time," I suggested. "Rest up somewhere."

"Where?"

"I saw a sign on the way here for the library. Somewhere like that might be good. We could thrash this out while the kid does her thing in the kids' book section."

"What if we get seen?"

"What happened in the lay-by occurred too late for anything to have made the daily papers. So it'd only be the TV news, which I suspect is now running our photos. But this is serious and we have to create some space for you and I to talk. We can't do that sitting in the car. And while we're on that subject, I think we need to dump the Beemer."

Melissa dipped her head. "Do we have to decide something like that right now?"

I nodded. "Yes. I know you're tired, Melissa. So am I. But we simply can't delay any longer. Things are happening out there, and we're no closer to making any firm decisions as to what we do next. We have to find that time. And we have to do it as soon as we can."

Melissa turned her head to gaze out of the window by our booth. The sky was low and a little overcast, but the sun was pushing its way through and already starting to warm the day. Another humid one lay in store. She sighed, looking as weary as I felt. The huge weight of responsibility caused her shoulders to sag, and she gave a single nod of resignation.

It was still too early for the library, so once we had outstayed our welcome at AJ's, we paid up and left. Barbara was busy serving, but I left our waitress a tip. Decent enough to show our appreciation for her attitude and service, not too big to stick in the mind. We drove for a few minutes, before I located a large DIY store on an industrial estate on the edge of town and parked up again. This was better than a side street outside someone's home. No one would bother us, no one would consider it odd for us to be there; anyone who spotted us would probably assume we were waiting for someone inside the store. We were safe here. Relatively so.

Except from the kid.

First, she had to take a leak. She'd had one at the diner, but clearly one was not enough. Melissa took her into the store and asked to use the staff toilet. They were reluctant, she told me afterwards, but the kid's howls of protest had won the day. It seemed being little, loud and obnoxious had its merits. Prior to taking Charlie, Melissa had reached over and grabbed the keys from the BMW's ignition.

"I'm not in the mood to take chances," she said.

I didn't blame her for thinking the worst. In her place, I would have done exactly the same thing. A short while after their return, the kid was back on to the subject of her father. No sooner had Melissa talked her out of that, than she started to complain about being bored.

Her voice drove steel-tipped spikes into my brain. I had lived through it before with my own child, yet there is something about the incessant complaining that drives even the sanest people crazy. I was already most of the way there, so it was easy to tip me over the edge. In a flurry of arms and legs and grunts of disapproval, I got out to stretch my muscles, leaving the two of them to it for a few minutes. I went and sat on a small wooden fence that enveloped the site, watching the traffic hustle by.

Did any of those drivers have my kind of worries today? I wondered, glancing back at the car. For a moment I considered walking away. Just standing up, heading off down the street, and never looking back. Separately we were sad cases, together we were a liability. But the thought of that murdering cop and what he might have in store for Melissa and the kid reined me in. That and the fact that, as I had mentioned to Melissa shortly before falling asleep that morning, she was the only one who could get me out of trouble with the Dawson family. I wasn't sure which of these I gave greater weight to, and didn't dwell on it for too long, either. I was going back to the car, and that was all that mattered at that moment.

TEN

Hendricks hated taking shit, and he particularly hated taking shit from fellow cops. Jurisdictional pissing contests were a fact of life in law enforcement, with all agencies constantly craving their own slice of major case pie. Under normal circumstances, anything related to Ray Dawson would fall within his own purview at the NCA, but not when it came to murder. That was local CID or murder squads all the way. There was a place for him here somewhere, though. He was determined not to be shoved aside.

Having endured scepticism if not outright suspicion from even his own boss, it came as no surprise to Hendricks when the more senior detectives who arrived on the scene tried poking holes in his story. He was certain they were not looking hard at him for actually carrying out the hit on Dawson, but they were sharp enough to consider his presence to be more than coincidental. Not that this bothered him too much. He had NCA credentials and the support from his immediate superior. It didn't matter what the cops thought. Only that they kept out of his way. A tough ask when it was their investigation, not his.

Throughout the events unfolding around him and the time passing, Hendricks never strayed far from his own car. It wasn't that he was considering fleeing the scene, more that he felt more comfortable being in the best possible place should he choose to do so. He was leaning back against the Mondeo's bonnet when Detective Chief Inspector Randall from Taunton CID walked across to chat with him.

"I don't suppose you'll be losing sleep at having one less villain around, eh?" he said. Randall was the Senior Investigating

Officer. Tall and slim and built for a decent suit, the detective fidgeted with the knot of his tie as he spoke. His voice was deep and cracked from recent overuse. Hendricks suspected the DCI had a good nose for sniffing out bullshit. Which meant he had to be on his own game. At all times.

"Not so's you'd notice," he admitted. Hendricks continued to slouch against the Mondeo, affecting a casual pose. "Ray Dawson was the worst kind of garbage, believe me. But it won't be long before someone else takes his place. Down the years it's come to feel like an extended game of whack-a-mole."

Randall nodded. "True enough. You think this could be a turf war?"

"Dawson had a habit of crushing those sort of efforts early on. I was thinking more of his brother, Chris."

"I have some vague recollection of seeing Dawson's name at some point, but I know little about him or his business. I guess if you lot are involved then he must be up to his neck in some serious shit. Well, was."

"The man was a poisonous bastard, that's for sure. Chris is even worse. My guess is he'll look to expand their empire."

"Which won't go down well with other villains."

"Right. People smuggling, knocking shops, drugs. You name it, they do it. But people just like the Dawson family also want their share of the action. If it goes the way I think it will, bodies will be piling up on the streets."

Randall winced. "So, in some ways, then, tonight's murder didn't do you any favours after all."

Hendricks spread his hands. "Well, when you put it like that…"

"You must be feeling a bit put out. In many ways, Dawson is your target, but you don't get to investigate his murder. That must seem a bit unfair to you."

"It is what it is. Those are the rules, and it's hardly the first time something like this has happened. We do our level best at the NCA to prevent them from operating, and when they are out of the picture we move on to the next. No matter how that is achieved."

"You're a better man than me," Randall said. "I'd be thoroughly cheesed off, especially if, as you say, his murder actually makes your job harder in the long run."

Hendricks was trying to play it cool, but he saw an opening of sorts. "Don't get me wrong," he said. "I'm as keen as anyone to find out who did this, even if it's only to see where it leaves me and my team."

"Well, we can have a chat later about how and when we keep the NCA informed. For now, though, please, stick around."

With Dawson's body now on its way to the mortuary in nearby Yeovil, the crime scene still being examined in minute detail by dozens of officers and CSI technicians, Hendricks looked on as Mike Lynch's Saab was hauled up onto a transporter, ready for relocation to the closest forensics yard. As he watched the mundane task, he thought about how to handle things from this point on. He wasn't fooled by Randall. The DCI's last words were more instruction than invitation, Hendricks thought. But it played into his own hands. He needed to remain involved, liaising with the investigation team, pathologist and the CSI crew. At least until the first lead on the whereabouts of Lynch, Dawson's kid or her nanny came through. But as the man responsible for Dawson's murder, he also knew he had a lot of shit to tidy up.

Not for the first time he asked himself if he had covered all the bases. The gun would not be found, of that he was confident. So far none of the detectives had summoned up the nerve to request a check of his clothing or a GSR swab. There was no legal imperative as he was not known to have been involved in the shooting or to have been anywhere close to it when it occurred. Hendricks didn't see any of these locals having the balls to even suggest it. Even if they did, he could refuse. The gunpowder residue bothered him. He'd washed his hands with some bottled water, had swapped out his suit jacket for official NCA attire that he carried in the boot of his car. But it would require only one person to take their suspicions further for his situation to worsen considerably.

Mike Lynch's abandoned car and the absence of Charlotte Dawson and her nanny, Melissa Anderson, lent credence to the theory that Lynch was the man they were hunting down. But Hendricks was convinced that Randall was putting two and two together and arriving at something approximating the correct answer. As yet there had been no formal interview. It would come, though. And he needed to be prepared.

"So listen, I have a favour to ask," he said to Randall. "You know the score. Behind the scenes, calls at a high level will be made. One way or another I'm sure the NCA will be asked to consult on this murder, simply because we know so much more than you do about the Dawson family and their entire enterprise. I'd appreciate it if we could arrange something between us now, rather than wait for it to trickle its way down through various channels."

The DCI met his gaze. He took a moment. Nodded once. "I'll discuss it with my team. We've kept the media at bay so far by insisting they remain behind the barriers we've erected further up the road. But they'll have their turn. This is a major enquiry, and we have to make sure we run this by the book because the scrutiny will be tremendous."

"And you think my request is out of order?"

"No. I think it's perfectly reasonable that we would ask the NCA for advice on someone like Ray Dawson. And his family, for that matter. But – and don't get me wrong – as the person who discovered the victim, we haven't even cleared you as a suspect yet."

Hendricks kept himself in check. No eye flicker. No nerve pulse in the cheek. He knew the tell-tale signs every bit as much as Randall did, so it was important not to reveal any unwarranted anxiety. However, some was entirely justified.

"Of course. I accept that. But we both know it's just a matter of ticking boxes, right? Whilst you haven't formally cleared me, you're not actually treating me as a suspect. At least, I would hope not."

"No, not at all." Randall gave a relaxed grin. "Trouble is, coincidental or not, you are our only witness, of sorts. I need to run it by my team, and at least one rank higher, before I can sanction sharing information with you. You understand that, I'm sure."

"Of course. Just let me know the score when you can."

As Randall walked away, Hendricks closed his eyes and tried to capture the conversation in his mind's eye. *Had the DCI demonstrated any genuine suspicion?* He was an experienced detective, so he was almost certainly proficient in playing the same games Hendricks himself was familiar with. Time would tell, he supposed.

As the transporter disappeared into the distance, a chatter went up around the scene. One of the cops, a uniformed sergeant by the name of Shaw, sauntered across to him and gave him the news that Mike Lynch's bank card had been used at a motel off the A303. Hendricks had to choke that down and fight off the urge to jump in his car and speed away.

"Are you heading off over there?" he asked the sergeant.

Shaw shook his head. "Let's wait and see if they're still there. If it's even him. Way I see it, he'd have to be pretty dumb to use his card just hours after killing anyone, let alone someone as high profile as Ray Dawson."

Hendricks had no choice but to agree. "Okay. Keep me up to speed, yes?"

Shaw gave a shrug. "I'm sure somebody will, officer."

Putting a red flag against Lynch's credit and debit cards was a standard move, but still Hendricks was surprised they had given the order so quickly. They had also been swift to deal with the media and keep them at a real distance. He realised now that he could not underestimate this team. To do so would be a huge mistake.

Mulling it over, something occurred to him. He used his work phone to first access and then sign in to his NCA account. He pulled up a specific database to run Lynch's family information. It took a few minutes, but eventually he discovered the man's wife and daughter exiting the country, bound for the USA. No release valve for Lynch there. The net was still loose, but tightening all the while. When he was done with the phone, Hendricks crossed his arms and leaned back against his car once again. There was nothing for him to do now but wait.

Thirty minutes later, DCI Randall broke away from the group encamped within a portable crime scene control room and jogged across to him.

"Bad news," he said, his face a picture of regret. "A night porter confirmed Lynch booked the room. But when armed officers breached it, they found it empty. Dawson's vehicle is not in the car park, either."

"Damn!" Hendricks tried to portray anything but the elation he felt. "Were the child and the nanny still with him?"

"The porter never saw them. However, three cups were found to have been used."

"That's interesting."

"Isn't it just."

Hendricks shook his head. "So, he somehow managed to smuggle the woman and girl into the place and then back out again. Without either of them apparently kicking up a fuss. Now that is worth some further consideration."

"You bet it will be. Oh, and I've had a word with the team. This Lynch character is clearly our number one suspect, so we don't have a problem with you tagging along. For the time being, anyway."

"That's great news. Thank you. It's much appreciated."

The DCI shrugged. "Well, like you said, the order will come down from on high at some point. And, to be honest, your perspective might come in handy."

With that he was gone again, dashing back to the long and narrow mobile building.

***

Hendricks became more agitated as the night wore on. Further discussions with Randall had been benign, but those with others in the investigation team began to feel more like interrogations. He knew he was being paranoid, but then the trump card against him was a car containing three people, two of whom may well be able to identify him as the man who shot and killed Ray Dawson. And that car was getting further and further away.

Dawn was still no more than a promise when he noticed a new vehicle roll up onto the scene. He watched with interest as a suit exited the dark, plain saloon, spoke a few words to a female uniform, who then pointed in his direction. The newcomer reached him with one hand extended, the other holding up a NCA warrant card.

"SO Hendricks. I'm Officer Nutton," the man introduced himself. "I've been sent to provide you with some assistance."

Hendricks bit down on a rush of anger. It was hard not to take immediate offence. Sure, Robin Dwyer may well have suspected something to be amiss, but could not have known for certain. Dispatching someone out here to hold his hand, perhaps even to report back on him, was clearly an unspoken rebuke.

"I wasn't expecting anyone," Hendricks managed to say, though he barely opened his mouth to do so. "I mean, I wasn't told to expect anyone."

Nutton shrugged. "What can I say? You're lead officer, of course. I'm just here to back you up and help out in any way I can."

Hendricks nodded. Realised the man still had his hand out. A swift, reluctant shake later, Hendricks turned on his heels and stepped across to his own vehicle. Door open he paused. Every nerve end was screaming at him to get the hell out of there. For all anyone knew he had legitimately stumbled upon a murder scene, but that wasn't how it felt at that precise moment. The wagons were circling around him, but it seemed very much as if they were penning him in rather than fending others off.

"No offence, Nutton, but I don't see any need for two of us to be out here. This is a police investigation, after all. If the NCA get any purchase here, it will be as a spare wheel. They'll allow us to tag along once some pressure from above is applied, but as a silent partner only. Two bodies on that sort of detail seems like overkill to me."

"No offence taken. Manager Dwyer made some calls and it was thought that, given you discovered the crime scene, the detectives in charge might want to keep you at arm's length. I'm here really to try and grease the gears if at all possible. Dwyer said to call him if you had any issues, but that he would be tied up in meetings for most of the day."

Pursing his lips, Hendricks saw the sense in Dwyer making that call. It wasn't necessarily a slight, rather a sound strategic move. Having done so he had then gone to ground. Making himself unavailable was another wily ploy on Dwyer's part. There really was no option but to accept the situation and move on.

Which raised a further problem for him – as if he needed more. It was always going to be hard enough trying to both keep up with and ahead of the local cops. Having a partner now made it virtually impossible. Hendricks nodded to himself. He was going to have to shake Nutton at some stage. All he needed now was the right opportunity.

***

The lay-by was crammed with vehicles and people. The portable control room took up much of the available space, yet spread around it were seven liveried police vehicles, and four unmarked cars. In the mix, uniformed officers, suited detectives, and forensic investigators clad all in white scurried back and forth like worker bees.

Rhino looked down the hillside at the scene through a pair of binoculars whilst thumbing a number on his phone. "We're on site, boss," he said when his call was answered. "Not close, but we can see what's going on. Not near enough to hear anything, though."

He listened to Chris Dawson's response, then replied, "Yeah, we're starting to figure out the main players. None of them have left the scene so far. No one getting too excited, either. All pretty routine. Any word from your man?"

"As you suggest, Rhino," Dawson said, "there's not a lot happening just yet."

Rhino wanted to press a little harder. Felt as if he needed to be aware if the boss's bought-and-paid-for cop was somewhere down there at the foot of the hill. It seemed to him they were missing a trick if so. He could see no advantage in him and Haystacks being in exactly the same place as an informant who was balls-deep in their midst. On the other hand, he was a man who followed orders and got on with the job. The less he knew, the less he could tell if he was questioned.

"So what's the play here?" he asked instead. "Your man gives us a heads-up when they get a line on this Mike Lynch guy, yeah?"

"That's the plan, Rhino."

"How much of a head start do we get?"

"As much as circumstances dictate. Could be five minutes, could be an hour. Bank on the former, Rhino. Or somewhere in between."

"And the job – no change there?" He and Chris had discussed privately the parameters and expectations of what was required.

"None. Don't worry, Rhino. If I change my mind you'll be the first to know. But don't hold your breath."

Rhino glanced at the time on his phone's display. Something had to happen soon. It had been a few hours since Ray had been gunned down. "Anything else, boss?"

"They had a spot of excitement earlier, before you two arrived. This Lynch fuckwit booked a room using his bank card. Dumb bastard. He was gone by the time the filth arrived. The room was empty, and no sign of Ray's Beemer, either. But if the bloke is that stupid, they'll have him soon enough."

Rhino let that sink in. "Which way is he headed?" he asked.

"Hard to tell, Rhino. East of you, but there's no knowing which direction he took when he left the motel."

"Any further thoughts on Melissa, boss?"

"Plenty. And none of them good."

"If any of the lead players move out and we haven't heard from you, you want us to go with them or wait here?"

"Use your initiative, Rhino. But make the right choice."

"Prick," Rhino said after the call ended.

ELEVEN

The kid had settled down by the time I returned to the car. When Melissa then got out for a smoke leaving me and the kid alone, I feared the worst. Instead I was caught by surprise when Charlie sat forward, peered up at me from between the seats, and said, "Do you like cartoon films, Mike?"

Grinning and grateful for a reprieve from the bleating, I turned and replied, "Yes. Actually, I do. Which are your favourite ones?"

The kid wrestled with that for a while. "I like *Toy Story*. I like *Ice Age*. I like *Moana*. I like *Frozen*. Oh, and I like *Shrek*." Her eyes flared at the thought of this film.

"Well, who doesn't like *Shrek*?"

"Amanda Wilson. She thinks he's silly."

I chuckled. "Maybe it's Amanda Wilson who's the silly one. I like *Up*. Have you seen that one? You know, the old man, the boy, the house and the balloons."

"And the dogs," the kid said, giggling and nodding.

"Squirrels!" we both cried at the same time, which set Charlie laughing harder still. She made a sweet sound.

"You're like the man in *Up*," she said.

"I am? I don't look much like him."

"No, but he was very grumpy, too."

I had to laugh at that. "He was, I suppose. But he did have rather a lot to be grumpy about."

"Roger was never grumpy."

"I'm sure he was from time to time, but he probably just hid it from you. Would you like me to do that, Charlie? Hide it from you when I'm feeling grumpy?"

She nodded. So serious was her look that I wanted to laugh again, but I sensed this issue was important to the kid. It made me wonder whether Ray Dawson had managed to keep his world from her as much as Melissa believed.

"Tell you what," I said. "How about I try my best not to be grumpy? I can't promise I won't be, but I will try my hardest."

"Okay. So, do you want to watch a cartoon now?"

"Now? We can't at the moment, not while we're in the car."

At this, the kid nodded enthusiastically, rummaged around inside the pink backpack that had been sitting in the footwell, before emerging with an iPad. "I watch them on here. Do you want me to find *Up* for you?"

I was touched that she would allow me to choose rather than opt for one of her own favourites. I shook my head, but gave her a smile and a wink. "I'll have to drive as soon as Melissa gets back in the car. But thank you, Charlie. You choose what you want for now, and maybe we'll watch it together later, eh?"

That appeared to pacify her. Moments later the BMW rocked slightly as Melissa climbed back in. "What were you two talking about?" she asked. "I could hear you both jabbering away."

"Cartoons," I answered. "Cartoons and grumpiness."

"No surprise on either one."

"That hurts. Anyhow, Charlie and I have reached an agreement. I'm going to try and be a little less grumpy around her, and if I am my prize will be I get to choose a cartoon to watch."

Melissa raised her eyebrows. "Impressive. Let's see how long that lasts."

I couldn't fault her scepticism.

***

A few minutes later, I set off for the library. I followed signs once I reached the river. Traffic was dense, but flowing nicely enough. I noticed a couple of car parks, but then saw a different sign and something occurred to me. I checked to see that the kid was engrossed in her film, small headphones worn over her ears.

"How about I drop you two off first," I said over my shoulder. "I could take the Beemer to the train station and leave it in the car park there? That way, if it's found they might assume we caught a train out of here. Could be a useful bit of misdirection."

Melissa nodded. "Even better, you could use a credit card to buy three tickets. If your card is being traced, that would work perfectly."

"I'd thought of that. The problem is, they may well have already put a block on my cards. I do have a business one that I use for emergencies, and they may not have got round to tracing it yet. I'll try it at the station, and if it works I'll also get as much cash as it will allow me."

"You know, it's possible they will leave your cards unblocked. It's a way of tracing you, so I think they'd be reluctant to cut it off. In fact, they'd probably love for you to use one."

I jabbed a finger in her direction. "You could be right about that. I'll try my usual card, and only use the other one if it fails. We may need something for emergencies."

"Why drop us off first?" she asked me. It felt to me as if there was a small note of suspicion in her voice. "Why not just drive straight there now?"

It was easy to understand Melissa's concerns. She and I had begun to relax a little around each other, found some common ground. Her trust was something I had yet to earn. "It will be a lot easier for me to get back to the library on my own. The sign back there said four miles to the station, and we're almost at the library now. Once I've parked up the car I can hike it back in under an hour, but it would be a long walk for Charlie."

"We could get a taxi."

"No. The police are bound to check once they find the car."

I saw the doubt in her face. I thought I knew why. "You're wondering if I am going to come back, right? You think I'm going to say goodbye to you both and then just keep on driving?"

"Something like that. Can you blame me?"

I let go a frustrated sigh. I dropped my voice lower. "To be honest, if I wasn't in the frame for murder I wouldn't be here now. That makes me sound like a complete bastard, I know, given how you and the kid are caught up in all this with me, but that's me. My problem is, as we have already discussed, that you are my alibi. The way I see it, only you can get me out of trouble with both the police and your boss's brother. I need you, Melissa. Far more than you need me, in fact. And until we've worked out exactly what we're going to do next, that's the way it will remain."

Still she seemed uncertain. There was a sadness in her eyes I had not seen before.

Traffic was a little backed up so I had to concentrate harder for a few minutes. When it started easing I glanced behind me again. "Why would it be so bad for you if I did do a runner anyway?" I asked her. "I'm hardly any help."

Melissa shrugged. Hugged herself. "I suppose part of it is the same as your reasoning: you are also my alibi, and the only one who saw what that NCA cop did. But I suppose I was also hoping you would somehow find a way out of this for us."

"Why? Because I'm a man? Because I'm more mature?"

"Yes. Both of those."

I gave a cough-cum-laugh. "Yes, well I think you've already got a pretty good idea of what kind of man I am. As for maturity, that just makes me more fearful and self-absorbed."

Eventually she surrendered. "Just come back, Mike. Maybe then we'd have got some idea of how to handle this."

"I promise you, Melissa, I will come straight back."

"In that case, when you do, you can start calling me Mel. That's what my friends call me."

I nodded. Surprised and pleased. We seemed to have reached a level of understanding that we could both live with. Neither of us were enjoying our time together, but we *were* together, and destined to be for a while yet.

Three minutes later, I nosed the BMW off the main road and pulled up outside a smart, single-storey building that looked only a few years old. It was a quiet street, clean and easier on the eye than those around it. "I'll find you in the kids' section," I told Melissa. I glanced around as the two climbed out, fearful of a beat cop or a patrol car drifting by. Melissa steered Charlie ahead of her, her arms burdened by the straps of one holdall and one pink backpack. Moments later, I drove off on my own in a gangster's BMW.

It never once occurred to me to run. That was last night's attitude, born of panic and fear and the loss of control that comes with those emotions. I still wanted to be far away, free of the shackles I felt had been imposed upon me by having to take care of Mel and the kid. Nothing had changed there. The difference was that, in the early hours of the morning my mind had been in such a state that I would have left the two of them to their own devices and not thought twice about it. Time has a way of restructuring priorities, of paving the way for our natural instincts to find a way through.

I found the station easy enough with the familiar logo guiding the way. I'd had to cross back over the river Avon, and as I hung a right at a small roundabout an Audi with police livery slipped in behind me. I felt my cheeks flush as I tightened my grip on the steering wheel. My focus switched back and forth between the road ahead and the road behind. At one point, I wondered what might happen if I just stopped, pulled up the handbrake, got out and turned myself in. It felt like anything had to be better than this torture.

One glance in the rear-view revealed the cop in the passenger seat speaking into the communication device pinned to the breast pocket of his bright yellow jacket. I wondered whether the BMW's number plate had raised a red flag to those behind. If the cop might be calling it in right there and then, summoning backup; armed officers, not just prepared but eager to take down a suspected gunman. The longer it went on the more I became certain of it, and I started preparing my story.

I turned off towards the station car park, believing with utmost certainty that the Audi's indicator was going to flash, that the police car would follow me up towards the station and into the car park. But even as a tremor started juddering its way along my extended arms, I saw the vehicle continue on its way along the main thoroughfare. I let go of about five minutes' worth of breath. Sweat trickled down from my hairline. I could not recall having been as frightened as this in many years.

TWELVE

Melissa was proven right – my credit card had not been frozen. From the ATM outside the station I withdrew the maximum amount of cash allowed, and then used the same card to purchase three one-way tickets to Paddington. I chatted briefly to the women behind the ticket counter, hoping she would remember me when questioned later. I made some lame joke about my daughter hoping to meet the famous bear who wore a hat and ate marmalade sandwiches. From the adjacent coffee bar I bought a coffee and deliberately screwed up my order on three occasions.

The pavements on the way back to the library were as busy as the roads, and though I kept my head down, shoulders hunched forward as I walked, my paranoia soon kicked in. It was not long before every man and woman who came towards me was a plain-clothes cop, every step behind me the last I would hear before having handcuffs snapped on. Every movement around me was aggressive, every building somehow hostile. When I rubbed my brow it came back soaked with sweat, and each step seemed to take me further away from my destination. It was like walking on a conveyor belt travelling in the wrong direction.

I had travelled barely a mile before I felt a familiar panic clamouring in my chest, closely followed by a yearning which never strayed too far away even at the best of times. I forced myself to focus on the paving slabs, taking no notice of the shops, I passed along the route. My head wasn't right, and it would be hard to pass an off-licence or pub or bar. It might even prove impossible. Finding oblivion courtesy of alcohol was not *the* answer, but it was *an* answer. One that had done the trick for me on so many occasions. Yet with each step taken I silently managed to talk myself down off the ledge, began to turn my mind away from those unwelcome desires. It was with no small measure of relief, however, when I turned towards the side street that would take me back to the library.

Its interior was plain but pleasant, a vaulted ceiling lending the place an airy, open feel. There were posters and framed pictures on every wall, advertisements for events, some local photography. The librarian was busy with a customer when I entered, which saved me from smiling a greeting. I worked my way around the numerous sections until I located the area set aside for children's books. When Melissa looked up at me with what I imagined was genuine relief, I was touched by this small show of faith.

The kid was sitting on a small plastic bench, a large colourful book splayed open in her lap. "Sometimes it's the only way to shut her up," Melissa confessed. "That or her iPad or Pod. She could be lost in either world for hours if I let her."

"Well, let her. For now, anyway. We have things we need to sort out."

She was seated close to the kid on her own at a small adult-sized table, a *Private Eye* magazine in front of her. "Did everything go smoothly?" she asked.

I nodded, taking a seat opposite. I explained what had happened, omitting my thirst for alcohol and hunger for release. "I got us out some cash, bought the tickets as well, so hopefully they will eventually look in one direction while we're disappearing the opposite way. What we have won't last long, but long enough. If we don't put an end to this today, then it has to be tomorrow at the latest."

"I feel as if I could sleep for a week," she said. Her clothes were more crumpled, hair a little more unkempt, but the biggest change was her eyes. She appeared harrowed, cheeks pinched. "I can't believe it's been less than twelve hours since the lay-by."

"I take it you didn't get any kip last night."

"Not a wink. You did, though. Snored all the time."

"Sorry." My wife had complained about that. An operation on my septum had contained it for a while, but it was a hopeless case. For some reason I related this to Melissa.

"Is that why she left you?"

"What makes you think she left me?"

"I just assumed."

"Because I'm such a prick?"

She shrugged. "You told me you were a drunk, that your marriage ended. Your ex-wife and daughter live on another continent. I threw the dice."

"I could have left her."

She shook her head this time, offering a strained smile. "I doubt it."

"Well, it just so happens that she did leave me. A lot of shit rained down on me in a very short space of time. It was hard to take, and I didn't handle it well. I lost a decent job, and for some reason that was the final straw. I drank. I changed. I would have left me, too."

"What other shit? You lost your job, but what happened before that to make your life so miserable? Was it the death of your parents?" Melissa regarded me with what felt like genuine concern.

"That. And other things. It's a long story. For another time, perhaps."

"I'll hold you to that."

I spread my hands. "How about you, Mel? What did you do before you started working for Dawson?"

"I got a job straight out of sixth form college. Worked as a PA for a businessman. Very successful business, too. It was a decent job."

"Sounds like it. Why the switch?"

Mel turned her face away. "Let's just say he wanted me to be more than a PA to him. It wasn't an amiable end to that career. He couldn't exactly fire me, because I knew too much about him and his business and he didn't want a wrongful dismissal case on his hands. But he didn't have to sack me, he just had to make things so uncomfortable that I would walk. Which is what I did."

I nodded. It happened to women. Always had, and probably always would. The casting couch spread far beyond the movie world. I felt for her, but decided now was not the time to probe any deeper. It was time to get our heads on straight anyway.

"So, have you given any thought to a way out of our current predicament?" I asked.

"You must have some suggestions."

"As it happens, I do. Two actually, but neither of them are ideal."

"What are they?"

"We've been through them before, Melissa… Mel." I smiled. "I think we need to accept that our options remain the same as they have been all along. There is no magic bullet. We go to the police and tell them everything we know. The problem there, of course, is that the cop who murdered your boss will have considered that eventuality, and will be doing his utmost to make things look ugly for me. You, too, possibly. Planting evidence, coming up with a fake eyewitness. Something along those lines. What he's not going to do is sit on his arse and wait for us to hang him with the truth.

"Or we could try and track down your boss's brother, and at the very least get him off my back. Maybe he can sort out the whole matter for us, bearing in mind he's the kid's uncle. I can only guess at how he will deal with the cop, but of the two options it's probably the best."

"And that's it? You've come up with nothing else? That really is no different to what we considered before."

"I realise that, and I said as much, but what the hell else is there? What would you have us do?"

"I don't know, Mike, but there has to be something better."

"Just saying it's so doesn't make it so, Mel."

"I realise that. I'm not a child."

I shook my head. "Why are you so reluctant to go to Chris Dawson? Surely, he will do everything he can to help. We have his niece. When we tell him what really happened, he's bound to do everything in his power to make things right. He can maybe even come and collect us, give us a place to hide away until something gets sorted out."

For a moment she said nothing, seeming to consider her response. "He's not as nice as Ray is. Was," Melissa said finally. "He's much more aggressive. He has a volatile temper, and can be very nasty with it. Vicious. He's unpredictable, too. I don't know what he would do. He would need convincing that our version was the truth. In fact, he might not even wait to hear our side. His brother has been killed, and Chris does not take prisoners. Anyway, it's moot: I don't have any idea where he lives, other than it's in Chigwell somewhere. And I doubt he's in the phone book."

Now it was my turn to pause for thought. I didn't like the sound of the man, and knew a little of his reputation, but the situation wasn't as hopeless as Melissa imagined. "I can find out where he lives. If that's the main problem, I can make one call and get his address within minutes."

She looked up at me, eyes wide. "How?"

I glanced around us, as I had done every few minutes since walking into the building. Mainly to ensure we could not be overheard, but also searching for signs that we had been compromised.

"I told you before, I used to be a journalist. I still have contacts in the business."

"But the cops and NCA will be watching him, surely. Maybe even listening in. The officer who killed Ray is bound to work out that Chris is our only option. We could walk right into their hands."

"So, we give it some more thought. Think of a way we can contact Dawson without anyone being tipped off, and arrange for us to meet with him elsewhere."

"It's risky. He's so unpredictable."

"Yeah. And sitting here doing nothing is risky as well. If the situation can be explained to him, if I can get to talk to him somehow without needing to meet, we may be able to figure things out."

"I… I'm not sure, Mike. I need a little more time to think about it."

I wasn't in favour of putting it off any longer. The more time that passed, the more likely it was that someone would recognise us. "Thing is, Mel, I don't know how much time we have. And what is there to think about? Yes, we take a chance that we'll get grabbed up by the cops if we get as far as meeting Chris, but if the alternative is to walk into a police station…?"

"I see the sense in what you're saying, Mike. I just want to take a little while longer to think it through. I'm really tired and not at my best right now. It's all so confusing. I have Charlie to consider as well, remember."

I nodded. How could I possibly forget? We had grown a little closer, and I did not want to push her away again by forcing the matter at this juncture. "Well, while you're doing that there's no harm in my getting the information we need. Once we have it we can choose to use it or not. But it will save time if we already have the address and phone number when we finally make a decision. How does that sound?"

This time Melissa was not shaking her head. Perhaps I was getting through to her. "That's logical, I suppose. But won't your contact have seen the news? Won't they be suspicious of your motives?"

I had not considered that, but trusted that both my personal friendship and my previous reputation in the business would be enough to at least open the door for me. "I'll get the information we need. I'm confident of that. But whatever we decide, we have to get out of here and move on as soon as we can. It's quiet enough at the moment, but the longer we stay in one place the more chance we have of being identified. Especially if the librarian gets a bit nosey."

"I suppose." She shivered as if caught in a sudden frosty cross-breeze. "I hate the thought of leaving here and going back out on the streets, but you're probably right. We can't stay here all day."

That settled it. I was about to stand when my eyes flashed across to Charlie and I recalled our conversation about which film to watch. Something had nagged me at the time, but it was a fleeting thought and I had dismissed it. Now it swam back into reach and I grabbed at it.

"Mel, does Charlie's iPad have Wi-Fi?"

"No. Ray had it disabled. Didn't want her accidentally finding something unsuitable on the internet. Why do you ask?"

"I thought I might be able to use it to run some searches, perhaps even mail my daughter. By now she and my ex will be both worried and under some pressure from both cops and possibly FBI agents. I can't imagine how Wendy is taking it if so."

"There are computers here in the library," Melissa said.

"I know. I don't like the idea of using them. Who knows who is watching what these days. I hear they work miracles over at GCHQ."

"Still. You should consider it. You're right about your daughter. She'll be very frightened, and concerned, I imagine."

"I am worried about that. But I'm pretty sure if they are running a trace on her account they can pinpoint exactly where we are the moment my mail drops into her inbox. The IP address of the sender is contained in the mail's header. It won't take them more than a few seconds to identify the library system. We can't have them know we're here long after we're supposed to have left for London on the train. I thought if the iPad had a connection it would make it much harder to trace, especially if I switched it off as soon as I sent the mail."

"Sorry. I don't know what to say." To her credit she seemed genuinely concerned.

"Do you know if it was disabled or removed?"

"I'm not sure. Knowing Ray, I'd say he left nothing to chance."

"Okay. I'll give it some more thought. Meanwhile, there are some public phones just outside the entrance so I'll go and make my call now."

Melissa managed a weak smile. "I hope your friend can help us, Mike. To be honest, I don't know how we'll manage otherwise."

I gave a single nod and turned to go. I said nothing more because there was nothing left to say.

THIRTEEN

Two men stood together on Lambeth Bridge facing Westminster. The London Eye rose up like a halo in the distance. Beneath them the river's flow was steady. A single small boat was chugging away towards the east. The bridge itself was teeming with traffic, commuters and tourists. It was a little after ten in the morning and London was in full swing.

"How are things at Thames House?" the man from the Home Office asked. His name was Robert Parks, Knight of the Realm, and he was a senior officer within the lavish new Home Office accommodation on Marsham Street. He was sixty years old, trim, tall, with waves of grey hair swept back casually as if to emphasise their rude health. Immaculately dressed in a dark grey pinstripe suit that could never have been purchased off-the-peg, he cut an imposing figure.

His opposite number at the Security Service, whose MI5 building almost cast a shadow over the two of them, gave a curt nod.

"Busy as usual," he replied. Unlike the man standing by his side, whose accent was pure Home Counties, Darren Hedgeman was proud of his Yorkshire roots and had a voice that suggested no privilege in his upbringing. His own suit was more Marks and Spencer than Gieves and Hawkes, but it was a sharp fit. He carried himself upright, like the ex-soldier he was.

"I dare say you could have done without this latest… disappointment, then?" Parks remarked.

"Admittedly, it hasn't helped. I would rather have maintained my focus on counter-terrorism, that's for sure."

"Naturally. But we all have to react to demands as and when they arise. I have to say, Darren, this seemed a simple request when it was made."

"Nothing like this is ever simple. That said, only misfortune prevented a successful outcome. I have confidence that the matter will be resolved today."

"Do you indeed? I'm not sure I share your optimism. I think we would all feel more comfortable if different personnel were involved from here on in. Someone more suitable and experienced. An outside agency, even, one more step removed than the last."

Hedgeman inclined his head. "Suitability was not an issue. I seem to remember we agreed upon that at the time. As I said before, what happened was unfortunate, and could not have been predicted."

"And still the end result is failure. So, one must question either the plan, the operative, or perhaps both. From your brief report, I would suggest there were other ways in which this operation could have been carried out. Ways which would have had a better chance of success and left less opportunity for, ah, shall we say *misfortune* to intervene."

The rebuke was clear.

Hedgeman took a moment to respond, shaping his thoughts carefully. The dirty brown water of the Thames was a familiar sight and sound, yet still it had the capacity to relax him. "Hindsight is a wonderful thing, Sir Robert. Assuming we are not rewriting history here, the basic plan was given a green light. Reproach can surely follow at a later date. For now, our attention is on rescuing the situation and achieving the desired result."

Parks shot his cuffs. Gold cufflinks gleamed in the sunlight. "Of course. And I am confident lessons will be learned. All the same, whatever the reason, the situation has changed and now would be a good time to introduce an alternative."

"I'm not sure I can agree with that assessment."

For the first time since the two men had begun their conversation, the man from the Home Office removed his gaze from the river and turned to Hedgeman. A slight tic around his left eye gave an indication that his calm demeanour had been altered.

"I don't mean to be brutal," he said, "but neither your assessment nor your agreement are being sought at this juncture. I have my own paymasters, Darren, and they have instructed me to organise something more appropriate to the revised conditions. I am passing that along to you in your role as the person who can facilitate that for us. Good enough?"

If it wasn't, it had to be. Hedgeman knew that if he took this matter to his own boss, even the most secretive and informal Home Office directive would have to be followed through. This was not a governmental edict, but Parks *was* the Home Office.

He gave a reluctant shrug. "You said something about 'appropriate to the revised conditions'? I have already relayed my insistence that affirmative action be taken on the new player."

Parks drew himself upright and let go a deep breath. He glanced down at the Thames once again before allowing his gaze to wander back up along the embankment towards Westminster and the seat of power.

"The situation has changed significantly. The thinking from on high now is that it is best to eradicate any possibility of this coming back to bite us."

Hedgeman frowned. "You mean we now include our initial operative?"

"I mean we now include everyone involved."

The man from 'Five' turned his head to stare at Parks. "This comes from the top?"

"It does."

"Severe, don't you think?"

"It has to be managed. Controlled. It's what we do."

For a few minutes after Parks had left, Hedgeman leaned on the handrail of the bridge and stared down at the murky water beneath him. He wasn't a naïve man. He knew that operations sanctioned by his office in the past had resulted in collateral damage. That children had been caught up in maintaining the security of the nation. There was a good deal of blood on his hands. More than he cared to reflect upon. But he had never knowingly ordered a hit on a child before. There were enough ghosts in his life. He didn't know if he had room for even one more.

He looked up as someone drew alongside him.

"Did you get all that?" he asked.

The newcomer nodded. "Recorded. File sent to the secure cloud e-mail account."

"What do you think, Simon?"

"Not entirely unexpected. After all, why else am I here?"

Hedgeman turned his head. Shook it momentarily. "I saw the video, by the way. A bit over the top wasn't it? Using a water pistol?"

"Better than the real thing."

"Naturally. Which I assume was the next logical threat."

"It was. And it got us the information we needed."

"Indeed," Hedgeman said. "All of which leads us back here."

"I'm sorry. Orders are orders, though."

"But all of them? I didn't anticipate this going so far."

"Nothing you can do about it now, Darren. Be pragmatic, and consider what happens if you aren't. If it's not you ordering me, it'll be your replacement ordering someone else."

"Well… maybe that's the way it should be, then."

"They're still going to be every bit as dead. This way, someone it matters to is in the game. Maybe one day you'll be able to use these recordings. Your replacement might not have a conscience."

"But a little girl…?"

Simon shrugged. "Who knows, she could be the final straw. When all the shards of this little puzzle are finally snapped together, she could be the piece that sticks out. The alternative – to be blunt – is that you get added to the list. Then what?"

A cloud passed overhead, temporarily fending off both the light and the heat. Hedgeman felt as if something similar had happened to his heart. Perhaps even his soul. But that it might be more permanent. Running a security service, even one as benign as MI5 mostly was, came with price tag. It consumed morals, stripped away dignity, devoured self-respect. A few moments passed before he hung his head again and said, "I can't save her now, can I?"

"No," the other man said. "But if you hang in long enough you just might save the next one."

FOURTEEN

There was a group of four public telephones on either side of a large square pillar directly outside the library entrance. Fortunately, one of them still accepted good old-fashioned money. I dialled a number I had long ago committed to memory, and hoped it was still in service.

"Susan Healey," announced a bright voice after only two rings.

I felt my chest tighten. A heady mix of both relief and anxiety caused my stomach to churn. "Susan, please don't say my name or let anyone around you see there's something wrong."

After the slightest of pauses, my closest ex-colleague and friend said, "Oh, hello. How are you?"

We had not seen one another for more than five years, hadn't spoken in almost two. I wondered if her instincts had kicked into gear and she had used the pause to start recording our conversation. On balance, I didn't think it mattered.

"To be honest, Sue, not so good. In fact, things are about as lousy as they could be."

"So I gather." Her manner was calm, perhaps even a little cool. I briefly considered spilling the whole story there and then, but was certain that doing so would spur on those journalistic instincts, which might result in Susan putting herself in harm's way.

"I can't tell you exactly what happened right now, Sue. For your own sake. I don't want you sniffing around the wrong people. Or worse, them sniffing around you. All I *can* say is that you shouldn't believe everything you hear. You will get to learn the truth, hopefully very soon, and perhaps you will even get the exclusive. But before that, I could really use your help."

"Tell me how. I'll tell you if I can."

"I need contact information relating to Chris Dawson. I need his address, telephone numbers and those of his favourite haunts, mail addresses, plus the same for any close known associates, that sort of thing."

A second pause. When she spoke again, her voice was more hesitant. "I'm not sure I can do all of that. Any of it, in fact. Given… given the circumstances."

There had to be other people close by her desk. I thought about what she might be trying to tell me. Or ask me.

"Sue," I said, injecting softness into my voice despite my anxieties. "If you are asking yourself whether I want that information in order to whack the other brother as well, then I'd say we were not as close as I always believed we were. That we never had been. That would upset me about as much as anything that's happened to me since the early hours of this morning. I didn't do it, Sue. Any of it. And I hope deep down you know that. The thing is, I need Chris Dawson to understand that, too. Otherwise, he might just send someone to pay me back for something I'm innocent of."

"You could explain."

"I may not be given time."

She seemed to get my meaning. "Do you still have company?"

"I do. And they are just as desperate as me to put an end to this."

"And the… authorities?"

"Can't be trusted at the moment."

I gave her time to digest the implication of those words.

"Are you certain about that, or just concerned?" she asked.

"Absolutely certain. That avenue is blocked to us right now."

"You could come in. Your version of events could be put to the editor, and running your own story will provide protection. Nothing could be swept under the carpet then."

"I did consider that, Sue. And believe me I was sorely tempted. But only briefly. On the surface, it sounds like the way to go.

Get my shot in first, start a formal investigation. Fact is, though, I have no idea what sort of evidence they have against me. Whatever it may be is entirely fabricated, but it could be considerable, and it may well be impossible to unravel. I need to know what that is before I put myself at risk."

"And how does the information you want help with that exactly."

"It doesn't. But it may just buy me some time. We're too exposed right now. I need an ally, not another enemy."

I heard her take a long, deep breath. I could only imagine the thoughts twisting and turning inside her head, buffeted like a plastic bag in a strong wind. I rested the phone against my forehead for a moment, then glanced around. The street was quiet now, with no foot traffic. Still I felt terribly vulnerable.

"Sue, I guess in the end this will come down to friendship. I know I let you down. I know I hurt you. Just like everyone else who knew me, trusted me. I've paid for it in spades, believe me. But if you ever knew me, truly knew me, you will believe that I could not do what's being said about me."

Just a heartbeat skipped by this time. "Give me your number. I'll call you back."

"No, I'll call you. Ten minutes enough?"

"Trust doesn't work both ways, then?"

Hurting her again. I swallowed it back. "I have more to lose."

"Ten minutes," she said, and ended the call.

***

I chose not to go back inside the library. Instead, I moved out onto the pavement and took in my whereabouts in more detail. It seemed to me that small town centres in England looked pretty much the same wherever you went. Such places were interchangeable. Narrow, often winding streets with nothing much going on, which suddenly, and with no clear boundary, merged into a whirlwind of activity and consumerism. This area was different, and had a relaxed feel about it. It felt safe somehow. Amidst the plethora of betting shops and charity stores, there was still time for old-fashioned charm, with antique markets and quaint tea shops jostling for business alongside the coffee and fast food giants. It was interesting taking time to really look at my surroundings. Odd the things you noticed when you did so.

When I called her back, Susan gave me her mobile number instead of the information I had requested. "Give me another ten minutes," she said.

I left it exactly that amount of time before using the new number. Every time someone walked past, I turned towards the library, shielding my face. "Can you talk now?" I asked.

"Yeah, I'm out of the office. Christ, Mike, what the hell have you got yourself into?"

"As much shit as a person can be in and still be able to breathe."

"I can't believe what I'm hearing. It's so wild. Outrageous."

"What *are* you hearing exactly, and can you find out more?"

Susan rattled off what she knew: that the police and NCA were looking for me in connection with the murder of Ray Dawson. In addition, there was the possibility that either I had also abducted Melissa Andrews and Charlotte Dawson, or that Melissa and I had acted together. The latter option was the lead police were currently focussing on.

"They're actually saying that?" I felt myself wince, my face contorted by an almost physical pain. Senior Officer Hendricks had been busy. Now he was laying the foundation for a conspiracy of sorts.

"It's top of the pile of several theories. None of which are good for you."

"Has anyone offered a scrap of evidence to back up those theories?" I asked.

"The investigating team are keeping things pretty close to their chest, Mike. Leaking one or two things at a time. The suggestion is that something may have been found in your car that implicates you in the murder."

"Fuck!" I licked my lips. They'd never been this dry. Aware that I had cursed aloud, I cast a furtive glance around me. I remained alone.

"Fuck indeed. What happened, Mike? Please tell me."

"I've already said it's best you don't know."

"Yes, and I'd remind you I'm a big girl now, Mike. I worked on many similar stories with you, remember. It's what I do."

I took a moment. Susan was right. We had taken chances together before. There was no good reason why I should not tell her everything this time, either. So I did. Every detail from the moment I saw Hendricks gun Dawson down.

"Now you see why I am in the mire," I finished. "That prick of an NCA cop murdered Dawson himself but is now finding ways to lay the blame on me. Maybe even me and Melissa both if necessary."

"Jesus, Mike," Susan said after a stunned silence. "I don't know which version is more crazy right now: you killing Dawson or an NCA officer doing so and then laying it all off on you."

"I was in the wrong place at the wrong time is all. He obviously intended to kill Dawson and then just leave. Given who the victim is people would have suspected a gangland hit. But I saw him, Sue, and he knows I can hang him for it. My word against his won't do if he has planted solid evidence. And he's had the time to do just that."

"It depends on what it is and how solid he's made it. He can't have been planning for this, so he hasn't had a lot of time to adapt."

I thought about that. Looked around once more. The sun had broken through the cloud cover and was virtually pulsating in the sky. One or two pedestrians passed by. I turned away again, ensuring my face could not be seen from either inside or outside the library.

"I guess you're right," I said. "But he's clearly done more than enough to steer things in my direction. He's probably still working on it as we speak. Which is why I need you to help me, Sue.

I need to know what they have, how he's twisting the story against me and away from himself. We need to figure out where to go from here, and it's impossible without knowing exactly what we're up against."

"So, not only do you want contact details for Chris Dawson, you also want me to dig around inside a police investigation?"

"It's what you do. You just said as much yourself. Remember? And you're bloody good at it."

"Sure. Skip the flattery, Mike. This is something out of the ordinary, you must see that."

I nodded to myself. "Of course I do. But this is the Dawson family, Sue. Big time. You have every right to be involved, asking questions. It's a major story, with the potential to explode into some kind of conspiracy. Sweet talk your editor. I know you can twist him around your little finger."

"Yes, I probably can. The real question is, do I want to?"

I felt my heart flutter. Began to feel vulnerable all over again. I was counting on this. Needed it. Melissa and Charlie needed it as well. My feeble grasp on hope was all but shot. I doubted Melissa had much left in her tank, either. I was no longer used to caring about anyone other than myself; hadn't done so since Donna and Wendy left my everyday life. I felt it now, though. An intense sensation I could not let go of.

"Maybe not for me," I admitted. "And if that's the case, I can understand why. I respect it even. You owe me absolutely nothing. But for the story? How massive would it be for your career if you blow the lid off this, Sue?"

"You're playing me, Mike. I'm not stupid."

A clutch of pedestrians had turned off the pavement and were heading up the path toward the library. I turned away, hunched into myself protectively. I felt exposed. And so alone.

I did indeed need this.

More than that, though, I needed my friend.

"Yes, I am playing you," I admitted. "And no, you're not stupid enough to fall for it. You are anything but stupid, Sue. But you must admit there is something major going on here, whether I'm telling the truth or not, and I know you won't be able to let that go. It's not in your nature. Even if you take me out of the equation, this is big time. With me in it, with what that cop is trying to do to me and, perhaps, the kid's nanny, it would be the biggest story you've ever had. And let's not forget the kid and everything she is about to be put through."

"I take it she knows? About her father, I mean." Susan's tone was more gentle now, the topic having switched to Charlie.

"No. Mel thought it was best to leave it for now." I wondered if that had been the best decision even as I said it. "I think she's probably right to err on the side of caution. It's hard enough at the moment having to cater for the kid. It would be impossible if she knew her dad was dead."

I heard Susan sigh. Then she said, "Okay, Mike. I'll see what I can find out."

I could not recall the last time I felt so relieved about anything. "Talk to the right people, Sue, maybe even including this NCA bastard, and ask them all the right questions."

"Such as?"

"Such as how big a coincidence is it that NCA Officer Hendricks just happened to be in the area where this major criminal was gunned down? And how much more of a coincidence is it that Hendricks was the one who happened to stumble upon Dawson's body? Those are two good questions to start with."

I was pleased with myself. They *were* good questions, and they needed exploring. Even if they were summarily dismissed or explained away, it would at the very least put the notion out there.

"I'll talk to the boss," Susan said. "Get the ball rolling."

"Good. And… thank you."

"I'm not promising anything, Mike."

"No. I mean thank you for not asking me."

"Asking you what?"

"If I did it. If I was guilty."

She gave a light laugh, and I could almost see her smiling face. I remembered it fondly. The two of us had come close on several occasions to becoming lovers. We had worked closely together, spent long hours forging a friendship that went beyond the mere collegial. In truth, I always thought Susan wanted it more than I did, but at the time my marriage had meant something to me. Even if at that point it had been a faint glow amidst its dying embers.

"You're too much of a wuss to murder someone, Mike," she said now.

I chuckled. "I'll take that as a compliment."

"I can certainly get you those details for contacting Dawson," she told me. "But it will take a bit of time. As you can imagine, I can't afford any leaks. The source I need the information from isn't available right now. I've left messages, but it's a waiting game and clearly you're up against the clock. But listen, on that subject, I've just had a thought: how about I put the wheels in motion here and then come to wherever you are and meet up with you?"

I had wondered when she would get around to asking that question. A part of me screamed out for the presence of someone who would be firmly on my side. To be with my friend once more. But another part, a bigger part, recognised the danger.

"No," I replied, reluctantly. "I don't like that idea at all. There's no need to put you in the firing line as well."

"That won't happen, Mike. It may be off my beat, but you said yourself that this is something meaty enough for a reporter like me to get my teeth into. There's no reason for me not to investigate, and I won't be alone. Hundreds of journos are looking into the same story right now."

"I guess," I said. I felt weak not insisting she stay away.

"Look, it makes sense, Mike. You are limited by whatever agreement you make with Chris Dawson eventually. If there's even one to be reached. You are still going to be wherever you are now, still watching your back. I could drive down and then take you where you need to go, bring some cash for you and a burner phone as well. You could tell me everything, and I can record it and send it on to my editor, save it all to the cloud. That way you remain beneath the radar, but your version of events is out there."

"It's too risky."

"How? Neither the police nor Dawson will know about it. Not until it's too late. In fact, how about I get us all a room for the night somewhere, away from the public glare. Mike, it doesn't take a genius to recognise how big this story is. It's the kind you and I used to dream about landing on our desks. Now it's here, and you are involved in it. But now so am I. You don't have to do this on your own any longer."

I turned it over – a furious internal debate. Myself, Mel and the kid would be exposed once we left the library. And at the moment only Mel and I could tell the true story about Ray Dawson's murder. Having a room to hide away in, someone to share this nightmare with, someone to work on our behalf, felt like a great plan. There didn't seem to be a downside.

"Okay," I said eventually. I walked a few options through in my mind, thought back to the earlier drive as I had made my way to the station, and then suggested the meeting place. I asked Susan how quickly she might be able to get here.

"I'll need a good few hours, Mike. There's a lot to do first, and then the drive itself of course." She suggested a time. "What will you do in the meantime?" she asked.

"I have no idea. We have to find somewhere else to lie low for a few hours, and then figure out what we do and where we go afterwards. We may have to tough it out another night maybe. Hopefully tomorrow will bring better news."

I really didn't want to think that far ahead, but knew I had run out of options. I was still debating with myself when I heard Susan speak again.

"In that case, Mike, I need to make a confession. I used a look-up service to find the payphone number you're calling me from. Don't be angry with me; I did it not for the story but because I care about you and the mess you're in right now. After I tracked the number to Chippenham, I booked a room at a Best Western hotel as close to you as I could find. I booked it in my name using the paper's credit card, told them a colleague would be arriving before me, and I have a booking reference number for you to quote when you get to reception. I thought perhaps this Melissa woman could use it, then you would figure out a way to get you all in there to wait for me."

After a brief flare of anger at my friend's betrayal, I could only feel a further surge of relief. It was exactly what we needed.

"We won't need the card you booked the room with?" I asked.

"No. I settled up. You just need the reference number. You can't check in until 2 pm or so, although you might try a little earlier. Having Charlotte Dawson with you makes it difficult, I know, but you'll figure something out I'm sure."

Once Susan had given me the details, I cut her short. "Look, Sue, I don't want to rake all this up again in front of Mel and the kid. There's a lot to discuss, and the kid will get antsy with another stranger in the room. Plus, there's a lot she shouldn't hear. We need to get a few things sorted out on our own first. So how about we meet up at the place I first suggested, huh?"

Susan agreed. We said goodbye and she told me to take care. That was the second time she had said that to me, and the second time she had meant it.

"I'll never be able to thank you enough, Sue," I told her. "But I hope to at least try one day."

I killed the line before she could hear me choke back my tears of gratitude.

FIFTEEN

We walked slowly beside the river which meandered its way around the edge of Monkton Park. Many other people were doing the same that humid afternoon in Chippenham. Charlie skipped ahead, waving her arms and calling out to the ducks and swans drifting aimlessly nearby, her life apparently back on track. The ordeal seemed to have left no mark upon her at all. I reflected on the ability children had to recover from adversity, wishing some of that magic dust would sprinkle my way.

After returning to the library, I told Melissa all about my conversations with Susan. Mel seemed both excited and cautious about having someone on the outside with whom to share our situation. The Best Western was located centrally between the library and the park, which felt like another favourable twist of fate. We could not check in as it was still too early, so we were still left in a bit of a bind. It was Mel who suggested going for a walk alongside the river, having studied a map of the town while she was in the library waiting for me to return. Before setting out, we debated the merits of the exposure. On the one hand, neither of us could think of anywhere to take Charlie at that time of day that would keep her happy and relaxed, and would also keep us away from the public gaze. I reasoned that our faces, even if they had been revealed in old photographs on the Internet or TV news stations, had not yet had sufficient time to seep into the conscious mind. I also suggested that even if people were aware of what had happened and our role in it, no one would be expecting to find us strolling by the river. Mel offered the view that so many people walk around with their heads down looking at their phones that we would probably be better off amongst so many, rather than risking a smaller, closed-in environment again. That combination of arguments seemed to do the trick, but I also knew that Melissa was desperate to spend time outdoors again.

Decision made, it had taken us only fifteen minutes to get here, and now I was enjoying the feel of fresh warm air on my skin.

"Tell me about her mother," I said, nodding in the kid's direction. "What happened there?"

Melissa hugged herself with one arm as she walked, her other hand busy with a cigarette. She strode confidently, with a young woman's athleticism and vigour. A dove-grey scattering of cloud hid the sun briefly, but the temperature continued to climb and the sky still retained a good deal of moisture. A light wind blew our way across the still water, flushing Mel's smooth cheeks.

"I never met Cassie Dawson, and I don't know a lot about what went wrong between her and Ray. They were childhood sweethearts, from what I understand, even though she was the daughter of a lesser rival. Their union brought the two families together, or so I was told. But from what I can gather, Cassie had an affair and Ray found out. The marriage ended badly."

"She must have fought for her kid though, right?"

"At first." Melissa nodded, casting a swift glance at the child, who remained enthralled by the wildlife. "But when Ray wanted something he usually got it. There were a number of threats, apparently. Enough to make Cassie step back. That wasn't enough for Ray, though, and he dragged her through the courts to prove she was an unfit mother. He bought a few witnesses to her so-called drink and drugs habits and of course the sleeping around. The end result was that Cassie was allowed to see Charlie only at Ray's discretion. Which meant hardly ever."

"That must have been hard for her to take."

"It would be for most mothers."

"And then she died. Cancer, right?"

"Yes, I believe so. She moved to the south of France and died there."

From my time at the newspaper, I knew of Ray Dawson's failed marriage, but was hearing these specific details for the first time. "How do you know even that much?" I asked. "You said you knew little of what went on with the business, yet you were aware of some of his criminal activities, and now these issues with the kid's mother. You appear to know a lot more than you first let on."

"Most of what I know comes from Roger, really. He's been with the family for many years, right from the very beginning, and he opened up to me now and again. He and I got on really well, and he was always around the house."

I knew exactly who Roger was, and he was no mere chauffeur. He was someone Ray trusted implicitly, a man close to everything sordid the Dawson family were involved with. The name had come up from time to time, although we had never been able to nail down Roger's precise standing within the organisation. I now wondered whether his absence last night was something other than a simple coincidence.

"Is there really no way we can get in touch with Roger?" I asked.

Melissa shook her head. "Again, I've never had cause to call him, so I don't know his number. I have no idea where he lives, other than it was within a short drive from us."

"Which pretty much leaves us back at square one."

I glanced across at her. "None of this put you off working for Dawson?" I asked. "The way he treated his wife, the way he cheated in order to keep Charlie to himself?"

Melissa frowned, perhaps reflecting on her decision. "Taking care of Charlie was and is my job. I love it. By the time I found out what Ray had done, I was in too deep. Charlie had worked her way into my heart."

She stopped walking, calling out for Charlie not to stray too far away. A caravan of cyclists eased past, a nuclear family bedecked in the finest safety equipment money could buy. Rather too much garish lycra for my taste. I watched them head along a path that led away from the river towards a housing estate.

My attention was drawn abruptly back to Melissa when she suddenly took hold of my arm. She looked horrified. "What is it?" I asked. "What's wrong?"

"Don't look now, but there's a man moving alongside us by the river. I'm sure he has been in step with us ever since we got here. Every time I've looked over towards him, I've caught him turning his head away sharply, as if he'd been looking straight at us but didn't want us to know."

I nodded and licked my lips. In an exaggerated manner I stretched and yawned and took in our surroundings, which included the man by the water's edge. He was not looking at either us or Charlie, but I thought I recognised him from the entrance we had used. He was dressed casually, and from what I could tell was a little portly and out of shape. I had to assume that if we had been spotted by the authorities they would have come in with armed officers to take us down. If this man had any interest in us at all, I was betting it had to be as a member of the public who had somehow recognised us.

"Let's move on," I said to Mel. "Keep it steady, just as we have been all along. Carry on talking and just act naturally. I'll keep an eye on him."

"Okay. I'm probably completely wrong, anyway. Just nervous I suppose. So, what do we do after we've met up with your friend?" Her turn to probe.

"I'm really not sure. For all the idea scares the crap out of me, Chris Dawson still seems the most likely route through all this. Even after Susan gets our story on the record and makes her editor aware, I'm not convinced we can put any faith in going directly to the police. And the NCA are to be avoided at all costs. I just need to figure out how Dawson can put things right for us. Or even if he can."

She appeared to give that some thought, eventually nodding. "You may be right. But why do you think telling our story to your friend's newspaper won't help? Once we have, you could let them find you a good solicitor, and then we hand ourselves in to the local police. That way there will be no chance for any investigation to be carried out on the quiet. Without representation. They will have to do it by the book, including investigating the officer who killed Ray."

"I don't have your faith in either the power of the press, or the UK justice system, Mel. That Hendricks character is obviously no fool. He would consider all the same options we are. If I were him, by now I would have planted all kinds of evidence, have any number of witnesses lined up just in case. A man who can shoot and kill a major crime boss is capable of anything. My bet is that if we walk in and give ourselves up, no matter what our story, he will have an alibi for himself and we will have all kinds of fingers pointing back at us. We'd look like fools. Worse, liars. And worst of all, murderers. Either separately or, more likely, together."

"But they can't put the two of us together before last night. You have no reason to murder Ray, and nor do I. I don't see how they could imply anything of the sort."

I had been asking myself the same thing. I'd come up dry. "Me neither, to be honest. But I don't want to find out from a position of weakness. Do you? Sitting in a cell is no place to realise they hold all the best cards."

Melissa nodded and gave a long sigh. She pulled out another cigarette and lit up. It seemed to relax her immediately. "I suppose you're right. How about your friend, Susan? Do you think she can find out what's being said, about how the investigation is being handled? At least that way we will know as much as possible, and we can judge from that what to do next."

"It can't hurt. Once we've filled her in with the details, once we have a way to contact Dawson, and once we know more about the investigation against us, we can figure out the next step. As for who can be trusted, I think we have to go back to the beginning, to what started this whole shitty business for us."

"What do you mean?" She looked up, regarding me with interest.

"I mean, who stood to gain from Ray Dawson's death?"

"What does that matter? We know the NCA killed him."

I nodded quickly, spurred on now by the paths my thoughts were travelling. "Yes, that officer shot Ray. But he didn't do it just because he wanted him dead. I don't see what he stood to gain from that fact alone. No, my guess is he was paid by someone. It was a hit. Pure and simple. The question is, who paid? Who has the most to gain from Ray no longer being around?"

Charlie came running up to us, which kept our conversation in check for a while.

"Did you see me with the ducks, Mel?" she asked, almost breathless and completely giddy with excitement.

Melissa bent forward and ran a hand through Charlie's hair. Her smile was broad and unreserved. "I did sweetheart. They're lovely, aren't they?"

I took the opportunity to check on our suspected shadow. As I turned my head our eyes met. He did not look away. His only reaction was a slight raise of the eyebrows, followed by a nod and a smile. The kind of thing you do when it's a gorgeous day and you encounter other people. I replied in kind.

My attention was snagged by the kid as she posed the same question to me. I asked her whether she preferred the ducks or the swans. After a full thirty seconds of deep consideration, she decided she liked them both equally. I told her I agreed. Ducks and swans rocked. Charlie bounced up and down on her tip-toes, enthusiastically begging us to go down to the water with her.

"In a few minutes," Melissa told her. "You go on and enjoy yourself. But don't go right up to the edge."

The kid trotted and skipped back her way back to the river. We watched her go, and I felt a tug of emotion. Wendy and I had often fed the ducks together, always choosing the same shaky wooden bridge over a narrowing of the lake close to our home. During our visits we gave names to the ducks and swans, and I had always regarded those times as my fondest memories.

"I just had a visual encounter with the bloke you mentioned," I told Mel. "I'm not saying for sure that we're in the clear, but I think he's just out for a walk like we are."

"Why did he keep turning away when I caught him looking?"

"Perhaps he's attracted to you. He's on his own, sees a pretty young woman… sneaks a few peeks and gets embarrassed when he gets caught out. It's been known to happen."

"Are you kidding? Have you seen the state of me?"

"You look fine."

"Fine but not good?"

I smiled. "You look okay. That's all you get from me."

"I suppose that will have to do then."

She smiled back at me. It was a nice moment.

SIXTEEN

"So where were we anyway?" Melissa asked.

I thought about it for a moment. "I was wondering who had the most to gain from Ray's murder."

"Right. As we discussed before, Ray had enemies. Other criminals who wanted part of his business, or whose business he'd previously taken. I heard him talking to Chris one day about the various gangs trying to muscle in on their turf. Having rivals was considered par for the course. And in that line of work, they could be people who would turn violent."

She tilted her head to the side, her long straight hair falling across her cheek. The sunlight and fresh warm air were improving her demeanour, but nonetheless Melissa looked weary.

We had been alternating between walking at a gentle pace and standing still every time one of us wanted to make a point. This time it was my turn, and I lingered where we stood. Melissa was correct in everything she said, but I wasn't seeing this as a gangland hit. I breathed in some of that clean air and said, "The local thugs would have done their own dirty work, because they love thinking of themselves as gangsters shooting up the town. Thing is, strange as it might sound, I can't see it being one of his enemies. Killing Ray leaves Chris as head of the family, and from what I know and what you've confirmed, Chris Dawson is much more of a hothead than his brother. Ray talked first, acted when words did no good. Chris does it pretty much the other way around. No, the way I see things, the Dawsons' enemies would rather have kept Ray in place."

"Then maybe they're gunning for Chris as well."

I shook my head, having previously given that some thought. "If they were going to do that they would make sure the two brothers were hit at the same time. Doing it this way puts Chris on his guard, allows him to hole up and tool up."

Melissa gave a slight chuckle. Her eyes fixed upon mine. She took a long draw from her cigarette, but did not release a great deal of smoke. "Now you're sounding like a bit of a villain yourself," she said.

"I know the lingo. I've been around enough of them in my time."

"When you were a journalist, you mean?"

"Yeah. That and growing up. Back in London. I was raised in the Whitechapel area, and the place was wall-to-wall villains. Not all big time, of course, but there were a few people I knew who became faces."

"Faces?" Mel threw me a puzzled glance. We started walking again, both keeping Charlie within view, the kid subconsciously moving along to our rhythm.

Grinning now, I shrugged. "Just a saying. It's what London villains became known as. And there were plenty of them."

"Sounds as if you are from your own 'hood'. Were you ever involved? Even slightly."

I hadn't been. Not really. I'd done a bit here and there, mostly when I was a kid. Strictly chicken feed. Cars, mainly. The money and the glamour was enticing, but it was far too dangerous a living for my liking. Then there were my parents, who would have nothing to do with that sort of life. My dad didn't beat his chest or put his foot down or anything like that; he just made me see the error of my ways with sound common sense and non-judgemental dialogue. Both my mum and dad had been pretty stoical people. They allowed me enough time to make my own decisions, albeit drumming into me every day their own beliefs and morals. I said as much to Melissa.

"They sound like lovely people. Caring."

"They were. I put them through a lot. They never got to see the worst of my drinking, but they were around for the beginning of it. They were never anything but supportive."

"You must miss them terribly."

I nodded. "Very much so. You're in a similar boat, of course. Estranged, in your case. Were you not close to your parents?"

"Not really. Not as much as I would have liked."

"But you have a brother, right?"

Melissa smiled. This time it hit her eyes. "I do. At least, I hope I do. He could be anywhere. Anything could have happened to him."

"You never know, this publicity might draw him out."

"I hope so, Mike. I really do." Then she swiftly changed the subject. "So, you were talking about growing up in and around a criminal environment."

I told her a little about how my background gave me an insight, and a little access to the London underworld in particular. It was partly why I could not imagine any of the Dawsons' competitors being responsible for what happened.

We came to a halt once more as the path we were on met another that set off at an angle and led over a bridge, back towards town. I glanced around, happy to see that the man who had been keeping pace with us had opted for a seat on a bench, his attention fully on the river. Mel checked on Charlie, who was lost in her own world down by the riverbank. She watched the girl in silence for a few seconds, then said, "So, what if it's actually far more simple? I know you said otherwise, but what if that NCA guy Hendricks just wanted to get rid of Ray?"

I wedged my hands in my pockets. "I don't know what to tell you, Mel. I doubt it. I just don't see it that way. It makes little sense to me. Unless it's purely personal, then surely better the devil you know. Hendricks may well have been getting the runaround from Ray over the years, but Chris taking over would be a damn sight worse."

Then it struck me. So forcefully that I couldn't imagine why it had not occurred to me before. There was one person who stood to gain a tremendous amount from Ray Dawson's murder. I turned to look at Melissa.

"How well did they get on?" I asked. "Ray and Chris? You said you didn't see Chris much, which suggests their meetings were probably mainly business. Was there any animosity between the two of them? Any disputes?"

"Not that I know of. Wait a minute, you think Chris…?" The shake of her head was resolute. "No. No way. Why would you even consider that?"

Because power can be overwhelming. The lust for it even more so. I had seen it many times before.

"Ray was head of the family by virtue of the fact that he was the eldest, and when their old man died in prison it was the natural move. It always seemed to me that Chris Dawson wanted to do more, to be involved with other things, to expand the business and take on other firms. Ray was mostly content with what they had."

"I still don't see Chris paying some cop to kill his own brother."

"A hit's a hit, no matter who takes the money. Plus, it makes an awful lot of sense if the guy who does the killing is also allowed to run the resulting investigation."

"But they were brothers."

"Yeah, and ever since Cain and Abel, brothers have been known to disagree, Mel. Sometimes with violent consequences."

Melissa looked over at the kid, gazed out across the river, then turned back to me. "I understand what you're saying. I do. And yes, in some twisted way it may even make sense. I just can't see him hurting Charlie that way, making her an orphan in the process."

I made no reply. I wondered how much Melissa was prepared to face the reality of our situation. Part of me thought I should leave her in blissful ignorance, but in the end, I thought she deserved to know how bad things might really be.

"Mel, what do you think Hendricks was going to do once Ray was dead? You think he was going to just drive away afterwards and risk you identifying him as the shooter?"

I could tell by the startled look on her face that she had not given that any thought. Now she was, and I could almost see the blood drain from her smooth skin. She shook it off quickly, though.

"Then Chris didn't set it up," she said defiantly. "He wouldn't do that to Charlie."

"Are you sure? Is there a possibility the kid will inherit Ray's money, plus a share of the business when she's old enough? Might there be a will out there that says just that? Power, control and money are strong motives, don't you think?"

"No. I'm telling you straight, Chris is not a nice guy, but he's not that evil."

I knew a lost cause when I came upon one. I had my own views on the subject, but respected the fact that Melissa probably knew Chris Dawson better than I did. The suggestion I had presented was just a theory, and one I was not about to dismiss entirely.

"So, if not Chris, then who?"

Melissa rolled her eyes. "We've come full circle. Again. This is like Groundhog Day, Mike."

She turned away, but before she did I saw her expression change. Same as earlier, she seemed bemused more than curious. Puzzled rather than frightened. I sensed something was playing on her mind, something she clearly did not want to share with me, but then considering everything we had all been through, it would have been odd if she was able to simply take it all in her stride.

The kid was squatting now, chatting away to the nearby ducks. Melissa called out to warn her yet again not to get too close to the water. I looked on. How nice it would be if adults could continue to adapt the way they did when they were children, I thought. You got scared and confused, hurt both mentally and physically, yet you bounced back in the time it took to snap a finger. Finding the park and the river had been our saving grace, because the way the kid had been playing up after leaving the library, I had been certain we would draw unwanted attention. Now Charlie seemed both as relaxed and happy as we'd hoped she would be. I envied her resilience.

We were still exposed, however. There were a lot of people around, the numbers starting to swell. I became more aware of their presence, and my anxiety levels immediately increased. I looked back at the bench, but the man was no longer there. I searched for him, and was relieved to spot him headed back the way we had all come.

"We can't stay here much longer," I said to Melissa. "We have to make some decisions. And make them soon. We should try checking into the hotel."

Melissa puffed out her cheeks. "I know. Such a shame. For the first time since the shooting, I feel safe. I know we're not, and I realise being out in the open like this is risky, but it's so peaceful I can't help but feel calm."

"Yeah. It lulls you, a place like this." I lowered my gaze. "The last time I saw my daughter was in a park. By a lake rather than a river, but it was a nice place. Seemed like my life was coming together again. I couldn't have been more wrong."

"What happened?"

I looked at her, and damned if she didn't seem genuinely interested. I gave a single shake of the head. "Some other time, maybe. When I know you better."

"Don't take this the wrong way, Mike" she said, "but I hope that doesn't happen. If we get to know each other better it will probably mean we are still not out of this bloody mess."

"Hey, language."

She smiled. It was a nice smile. My own smile was less genuine. As I had said before, places like this could lull a person.

It was time to go. Melissa called Charlie over. When the kid re-joined us, her hand sought mine as the three of us began to walk across the bridge. I said nothing. Neither did I shake it off. Instead I smiled to myself and carried on walking.

SEVENTEEN

By the time the call came in to move, Hendricks felt as if he had been driven borderline insane by the seemingly never-ending wait. Aimlessly kicking his heels had never been his favourite way of passing time, but today he felt like a caged animal. He padded around like one; back and forth, forming tight circles or squares, never straying too far away from his vehicle. Nutton holding back, yet watchful.

His fellow NCA officer's eyes were not the only ones that fell upon him, Hendricks noticed. The cops and detectives milling around seldom switched off from observing him. He did not believe it was paranoia, and given the situation he was in few would blame him if that became the diagnosis. No, Hendricks knew when he was being watched, mistrusted. Doubted. He rose above it, meeting their gaze whenever it became overt. *I see you.*

The morning was halfway done when Nutton sidled across to him. The two had barely spoken, but Hendricks could see in the man's eyes that something was sparking behind them. "There's activity over in the control room," Nutton said.

"Has been all night as far as I can tell."

The younger man was not deterred by the attitude. "Not like this. You can almost feel the tension level spreading out in waves. Something's up."

Something *was* up. Randall came bursting out of the door and headed to a waiting vehicle. Another suit came running over to them. "They've found Ray Dawson's car, sir. Chippenham railway station car park. We're all headed that way now."

Without a word of thanks for the information, Hendricks turned away and said to Nutton, "See you there."

***

Haystacks was getting antsy. With biker blood oozing through his veins like two-stroke engine oil, he hated being cooped up in a car. In the periphery of his vision, Rhino noticed his companion fidgeting in his seat, and was struggling to think of a way to keep the man occupied. It was like being with a child.

After yet another long and steady sigh, Haystacks said, "This is bullshit, man. What are we expected to do with all these pigs around us?"

Despite the retro terminology, Rhino had to agree. He had observed what he believed to be the decision-makers heading for their vehicles back at the lay-by. This was no doughnut run. The pack were on the hunt. Rhino gunned the engine on his C-Class Mercedes, pushed hard down the hill, which eventually looped its way around to the road on which the small police convoy was travelling. Within a few minutes he had taken up a comfortable position behind them, maintaining the distance at a steady sixty. An hour and a quarter later the police vehicles pulled up outside Chippenham railway station. Rhino circled around and found a spot in the car park where he could observe both the station entrance and the gathering of officers and CSIs now grouping around Ray's vehicle.

"What d'you reckon?" Haystacks asked, nodding towards the station entrance. "Dumped the motor and trained it to London?"

"I hope not," Rhino replied, after a lengthy pause.

"Why's that?"

"Because that would suggest Mel was complicit. Lynch might be able to control her easily inside a car, but not exposed like that on a train journey. If she's on a train with him, she's there willingly."

Haystacks nodded. "Complicit's a good word." He considered himself a student of language, if not a master of it when speaking.

Rhino wanted to focus his attention on events over the other side of the car park, and the chatter was distracting him. "Tell you what," he said. "Take a walk over to the station. Hang about for a while as if you're waiting for someone to arrive. See if you can pick up on anything being said or done. Get us a couple of coffees while you're there. And a blueberry muffin – I'm starving."

Haystacks chuckled. "Starvin' Marvin," he said.

"That some racist shit?" Rhino asked.

"Fuck you."

Starvin' Marvin was a little black character from the TV show *South Park*. Every time Rhino mentioned he was starving, Haystacks made the same chuckling sound and said the name. Querying the racial overtones in his colleague's remark was Rhino's customary response, as was the barked rejoinder.

Rhino shook his head. "Just go get the breakfast and listen out for information," he said. He did not for one second believe that Haystacks would return with anything valuable for them to use. He just wanted rid of the man so that he could concentrate. Plus, he really was very hungry. He thought of Starvin' Marvin, and chuckled. He loved *South Park* every bit as much as Haystacks did.

"While I'm gone," his companion said as he climbed out of the Merc, "call Chris again will you? Tell him we need to be ahead of this lot, not behind."

"He knows. You think he doesn't know?"

Haystacks leaned through the open passenger window. "Yeah, well if he has this cop in his pocket, why have we heard fuck all from him?"

Rhino had no answer to that.

"Get the breakfast, fuck you!" he snapped.

In truth, he hated duties like this. He didn't quite know what he thought about the murder of his boss's brother, but following in the footsteps of the cops was ridiculous. Haystacks was right about that much. So exactly where was this cop who was supposed to be helping them?

***

They showed Mike Lynch's photograph to every member of staff. No one recognised him. However, when the machines at the ticket counter were checked there was only one that had sold three one-way tickets to Paddington, London. A young woman by the name of Sally Wainwright had sold them. Randall interviewed her, allowing Hendricks to sit in. DCI Randall showed her photos of Lynch, Melissa and Charlotte Dawson. This time there was a flicker of recognition.

"Maybe," she said. "Now that I see him again, the man is familiar."

"Have you watched any news broadcasts on TV this morning, Miss Wainwright?"

"No. Why do you ask?"

"Just to rule out the possibility of you having seen him on there earlier today. So, just the man, then. You saw no one waiting for him, not the woman and the little girl?"

She shook her head. "No. Sorry. It wasn't rush hour, but it still gets pretty busy in here."

The woman was starting to become defensive. Unable to help himself, and desperate not to lose the possible witness, Hendricks raised a placatory hand. "No worries. In a while we'd like you to provide a more formal statement, and it's possible something will be jogged loose then."

He earned a glare from Randall, but felt he could live with that.

They were sat around a table in the staff rest room. Just the three of them. The woman sat forward in her chair, clearly a little distressed.

"That's fine," she said. "I'm not in any sort of trouble, am I?"

"Not at all," DCI Randall reassured her. "You're being very helpful, and we thank you for that. So, have a think about this now: the man bought the tickets, and then left your window. Can you recall which way he turned?"

"Which way…?"

"Yes. Did he head for the platforms, or did he make his way back outside again?"

Sally Wainwright frowned. Her eyes shifted to one side for a moment as she attempted to access that memory. It was an astute question, Hendricks thought. Finally, she shook her head. "No, I didn't notice. I'm pretty sure someone was waiting to buy a ticket so my attention was all on them next. But, if it's the man I think you mean, he did speak to me."

Randall was alert to this. "He did? Can you recall what he said?"

"He asked me which platform he needed. And now that I put it together with the other photos you showed me, he did mention a wife and daughter I think. Some joke or other about Paddington bear."

"But you definitely didn't see them? His wife and daughter, I mean?"

"No." The shake of the head was firm this time. "Only him."

A short while later, Hendricks and Randall were joined by officer Nutton and Randall's colleague, Detective Sergeant Buchanan. Sally Wainwright had been taken elsewhere by a DC to provide a full witness statement.

"What do we think then, gentlemen?" Randall asked, having laid out what they knew so far.

"I'm not buying the trip to London," Buchanan said. Unlike Randall, who sounded very local, the DS spoke with a thick Scottish accent.

"I agree," Hendricks said quickly. "If he was doing that legitimately he would want to blend in, not stand out by providing unnecessary information. He wanted to be remembered."

"Unless nerves got the better of him." This from Nutton. "Some people blurt out all kinds of rubbish when they're put under pressure. It's human nature."

Randall nodded. "A good point. However, I think my DS and Officer Hendricks are correct. It's more likely, I feel, that Lynch drew attention to himself deliberately, believing we would be convinced they had travelled to London."

"So where do you think they are now, boss?"

"Well, the Beemer is sat out there in the car park. They didn't get the train, I'm pretty certain of that. My guess is they've found somewhere to hide out right here."

Which was precisely what Hendricks believed. The exact reason he then said, "We need to explore other possibilities. We don't have any idea how much money Lynch had on him. He could have bought other tickets, using cash rather than his card. This time, keeping a low profile, perhaps buying three separate tickets with three separate purchases. Could be a double-bluff, and they really have gone to London. Or they've headed off in the other direction."

Nutton was nodding. "Any of those are genuine possibilities. It's hard to imagine them remaining static in one place. Having dumped their vehicle, a train is perhaps the more likely route out."

Randall nodded and stretched out his legs. "You could well be right. We'll make sure to follow up on that. It does beg the question as to why they dumped the car, given we know its anti-theft device was not functioning."

"The Dawsons' and their crew have the Lo-Jacks, or whatever system their vehicles use, disabled as soon as they purchase them," Hendricks said. "But I imagine Lynch was wary of ANPR. The more he drove, the more he risked having his number plate ping your system."

"This opens up the wider debate concerning the relationship between Lynch and the nanny, Melissa Andrews," Randall said. "I would hope for access to the car park CCTV shortly, as well as the station footage already requested, but until then we have to speculate. What doesn't change is that if the woman and the girl remained in the car while he booked the tickets, or went voluntarily with Lynch on a train, then we have to ask how that can be."

"Indeed," Buchanan said, nodding enthusiastically. "Is it possible that this nanny knew Lynch prior to these events? That she is in some way part of it?"

As the senior NCA officer in the room, Hendricks guessed the question was aimed at him. He shook his head. "Your guess is as good as mine, I'm afraid. I ran Mike Lynch against our list of Chris Dawson's known contacts, and nothing sparked. There's no way for us to tell whether Lynch and Melissa Andrews were in prior contact. Not until we do a phone dump on their mobiles, but that won't be for a day or so yet. Even then, I doubt they used any form of communication we can trace."

"So, the NCA doesn't keep tabs on those within the Dawson household as well?"

"Not allowed to. Not employees. Had she been identified as Dawson's girlfriend or some such, then yes, we would have a folder on her. But not his daughter's nanny, no."

Randall cleared his throat. "How about the more informal information? I'm sure my team and I are not alone in keeping two sets of records. One for officialdom, one for our eyes only."

Hendricks smiled. Nodded. "Yes, she was checked out. But only basic stuff. Nothing popped, so her file was closed. However, whatever happened here, it does make her appear more involved than was first thought."

"It makes sense," Nutton said. "She may even have had the task of getting Dawson to pull over."

"Well, let's not lose sight of the fact that, had there not been a pile-up on the M5, we'd not have ended up on that road in the first place."

"True." Nutton nodded. He took a pull from a bottle of water. "She still might have done so simply because they had diverted. You were there, sir, so how busy was the road? I mean, you can't have been the only vehicles to take the same alternate route."

"It was surprisingly quiet." Hendricks did not appreciate his colleague dropping the spotlight back onto his part in what had transpired. "I got the impression the accident had not long happened, so Dawson may have been one of the first to find a different route. I noticed it got somewhat busier a while later."

DCI Randall had been jotting notes on a pad inside a folder. He snapped the folder shut and popped the pen inside the breast pocket of his jacket. "I think we've speculated enough. We know for certain that Andrews is not a name or number in the contacts list on Lynch's mobile. I myself spoke with Lynch's ex-wife, and she denied ever hearing the name before. It sounded genuine enough."

"I'd like to get sight of that," Hendricks said. He had already been through it, long before anyone else arrived at the scene. It didn't hurt to throw Randall off the scent, though. "There might be a name on there I recognise that you would not. One of Dawson's crew, perhaps."

Randall nodded. "It'll be in evidence by now, but we can arrange that for you. Myself and DS Buchanan need to go and feed back to our team, and catch up on anything new they might have. I have one officer going through CCTV footage from the platforms. The car parking company are giving us grief over acquiring footage from their system, but, as I mentioned earlier, I do expect that sooner rather than later. Hopefully, either or both will tell us what happened after the tickets were purchased. I suggest we meet up again afterwards. I have your details, Officer Hendricks, so I'll call or text you. Thank you both."

The two detectives stood at the same time, and seconds later Hendricks and Nutton were on their own. They were silent for a few moments. Hendricks was processing information, whilst at the same time planning his own next steps. It felt as if what had taken place right here at the station was key. He firmly believed DCI Randall was correct, and that Lynch, the nanny and the girl were still in Chippenham. Purchasing the tickets had been a ploy. They had found somewhere to lie low. He wondered why. What might the three of them be waiting for?

Nutton was becoming an irritant. The young man was pleasant enough, and had given him room when he needed it. Nutton did not appear at all phased at Hendricks putting distance between them, either. In different circumstances he suspected he would even like the man. However, if the investigation was going to take a major step forward – and it seemed like only a matter of time before it did – then it was crucial for him to be in an ideal position to slip the leash and just take off on his own. To do that, he had to somehow keep his colleague busy.

"I have some tasks for you," he said to Nutton. "I need to keep close for obvious reasons. But whilst the investigating team seem to have most things in hand, I think there are several avenues we can explore at the same time.

"Get a list of train times, destinations and stations they stop at en-route. Start from when Lynch bought the tickets right up to when the BMW was reported. Also, Randall has requested CCTV from the car park and this station, but I wonder if he thought about the trains themselves. Find someone who can help us with that. And one more thing, if they didn't take a train, and the Beemer is here, they may have taken a cab. Check with local companies, please."

Nutton was making notes. He looked up as he flipped his pad closed. "Where will I find you when I'm done?" he asked.

Hendricks glanced at his watch. "I have something to attend to, and then I'll get hold of Randall – no way am I waiting for him to bother to find me. I suspect we'll remain close by for a while yet, so sort us out a couple of rooms somewhere in town and text me with the details. We'll meet up there later this evening."

"Unless there's movement on Lynch, right?"

"Of course."

For the first time since he had arrived unexpectedly, Nutton stepped up to confront Hendricks. "You're not looking to side-line me, are you? I mean, I accept you didn't really want me here, but now that I am, and I'm making myself useful, I hope you wouldn't just take off if the police get a decent lead."

Hendricks raised his hands defensively. "That's not it at all, and I'm sorry you think that of me. It's not the way I work, Nutton. But I am used to working on my own, so I do need my own thinking space. I have my routines for working things through.

That's all. I hear anything, you hear it a second afterwards. Same goes the other way, of course. I'd expect that in return. Okay?"

Nutton nodded. "Fair enough. I'll get cracking on this and we'll meet up later."

"Oh, something I just thought of. Check on car thefts within the same time range. He might just have nicked himself a set of wheels."

"Will do. Good thinking."

Hendricks watched as the junior officer walked out of the room and into the ticket office. Whatever happened next, it was his firm intention to never see the man again.

***

The problem with following a decent sized group of people was that sooner or later they always split up. Rhino thought about how that was playing out right now. He called his boss immediately. "Chris, we have movement. I know I'm your eyes on the ground, but we may need some extra hands down here."

"What's your problem now, Rhino?"

Now? The word rattled Rhino. He had called Chris once so far to complain, and somehow this had earned him attitude. He let it pass. For the time being. "The problem is they're splintering. At the lay-by they formed three distinctive groups. All three came here to Chippenham railway station. What we've got now is one group – which seemed to have two men working together, but each with their own car – now about to go their separate ways. One is headed to his motor, the other is still somewhere inside the station. The second group, larger and definitely the men in charge, are gathered out by their vehicles and to me they look set to move off very soon. Another group, lesser detectives I'd say, have not emerged from the station since they went in."

"So, you want to know who to stick with?"

"I do."

"No, you don't. You don't want to know, you want to be told."

"Well… that's how I end up knowing."

"No, Rhino. That's how you end up doing what I suggest. That's how you end up evading responsibility for anything. The only one who can really know what to do is the person down there watching events unfold. Who might that be, Rhino?"

The big man hated being spoken down to. "Haystacks?" he suggested.

"Don't fucking wind me up, Rhino. You're on the spot. Make the decision. But, Rhino…"

"Make the right one?"

Chris Dawson laughed. "You got it."

Rhino did not like the way this was shaping up. It was a hard enough task as it was without Chris acting like a prick. He thought about what he had witnessed from up on that hill, how that fit in with what he'd seen since the circus had moved here. The middle group – larger, more cohesive. They were the ones in the know.

Haystacks had returned to the Merc an hour earlier, drink and muffin in a white paper bag, scrunched up at the collar. What he had managed to pick up was not quite as useless as Rhino had expected. Apparently, three tickets had been purchased by someone fitting Mike Lynch's description. Cash had also been withdrawn. The story being told was not being bought by the cops however. They were convinced that the three had remained in the town.

"Haystacks," Rhino said now. "We have to split up for a bit. I need you to get back to the station. Linger, but blend in. I may have to follow that bunch waiting out by the unmarkeds. I reckon they're looking set to move any moment now, but a whole bunch are staying behind. You go, I'll stick with them. Call you later."

His colleague slipped out of the vehicle without another word.

Now that was the Haystacks Rhino enjoyed spending time with.

EIGHTEEN

On leaving the park and the tranquil river behind, I began to feel curiously detached. On the one hand, I felt we were more exposed; on the other, just knowing my meeting with Susan was only hours away somehow made me feel invulnerable. For the first time since leaving the motel I wasn't expecting to be snatched up by some armed squad dressed like Robocops. Charlie was happy enough, having enjoyed herself in the park, but it was only a matter of time before she started bleating again. Her chatter for now was idle, the mindless ramblings of a small child coming to terms with new surroundings and a change in routine. I dreaded that whining starting up again. She'd had an ice-cream, but she would soon be hungry. Plus she was getting tired. A combustible combination.

Melissa was not in a good place, however. Understandably she was apprehensive, but moving away from the wide-open spaces unnerved her. She explained that she felt the tight streets were closing in, the taller buildings looming over her. I thought I understood what she was going through. I had experienced something similar on my walk back to the library after I'd dumped the car.

"It's natural I think," I told her. "You're starting to feel hemmed in, a little paranoid. That's no bad thing, as it keeps you alert."

"Oh, I'm that all right. I feel jumpy. My flesh is crawling."

"You feel watched, right? Eyes everywhere."

She turned to look at me as we walked on. "Exactly that."

"Don't fret about it. It comes with the territory when you feel you're being tracked." I deliberately avoided using the word "hunted", despite believing that's exactly what was happening.

I turned the conversation around to how everything would feel better once we were safely ensconced within a hotel room that no one could track us to. A place where we could rest up and feel safe while we planned our next move.

"Sue will be bringing us some more cash," I told Melissa as we turned into Gladstone Road, where the hotel Susan had booked was located. "And maybe by the morning she will have dug up some news we can act upon."

I tried to sound more confident than I felt. It was just as likely that a further night would allow Hendricks to plant and create more evidence as it was for Sue to find a weakness we could exploit. But Melissa didn't need to know this. She was coping remarkably well, but there were recent signs that the stress of our desperate situation was getting to her.

"Why is she not coming directly here to the room?" Mel asked me as we approached the Angel Hotel courtyard. "Why meet elsewhere first?"

"Because at this stage we can't be too careful," I explained. "I want to make sure she really is okay with all of this before putting the four of us in the same room together. Also… and I hate saying this, hate myself for evening thinking it, but I have to consider the fact that she might bring the police with her."

"Why would a friend do that?"

I shook my head. "Oh, not out of malice. Not Sue. But if she genuinely thought it was the best solution then she might just go for it and to hell with facing my wrath. What's that old saying: 'better to beg for forgiveness than ask for permission'. Something like that, anyhow."

Just then Charlie stopped in her tracks. Her face was set, sullen all of a sudden. "How long do we have to stay here?" she demanded to know. "I want to go home now." She folded her arms across her chest.

"It's just for one more night, sweetheart" Melissa reassured her, crouching down so that they were eye to eye. "Think of it this way, you'll go to sleep later on tonight and then when you wake up we'll be heading off."

"Home?" The kid raised her head, her eyes imploring her nanny and guardian to end this misery. "Will Daddy be there?"

Melissa looked back over her shoulder. I shrugged. I didn't know what to tell the kid. Mel looked away again and stroked Charlie's hair. "We'll see, sweetheart. We'll see."

"Will Roger be there?"

"I'm sure he will be."

"Is Mike coming with us?"

"Is that all right by you if he is?"

Charlie nodded. No second thought necessary. I was touched by this small show of affection. It was like the hand-holding earlier. Once again it made me think about my own daughter, now almost six thousand miles away. I felt a twinge deep in my stomach. An ache I knew I would never truly be without.

We still had time to kill, and I saw an advertisement hoarding that made me grin. "Hey, Charlie," I said. "You like *Ice Age*, right?"

The kid nodded. Interested, but not ready to fully commit.

"Well, the new one is on at the cinema, and that's just a short walk away. How about it?"

The look on her face told me I had come up with just the right idea. Melissa, too, appeared relived by the suggestion. We blew a decent wad of money on the tickets, tubs of popcorn, large drinks, and a bag of M&Ms to share around. The movie series had run out of steam a long time ago, and this one was yet another rehash of the familiar. It didn't matter. It got us off the street, and in the dark where nobody would take notice of us. It was a perfect way to pass the time.

Afterwards, we took a slow walk back in the direction of the hotel. Charlie's mood was greatly improved, and for that I was grateful. As we reached the street on which the hotel stood for a second time I stopped in my tracks.

"I'd better go," I said to Melissa, checking my watch. It was a little early, but I didn't want to be around the kid if she kicked off. "You head to the room. I'll see you in an hour or so."

Melissa gave me the strangest smile.

"What?" I asked.

"You seem different somehow. There's no panic anymore, no stress. It's like you're a whole other person."

"Well, don't bank on me being a better one," I scoffed. "There's not even a tiny part of me doing this for you or her."

The kid jerked her head up, suddenly very much alert and scowling at me. "You're mean," she snapped. "I don't like you anymore. I want Roger back."

Melissa glared as she stood upright, turning to confront me. "Why do you do that, Mike?"

"Do what?"

"Let people in just enough to have them start believing you're a decent guy, only to prove yourself the arsehole they originally thought you were."

"Hey," I said, spreading my hands. "You're the one who made the mistake. I never said I was anything *but* an arsehole."

I regretted the sentiment more than the comment.

Melissa stared me down. Fierce disappointment blazed in her eyes. "True enough, Mike. I won't make that mistake again, believe me."

I met her angry gaze. "But you are confident there will be an 'again'? I mean, you do believe I'm coming back? You think I'm at least decent enough to do that."

"Of course. I'm your alibi, right? You need me to help get you out of this."

I raised a finger and wagged it in her direction. "You got it, darling."

She leaned forward and lowered her voice to a whisper. "Well, me and Charlie come as a pair. Remember that. If you need me, you need her, too. So be nice. It won't kill you."

I turned and walked away, already regretting my outburst and putting an end to the good will I had earned throughout the day. I hadn't meant a word of it.

***

That was a little under an hour earlier. Here in the high-rise car park for my meeting with Susan, I was aware of my every sense opening up like a budding flower. I wasn't exactly afraid, more anxious. Excited, too, at the prospect of seeing a good friend again.

My thoughts turned back to the disagreement with Melissa. She had been right. I did need her. Far more than she needed me. She and the kid came as a package deal, and I was okay with that now. I no longer felt any antipathy towards either of them. But my focus at the time, as now, was on meeting with Sue and trying to get our three lives back on track. I had not handled things well, and I made a mental note to apologise later. Try and put things right between us. Not for the first time, I had acted like an arse. No great thespian qualities were required on that score.

Susan Healey was – had always been – the brighter side of humanity. The very opposite of me, in other words. She could almost always offer a positive spin on any situation, no matter how bleak it might appear at the time. I recalled that I had initially considered her to be naïve, yet our time working together had eventually dissuaded me of that notion. Susan simply refused to embrace the darkness that seemed to so overwhelm most people. I decided I had been right to contact her, and was absurdly pleased that she had suggested coming to meet me. It implied she had forgiven me, and for that I was more grateful than I could ever express.

At the end of a grim concrete walkway, intended (but failing) to make pedestrians feel safe and separate from the vehicles entering the car park, was a blue door. It looked heavy, but when I applied most of my weight to it, it flew open and I found myself in the stairwell which, as car park stairways always do, had a strange chemical odour and a particular dirty light quality.

I made my way up two flights and then out into the parking area itself, which was about the size of a football pitch. I crossed over to a circular column and leaned against it. It seemed a good place to wait, because under the meagre lighting the concrete pillars cast deep shadows. This provided plenty of places to hide in the gloom, from where I could see the ramps that directed the vehicles from floor to floor. I stood with my back against the column and took a breath. By my watch I was a few minutes early, though I had dragged my heels after I'd left Mel and the kid. There was no sign of Sue's Mini Cooper. I hoped she wouldn't be too late, because only now was I realising how out of place I looked standing there. You did two things in car parks: you drove in, exited your car and went about your business; or you got back into your car and drove away. Loitering by one of the support columns would draw unwanted attention.

Not good planning on my part.

Rusty, I thought.

The first vehicle that came up the ramp continued on and up to the next level. The second, a silver Audi, took a space close by the ticket machine. The driver claimed his ticket and walked off down the ramp he'd just driven up. The third, just a few minutes later, was a red Mini Cooper. I had told Sue to look for the stairwell exit sign and park close to that, which she did. I tracked her progress and gave it a few minutes. No other vehicle followed. I saw nobody else taking any interest in the car, nor was anyone studiously avoiding looking at it. As I started slipping between cars, moving in the direction of the Mini, I took one more quick look around, and then jogged the last few yards over to her car.

NINETEEN

The moment our eyes met I felt it all over again; whatever we had once shared was still there. It was as if the intervening years had not occurred, or at least had melted away to the point where they did not matter. Sue looked exactly the way I remembered. Same angular features and high cheekbones, same wavy dirty-blonde hair flowing over her shoulders and halfway down her back, same piercing blue eyes. Even the same wide smile; which I hadn't entirely expected. She wore a navy linen jacket over a grey top and blue jeans, which were tucked into leather boots, and was apparently no older than the last time we had met.

We hugged one another like the long-lost friends we were. When I pulled back, I was almost overcome with relief and regret in fairly even doses.

"You're still as gorgeous as ever," I told her. I was aiming for something light-hearted, but I also meant every word.

"Hmm. Flattery will get you nowhere, my friend. Not this time."

I smiled. Her words were tough, but I could tell her heart wasn't in it. "Seriously, Sue, you look great. Damn! It's been too bloody long."

"Hey, that's not down to me, Mr."

"I know, I know. My fault all the way. No arguing with you there."

She pulled her head back, eyes widening. "Good grief! Michael Lynch, sincerity, and an apology are not three things that often occur at the same time."

"Okay. I deserve that. But for what it's worth, it *is* good to see you again. I've missed you so much."

She forced out a long sigh as we got into her car and sat there looking at each other. "You, too, Mike. You can't believe how much I've been rehearsing on the way down here. All the home truths I was going to tell you. All the finger wagging, all the… disappointment I was going to express and get out of my system. But now that I'm actually here, it just feels a bit petty and unnecessary."

I hung my head a little. "I know I let you down, Sue. I know I may even have hurt you. It's no excuse, but you know the state I was in at the time. The drinking got a real grip of me. I'd like to blame it all on losing both my career and my marriage, but of course I lost both *because* of the booze, and I hurt everyone who was in my professional and social orbit at the time. Whatever I said, whatever I did, I apologise. That's all I can do."

I felt her hand on mine. A light touch. The touch of a friend. But electric all the same. "It's okay, Mike. It was a long time ago. I won't deny that you hurt me. It was hard to take, but life moves on. We all move on."

I nodded my agreement. "It's easy to forget that. When you leave behind a life that had been in your blood for years, leave people you care for behind, somehow you still think about them as they were, not how they may be now. You still look terrific, though. I've read your columns and you're writing better than ever, too."

"I'm happy enough," she told me. "Professionally and personally. But we'll have time for that later. Right now, I think we ought to concentrate on getting you out of this mess you find yourself in."

I cleared my throat. It took two attempts. "Easier said than done, I'm afraid. Is there anything new since we spoke last?"

"Not really. Because of who and what Dawson was, plus the fact that an abduction cannot be ruled out, the investigation has gone up through the gears. I'm not aware of them chasing any fresh leads, though. Not since discovering the car."

"How about Chris Dawson?" I asked. "Has anyone put his name in the frame for it?"

Sue nodded. "It's been suggested. But only by a few sections of the media. The police and NCA investigation is firmly focussed on you."

"I really need you to find out more if you can, Sue. I'm sorry I have to ask, but I could do with you being there at the next press conference if at all possible, to get close to the team investigating this. Hendricks can't be controlling everything. For one thing, it's not the NCA's place to take a lead. Plus, there's only so much evidence he could have planted before the police rolled up on the scene. Only so much he can do now, especially as he's not running the case."

Sue patted my hand again. "Mike, take it easy."

"Sorry. Was I getting heated?"

"Just a little. Your voice was going up a notch or two, and I could see a big vein in your neck start to throb."

I hadn't realised. "I got a bit carried away. I think the pressure finally got to me, and I vented the moment I had a friendly ear who would listen."

"I remember that vein well, Mike."

I nodded. "If anyone would, you would. I was… combustible in those days."

"Look, it's all right. You can relax now. I'll do it. I don't need any more convincing. You were right, the official story as it stands is enough to warrant some serious interest. The twist I can put on it makes it front page headlines for days." Susan broke off, looked into my eyes and grinned. "To be honest, Mike, even if it weren't, now that I've seen you again I would still be getting involved. You're in a jam. You're my friend, and you need my help."

I put my head back, released a sigh. Tension that I had been carrying around for hours ebbed away. "I can't think of anyone I'd rather have in my corner than you, Sue."

She squeezed my hand this time, our fingers intertwined. "Okay, I'll drive you back to the hotel and then as soon as we've discussed a strategy with Melissa I will call the investigation team. I'll start on this as soon as I can." She reached inside her jacket pocket, took out a bundle of notes and handed them to me. "Meanwhile, here's some money to tide you over. There's a burner phone in the glove box for you, too. I charged it up on the drive down, put the SIM card in for you. It has my mobile number punched into it, and I have its number in mine. When we're not together I will call you as soon as I have anything for you."

I grabbed up the mobile from the small compartment and pocketed the cash. "Thank you so much, Sue. Seriously. You have no idea how desperate we've become."

"I think I do. You called me, after all."

I managed a small chuckle. "The sad thing is, even after what I did to you, even after all the time that has come and gone since, you were still the first one I thought of. Still the person I knew I could rely on."

"That is sad," she agreed. Her wide smile flashed again in the gloom. "But also nice to hear in an odd sort of way. To be honest with you, Mike, it's good to be–"

Susan Healey's smile disappeared in a fine maroon vapour before I heard both the back window and windscreen shatter. I felt the warm slickness of her blood and tissue splash across my face, as hers became a jagged, flapping maw. My eyes barely registered the horror before a scream erupted from deep inside my core and filled the vehicle with my pain. Hands scrambling frantically, I hooked something from my eye, and as my fingertips scraped against the hard nub, I knew immediately it was a fragment of bone.

I acted by instinct.

I ducked low into the footwell of the car, then in one fluid movement I pushed open the door, threw myself out and scuttled around to the front of the Mini, seeking protection provided by the engine-block. When no further shots followed, I raised my head a little, trying to see beyond the vehicle. Other than a couple of parked cars I saw nothing in the vague amber light.

Curious.

Not right at all.

After the kill shot I had expected more to follow. That or the sound of the gunman rushing towards me.

But there was nothing to see and only silence out there to dampen down the screaming inside my head.

Run, my mind insisted.

But I couldn't.

Instead I waited. Looked and listened.

Still there was no movement. No further shooting.

Something that felt like acid squirted in my stomach. Blood pounded in my temples. My legs felt like I was wearing diving boots, but I knew I had to move. Impulse once more insisted I run, just as it had back in the lay-by, but this time I couldn't. Not yet. Not until my brain knew for certain what my heart already believed.

Keeping low, I edged my way back around to the door from which I had so swiftly exited only minutes earlier. My eyes scoured the car park, but I understood that I would almost certainly never see the shot that would kill me. I would be dead even before the flash of gas igniting in the weapon's muzzle lit up the dark recesses of the structure.

Ignoring the sense of exposure, I leaned through the passenger doorway and reached out a hand. Like the coward I truly was, I could not bring myself to look. Instead I put a finger to my friend's wrist, feeling for a pulse. There was no way Sue could have survived such a massive impact from a head shot. My mind was aware of that. But I owed her the time it would take to be certain.

Still expecting that second shot or the appearance of the killer by my door, I tried the limp wrist in my hand one more time.

Nothing.

Susan was gone.

And this time it would be for good.

I backed out of the Mini. The urge to run was now almost overwhelming. I turned to look at the exit that would take me to the stairs. It was close, but far enough away that I knew I could not escape unless the shooter allowed me to. Instead of heading towards the exit, I turned to look back once more at where the shot must have come from. One level up, either side of the ramps.

Still no movement.

Still only silence.

"You bastard!" I cried, rage spilling out unchecked. Tears now streaming down my cheeks, dripping from my chin and falling to the car park floor. Emotion erupted from deep within my chest. "Why her and not me you fucker? Why her and not me?"

I rose up, and this time I did run. But away from the stairs, directly towards the ramps. There was no conscious thought. Only raw anger and outrage. It didn't matter that I was presenting an even bigger target of myself with every movement. My friend had been murdered and grief threatened to engulf me. At that moment, I did not care if I lived or died.

My fight or flight response was screwed. Perhaps terminally so.

I stopped out in the open, listening keenly.

Nothing.

"Where are you?" I called out. "Show yourself. Is that you, Hendricks? Come on, you fucker. I'm right here. This is what you want, isn't it?"

Nothing.

Then a sound to my right. I whirled, fists balling, spittle flying from my mouth. The door of a narrow lift juddered open and an elderly couple stepped out. I stood no more than ten yards from them, caught directly beneath one of the caged ceiling lights. The three of us looked at each other.

I turned on my heels and ran, this time for the stairway.

Something drove me. It could not have been either my head or my heart, for the former insisted I slowed and took a breath, whilst the latter wanted to head back and take the car park to pieces, car by car. Thankfully, it was instinct that took over. One floor below I switched direction, sped across the parking area and changed stairwells. The exit door was closed, and I had no idea what was waiting for me out there. Nature won the day there, too, as I flung myself through the door without hesitation.

The man I slammed into was wearing a black zipped jacket with a hood raised up and drawstrings pulled tight, black combat trousers and black ankle boots. On one shoulder hung a black backpack. The door had crashed open hard, striking the man a glancing blow from shoulder to face, sending him tumbling to the floor. He turned to look at whoever was responsible. What I saw in his eyes, more than anger, more than any surprise, was recognition.

This is one of them, I told myself. No obvious weapon on view. A man tasked to trace and delay if necessary. Perhaps to apprehend, but not to kill. There was a narrow advantage, one that was closing with every split second that passed. Once again I did not hesitate. I slammed my shoulder into the man in black, just as he raised himself onto one knee. This time the man rolled backwards and sprawled wide on the hard surface. Narrow advantage or not, I used it well.

No point in trying to tackle him physically. He would be combat-ready. I was not.

I aimed one swipe at his head with my right foot, felt a satisfying crunch beneath it. His head jerked backwards, and I saw his eyes roll back. Then I ran.

I cut through a short, narrow alleyway, heading into the rear of a Marks & Spencer store. I flitted between aisles of female attire and footwear, finally emerging on the far side of the building by the underwear and lingerie. The main doors led me directly onto a wide and busy road, where I was quickly able to get my bearings.

When I turned to glance over my shoulder, the man I had struck with the door was nowhere in sight. As for Susan Healey, I did not think she would ever stray too far from my nightmares.

TWENTY

Rhino had known he'd backed the wrong horse after less than a couple of minutes on the road. Their two cars moved away from the station, took a right back out onto the main road, then on to the one-way street on the left where Tyre City stood on the corner. He followed at a discreet distance, but having rounded a bend he came out onto a wider stretch of road to find that they were gone from view. He stopped the Merc. It rocked a couple of times. As it did so, Rhino checked the rearview, and only then did he see the entrance to the local police station, which stood on the banks of the river. He watched as the cars he had been following crawled their way around to find parking spaces in the shadow of the large building.

It was time for decisions. One of the two cops he'd thought might be part of a pairing had driven off before this crowd. He was long gone. So, it was either sit here and wait for them to emerge from the nick, or return to the railway station and Haystacks. When he ran that option through, his mind drifted to the second of the supposed pairing. He had remained at the station. He had his own vehicle. There had to be a reason why he had stayed. Rhino tapped the fingers of his right hand on the steering wheel. Nodded to himself, and removed his foot from the brake. You didn't always play the hand you were dealt, especially if you dealt it yourself.

***

Two hours later, still sitting in the station car park, Rhino realised the beauty of this sort of work was that while it was happening you never knew whether your decision was right or not. It was only afterwards, in retrospect, that you found out one way or another. Unfortunately, the downside was that also happened to be how you were judged. He carried some weight with Chris, and had stockpiled plenty of markers in his favour for all the things he had done with, and on behalf of his boss. Screw this up, however, and there was a chance those chitties would count for nothing.

Whilst Rhino turned all this over in his head, Haystacks was of course verbalising pretty much the same thing. He didn't think it was at all fair that he had been put in this position, insisting that the odds had been stacked against them.

"It's his fault, man," Haystacks said. He stroked his long beard, as he often did when he was contemplating. "Chris's fault. He should have sent more men. That way we could have covered every move."

"Are you going to tell him that?" Rhino could not fault his friend's logic, but was sick of hearing about it.

"Yeah. I'm going to tell him exactly that if he starts pointing a finger in our direction."

Rhino appreciated the 'our'. He sighed and turned to Haystacks. "You're one tough fucker, and I wouldn't put it past you to go one-on-one with the boss. But he's the boss. You need to shit or get off the pot with him."

Haystacks was quiet for a few moments. Then he muttered, "I don't mind being someone's right-hand man. Don't mind being told what to do. I respect Chris. But if we missed something here today, all I'm saying is it's not our fault. I don't want to pay for something I didn't do wrong. That's cool, right?"

Rhino had been watching the entrance to the station, hearing perhaps only every other word. "You notice that cop who was with the other fellah at the lay-by, the one who drove away on his own earlier. He keeps popping out to make calls. Why do you suppose that is?"

Haystacks paused midway through a two-handed beard stroke. "I don't understand the question."

"My point, Haystacks, is that his phone will work just as well inside the station. So why does he keep coming outside to use it?"

Haystacks sat more upright. Peered out towards the entrance and the non-stop movement of bodies in and out, all eager to go somewhere it seemed. "You think he could be speaking to Chris? You reckon he's the bent cop?"

Rhino spread his enormous hands. "All I'm saying is, he looks like a man who doesn't want these conversations overheard."

The two of them watched the entrance closely. Sure enough, within ten minutes the cop was out there again. Fidgeting with his phone and yammering on it. Rhino and Haystacks glanced at each other.

"We follow him when he leaves," Haystacks said.

Rhino smiled. "We do indeed."

"You were wrong about this last time."

"I was."

"So, you won't want to be wrong again."

"No, Haystacks. I won't want to be, and I won't be. This is our bloke. So, you can stop stroking your damned beard."

***

Hendricks sat in his hotel room. He had tossed his jacket across the edge of the bed, and his tie had followed swiftly after. He sat in one of the room's two chairs, heels resting on the other. He had made several calls, logged into his network and checked numerous databases, but could find no leads on Mike Lynch's potential whereabouts. Finally, he called his manager and updated Dwyer on developments.

"How are things with local police?" Dwyer asked immediately.

"We came to an amicable arrangement, sir. Downward pressure obviously helped, so thank you for that. I really want to stay with this."

"Let's see how it plays out over the next forty-eight hours, David. Ray Dawson is now history, and there's plenty of work back here to occupy you."

"I'm sure we will have resolved this inside two days, sir. Mike Lynch is unknown to us, so despite having managed to murder Dawson, he is, nonetheless, inexperienced. Plus, he has a woman and child in tow."

"Hmm. I wonder, David. You and DCI Randall seem to be of a mind that Lynch and Andrews may now be colluding. The alternative being he stashed the woman and the girl away somewhere whilst he purchased tickets at the station. I wonder have you considered a third option: that Lynch is no longer with them."

Hendricks paused long enough for him to raise an eyebrow. The thought had not occurred. There was some confusion in his mind as he juggled the two storylines: one that had Lynch marked as a cold-blooded killer and abductor of two people, and the other the truth. Other than Lynch himself, and perhaps by now Melissa Andrews, he was the only one who knew Mike Lynch was an innocent bystander, a man in the wrong place at a very wrong time. Hendricks had to assume that Lynch would do everything possible to keep Melissa close by, she being the only other witness. Yet at the same time he had to follow the logical conclusions others were drawing.

"I had not considered that, sir," he admitted. "But if we follow that thought process through, then either he does have them both secured away somewhere, or they are both dead. Any other scenario and the woman and child would by now have been discovered, or handed themselves in to us."

After a moment, Dwyer said, "Tread carefully, David. You talk about 'us' and 'we' a lot, when in reality you mean 'them'. The investigation team are allowing you to tag along. Not the other way around. Don't forget that."

"Of course."

"Has anyone given you a hard time? Asked some complicated questions?"

"Not really, sir. Of course, they have questioned me, but it's been a box-ticking exercise for the most part. They know the man responsible drove off in that BMW, so they don't want to waste more time than necessary."

"Well, that's excellent news. And it's a good sign that they have allowed you on the inside, David. They didn't have to."

"Agreed. Though I'm not sure it helped matters having a second NCA officer attached. Randall was sniffy enough when it was just me."

Right at that moment there was a knock on the door. "I have to go, sir. Someone here for me, it could be important. I'll call you right back."

Hendricks killed the call and tucked the phone away in his trouser pocket. It was Nutton at the door. Hendricks stepped aside to let the man into his room. "You could have got a better place for the night," he complained. "This is a bit of a dump, even for NCA standards."

Nutton did not respond. When both men were in the main part of the room, Nutton turned. In his hand he held a pistol. It was aimed at Hendricks.

Hendricks frowned, and then laughed. "What the fuck is this?"

"I heard you on the phone. Were you talking to Dwyer?"

"What the fuck does that have to do with you? And would you mind telling me why you're playing at being Clint fucking Eastwood all of a sudden. You'll make my fucking day when I send you back off to wherever you came from with a hail of bullets aimed at your arsehole. Arsehole!"

Nutton smacked a hand against his side. "Damn! I played my hand too soon. I thought you might have asked Dwyer why he sent me."

"That's exactly what I was just…" Hendricks did not complete the sentence. It dawned on him, slowly at first, then the entire picture suddenly became clear. He took a step back, his leg striking the bed.

"Oh," he said. "I see. I asked him why he sent you. I never had a chance to hear his response. He would have told me he didn't send you, right? That he's never even heard of you."

"Right."

"Because I fucked up?"

"Because you fucked up."

Hendricks took a long breath. "I can still be useful to them. We, you and I, could still be useful. There's a whole reservoir of information out there to be drained off."

"I guess this time I also fucked up. Only, there's no one left to tell."

Hendricks was about to disagree on that point, when the gun was raised.

Three shots later – two centre mass, one to the head – and Hendricks stopped thinking altogether.

***

Rhino and Haystacks watched it all unravel from a safe distance. The lone cop eventually quit whatever he was doing inside the station and headed for his car. As his Mondeo edged its way into town, Rhino's Mercedes followed. It irritated Rhino that his boss refused to let them know who his inside man was. Chris referred to it as 'compartmentalising'. Rhino considered it just plain old bullshit. He had an idea it could be this cop, but that was just a guess.

The cop drove out to the motorway and pulled into the services. He sat there for twenty minutes, at which point another vehicle pulled up alongside. The passenger in that car, a Jaguar XK, joined the cop in his Ford, where they talked for a little over ten minutes. When they were done, both pulled back out of the services. Rhino watched all this with great interest as he followed once more. The Jag driver had status; during the conversation, the cop had come across as deferential. That could only mean the Jag man carried some weight. When he reported it all to Chris, his boss listened but made no comment. He simply told them to stick with it and wait for the go command, or to call it as they found it.

They drove back into Chippenham. The cop ate at a Burger King, went for a pint at a crowded Wetherspoons, and then made his way to a Premier Inn. Rhino reported on their status once more, having chosen a spot with the best view of the building and its grounds. The next thing of interest to occur was that the cop they believed to be their guy's partner exited the same hotel and slipped away into the gathering gloom. As the partner's vehicle was lost from view, Rhino looked across at Haystacks.

"Did you notice that other cop's car parked up?"

His companion shook his head sullenly. He wasn't in a talkative mood. He had bent Rhino's ear for most of the afternoon and early evening about how he was sick of boring jobs like this. To Rhino's memory, this was the first such job they had ever done for Chris.

"Maybe we should've followed him. Earlier and now. At least he's doing something. More than any other fucker from what I can see."

Haystacks shrugged.

Rhino sighed and shook his head. It felt as if they were set for the night. He was prepared, having done it before. But Haystacks snored like a freight train, which meant a poor night in store for both of them.

"I'll take first watch," he said. He was tired, maybe a little weary, But at least he would be ready to sleep when it was his turn.

A few minutes after Haystacks had settled back into his seat, head propped up against his balled-up jacket resting against the side window, an ambulance came sweeping up outside the hotel and stopped immediately outside the entrance. Moments later the circus was back in town, with three marked and two unmarked vehicles, each with lights pulsing. Armed officers piled out of one vehicle. It wasn't long before they had the entire place sealed off.

Rhino was so glad he had decided to park in a street directly opposite the hotel. If he had chosen its car park instead, he and Haystacks would now be trapped. He glanced across at his colleague. "This has got to be about our cop, right?" he said.

"No question."

The big man shook his head, pulled out his mobile, and called Chris. When he was done, he turned to Haystacks and shrugged expansively. Shaking his head he said, "Chris says we're to stay put. Looks like his man is not the poor sod who needs that ambulance."

Haystacks returned to pulling at his beard.

TWENTY-ONE

I was out of my mind.

Not on either drugs or drink, which would have been fine by me. I was demented by reality. In the space of a heartbeat, a person's life had been snuffed out so brutally just inches away from me. Not any person, either. A friend. Perhaps the last real friend I had. A friend whose blood had sprayed down on me in a shower of horror.

Wherever my gaze fell, it fell upon the same thing. It didn't matter what my eyes were showing me, for within my head a gout of blood erupted from a burst balloon and rained down upon my upturned face. It was a nightmare whilst more awake than I had ever been, one that replayed over and over and over again. A spool of violence, unrelenting and obscene. I stumbled along the streets, aware of the sight I presented to other pedestrians, fully understanding that I could not carry on in that state, yet pursued through the streets by vivid and garish images of a lifeless face torn to pieces by a single projectile.

The revulsion felt as if it continued for hours, but the whole thing was over in a few minutes. Even so, I swiftly realised I had completely lost track of time. My awareness of surroundings, of people, became peripheral, which made me vulnerable. I had a sense of being outside of myself, looking on at this blood-spattered creature lurching along the pavements. It was a panic far worse than that caused by witnessing the murder of Ray Dawson.

Not again, I thought. *Get a grip of yourself, Mike.*

I had to find a way out of this maelstrom, back to myself once more.

First thing to address: it wasn't just my shambling gait that was drawing attention. I buttoned my jacket all the way, but still the vivid scars of Susan's death remained on my shirt in smears and ribbons of crimson red. I spotted a Tesco supermarket and ducked inside. I found the clothing section, snatched up a polo shirt in my size. Wedged between the ends of two aisles of racking I removed my suit jacket, tore off the once pristine white shirt and balled it up. I used it to wipe blood and tissue from my face and hands and hair as best I could. Then I wriggled into the new grey top and paid for it with some of Susan's cash.

I ignored the woman behind the counter, her severe frown indicating how irregular it was to carry out a sales transaction in this way. I asked for a bag anyway, into which I stuffed my soiled clothing. The whole thing went into a large rubbish bin which stood at the exit from the store. I felt the eyes of the cashier on me.

It wasn't perfect but it would do. Both to avoid drawing attention, and if anyone had been following me the change of clothes would help. Despite my head screaming at me to hurry, to find sanctuary as quickly as possible, I forced myself to take extra precautions the closer I got to the Best Western, making sharp about-turns, ducking in and out of alleyways, criss-crossing streets. Still frantic, I nonetheless had the presence of mind to run through the hotel entrance when it was at its most obscured by passers-by. The receptionist said nothing but the room number when I mentioned Susan's name, yet she had to have been aware of my agitated state and whatever residue of blood I had been unable to entirely eradicate. I decided it didn't matter anymore. The precautions I'd taken had to be enough – I had nothing else to give.

When Melissa let me into the room, I brushed past her and sat down on the bed without a word. I drew my knees up to my chest, lowered my head into my hands, and silently but steadily wept, shoulders heaving, a low keening escaping my lips. It went on until I was drained and only the torment of loss remained.

"Mike?"

Melissa whispered to me, a hand resting upon my shoulder. I glanced across to see that Charlie was, thankfully, sound asleep on the double bed. Without looking up I said, "Susan was killed. Shot dead while she was sitting right beside me."

Without a word, Melissa wrapped her arms around me and rested a cheek on my head. This stark and unexpected moment of tenderness caused me to sob again, and I felt the fresh strain of bone-deep anguish ripping through my body. Somehow shielded by Melissa's comforting embrace, the emotion flooded out of me until I was drained. I felt weakened by all that had happened. Perhaps even broken by it.

"I killed her," I told Melissa, staring up at her, blinking away my tears. "I killed my best friend."

I felt her shrink away from me, and I shook my head urgently. "No, I didn't have anything to do with shooting her. I just may as well have done. I allowed her to come down here and meet with me. I wanted it. I put her in harm's way. I knew it was dangerous. I knew it, and I let it happen anyway."

I started crying once again and put back my head, not wanting to close my eyes and see Susan's shattered face staring accusingly back at me. I heard myself wailing softly. I began to rock back and forth.

"I'm so sorry, Mike," Melissa said gently. Her breath caressed my cheek. "I really am so very sorry for your loss. Are you hurt at all? You look as if you might be bleeding."

I did not want to think about the jagged bone shrapnel that had pierced my own flesh. I shook my head. "This is Sue's blood. We were inches apart when…" I couldn't bring myself to complete the sentence.

"How did you manage to get away?"

"That's what I've been asking myself ever since I… since I left her there. Oh, God I left her there, Mel. Left her body sitting in her own car."

I shook my head, desperately trying to clear my scrambled thoughts. "The thing is, there was just the one shot. I managed to scramble around to the front of the car, then check back on Susan, and then I completely lost it and walked towards where the gunman must have been standing to take his shot. I had no chance. I was an exposed target. But there was no second shot."

"Do you think the shot that killed your friend was meant for you?" Melissa asked.

I shrugged. I had considered that same question on the long walk back. "I don't know. If I had to guess I would say no. To anyone watching us through a scope it would have been obvious who was in the driver's seat. If I was the intended victim, then whoever killed her certainly could have taken me out as well."

"But why? Why kill her?"

"To keep her quiet, perhaps. To get her out of the way? I can think of at least one man who wouldn't want our story to be front page headlines."

Melissa frowned. "But if they had killed you instead of her, it would have solved both problems – you out of the way and Susan left with no story. Well, a story that would have to rely on hearsay. Come to that, they could have murdered you both."

My eyes shifted towards the door, across to the kid, then I switched my attention back to Melissa. She appeared distraught, stress etched into her soft features and perfect skin. When I spoke, my voice was low, more in control.

"Assuming the person who murdered Sue is the same person hunting for us, I suppose it could have been done to make me panic. To force me to run, head back to you two without thinking. Lead them to you both. After all, taking me out would still have left your whereabouts unknown."

It was rational. Logical. Perverse. It had the feel of truth about it.

"And did you panic?" Melissa got to her feet, casting a fearful glance at the door. "Could you have been followed, Mike?"

"I can't be certain, but I did everything I could to make sure that didn't happen. I was very careful."

"But is that enough?"

It took me only a few moments to arrive at a decision. "No," I admitted. "We can't take that chance."

Melissa sat back down, her face crumpling. "So, what now? Where do we go, Mike? Where?"

"I have an idea. It's not quite a last resort, although it is something I did not want to even contemplate. I am certain it can solve our immediate problem. Provided I wasn't followed back to the hotel, I think we are safe as long as we stay in this room. Even if they followed me here, they wouldn't know which room we're in, so that would require handling on their part. My guess is if they are out there, they will wait for us to leave. So, I'm going to make a call, and I'm going to get us some help."

I took out the mobile phone Susan had bought me. I keyed in a number I had long ago committed to memory. I had no idea if it would be answered, or even if it was still in service. But although I had told Melissa that it wasn't our last resort, I now believed it almost certainly was.

The call tone was interrupted on the fourth ring.

"You know who this is?" I asked.

There was only the slightest pause to lock in the voice.

"I do."

"Have you heard about me?"

"Should I have?"

"If you've been watching TV or listening to the radio, then yes."

"I haven't. Are you in trouble?"

"Yes. Look, I don't–"

"Don't waste time explaining. Tell me where. I'll tell you how and when."

***

The roads around the multi-storey car park were heaving, nose-to-tail traffic inching towards various destinations. It was Haystacks who had taken the call from Chris, Rhino having nipped out to take a piss somewhere. When Chris mentioned a shooting, Haystacks was initially intrigued to learn the identity of the victim.

"So is this Lynch guy in the frame for Susan Healey's murder?" he asked.

"That's certainly being considered, yes. Lynch was seen, both near the victim's car and fleeing the car park. Covered in her blood apparently."

Haystacks immediately saw the flaw in that theory. "You said the police were considering whether a rifle was used. How does that tie-in with him having blood on him?"

"It's early days. Witnesses mention the blood. Passenger door was open. No mention of finding the bullet as yet, but I'm told the back window was shattered. Too soon for an in-depth report, so all options are being considered at the moment."

"And the incident here?" The Mercedes was still parked up opposite the hotel.

"Confirmed as Dave Hendricks, NCA officer. He discovered Ray's murder scene."

"And now he's dead. Either Mike Lynch is a very busy, very aggressive guy, or something else is going on here, boss."

There was a momentary pause before Chris Dawson said, "I'm starting to wonder about that myself, Haystacks. Anyhow, when Rhino gets back from his slash, drive over to the car park and have a nose around."

Haystacks sighed. "But your man is there, I take it? Isn't it a waste having us there as well?"

"He's not on scene. It's going to be harder obtaining regular updates, so drive around, see what you can see and have Rhino call me when you have."

The call was ended abruptly before Haystacks could complain further.

So now they were stuck on the road going nowhere, unable to get anything like close to the murder scene. Haystacks suffered in silence for a change, whilst Rhino tapped his fingers and cursed aloud every few minutes. They had moved about one hundred metres in ten minutes when Chris called again.

"My contact has been reassigned. All he can do is update me on the database records as and when they change, so we won't hold our breath. You getting anything?"

"Nothing," Rhino replied. "As good as useless. Can't get anywhere near the place."

"Word is that Lynch has had it on his toes. Did what he had to do and got out of there. Still no word about Charlie or Mel."

"So, what do you want us to do now, boss?"

"Find somewhere to stay overnight. If I haven't got back to you by mid-morning tomorrow, come on back."

When the call was over, Rhino caught his colleague silently nodding to himself. "What's with you?" he asked.

"I prefer 'in the wind'."

"What?"

"Chris said Lynch has had it on his toes. The Yanks say he's 'in the wind' instead. I'm just saying I prefer that."

Rhino shook his head. "You are one strange fellah, Haystacks."

Haystacks laughed and nodded. "You have no idea," he said.

TWENTY-TWO

When I put the burner phone back in my pocket, I felt the tension drain from my face and neck. A headache that had been building all day was suddenly gone. Still my mind replayed what had happened back in the car park, and my chest rose and fell rapidly at the thought of my murdered friend.

Dear Susan.

Her awful death made me feel more determined than ever to see this through. This wasn't just about me anymore. Nor Mel or the kid, either. Now I owed a debt to a friend. A friend whose last mistake had been to try and help me.

Worn out from our trip around the park and alongside the river, Charlie remained fast asleep and oblivious to the profound tension within the hotel room. Perching on the end of the bed, Melissa looked up expectantly at me as I drew in a deep breath.

"He's coming?" Melissa asked. "Your friend."

"He is. It'll take him a few hours, but he's on his way."

"He must be a very close friend. That was a strange phone call."

I smiled. "More an old friend who owes me."

"It must be one hell of a debt."

Making a snap decision, I sat down by her side and told her about Terry Cochran. Partly to let her know something of the man I had requested help from, but mostly to try and erase the haunting images of Susan. If only for a few minutes.

"We did a tour of duty together," I said. "Our separate units were shipped out to the arsehole end of the universe. We worked together several times. We hit it off right away."

"You were in the army?"

"Yes. Royal Marines. Commando unit. That surprises you." It was not a question.

"A little. No, a lot if I'm being honest. You don't seem the type." Melissa tilted her head and stared at me as if a different person now sat before her.

"I know. It surprises most people these days. Not back then, though. For me it was join up or find more and more trouble to get into. I signed up on the dotted line the day after my eighteenth birthday."

"How long were you in the… Marines, was it?"

I nodded. "Only three years, unfortunately. I was wounded in Iraq, invalided out. A stray bullet caught me in the back, did some nerve damage. Nothing life threatening, nothing anyone would even notice by looking at me. It was life *changing*, though. I couldn't go into the field anymore, and I didn't sign up to sit behind a desk."

"I'm sorry, Mike. That must have been awful for you." I saw genuine sympathy in her eyes.

I remembered the day well. The battle of Umm Qasr was fought in order to secure the port. My squad, plus another Marines unit and the US Delta team were pinned down by sniper fire. My team and I were given the task of providing cover so that our own sniper could take out their opposition. During a particularly gruelling exchange, I took out two activists, covered the wounded until help arrived, and then felt the jolt in my back just as a snatch Land Rover came to sweep us up and return us to the safety of numbers. I recalled too the interminable months of physiotherapy, the pain, sweat, blood and tears that followed. The words of the doctor who informed me that the nerve damage was too severe to repair adequately.

It was all still so fresh in my mind because that was pretty much when the real drinking began.

"It was hard graft," I admitted to Melissa. "But those three years with the unit taught me discipline, at the very least. How to avoid trouble if I could. I suppose that's why I have acted instinctively at times over the past day. Old habits, I guess. Anyhow, I quit the Marines and Terry Cochran remained. He later went on to join the SAS."

"I bet that hurt even more," Melissa said.

"Not really," I told her. And it was true enough. "I wasn't cut out to be that ruthless. Nor that hard, or savage, or brutal, if I'm honest. So, I put my savings and pay-off to good use on a journalism course, and from there went right on into the job."

"But you don't do that any longer. Why not?"

"No. That ended… badly. I fucked up, and was lost for a while. Too long. These days I'm just a self-employed graphic designer."

"So how did this debt to your old colleague arise?"

"That's not important." I swiped the air as if physically brushing aside the question. "The thing is, every year on its anniversary he contacts me in some way, and asks what he can do to repay the debt. And every year I have told him not to be stupid and to just get on with his life, that there never was a debt. That he owed me nothing."

I broke off from speaking, remembering those days fighting alongside Terry Cochran, the bond between us that was strong and fierce whilst going about our work, yet merely casual away from it. I had not told Melissa every detail. She had no need to know.

"But now you've had to call in that debt, right?" Melissa prompted.

"Yes. Mine was an act of friendship, and he owed me nothing. Still, when I now need it to be more than that – or perhaps less than that – I made the call. I'm not sure what that says about me."

"That you needed help," she said. "That you asked your friend for help, just as he asked for yours."

"I wish I could see it that way."

"You should. I'm sure he does. So what was his reaction, anyway? I only heard your side of the conversation. If you can call it that."

I gave a narrow smile. "Immediate. Automatic. Asked me what he needed to know, told me what I needed to hear. You heard my side and it must have come across as stilted. But that's how it is. He's retired from the regiment, was working with some dark security types last time we spoke, but this would have been just another op for him. Something to pull him away from whatever haunts him these days."

Melissa glanced across at the kid, checking that she was still sleeping. Returned her gaze to me. "So, what's the plan?"

"As usual in circumstances like these the first stage is to remove us from harm's way and get us to a safe location. That's the only plan necessary right now. After that, the three of us sit down and discuss our options."

"And your friend has one of these safe locations?"

I gave a single nod. "Knowing Terry as I do, I fully expect him to have a list to choose from. No one will tie me to him, so it's safe for us."

She was silent for a moment, then asked, "What do you mean by something haunting him?"

"I don't mean ghosts, if that's what you think. Thing is, when you do the things we did, you can't afford to think about those you kill in the line of duty. I'm really talking about retribution. Relatives and friends of those you have killed. Sometimes more than that – the nations of those you take out will occasionally want to exact revenge. I know Terry worked in Afghanistan, South America and several countries in Africa. If his identity were revealed, his life would certainly be in danger from someone."

"What a way to live," she muttered.

"Yeah," I said, nodding slowly. "And now we're getting a taste of it."

***

We were packed up and ready to leave by the time I gave the nod. It was still light out and Charlie was obviously tired and a little ratty at being dragged away from her cartoons, which she had been watching on TV since she woke up. Melissa did her best to soothe the kid by insisting that it would be for a short while only, that we could all settle down just as soon as our ride came to an end and that the next day would be better all round. As usual, Charlie asked about her father. Once again, Melissa told the girl a lie.

"I leave first," I had earlier explained to Mel. "When you follow, five minutes later, you turn right when you come out of the hotel entrance, first right again, then second left. I will be leaning with my back against the vehicle. If I'm not there, if I'm facing it instead, if I'm doing anything other than leaning back against it, you keep on walking."

"And then what?" she had asked.

"Hope that we can somehow figure things out and locate you."

"And if you can't?"

"Then if I were you, I would throw myself at the mercy of the police. It's your best hope, to be honest."

"And you? What will it mean for you?"

"I have no idea. It depends on who or what has prevented me from meeting Terry. But what you don't do is stop, not even to consider. You keep on going and you don't look back. You understand me? You do absolutely nothing to draw attention to yourselves at that point."

I had cleaned myself up before Charlie woke up. My face and hands and hair, at least. Blood and tissue was easy enough to wash off. As for the taint...? That was a different matter entirely. A couple of times, Charlie had asked me what was wrong. I brushed her off. She then reminded me that I had told her I would try not to be grumpy. At any other time that would have made me laugh. On this occasion, I simply lowered my gaze and turned away from her.

Now on my way out of the hotel, I was nowhere near as clear-headed as I had sounded an hour or so ago when Mel and I were talking. Out there somewhere were the murdering NCA officer,

Dawson's men, and perhaps even another group of people who had already murdered Susan.

Jesus, Sue!

I felt tears welling up once more. Seeing my friend so brutally and instantly murdered was the worst thing I had ever witnessed. I had once been scrambled to the scene of a bomb attack on one of the UDR vehicles, and the aftermath of that explosion had been horrific. So too the various battles on numerous foreign fields. But this had been personal.

And I had asked her to walk right into the trap that killed her.

Nothing would ever make me forget that. And yet at the same time, her murder had changed me in another way. Now this was not only about emerging from our predicament unscathed, wasn't merely about getting away and clearing my name. Now I wanted the responsible person or persons to pay for what they had done. Now my impulse was to fight rather than run. So, whilst I was still wary of what awaited me, this time it was because I didn't want anything to get in the way of what I had to do.

The night air was warm, the air clean and dry. There were a few bars and restaurants close by, so the area was teeming with people. I spent only a few seconds scanning the pavements for anyone paying particular attention to me. Other than the cop I had no idea who to look out for, and if others were involved and they were professionals, I almost certainly wouldn't know they were there until it was too late.

It was only a short distance to the first street. Still close enough to the main road, and if anything was going to happen it wouldn't be until I took the street on the left. I listened hard, but did not look behind me. There were more people around than I had anticipated at this late hour, which came as some relief. My gut feeling was that those hunting me had no idea where I was, and that the most dangerous moment would come when I reached the vehicle. Terry Cochran was their only way in now. If they were around, that's where they would be.

On turning left, I immediately noticed how empty the street was. A group of teenage males about a hundred yards ahead, walking my way but on the opposite side of the road; on my side, a young couple heading away from me, arm in arm, their laughter carrying to me on the warm breeze.

I spotted the black Range Rover. As agreed it was parked facing towards me, a signal that Terry was confident he had not been followed. I pushed out a deep breath and continued walking. Ten yards on I saw a figure sitting behind the wheel. Ten yards further and I could make out the figure's features.

It was Terry Cochran.

Impassive. Calm.

As I drew level with the vehicle's windscreen, Terry gave a single nod. I stopped walking, and spent a few seconds dropping my gaze on every vehicle, every house, every front garden, plus both pavements. The youths had disappeared around a corner, the couple into a house at the far end of the street. I guessed I had less than thirty seconds before Melissa and Charlie appeared at the top of the street. Either I leaned back against the Range Rover or I carried on walking.

I gave it all the time I could spare. It was possible, though highly unlikely, that someone had made the link between myself and Terry Cochran. It was therefore equally possible and equally unlikely that someone had managed to track Terry down and follow him. More improbable, however, was that Terry had allowed himself to be tracked all the way here. A GPS device of some sort was not out of the question, but I had to assume that a man as paranoid about security and safety as Terry would have swept for one before leaving home.

A lot of possibilities.

But what I considered inconceivable was the idea that my old friend had allowed me to walk into a trap.

The Range Rover was facing the right way.

Terry had given me the nod.

I leaned back against the vehicle and waited.

TWENTY-THREE

Other than cursory introductions, little was said until the town of Chippenham was a distant dull light behind us and the kid was once more engrossed with her iPod, her head on Melissa's lap. Melissa herself seemed jaded and still in mild shock. I was astonished at how well she had held up, given everything we had been through in the past twenty-four hours. But everyone had their limits. Me included.

Shortly after hitting a stretch of unlit dual-carriageway that headed north-east, Terry turned to me and said, "So tell me why I'm here."

I glanced back to check on the kid before responding. "There's a lot to tell, Terry. None of it fit for certain ears."

"The child? She's lost in another world."

"Even so." I didn't want Charlie to overhear a single word, in case something unsettled her and set her off.

Terry took the hint. A turn-off was coming up and he went with it. The long decline took us down to a roundabout. He took the first left, drove for a mile or so along a minor road, before pulling over into a car park attached to a row of shops. Most of them were boarded up and unused, the parking area deserted apart from a few youths clustered together on bikes. Terry killed the engine, opened his door and climbed out. He jerked his head at me and said, "So now let's talk."

We spent the next ten minutes doing just that, having walked a dozen yards away from the vehicle, keeping our voices low. Using broad strokes, I took my friend through every significant aspect of the past day. Terry listened, commenting only when prompting for further details. His face remained impassive throughout. When I was done, he took a breath and scratched behind his ear.

He said, "In your old job, did you and this Dawson cross paths?"

"No. His name came up a lot across our desks, and I did a bit of research for Susan at one point, but I never met him or filed a story on him. Why?"

"I'm wondering if your involvement is entirely coincidental. Anyone who is looking to lay blame at your door will look at your past employment as a potential motive."

I took a few moments to process that. "I never thought of that angle, Terry. But I don't see any way that it could have been set up around me, judging by the manner in which the accident and the re-routing panned out. It was just rank bad luck. I was on that road by chance, I pulled over by chance. I don't know Dawson, and I certainly don't know Hendricks, the NCA officer."

"Still…"

"Yeah. I'll give it some more thought. I don't see why or how, though."

"Okay. Mike, I'm sorry about what happened to your friend, but I have to ask: do you think you may have been the target?"

I shook my head. Firmly this time. I'd had a long time to consider this one question. "No. If you're going to use a rifle then you're going to be good enough with it to hit your target. Believe me, I've thought about very little else since it happened. I think there were two reasons why Susan was the intended victim. First, she knew everything and she needed to be silenced. But secondly, I think the intention was to spook me into blindly running back to Mel and Charlie. The way I see it playing out, they tapped Susan's phone, they followed her to get to me."

Terry said, "I agree. They probably didn't have enough time to arrange a larger, better team to cover every possible escape route from that car park. That's why you encountered only one man when you exited. You did well to keep your wits about you, Mike."

"Maybe. But where does that leave us?"

"I'm not sure." Terry shook his head. "Let's just get you all secured away. Then we can do this again in more detail, see what pops next time around."

I had watched Terry take in our surroundings throughout. He must have been as aware as I was that the youths on bikes had taken to circling us, those circles decreasing with each pass. Something about us had emboldened them. I suspected they would regret their growing confidence. Terry and I went to move back to the vehicle. As we did, Terry stepped to one side and took himself closer to one of the bikes.

"Whatever you're thinking, think again," he said. He stood in the path of one cyclist. "My friend and I are going on our way. You try something on, and I'll snap your neck like dry kindling. I am not in the mood, so back the fuck off."

The young men with sour faces did not look the type to appreciate being ordered around by someone not of their crew. On the other hand, Terry did not look as if he gave a damn what they thought. The clash of wills lasted only seconds. That was all it took for the youths to turn away and ride off into the distance.

I smiled to myself, grateful he was on our side.

***

Less than fifteen minutes later we were heading east on the M4 motorway. Terry appeared completely untroubled, as if he were on a Sunday outing. I admired my old friend's ability to immerse himself in something so completely that it became all-consuming. I studied Terry's eyes as they flitted from the road ahead to the rear-view mirror to each door mirror in turn. He would not only be looking for a tail, but also retaining licence plate information. Just the first three or last three digits, perhaps, but enough to prick his memory if spotted later on in the same journey. A journey I knew would be circuitous.

"So how are things in the farming community?" I asked the moment I saw Terry start to relax a little. I thought we could do with a momentary break from our troubles.

"Busy enough," he replied without breaking his observational routine. "Not so much for me, of course, I just rent the land out to proper farmers. They are the ones who do all the hard graft."

"And your other business?"

"Demanding when it's offered. Nothing in the pipeline just now, though."

"You're a man of leisure, then?"

"Most of the time. What are you up to these days?"

"I'm a freelance graphic designer." I nodded and managed a thin smile. "Glamorous, huh? I could spend the next thirty minutes explaining what it is I do, but it would hardly make sense even to me. Plus, I need you alert, not comatose."

Terry glanced across at me for a second. Flashed a grin behind a ragged beard now more salt than pepper since the last time I had seen him. He was a big man, appearing taller than his six-one height, with a build of hard, disciplined muscle. As ever his hair was buzzed tight to the scalp. Scars from both shrapnel and fist fight wounds littered his face. He had a blue vertical arrow tattooed on his neck, pointing at his left ear, beneath which were the words *This Way Up*.

"I always liked that about you, Mike. You find something to joke about no matter what the situation. Often at your own expense."

For a moment, I thought he had me confused with someone else. Then I realised Terry's memory of me was correct. In recent years, I had found a different method of coping with stress and difficulty, and the bottle had been unkind to me in so many ways. It hadn't always been like that. I hadn't always been this man.

"That was me," I admitted. "The Jokerman. And you were always Mister Stoic. Some things don't change, do they Terry?"

"As I recall, you were hardly bursting with emotion yourself. In a battle of the stoics, I'm not sure which of us would win."

"Ah, well then maybe things do change, after all."

Terry was concentrating hard again as we pulled off the motorway and headed in the direction of Swindon. Minutes later we took the Oxford turn-off. After settling in to the new route, he spoke up once more. "We change according to our experiences, Mike. We're the sum of them, after all. You were out of the game before it got a real grip on you. You became a citizen again before the military had time to turn you into the kind of machine it likes to work with. The kind of person it can mould into shape. Me, I went deeper and darker, and for so long I hardly remember who or what I was before."

I turned my head, astonished. That was easily the most words I had ever heard Terry say in a single go. "You regret it?" I asked.

"No."

"You sure? Only you sounded as if you might."

"No. No regrets. Why waste time on things you can't change?"

"That's a good philosophy. I wish I could follow it myself."

"There was a time when you did. You can find that person again. Maybe you already have."

I gave a snort of mild derision. "How do you figure that?"

He nodded back over his shoulder. "When confronted with a man who had just shot someone dead, you first managed to get away and then evade capture. When saddled with baggage in the form of two extra people, you didn't abandon them, despite having had several opportunities to do so. You kept your wits about you, you made a plan, and you held firm. After witnessing a friend being killed you didn't panic, didn't head for the hills and as far away as you could possibly be, and you didn't dive into the first open bottle you could lay your hands on. Instead you lost your hunters and made your way back to keep your baggage secure. I'd say you coped far better than you want to let on."

I looked away, staring out of the side window into the night. The landscape rushed by in a darkening blur. If I was being honest with myself, there was nothing my friend had said that I could argue with. There had been moments over the past day when all I wanted to do was dump Mel and the kid and find the nearest bar. But I hadn't. Wanting had not been the same as doing. Instead I had kept them close and kept them safe. Maybe Terry had a point.

Perhaps the real Mike Lynch had finally stood up.

Not quite old Mike, perhaps. But not the new Mike, either. Someone in between.

TWENTY-FOUR

"So we're baggage now?" came a voice from the back seat. It was the first time Melissa had spoken since the brief introductions were made back in Chippenham, and she had found her fire again.

"It's just a term," Terry replied, sneaking a glimpse in the rear-view. "It doesn't mean anything."

"Well, it sounded like it meant something."

"Then we see and hear things differently. Charlie is your baggage. You two are Mike's baggage. You three are now my baggage. I don't know about you, but I take care of my baggage."

Melissa took a while to respond. Her tone was less harsh when she did. "I hear you. I understand what you're saying. I'm still not liking that term, though."

Terry smiled and gave a shrug. The conversation was over as far as he was concerned.

I turned in my seat, saw the kid had dozed off. She'd had one hell of a day. "So, in the time since I gave you the outline of what we're facing, what kind of plan have you come up with?" I asked Terry.

"Beyond getting you three squared away inside a safe house, not a lot. Once you are rested, when the initial shock of the past day has worn off, we need to assess your options all over again. We need to figure out what they want. And we also need to try and work out who the hell *they* are."

"Well, we know the first shooter was a cop. I think we can also safely assume that the sniper was also law enforcement, or at least working on behalf of Hendricks."

Terry shook his head. "I'm not so sure you can assume anything. Not from what you told me. To work this out, you need to go back to before the first murder. And the question you need to answer is, who Hendricks is working for? In my view there is no chance that he shot Dawson dead on NCA or any other official business."

"Maybe it was personal."

"It's a consideration. Certainly, we can't rule it out. If that's the case, then the logic of your assumption is sound. But let's put that to one side for a moment and look at alternatives. Say you're wrong. If not personal, and not a NCA sanctioned hit, then why?"

"A contract." I had considered the possibility before, but now it felt right.

"That's the way I'm leaning. So, that leaves the paymaster. Who would want Dawson dead and has a way into someone like Hendricks?"

"Hey!" Melissa snapped. "Could you please not use that name. Charlie may be dozing right now, but I don't want her overhearing something like that if she wakes up."

"Fair enough," Terry replied. "You're right."

The interruption had given me a moment to give my friend's words a stir. "Mr D's rivals are unlikely," I said. "They would have hit the brother as well, and at the same time. Unless of course it *was* personal after all, but just not personal to Officer Hendricks himself. Someone Mr D crossed, perhaps, someone who also happened to know Hendricks could be bought."

"Or persuaded in other ways," Terry mused. He nodded. "But yes, it's another line we have to consider. Either way, that leaves what happened afterwards open to doubt. We're missing something here, Mike. See, if I am the person who contracts Hendricks to take out Mr D, and Hendricks screws up, then I am going to punish Hendricks, not look to take out four more people, including a child. By removing Hendricks, you remove the problem. By hunting innocent people down, you exacerbate it."

His alternative theory made sense. Most of the way. "You could be right. But whoever is behind this, they probably have no idea what either Mel or I witnessed or did not witness, what we really know for certain. It kind of makes sense to me that they would feel a strong need to wipe the slate completely clean."

Terry allowed that to percolate, before he nodded his agreement. "True. I can buy that. Still, is it likely they would then allow Officer Hendricks to continue?"

"No. That doesn't make a lot of sense. But only if you see it from the paymaster's viewpoint, I suppose. If you are Hendricks, maybe you know that by screwing things up you have made yourself a target."

"So, if I'm now Hendricks, I will do anything to make sure the witnesses are silenced in order to buy my own life back." Terry pursed his lips. "Yeah, that sounds feasible, too. Hendricks busy cleaning up his own mess. As for the paymaster, the way things have worked out, I'm probably going to cover all bases. Remove *all* obstacles."

"But still we come back to who wanted this at all. Hendricks's motive is money, plus he gets to nail Daw… Mr D, who has been a thorn in his side for years. A win–win scenario for one lucky cop. Why does Mr D have to die in the first place, though?"

"We answer that and we move a step closer to understanding who set this whole thing in motion."

I regarded my friend carefully. I felt we were discussing things as if we needed to fill in all the blanks before we could move on. To my mind, what we needed at that moment was to focus on us. To determine what would happen once we were secure, rested up, to understand what Mel and I did then to claw our way out of this mess. I explained all this to Terry as best I could.

He shrugged. "What I'm saying, Mike, is that perhaps the only way through to the other side of this is to take the fight to them. Those responsible. I don't see an easy out for you. The one thing you don't do at a time like this is put yourself in an unpredictable situation. You take charge of it instead."

There was plenty of sense in that. I nodded. "But how do we get close to them if we don't even know who they are?" I asked.

"That I don't know, my friend. But we have time to work it out."

"Anyone interested in my opinion?" Melissa asked.

I turned my head to look at her. "Of course. We're in this together. If you have something to say, now's the time."

She gave a faint smile. "Then for what it's worth, I think this NCA officer is responsible for it all. I don't believe there is any conspiracy, just him. I think he messed up and is doing everything he can to save his career and himself. He wants to leave no witnesses. No trace. No comeback."

Melissa glanced down at the kid, who was sprawled across her lap as much as her seatbelt would allow. Then she put back her head and shook it once. "But what do I know? This isn't my world at all."

"That's where you're wrong," Terry said. He kept his attention on the road ahead. "You are very much a part of this world now, I'm afraid. But don't worry, it's my job to help you and Mike here to figure a way back out of it again."

"So exactly where are we going, mate?" I asked for the first time. "Not to your own farmhouse, I take it."

"No. I have a place in mind. We'll be okay there."

"Is it a secret?"

He glanced across. "Actually, it is."

I laughed. "But you're taking us there. What, you going to blindfold us?"

"That might be taking it too far. But there is a good reason for my keeping it from you. If something… unpredictable happens between here and there, I can't have you knowing the destination."

"You're serious, aren't you?"

"Deadly. What if we were to get separated? What do you imagine they might do to you in order to extract that information from you, Mike? You've been there. You know."

I looked back over at Melissa. "Terry here is paranoid. Even more so than me."

He gave a low chuckle. "Yeah, and with good reason. Paranoia is the only thing that has kept me and an early grave from coming together."

Hearing that, I wondered, not for the first time, just who my friend had crossed over the years. "Are you exposing yourself here, Terry?" I asked. "Making yourself vulnerable. I mean, to more than the immediate threat our predicament poses."

"I wouldn't think so. In fact, I would say it's highly unlikely. I suppose it depends on where this little adventure takes us."

"You chewed me out for not calling you first, but I'm beginning to wonder if I ever should have called you at all. Two people are already dead, one of them at least completely innocent. This is not your battle."

"It is now."

"But it shouldn't be. That's my point. It needn't be."

"And I say again, it is now. Exactly as it should be. Like I told you earlier, the only thing you did wrong in calling me was leaving it too damned late." Terry raised a hand off the steering wheel. "Don't say another word about it, Mike. I'm already pissed at you for not contacting me sooner. Don't make matters worse."

I smiled and shook my head. "Are you ever going to let that go?"

"We'll see. Let's find a way out of this shit first, then I'll have time to decide whether or not to forgive you."

Terry winked and then set his eyes on the road ahead.

TWENTY-FIVE

We took a cross-country route which skirted Oxford and Northampton and eventually came upon the A1(M). Terry headed straight over towards Peterborough, hit the Fletton and Frank Perkins Parkways, before taking the Boongate turn-off and negotiating his way through to a poorly maintained road that ran alongside a narrow section of the Nene river. We were less than two miles from the city centre, and now the land was flat and just about deserted.

Terry slowed as he approached a small copse of trees to our left, and only yards before reaching it he swung off the road onto a gravel drive, swept past a collection of forlorn-looking outbuildings, before pulling up in front of a two-storey house. It had evidently been extended. It consisted of a modern frontage that looked oddly disjointed and ill at ease with its past sheltering behind. He killed the vehicle's engine and silence enveloped our small group of weary travellers.

I stepped down out of the SUV, stretched out my aching back muscles, glancing all around. The air was cooler now, the night sky a black backdrop glittering with stars. It was a little after midnight, and only silence greeted us at the end of our long journey.

The kid came awake with a start as Melissa carried her across to the dwelling. For a moment, I thought Charlie might kick off – a sound that would carry across the flatlands on the faint breeze that was blowing in from the south – but she quickly snuggled back down into Melissa's neck and fell right back to sleep.

The front door of the house opened into a slight porchway, which in turn led directly into the lounge through another door.

It was a large room, with just a single sofa arranged along the far wall, a TV in one corner. Bare essentials.

Once we were all inside, Terry swiftly took charge. "There are two bedrooms and a bathroom upstairs," he explained to Melissa. "You and Charlie take the room on the left as you hit the landing. The bathroom is at the far end. Don't stray into the other bedroom. I want to know where I can find you if I need to."

He turned to face me. "You take the other bedroom. I'll be down here on the sofa. I have no provisions, but there's an all-night Tesco not far away, so if any of you need anything let me know. If not, I'll just pick up a few essentials. You'll be fine here, by the way. Nobody followed us, no one knows you're here. Mike, I'll show you a few things before I leave, but it's safe. Trust me."

Melissa thanked him and managed to squeeze out a weary smile. Charlie was now virtually draped over her shoulder, a thumb wedged inside her mouth. She said they could each do with a toothbrush, some toothpaste, bath or shower gel, and an anti-perspirant deodorant.

"No problem. We can go out tomorrow morning, get a change of clothes, anything else you may need. More supplies. For now, I suggest you get Charlie settled, maybe have yourself a relaxing bath – there should be some bath soap up there, clean towels in the airing cupboard on the landing. Try to unwind a little. When you're done, if you have the energy, join us for a drink and some food. If not, use your bed and use it well."

A single finger beckoned me. Terry led me behind the stairs, beneath which was a small cupboard that looked as if it functioned as an office as well as a storage area. Sitting on top of a built-in shelf sat an array of electronic equipment and two flat screen monitors. I wondered how many times my friend had used this safehouse before. Terry unlocked the top drawer of a filing cabinet, took out a locked box and used a different key to open it up. Inside was a Glock 19 pistol and a suppressor. He handed me both.

"I know you remember how to use this," he said.

I nodded and hefted the piece, feeling the weight of it in my hands. It had been a while, but yes, this was my sort of weapon.

"Take it with you wherever you go from this point on. You're safe as far as I'm concerned, but I plan for all eventualities."

"If anyone gets past you, I'll do the right thing," I assured him.

"They're not getting past me, but I know you have my back."

I wondered how it was that this man had more faith in me than I had in myself. Perhaps because the man Terry had known so well all those years ago was a very different person from the one I had become. Still, it felt good to be trusted again. It had been fun experiencing Terry taking charge. More than that, it had been an immense relief. A weight had been lifted off my back.

Terry switched on both monitors. Seconds later they revealed images split-screened into two views, front and back of the house. "The one on the right is thermal," he said. The green screen on the left was obviously using night-vision optics. "If you hear a series of low double-beeps coming from any room, check these screens first. We'll go over it a bit more when I get back. You won't need it right now."

"If you're sure."

"I'm sure. Now, get the kettle on and some mugs out. I'll be back before you know it."

After Terry had left to make the drive to the supermarket, I sat in the lounge for a few minutes, allowing my thoughts to catch up. Try as I might, I could not escape the haunting imagery of Susan's death. Only a few hours had passed since she was killed, but I doubted the effect it had on me would change with the passing of days, weeks, months or even years. Alone with my imagination I conjured up all manner of scenarios by which Sue's murder could have been prevented. It was a foolish waste of time. Nothing changed. She was still dead, and I remained responsible.

There was no inner peace to be found, yet a sense of calmness descended upon me. We were in good hands at long last, far away from prying eyes, and I had complete confidence in Terry's ability to find the best path, no matter how labyrinthine. Without emotional attachment, he would be able to see what neither Mel nor I could: a way out.

I felt myself smile, despite my misery and simmering fury. Terry and Mel were like oil and water, and she had not appreciated being referred to as 'baggage'. I sensed she genuinely understood his honest intent, just that it was in her nature to object. As it was in his not to care if she did.

My own impressions of Mel had altered as our time together increased. For a young women she had great presence, knew her mind and was unafraid to express opinions. That did not mean she was always right, but I knew Terry would appreciate her honesty as much as I did. Mel's allegiance to Charlie was obvious. It went beyond loyalty and devotion. The nanny loved her charge, and as the day had worn on I saw several examples of those feelings being reciprocated.

We were a collective, with collective responsibilities. Misfits thrown together by a series of events over which we had no control. Yet a bond had formed, in spite of our many differences, and I felt it growing tighter even as I sat there contemplating what might lie ahead for all of us.

Dragging my weary frame up off the sofa, I made my way upstairs to check on my baggage. The bedroom door to the left was ajar. Melissa stood with her back to the wall, gazing down at the sleeping child. There was a great deal of affection in that look, I thought. A tumult of warm emotions encapsulated within those eyes.

Melissa turned her head at my approach. I offered a tentative wink. "We'll be fine now," I assured her. "Here, I mean. Terry was serious. You, Charlie and me are all his baggage now, and he will take good care of us."

Melissa's eyebrows arched. "You're mellowing. You called her Charlie."

I chuckled. "Yeah, well she's still a pain in the proverbial, but it is her name."

"It's nice to hear you use it without anger or irritation in your voice."

"I'm in a different place now. In more ways than one. And my bark is far worse than my bite. Back in Chippenham you suggested that I erected barriers, even pushed people away. You were right. But that's nothing more than a defensive mechanism. It's not really my true nature. Anyhow, you doing all right, Mel? You feel safer now?"

She gave me a look I couldn't quite decipher. For a moment she said nothing, seeming to search deep within herself. Eventually she nodded and said, "I think everything will be okay now, yes."

I didn't quite know why, but the look concerned me. Perhaps she was still scared. I wondered whether she still did not trust me. Even if that were the case, surely, she had to have some faith in Terry Cochran. Maybe I was reading too much into it. Melissa had been through an awful lot. Myself and Terry were virtual strangers to her, yet she was being asked to put her life in our hands. She had every right to still feel both cautious and afraid. We all did.

"You turning in?" I asked.

"No, not yet. The bath soap I found was horrible, so I'll wait until Terry gets back and then I'll have a nice long soak."

I made a show of sniffing my own armpits. "I think I might hit the shower later myself. Starting to get a bit ripe."

Melissa took a step towards me. Her eyes met mine. "Thank you, Mike. I'm still not quite sure what kind of person you really are, but you've not let us down. Quite the opposite, in fact. And at a huge personal cost, both in losing one friend and calling in a debt from another. I get the impression that there is something solid and good beneath that veneer you wear. When this is all over, I'll make sure people understand that."

I was going to brush away her comment with a quip, but at that moment I thought my voice might break if I attempted to speak. Instead I just nodded and headed back downstairs.

TWENTY-SIX

When Terry returned, he and I unpacked the groceries in the small, but well-appointed kitchen. Ignoring the boiled kettle, Terry took two bottles from a six-pack of Stella Artois, uncapped both and handed one to me.

"No, thanks." I waved the beer away. "I'm on the wagon and this isn't the right time to fall off."

"Fair enough. I got tea and coffee and some milk. Oh, and a bottle of juice. Make whatever you want. How are the hostages?"

I laughed and started opening a box of tea bags. "Don't let Mel catch you calling them that. Charlie is still asleep. Thankfully. Believe me, you'll know all about it when she's not. I think Mel is just gathering herself and waiting to have a bath."

"It's a hell of a lot to take in," Terry observed. He gulped his way through half the beer and backhanded foam from his lips. "Melissa looks as if she doesn't know whether she's coming or going."

"From what she tells me, Dawson kept his home life and his business completely separate. She's not been around this sort of thing before. Not this close, anyway."

"Few people have."

I poured hot water into a mug. "Thankfully."

Melissa padded barefoot into the kitchen. Her shoulders were slumped, hair dishevelled. Dark rings had settled around her eyes. I could empathise.

Terry handed her a carrier bag. "Toiletries," he said.

"Thanks. What do I owe you?"

"We'll settle up later. You want a beer and something to eat before you go back up?"

The look she gave him was hollowed out. "No, thanks all the same. I'm all in. I need a soak and then I'm going straight to bed." Mel turned to me and said, "Would you watch Charlie for me? If she wakes up while I'm in the bath, she'll panic."

"Sure, no problem. You go up. I'll get some of this tea down my neck and be right behind you."

I felt myself unwind as the hot tea worked its magic. The past twenty-four hours or so had been traumatic to say the least. That I, Mel and Charlie were here, alive and well, suggested I had not done too badly. I knew I would forever question some of the decisions I'd made, but that depth of self-examination went with the territory.

As if reading my thoughts, Terry said, "Don't do that, Mike. Don't second guess yourself. It's futile, pal. No one ever really knows what they would do in situations like this. In my view, you handled yourself well. If you made mistakes, you have to learn to live with them."

"Easy to say, Terry. Not quite so easy to do."

"I understand that. Doesn't make it less true. You can't change it. And no good will come of self-recrimination."

I could not quite get a handle on the way it all went down regarding Susan. Although I had warned her of the risk involved, had I not actually believed in the possibility of her coming to harm, or had I ignored it because I wanted her there? Needed her there. I did not recall at any stage thinking she might be in any real physical danger, but if that's really the way it happened then I had to question how I could have been so badly prepared. This much I revealed to Terry.

He reacted pragmatically. "From everything you've told me, Mike I don't see how you could have foreseen what happened. Logic suggests it was Susan who was followed. Could you have predicted that her number was being monitored, or that she herself was being watched? I don't think so. Either way, you can't change a damn thing. It's done. You move on. It's the only way you'll cope."

Moments later, I drained my mug. "You turning in?" I asked. "I'm guessing a sadist like you has an early start planned."

Terry grinned. "Tomorrow we're all up when we're up. No schedules to keep here. Not yet at least. Best if we all get the rest we need."

"I'll hold you to that. I'm popping upstairs to sit with Charlie until Mel is ready, then I'll come back down and join you for another drink and something to eat. I'm famished."

"Sounds good to me. It'll be good to catch up, Mike. Been too long."

I sat for only ten minutes or so watching the child sleeping, but it nonetheless carried me back in time to when my own daughter was the same age. To me there was nothing quite as vulnerable as a sleeping child. I felt myself becoming anxious whilst contemplating once again all that Charlie had yet to go through, especially after she learned of her father's death. Charlie was only a kid, but old enough to comprehend, old enough to be devastated, to feel the pain of loss tear right through her.

I knew all about such loss.

Never being given the opportunity of saying goodbye to my parents was one of the many sorrows in my life. To have those two good people ripped away from me in a senseless accident left me wandering in the wilderness for a long time. I did not have the tools to cope with such loss. I became immersed in misery, allowing it to dominate my life in a way that sent me spiralling downwards. Everyone I knew and cared about got caught up in the whirlwind of wretchedness I created. I was a stain, a blight, tainting the world and the lives around me. I emerged a weaker man; that much I could acknowledge.

It should not have taken murder and chaos to start bringing me back. Yet it had, and that journey had begun at last. I did not know what my destiny would be. The only thing I was sure of is that I would have a hand in shaping it.

When Mel stepped back into the room she had a towel wrapped around her, wet hair coiled and glistening against the nape of her neck and back. The sight of her bare shoulders and legs sent a swift jolt through me, and I jerked as if prodded with a taser. Until now I had not been able to see past our situation. Suddenly I was acutely aware of Melissa's sexuality.

"You'll... you'll be fine here, yes," I stammered. I nodded to myself and looked everywhere but directly at her.

"We will. Now all I really want to do is sleep."

"Yeah. You do that." I flashed a quick smile and got out of there.

***

"Any bright ideas how we extricate ourselves from this mess?" I asked my friend a few minutes later. We had eaten toasted cheese sandwiches that Terry had knocked up, and a second cup of tea had sated my thirst. We sat on the sofa, side by side. Terry upright, me slouched, my body craving slumber.

"Not as such," he said. "I think we can dismiss Chris Dawson and his crew to a certain degree. If we absolutely had to, I could find a way to reach them and let them know precisely what went on, but at the moment there's no real benefit to them becoming directly involved. I can be convincing, but with no obvious advantage I say we push them to one side. Your main problem is obviously the police. For me the biggest concern is whether this Hendricks guy is working alone or is part of a bigger problem. The shooting of your friend bothers me for more reasons than the obvious. You have to ask yourself how likely it is that this one cop who took Ray Dawson out at close range also happens to be proficient with a rifle? How could this one man have tracked and traced Susan?"

I shook my head. "I can't see it. He has to be getting some help."

"Agreed. So then, we have to wonder whether that help is official or off the books."

"The NCA would never sanction taking Susan out like that. Me, perhaps, if they believed I was armed and a danger to the public, or at least if Hendricks had somehow convinced them I was. But to kill an innocent in the hope that I would bolt for Mel and Charlie which would then allow them to follow me...? No chance."

"Well, we know that they do believe you to be armed and dangerous, because this bent cop has managed to persuade them of it. Even so, ordering an action to take you out seems most unlikely, let alone Susan. But let's just say the order on you was given, perhaps on the basis that you were an imminent threat to your friend. If handled and spun a specific way, her death might later be explained away as an accident during the hit on you."

"Okay, I can follow that line of argument."

Terry nodded and pushed on. "But if it was official then a specialist armed unit would have been called in. No way they're going to tell this lone cop he has the green light to take you out. I don't believe the NCA even has that kind of reach. So, either an entire armed response team is also in on whatever is going on here, or Hendricks is working both off the books and not alone."

The two of us were silent for a while. I ran through the permutations. The variables were numerous. Then I said, "All of which leads us back to the biggest question of them all, Terry. However, we ended up here with you in this house, just what the hell started the whole chain of events?"

And that was when the beeps started coming from the surveillance equipment in the cupboard.

TWENTY-SEVEN

"How many?" I asked.

Terry was standing in the cupboard beneath the stairs, whilst I remained by the door. He took a few seconds to study the night-view cameras, in addition to the two Silent Sentinels picking up thermal sources.

"Two out front, two out back," he replied. "Standard formation. By the book."

"Not ideal odds," I said.

"Not for them, no. They're taking their time, though. Approaching with a great deal of caution. My gut says this is a recon, getting the lie of the land, looking to identify what's going on in here before regrouping elsewhere to plan the strike."

I understood what he meant. There were many playbooks in combat situations, and you used whichever best suited individual purposes. There was no heat of battle raging here. All was still, and whoever was out there had to use stealth.

"They won't want to announce their presence to the whole area with a violent breach," I said. "I know your neighbours are not exactly close by, but across this open terrain the sound will travel far."

Despite the circumstances, Terry turned and flashed a grin at me. "Once a Marine always a Marine, eh Mike?"

"Up here, maybe," I responded, tapping the side of my head.

"That'll do for me. So, listen up pal. On this floor there are three rooms, two entry or exit doors, five windows. We can't cover them all if they go for a multi-personnel ingress – and they will. But there is only one staircase."

"We go for the high ground," I said.

"As always. So, you set yourself up on the landing at the point where it dog-legs back. I'll stick with the surveillance until I know for sure what they're planning. If they're using suppressors like us then it's a reasonably safe bet there'll be no flash-bangs or stun grenades coming our way. As you said, they'll be aiming for a swift and silent operation."

"What about their tactics?" I asked.

Terry was unlocking a cabinet in the cupboard. I guessed it held more weapons. "I think they'll wait for the house to go dead, so I'll kill the lights one by one. I reckon they'll give it thirty minutes. So after this, no more chat. If I'm them, I'll plant a listening device on one of the windows, and I have to assume they think like me."

"Do we warn Mel? Tell her what to expect?"

"Let's see how it goes in the next few minutes. Panic is the last thing we need right now. Especially with a child in tow."

I nodded. Without another word, I picked up the weapon Terry had given me, twisted the suppressor onto the barrel as I stepped out into the short passage and then climbed the first rise of steps. The calm exterior I hoped I was presenting was for the benefit of my friend. I wanted him to believe in me, to feel confident of my part in his plan. Inside I was screaming. My three years of service were a long way back in the past, and whatever training and experience had been ingrained was long forgotten now. These days I was a mere civilian. And I was scared, just as any other civilian would be. But Terry was my friend, I had got him into this mess, and I would stand shoulder-to-shoulder with the man.

A few minutes after I had secreted myself low in the tight corner of the landing, the downstairs lights were extinguished and Terry appeared moments later out of the darkness. He switched on a small pencil-beam torch with an amber bulb, illuminating a sheet of paper on which he had written 'ALARM BYPASSED. SILENT BREACH FRONT AND BACK IS MY BEST GUESS. LET THEM COME AS FAR AS POSSIBLE. WAIT FOR ME.'

The torch beam rose and I nodded my understanding. Our unwelcome visitors would not have bothered bypassing the alarm if they had intended on coming in heavy. It was likely that these people had no idea who was inside the house other than myself, Mel and Charlie. Whilst we were taking every precaution, I doubted they would be expecting any kind of retaliatory response. Let alone an armed one.

The beam flashed upon another note. 'WILL PASS MESSAGE ON TO M TO MOVE INTO BATHROOM WITH C, LOCK UP AND STAY SILENT. WILL KILL LIGHTS UPSTAIRS. BACK BEFORE YOU KNOW IT.'

Terry forced something bulky into my free hand. A pair of Cobra Optics Storm Pro night-vision goggles. Then he was gone. In the darkness and relative silence that followed, time dragged. I wanted no part of this, but at the same time I wanted it over and done with. Most of all, I wanted payback for what had happened to Susan. Terry and I were outnumbered, but the element of surprise and my friend's ability in a firefight would be enough. Had to be. It was crucial that every shot found its target. That way we might even end it before it had really begun. If not, I would put my faith in my friend.

Minutes ticked away, and then I was aware of Terry coming back down to the landing and setting up to the front and right. I pulled on the goggles to allow time for my sight to adjust, then hunched down and waited in the gathering silence. I did not have to wait long.

When it came, the sound of the breach was almost disappointing. The back door was too far away for any sound to be audible, but the noise of the front door being forced open was both muffled yet impossible to miss if you were listening for it. I ran it all through in my mind. We had to allow the men to reach the passage and start heading for the stairs. I had no doubt they would be wearing their own night-vision, and once they hit the stairs they would see they were not alone. We had to hope they would not notice anything untoward beforehand. It was all about timing. I had to stop myself from jerking on the trigger, silently telling myself just to wait for Terry to fire the opening salvo.

The entry team were good. I had to strain my ears to hear the soft scuffing of boots on the carpet and kitchen linoleum. I could not have been more focussed. It was curious, but whilst I had been close to hyperventilating just a few minutes earlier, I now felt no fear. An inner edge, a strength long forgotten, had somehow returned. I listened intently. I could hear their advance moving closer from either side of the stairway.

And then they were there. Distorted green, grey and white figures, almost close enough to touch.

Three of the team were in full view when one at the front turned his head to peer up the stairs. Instinctively, I knew Terry would take this man out first and then move on. The next natural target would be the second man in line. I felt certain Terry would take him as well. I adjusted my own aim accordingly, intent on hitting the third figure.

An abrupt flare of light in the darkness indicated the first shot before the muffled explosion of gases could be heard. The first was instantly followed by a second. Before the figures below had a chance to focus their own weapons, I double-tapped my own target. Virtually at the same time, the man in the middle went down beneath two more shots from Terry's weapon. The bursts of light were not significant enough to disturb vision, so within less than three seconds I could clearly see that all visible targets were down. From upstairs I heard Melissa cry out. I hoped she had the good sense to stay locked up in the bathroom as instructed.

Predictably, the fourth target had held back rather than rush forward and engage in the firefight. In my view, this marked them down as a wily foe rather than a cowardly one. They had weighed up their assault options quickly and rightly decided to err in favour of discretion.

I assumed Terry had come to the same conclusion, as my friend descended the stairs inch by inch, his head jerking from side to side as he attempted to peer around the corner of the wall close to the stairs. He had indicated nothing, but I followed him anyway.

I had my friend's back.

Once again, I heard a muted scream from above, and guessed that Mel was now starting to panic. I could hear Charlie muttering, asking what was going on. I had no choice but to dismiss it; there was a job right here to complete. Ahead I saw Terry remove the goggles, so I did the same. It was possible, likely even, that the final target would by now have removed his own and would hit the lights, causing momentary blindness for anyone still using night-vision. It was a calculated risk, but I assumed Terry was reacting to what he would do in his opponent's shoes.

Less than five seconds later both the hallway and kitchen lights came on. This was a mistake, because there was probably only one place where both switches could be reached simultaneously, and Terry would know exactly where that was. Barely a heartbeat passed before another two suppressed shots were delivered, followed by a soft thud as our final target hit the floor.

There was no screaming or shouting. The awful sound a wounded human makes was one I had heard more often than I cared to think about, a sound that would never leave me. Inside the house there was now only silence. There were no wounded.

Terry glanced back over his shoulder and jabbed a finger at two of the men lying on the hallway carpet leaking blood from two rounds each, parts of their faces now missing. As before, I knew what was required of me without him having to say. While he checked the third victim's pulse, so I did the same to number one and number two. Terry stepped away, inspected the slumped form wedged into a nook between the kitchen and hall, turned and gave a thumbs-up.

"Good job, Mike," he said. Terry wasn't even sweating.

I nodded. Exhaled for the first time in a while. "You, too, mate. That was intense."

"I'm going outside. I want to have a look around, see if I can find their vehicle. There may be more of them out there waiting."

"You think that's likely?"

He shook his head. "They will have been on comms and overheard everything that just happened. If that were the case they would be in here by now. No, I don't think I'm going to find anyone else out there, but I want to know rather than guess. Can't have anyone calling up the cavalry."

With Terry gone, I spent several minutes dragging the fallen bodies into the kitchen. I was used to being up close and personal with death. It may have been a long time ago, but some things you never forgot. There was no reason why either Mel or Charlie had to see them, so removing them from view was the best thing all round. When I was done, I hurried back upstairs. Knocked on the bathroom door.

"It's me, Mel," I said. "It's safe to come out now."

This time she did not scream. This time she sobbed, and fell into my arms. And Charlie joined in with her.

TWENTY-EIGHT

Terry drove hard across the flat terrain of the Fenlands. The sky ahead was gradually illuminating the farther reaches of the land as the ascending sun tipped the horizon. We headed into it, the road shimmering before us. Five miles north of Thetford, Terry hung a right off the main road, slowed and headed along a dirt track. The route was dusty after a dry summer, deeply rutted by tyre indentations left behind from the muddy winter. The Range Rover bounced and juddered along for just shy of a mile before turning left onto a long gravel driveway that led to a single-storey farmhouse with a large dormer roof. A yawning ditch encircled the property, and we had to cross a low wooden bridge to reach the wide, rectangular parking area. I noticed a large wooden barn set back and to the left of the house, and over to the right stood stables built from crumbling grey stone, and a small crop of outbuildings.

There had been little conversation during the drive. Melissa sat in complete silence, alternately hugging herself or twisting strands of her hair and coiling them around her finger. Perhaps for the first time in her life she was starting to understand that nightmares can come true. After initial petulance, Charlie had settled back to sleep. The kid was wasted without even knowing why. Terry appeared lost in thought throughout the entire journey. I could still feel occasional tremors rip through my own body. They were coming every few minutes. At one point, shortly after we fled Peterborough, Terry had noticed.

"You okay, Mike?" he asked.

"As right as I'll ever be."

"Taking a life up close like that is never easy. You'll feel the jolt for days."

Earlier, when Terry returned to the house, he revealed that he had found an empty SUV, but after a rapid search it had come up clean. No documentation, nothing that might tell us who the armed men were or where they had come from. Whilst Melissa calmed a bewildered and sobbing Charlie, myself and Terry searched the bodies of the four dead men. As with the car, they gave up no clues.

Probing their pockets felt obscene to me. I had done it many times before, but only in the aftermath to acts of open warfare. These particular dead bodies were different. They didn't even feel human to me.

"This isn't making sense," Terry said as he shoved one of the men aside.

"In what way?"

"The hit on Dawson I can just about buy. NCA officer goes all vigilante. The murder of your friend, however, doesn't feel right at all. That escalates matters, possibly to some kind of conspiracy. But this? Four well-armed, well-trained men, all wearing the same special ops combat gear. No way anyone is getting a bunch of mercenaries together at such short notice and have them make a strike as if they've been a unit for a long time." He shook his head and chewed on his lip. "No, this is something else altogether. Something much bigger."

I had felt it as well. A wrench deep in the gut. Terry was spot on. What had happened here was not due to one lone cop pulling the strings of a well-oiled killing machine or snatch squad.

"What are we going to do with them?" I asked.

"Someone out there will be waiting for a situation report. When one fails to come they'll send another team. There's too much mess and blood here to clean up before that happens. We need to go, leave these men where they are. Wipe down everything you touched."

Less than ten minutes later we were out of there, taking with us four extra weapons and spare clips of ammunition.

Now, in silence still, we disembarked and filed into the house. This was an older property than the previous one, and it immediately felt lived in. Terry led the way, I brought up the rear. In the cluttered, stone-floored kitchen, Terry filled a kettle and got it going. Five minutes later we were sipping our drinks at a scarred oak table in the centre of the room. Charlie perched quietly on Melissa's lap, a small glass of orange juice clasped in both hands, headphones wrapped tightly around her ears. Not for the first time I was grateful for the invention of the various Apple devices.

I glanced around the table. Terry's face was pinched, eyes dull. Melissa looked both wired and exhausted at the same time. Only Charlie appeared rested and at ease. Having initially succumbed to tears, tantrums and sullenness when snatched from her sleep, carried unceremoniously from the safe house and stuck inside a vehicle once more, her mood had improved considerably within mere minutes. I had been astonished – but so grateful – for the rapid and unexplained change in her disposition.

Before we were halfway finished with our drinks, Terry turned to Melissa and said, "There's a TV in the room at the far end of the passage. I suggest you get Charlie settled in front of it and then join us again. We have much to discuss."

It was the first thing any of us had said since pulling off the main road.

To my surprise, Mel complied without comment. "Nice place," I told my friend once we were alone. "You live here, or is this another safe house?"

Terry sipped from his mug before responding. "A bit of both. I use it more than I should."

"I don't envy your life, mate. Always on the move, always looking over your shoulder."

"And yet which of us is currently on the run from the police, a bunch of gangsters, and a heavily armed hit squad?"

I grinned. "You may have a point."

Melissa came back into the kitchen. "I managed to find some cartoons," she said. "Charlie will be fine on her own for a bit."

"Shut the door behind you," Terry told her. His voice had hardened.

"I thought I'd keep an ear out for – "

"I said shut the door. Let's not debate it."

I glanced across at Terry. He had eyes only for Melissa, whose cheeks were now flushed. She did as she was told without any further argument before taking her place at the table once more. She folded her arms beneath her chest and stared straight ahead.

"Good. Now, empty your pockets," Terry insisted. He raised a hand. "Don't ask why. Don't argue with me. Just do as I say."

For a long moment Melissa made no reply. Then she swallowed and said, "And what if I won't?"

"Then I will do it for you. And I don't do gentle."

"Terry, what's going on?" I asked, noting the tremor in Mel's body. "What's this all about?"

"You'll see in a moment, Mike. As soon as Mel has done as she's told."

Melissa got to her feet, saying nothing. Her mouth formed a pout. From the single pocket of her dress she took out an unopened packet of gum. From her left jacket pocket, she took out a set of keys. From her right jacket pocket, she took out a crumpled packet of cigarettes and a disposable lighter. Each of these she deposited on the table before her. Mel then turned to Terry, chin set proud.

He raised his eyebrows.

The silence of our surroundings was all too evident in that kitchen as the two continued to stare at each other.

It was Melissa who broke.

As I knew she would.

But I was not prepared for what she then removed from an inside jacket pocket and placed on the table alongside the other items.

The mobile phone should not have been there. Yet there it was. If Mel had seen the look I flashed her it might have terrified her all the more, but she was staring down at the table, arms re-crossed.

"Had to be," Terry said. He looked first to Mel, then at me. "It was the only way they could possibly have tracked us down."

It dawned on me then what my friend was saying. The crew lying dead back at the first safe house. Undoubtedly led there by the GPS on Melissa's mobile.

"When did you figure it out?" I asked him.

"The moment I saw them on the monitors."

I made a ball of my hand and slammed it down on the table. The mugs jumped, some of their contents spilling out across the hard wooden surface. "Damnit!" I glared at Melissa. I jabbed a finger in her direction. "You were in on it. You knew your boss was going to be shot and killed."

Melissa's eyes widened, her mouth hung open. Then she shook her head, eyes narrowing again. "No! No, that's not true. You have to believe me."

"Well then why have you been letting them track us down?"

"I haven't." She glanced back down at the table. Her voice was quieter when she spoke again. "At least… I didn't mean to."

"You told me you didn't have a mobile," I snapped.

"I lied." She shoved her hands into her pockets.

"Why? For what possible reason?"

"Because I didn't trust you." Now she met my glare, and this time she did not flinch. "I didn't know you from Adam. We've been over this. I was scared out of my wits, Mike, and despite everything you told me, despite everything that happened to us all, I didn't trust you. Once I'd said I didn't have a phone, I didn't want to take it back. I was afraid of what you might do. It was my one hope if you turned out to be a bad guy, and I couldn't let you know I had it."

I bit down on that. I was furious with her, but I also understood. Even so, her actions had put us all in danger. I told her as much.

"I know that now," she almost whimpered. Her lips were trembling. "Do you think I wanted that to happen back at the other place? Do you think I would have put Charlie though all that deliberately? Everything I have done since Ray was killed has been to take care of Charlie. I wanted that one bit of protection, and I didn't think of the consequences. That's all I can say."

I turned to Terry, frowning my disapproval. "And you let her keep it on her? You guessed what was happening and still you let her keep it so they could track us again?"

He nodded. "It's time we took control of the situation, Mike. Confront it head on. I chose to move on because we're about as well defended here as we could be. Rather than sit and wait for them to find us, we draw them in now, we take them down now."

"They were not prepared for *you* last time, Terry. They will be now. For someone, at least. For a fight. The kind of fight that can leave four of their men dead."

"That cuts both ways. And we also have the advantage that they won't have a clue we know they'll be coming."

I inclined my head. "I do hope you're right. You have to be right. Either way, you could have discussed it with me first."

He took another sip of his tea. "We didn't have time for all that, Mike. I knew we would need to spend some time finding out from Melissa here just what the hell is going on. I wanted to do that from a position of strength. Here is where we are strongest, believe me."

Have I got any choice? I wondered silently. I couldn't blame Melissa for keeping quiet about the phone, could hardly blame Terry for taking the fight to those who were hunting us, but neither was I about to welcome the situation with open arms.

"I suppose the question is," I said, staring hard at Melissa, "have you done more than leave the phone on? Have you used it at all?"

She glanced at the device before shaking her head. The first movement on her part told me her mute denial was another lie. When I spoke again, I lowered my voice, leaning in towards her. "Melissa, you have to be honest with us now. It could be nothing, but it could be everything. The difference between life and death. For all of us, Charlie included."

Melissa bit her lip. Closed her eyes. "Okay," she said finally. "I'll tell you everything."

TWENTY-NINE

The first time she made contact was whilst waiting in the car with Charlie at the motel, sending a text to Chris Dawson. She briefly explained what had happened to Ray. To us. The gist, anyway. The next time she risked checking the phone was while I was asleep in the car. By that point, Chris had asked her where we were.

"And you told him?" I asked.

"No. I didn't really know where we were for sure, so I sent back a message telling him I'd update him as soon as I could. I then had to wait until we were in that restaurant for breakfast. When I was in the bathroom. Only this time while I was checking my inbox another two messages came in. The first was from Chris again saying he would wait for me to confirm our location, but that as soon as I told him where we were he'd mobilise a crew to come and fetch us. The other text was from an unknown number. I can't remember the message properly, but it said something like 'The man who took you is very dangerous. Do not trust him. Trust no one. Not even family. Just leave your phone on and we will find you.'"

No one said anything for several seconds. Terry eventually broke the silence. "I take it you've deleted these texts," he said to Melissa.

She nodded, adding nothing.

"And that's it? Nothing more?"

"Two more from Chris, still wanting to know where we were."

"You responded to neither?"

"No."

"Tell me, Melissa, did the texts from Chris ask about Charlie at all?" Terry edged forward in his chair this time.

"I don't remember. I don't think so, actually. Why?"

"Nothing. Just a thought. And you have no idea who that other text came from?"

"None whatsoever."

Terry stared at her for a moment. He seemed to have nothing else to say.

I did, though. Yet again something was not sitting right with me. They had tracked us through the GPS on the mobile. We were now expecting them to trace us again. So, it occurred to me to wonder why they didn't do the same while we were in Chippenham. After all, that was the longest we had stayed anywhere since this whole thing kicked off. I voiced my concern at this anomaly.

"It may have taken them too long to activate a GPS trace," Terry said. "They would have needed to go through the provider, possibly even obtain a warrant."

I was still looking at Melissa, and I saw something flicker across her face. "Is that it, do you think, Mel?" I said. "Or could there be another reason."

She took a breath. She could barely bring herself to look at either of us. "No. No, that's not it," she said. "I got scared. My head was reeling. I remembered reading about how a phone could still be traced even if it was switched off, so I slipped the battery out. I only put it back when we left the hotel."

I had been certain there was something more, something Melissa had not revealed. I could not figure her out. At times, she appeared to be actively working against us. What she said about being wary of me, and then Terry, all made perfect sense. Yet so did the notion that she was part of all this somehow. Whatever *this* was.

"I think it best if you go spend some time with Charlie," Terry told her. "Mike and I need to discuss this alone."

Melissa looked from me to him and back again. She lowered her head. Tears welled in her eyes. "I'm so sorry for the trouble I've caused," she said in a soft whisper. "I really had no idea what I was getting us into."

"We deal with it," Terry told her. His voice was neither gentle nor harsh. "We can't change what's done. So, we'll handle it."

***

"'We can't change what's done'," I echoed when it was just the two of us again. "Nice philosophy, Terry. And accurate of course. But if I was afraid before, now I'm bloody terrified. I still can't quite believe you deliberately wanted to lure them here."

He stood, walked to the sink and rinsed out his mug. He peered out of the window for a second or two before speaking. "How did you imagine all this panning out, Mike? Did you think it would all just disappear provided we lie low for a while? Did you imagine putting your head in the sand for a day or two and then when you pulled it out again everything would have righted itself?"

"Honestly? Of course not. But after what happened back in Peterborough, I really did feel the need to regroup and take some time figuring out a plan. I thought we would do that together at the very least."

"You're annoyed with me."

"I am." I was. I felt more than a little betrayed. He had tossed a coin and not afforded me the opportunity of calling one way or the other. I wasn't sure what I had expected, how I really imagined our working relationship to go down. I had thought I would get a say in how we did things. Offer my opinion at the very least.

Terry came back to the table to clean up the liquid spills I had caused. As he soaked them up and wiped them away he said, "Mike, you called me to come and help you out of a jam. I always told you that when you called I would come. I have no problem with that. But when I help, I do it my way."

I licked my lips. As usual they were bone dry. "I understand that, Terry. You're the professional, the one with the expertise. I accepted that you would have overall control of the situation. Still, I had also expected you to discuss options before putting them into operation."

Terry was unapologetic. He explained to me that we could have taken all the time in the world, and still the outcome would have been inevitable. We had ruled out throwing me at the mercy of the authorities, because then the system would have had me in its clutches, and Hendricks would have had me wrapped up in a nice neat package just waiting for a bow. We had also ruled out trying to arrange some sort of deal with Dawson, because the original problem remained and needed to be dealt with. What took place back at the safe house meant that whatever was going on had taken a significant step up, not back down. The only remaining solution was confrontation.

"Fair enough," I said. "But are we really in the best shape to sit here and wait for them to show? We could have kept on the move."

"Whether it's people working with Hendricks, some sort of NCA hit squad, or persons unknown, these people will not back down and walk away. Especially not now we've put four of their own down. With or without Melissa's phone, these people would find us. I know this, Mike, because I could easily have been one of them. Trust me, our only advantage is to tackle it head on and on our own terms."

"And what exactly are our terms?" I demanded.

Terry took a moment before explaining. "Right now, they believe they can come and get us as and when they like. That we have no idea they are coming. And they will send their best men next time. More of them, too. Only way we turn that around in our favour is to make our own plans and be ready for them. Keeping on the move is not a valid alternative in my view. Not in the long run. I have something in mind, and as soon as I've ironed out a few wrinkles in my plan, you and I will go over it. Together this time."

I ran both hands down the side of my stubbled face. "I do understand what you mean, mate. And I am grateful to you, although it may not sound like it right now. It just feels as if you've drawn them on far more quickly than suits us. Or, to be more accurate, suits me. And Mel and Charlie for that matter."

"You think I should have snatched the phone off her back in Peterborough. Removed the battery, taken some time before switching it back on to alert them? Given us time to discuss it."

"That's exactly what I think."

Terry nodded. "I considered it, Mike. In my opinion, the more time we give them the better it is for them, not us. They have already sent one team. At some point, shortly after that team went unintentionally dark, they would have sent a second team to recon. Assembling a second team would have taken time. Then they would have had to travel. Once there, they evaluate, recon, then give the green light for further action. Eventually they breach and find their colleagues."

"And then they'll know I didn't put them down on my own," I said.

Terry shrugged. "What of it? Whether it was you, someone else, or a combination of the two, they won't make the same mistake again. They underestimated their targets. That was a onetime only opportunity for us. If I had planned for that, things might have been different. The main thing is, that entire reaction I just described on their part will have taken time. I sincerely doubt they even have a team on site yet. We have plenty of time to get this right. And yes, they will realise that you now have someone fighting your cause. That will throw them. All plans go to shit at first contact with the enemy, you know that as well as I do. But now they will be more defensive. That can only play into our hands."

I shook my head. "Hold on a moment. If they are tracking the phone then they will have seen it on the move, away from the previous location. Why would they waste time going there?"

"Because they have no idea what took place there. They have the GPS, so they can pick that up as and when they need it. But they have to find out what happened back at the first safehouse before actioning something else. For all they know, we tossed the phone onto the back of a lorry to lure them away."

I started to respond again, but it was a lost cause. If Terry's decision was in any way damaging, then that damage was already done. It was out of my control. What happened next was the only thing that mattered now. I looked at my friend and forced a thin smile.

"It's good to be working with you again, Marine," I said.

Terry raised a thumb. "You too, my friend. *Per mare, per terram*, right?"

My smile broadened. "By sea, by land" is the Royal Marines motto. I nodded. "Fucking right," I said.

The only correct response.

THIRTY

The sun was rising fast and the heat was rippling across the land that lay beyond the entrance to the farmhouse. It stretched out into the distance, flat and brown, for about a mile, before a collar of gorse introduced the rise of a hillside, ascending so gradually it was hard to tell whether the incline was more trick of the eye than a geographic feature. Lush woodland to the left and right was edged by waist-height log fencing, unpainted yet sturdy.

It was a beautiful day, and I had a glorious view to occupy my mind. Yet it was unappreciative of such splendour, dwelling instead on our predicament and the tragedies which had contrived to lead us here. I was afraid. For Charlie, Mel, even Terry and myself. More than that, I remained overwhelmed by grief. Eyes closed or open, I saw Susan at the moment her life had ended. There was no blinking that away, no amount of sleep capable of eradicating the numbness crawling through my body. Had it not been for my absolute desire for vengeance, I'm sure I would have shut down completely.

People were coming.

One of them had murdered my friend.

Of that I was certain.

I turned away from the view offered by the kitchen window. "If you were them, what would you be thinking?" I asked Terry.

He sat at the table, considering that for a few seconds. "I would be puzzled. Intrigued. Perhaps even a little concerned. No offence, Mike, but even if they were aware of your military service, four well-trained men with the benefit of surprise ought to have been enough."

"Still, they can't be certain what happened."

"No. They might wonder if Melissa gave them up, in which case you might not have been as unprepared as they believed. Even so, four against one is a win for them. So, they'll suspect you had help. They will want to know who owned that property, and this one when they come looking."

"What will they find?"

"Nothing in land registry, census, electoral role. Nothing to point them in my direction, that is. Which will leave them guessing. Something they will not like one little bit."

I followed Terry's logic, finding no fault with it. "So, if you are them, what do you do next? How will they approach this new situation compared to the last? You said before you thought with more and better men, yes?"

He stretched out his legs, seemingly perfectly relaxed. I wondered if he was as at ease with his decisions as he appeared. "At a minimum," he replied. "They will take longer to plan this time, and plan well. They will want to recce the land ahead of any strike, though I doubt they will try to do the same with the house. They will want to wait for the cover of darkness, maybe only twilight." He glanced at his wristwatch. "We're talking perhaps twelve or thirteen hours from now, but that may be too long for them. It's a big risk allowing the status quo for that length of time. Is the op time sensitive? We don't know for sure, but probably. Every hour lost is an hour in which you might call in the police, but I would rule that out as you've had ample opportunity to take that path."

"So, what does your gut tell you, mate?"

"My feeling is they will put in place a well-defined plan, put in place personnel early, aiming for the late stages of twilight to come at us, but anticipating the go command at any time."

"What might make them jump the gun?"

"Movement. If they see that phone move again they will act."

I nodded, thinking it through. "It's a long time to be out there," I said. "In the daylight, relative open ground to the front at least."

"And rear to a certain degree," Terry added. "There's a river that marks the end of the property. On the other bank it's mostly flat fields."

"So, they have that against them, plus the waiting time."

"Yes, but they are also professionals. They will be modifying as they go, looking for a way in much earlier if possible. But it's a clean, bright day, with cover only from the sides. If they come before dusk they'll have to come hard and fast, and that's a risk I doubt they will take."

"So, if they are not going to do anything for the next dozen hours or so, are we?"

He flashed a rakish grin. "Now that, my friend, is a really good question."

***

The single-storey building on the corner of Finchley Road and Queens Grove in north-west London, had once been a recognisable landmark in its days as a bar and restaurant serving cuisine from Peking. At one time, it had been named Lords Rendezvous, in reference to the nearby cricket ground. Now its tall, mullioned windows were boarded up as it awaited yet another transformation. The one thing it was unlikely to ever be again was a London Underground station. Marlborough Road, a Metropolitan line station, was closed together with Lords station in 1939 when the new St John's Wood deep-level Bakerloo station opened.

In part exposed to the elements, yet entirely hidden from view to any passer-by, the building's dereliction had led to decades of abuse from local youths. No window remained unbroken, no door on its hinges, and it was virtually impossible to find a section of wall that had not fallen victim to the blight of graffiti.

As Simon Faulkener made his way towards the slim figure of Allison Cooper, the peer of the realm with oversight of the UK intelligence community, he regarded the artwork with a neutral detachment. Whilst he failed to see any genuine harm in disfiguring something that could not be seen without a great deal of effort, neither could he imagine how anyone could get a thrill from debasing these walls with crude tags. It was one of many things he didn't understand about the younger generation, despite being only in his early forties himself.

Department D-150 exists only unofficially. A Home Office department whose officers worked for both MI5 – the Intelligence Service - and MI6, the Secret Intelligence Service. D-150 staff were responsible for organising and managing covert, undercover and clandestine operations both domestically and abroad. Allison Cooper had been involved for the past two years, having herself moved into the House of Lords from SIS. Meetings between Cooper and her operatives were held just about anywhere other than the Home Office room that bears their departmental name on the door. When official meetings have to take place, they do so within the walls of the architecturally remarkable building at Vauxhall Cross – a building referred to within Intelligence Services as Legoland, which houses MI6 – or the newly refurbished home to MI5 at Thames House.

But this was an unofficial meeting. With a private security operative. And such meetings were held in very different locations; none of them official

Approximately two hours earlier, Faulkener had surveyed the room in which the bodies of four men he had commanded now lay lifeless on the floor. Four men, eight shots. Not a bullet wasted. He bit down on his anger. Consistently being at least one step behind the game had caused his plans to go awry for a second time now, and he was neither used to nor accepting of failure. It was at that point that Faulkener began to wonder for the first time just exactly who Mike Lynch was.

Still gazing down at fallen comrades, he had punched in a call. "It's me," he said when the line was connected. "We have another problem. Worse this time. Much worse." He had gone on to outline the situation, and to make his demands for information. Arriving at the meet, he had expected to find Hedgeman, the man with whom he had been dealing up until now. Upon seeing the Baroness herself, Faulkener immediately began to feel uneasy.

They shook hands. He had met Cooper on two previous occasions, yet once again he was struck by her sheer presence. Elegant without being showy, she wore a crimson jacket over a navy-blue dress that showed off great legs and a full bust. The woman oozed class and sexuality.

"Baroness," he said. "I wasn't expecting you today."

"I don't doubt it," she responded. Her Oxford-bred, Oxford-educated voice matched the stature of her appearance. "However, I was not at all convinced that our esteemed Chief Hedgeman had managed to convey the seriousness of this operation to you. I came here today to put that right."

Faulkener bristled at her comment and stood his ground. "I wouldn't say I was unaware of the serious nature of the op, Baroness. More that the ops themselves have been rushed, and clearly, I have not been provided with enough relevant information. Or time, for that matter."

Cooper smiled. She stepped close enough so that Faulkener could smell her perfume. "Oh, Simon. What's all this Baroness nonsense. Last time we met I had the distinct impression that we had become good friends."

He shook his head and laughed. "I didn't know if you were wired. Or, for that matter, whether your security detail might be close enough to be listening. Didn't want to appear too chummy."

She dismissed the observation with a single shake of her head. "Oh, they watched you on your way in, and they will watch you on your way out, Simon. Only the very best get to be my close-quarter protection. But they won't care about any lack of formality. How are you, by the way?"

"I'm good. And you?"

"Very well, thank you. How's Kathy and the boys?"

"All healthy. And your husband?"

"Still impotent, unfortunately."

Faulkener breathed her in. Wide eyes, grey with flecks of green. Tanned, healthy skin for a woman nudging fifty, stark ruby red lipstick, blonde hair cut stylishly short. He licked his lips. "You know, when I saw you just now, I thought I might be walking into my last ever meeting?" he said.

"Really? As if we would dream of doing such a thing." A smile tugged at the corners of that glorious mouth once more.

"Cut the crap, Allison. Don't string this out if that's what you have planned. It would surely demean us both."

She pursed those lips. "Hmm, I don't see how it would demean me, Simon. But I take your point. No more silly buggers. So, let me assure you that today you get to walk away. It would be advisable, however, if you contained the situation by the end of it. There are others involved who take a less charitable view than I."

"Thanks for the heads-up." He had won a reprieve, but was on borrowed time. "So, I requested an in-depth background analysis on Lynch. Do you have that for me."

"I do. The only item of note is that he spent three years as a commando in the Royal Marines."

Faulkener put back his head and swore. "Fuck! A Marine! I could have done with that information beforehand."

Cooper nodded. "Though to be fair to Hedgeman, you failed to request an in-depth until your second op failed."

He couldn't argue with that. "Noted. On the other hand, unless he was a combination of Navy Seal, SAS and James bloody Bond, there's no way he took down four of my men on his own."

"Don't forget, he did have a young woman and a little girl with him. Perhaps they were both in the paramilitary wing of the Girl Guides."

"I've got four dead men on my hands, Allison. Save the levity for later, eh."

"Says the man who just this second mentioned double-oh-seven."

"Okay, okay. Look, the fact is, this Lynch character now has some help. That much is obvious. The house for starters. Then the fact my men were taken down so easily. Now that I know his background, his time in the commandos is a good starting point to find out where this help is coming from. We could be dealing with a small team of ex-Marines for all we know."

"What does your source have to say for herself?"

"Melissa Andrews is hardly my source, as well you know. She allowed us to track her, that's all."

"Did she? Or was she leading your men into a trap, I wonder?"

Faulkener shook his head. "No. Initially we got GCHQ to tamper with her phone, so that she believed she was texting Chris Dawson. Then we decided to add an unknown player into the mix, someone potentially neutral who would take care of her. I'm convinced she believed it at the time, and that she left her phone on hoping she would be tracked and rescued."

Cooper paused to consider this, pushing loose strands of hair behind her ears. "So, do you suspect Susan Healey passed a burner phone to Lynch before you took her out? And that it was this he used to contact someone from his past?"

"That's exactly my line of thinking. After which they were collected from Chippenham, taken to Peterborough. The surveillance equipment inside that house could not have been anticipated. Yet the team I sent took precautions. They did their job. And still they walked into a trap, but not one set up by Melissa Andrews."

"Which leaves us where, Simon?"

"Hendricks is no longer an issue, for a start. I had one of my operatives take care of that. He managed to get close to the investigation team, but unfortunately acted a little nervously, believing he was about to be exposed as a fraud. As for Lynch and his little posse, the phone was left on, and has remained on."

She frowned. "Doesn't that strike you as odd?"

"Of course. Whoever is helping Lynch, perhaps even the man himself, had to have figured out after the raid that they were traced somehow. I don't know how Andrews managed to convince Lynch that she had no phone with her, but in my opinion, that lie could not have survived the attempted strike action."

"So, they know then? Lynch and whoever."

"They do. They know something."

"And your next plan of action will be?"

"Different now that I am fully aware of what we might be facing. But still to take them down."

"Very well. By the way, I saw that video you showed the woman in the safe deposit bank. A water pistol, Simon? Really?"

He grinned. "It wasn't my idea, but it was a nice touch, I thought. It did the trick. Got me into that box. Got you the information you needed on our target. We wouldn't be standing here now without that info."

The Baroness stepped in and patted him on the arm. "Indeed we wouldn't, and believe me the data was illuminating. Anyhow, take care of yourself, Simon. But get it done by nightfall. Or else." Then she winked at him and walked away without a backward glance.

THIRTY-ONE

Terry and I remained in the kitchen. The stools were wooden with pads of covered foam. Not ideal for comfort, but acceptable. Melissa had come through to ask for drinks refills, but then without another word had returned to Charlie in the living room.

"I know you're angry with her," Terry said when she had gone. "And you have a right to be. On the other hand, she's young and was afraid of both the situation and you."

"I've already forgiven her," I said. "I'm just not ready to tell her so."

Terry nodded and continued explaining how he saw things taking shape. He knew the land well, which was a major advantage. We agreed it would not take our adversaries long to get a handle on it, however. They would position themselves at compass points and in between as much as possible, depending on numbers. Close enough to act as well as survey, far enough away to remain invisible to the casual observer. They would figure out the landscape.

"But not what runs beneath it," Terry said.

I looked up. "Beneath? You mean a tunnel?"

"Tunnels. Plural. My guess is this was a smugglers' cottage at some point. Some changes may even have been made during wartime; this area was used extensively for trench training. We are in a good position here, backing on to the river. Somewhere along the line it feeds into The Wash and The North Sea, and I don't anticipate a major strike from that direction. If anything comes from there, it will be diversionary. One or two of the tunnels have fallen in, others I have extended. There's a decent network going on down there."

"So, once we know they are here we leave the phone and use the tunnel system to escape while they are waiting for nightfall."

"Is one way to go," Terry said. He then shook his head. "But not mine."

"I know. But why is that?"

"You're forgetting why I came here at all, Mike. We're dealing with professional, determined people. They want you badly. We slip away today, we are safe for today. But what about tomorrow? Or next week? Next month, even?"

"So, your plan is to... what the hell is your plan?" I was confused.

"Take some down. Take one, preferably two prisoners. Persuade them to talk. Find out why you're being hunted down like foxes."

"But we know that, Terry. We witnessed something we should not have seen."

He screwed up his face. Scratched his beard. "And I think you know I don't completely buy that. There's something more in play here. Some aspect of the full story we just aren't seeing yet. Ray Dawson was murdered for a reason. You say they want you dead because you witnessed his murder. I say the reason they did it in the first place is what drives them on."

"You're sure of that? It could be just that simple."

"Yeah, it could be. But it isn't. Listen to your head, Mike. Mine is telling me a different story. I think yours is, too."

I let it go. It was all guesswork on our part. The whole thing. I knew all about gut feelings of the kind Terry was being guided by. In his case, the gnawing sensation relied an intuition borne of literally dozens of military operations and conflicts of one sort or another. I trusted the man's instinct more than my own.

"So, what do we do now. I mean, right now?" I asked.

"First up, I introduce you to the defences. Second, I show you a way out if this all goes tits up."

Rising to my feet, I said, "So I'm not coming with you on your scavenger hunt?"

"No, pal. I need backup of the kind that has to take place from here. Your job is to offer protection should they attempt a breach while I'm in the tunnels, or if they get in behind me. And if all of that starts to look dodgy, your job then is to take care of your baggage and get Mel and Charlie out of here."

I shook my head. "No way, Terry. My phone call dragged you into this mess. I'm not running away and leaving you just because things get a little hairy."

Now it was his turn to stand. The two of us faced each other. "Mike, nobody mentioned running away. Listen to me, who saves Mel and Charlie if you go down as well? Who? You want to leave them to their fate just to save face. I know what sort of man you are. If those two were not here, you would stand by my shoulder. I know that about you. But they *are* here. And your first duty is to them. And you'll abide by that. You won't want to, but you will. Because it's the right thing to do."

I glared at him. Everything my friend had said was true, but that didn't mean I had to like it. "I'm going to get some air," I said, turning and walking away.

Terry let me go.

***

A few minutes later, Melissa entered the kitchen. "Charlie is lost in those cartoons," she said.

Terry leaned back against the counter where he had been tidying things away. He looked up, took in her lowered head and clasped, fidgeting hands. "No need to be so sheepish," he told her. "There's no anger towards you anymore. You did what you felt was right at the time."

She smiled; faint, but there. "I'm not so sure Mike feels the same way, but thank you for that. I heard raised voices. Are you two okay?"

"Ah, a minor dispute. No problem."

"Mike clearly has a lot of faith in you. He was a wreck after what happened with his friend, but from the moment he called you he's been so much more relaxed. I need to thank you again as well, Terry. For coming to get us, I mean. That and… all that's happened since."

"No problem."

This time she coughed up a choked laugh. "Oh, I'm sure it's been a massive problem. One way or another."

"It is what it is. Mike called. That's enough. What followed, what happens now, it's all fine."

"If that's truly the case, then all I can say is that must be a pretty big debt you owe Mike."

Terry nodded. "He hasn't told you, then. That's typical of the man, Melissa. Not the man you think you know, perhaps, but the one I know for sure. To be frank, the debt I owe is bigger than I can ever repay."

"It is? How so?"

"He told you he was wounded, right? But what he obviously didn't tell you was that I was also injured in the same firefight. A lot worse than him. Mike stood over me and took three of them down, somehow managed to tend to my wounds, crouched by my side until the rescue vehicle came in and swept us up. I'm told I was down on the ground for the best part of two hours. Mike fought them off and stood guard all that time. We lost two of our friends in the first exchange, so only the two of us got out. That's why I owe him. Why I would do anything for him."

"Even give up your life?" Melissa asked him.

"Absolutely. I wouldn't have a life to give up if it weren't for him. He's the reason I'm still here. Mike bought me time by putting his own life at risk. The least I can do is reciprocate."

She was quiet for several moments. Finally, she nodded and said, "I think I have to consider him in a different light from now on."

"Up to you. He's done right by you so far. He might speak or act as if he doesn't care, but he does. About you and Charlie both."

"I'm beginning to see that."

Terry clapped and rubbed his hands together. "Good. Now, in a short while you and I have to go over a few things. Important things. As soon as Mike and I are done planning our next move."

"Okay. But we're in trouble, right? No better than the situation we were in earlier."

"Similar, but better. This time we are prepared. Or at least, we will be."

"I'm part of this," she said. "Me and Charlie, and I speak for her. You and Mike are the ones doing the fighting, but it isn't your battle alone."

"I understand, Melissa. For obvious reasons, decisions over tactics have to be mine and mine alone. But I won't leave you in the dark. You'll have your role to play. I promise you that."

When he was alone, Terry Cochran gave a sigh and turned his thoughts once more to what lay ahead. It was a long time since he had carried baggage other than fellow unit members. He hoped it was a burden he was able to bear.

THIRTY-TWO

I returned from a short walk around the perimeter of the house feeling a little embarrassed over my display of peevishness. I realised almost as soon as I left the kitchen that Terry had done all the right things so far, and that it was his duty to take a step up to cover both his friend and Mel and Charlie. The stroll had helped me to cool off, inside my head if not externally. The heat of the day climbed with the rise of the sun. Terry had thrown open several strategic windows to allow for a cooling through-draft, yet still I felt sweat falling from me and soaking my top. The draining, strength-sapping heat made me want to curl up on the floor somewhere and ride it out in torpor.

"Sorry," I said, eventually locating him in a small study. It was bare except for a desk, on which stood a laptop computer, and a spare fold-up chair leaning against a wall.

Terry shook his head as if my apology was unnecessary. He waited for me to make myself comfortable on the chair before swiftly outlining his plan. He would initially run surveillance from the roof space and identify as many positions as he could. He would then confirm whatever else he could using CCTV equipment. Finally, he would use the underground system of tunnels to put himself amongst them.

"You have a cloak of invisibility I don't know about?" I asked, half grinning.

"The tunnel exits are well-concealed. They would have to be extremely fortunate to spot them. They provide all the elements of surprise I need."

"So, the hope is that you can rise up from sheltered areas close enough to them that they won't have time to either see or hear you coming. Certainly not enough time to react if they do."

"Precisely." Terry nodded.

"Well, depending on where they position themselves."

"Okay, less precisely."

"I know we've been down this road before, but can I make a suggestion?"

"Go ahead." Terry folded his arms across his chest.

"Two of us can cover twice as many positions. Is it possible that by going down there with you it gives us a greater chance of success?"

Terry scratched behind his ear. "Mike, I'm not going to lie to you. The answer is yes. If we both attempt a coordinated strike, we improve our odds significantly. But in doing so we leave our flank uncovered. I mentioned this earlier, and that hasn't changed. My way, I can hit my priority target, quickly move underground again to strike at number two. I might manage a third before they realise what's happening, maybe not. So, I funnel back and re-join you here. That way, if they do happen to get past me, or go around me above ground, their numbers ought to be depleted enough for you to take them down. We do it your way, and they get behind both of us, then Mel and Charlie have no chance."

I shook my head. "The way you describe it, Terry, I don't like our chances at all. If two of us can't prevent them entering the house, why do you think you can on your own?"

"Mike, I'm not necessarily saying I can."

Now I realised the full ramifications of his strategy. It wasn't anticipating complete success. It was expecting only a limited version, one which offered greater protection for Melissa and Charlie, but made Terry himself expendable.

"This is your master plan?" I said. "One that has a high probability of you not making it back."

"I'm a great believer in myself, Mike. In my mind, there is only one outcome: I remove threats from a minimum of two, maximum of three positions, then you and I together remove the remainder. I'm not counting on sacrificing myself today or any other day, pal."

"I believe in you as well," I told him. "But I'm also a realist."

"We've been in tighter situations than this. You, more than anyone else I know, understand all about that. The odds are not in our favour, but odds are confounded all the time."

"And I assume you have a plan for me?"

"Of course. While I'm out there, I need you to keep them occupied as and when they approach. The loft area provides coverage of every side of the house, and there's enough height that you won't be bent double as you move. You can switch between firing positions, which will keep them busy and make them believe there are more of us. That alone is likely to cause a drawback and reassessment. That buys me more time."

"There is going to be a well-drilled unit out there," I pointed out, nodding towards the window. "With good resources, we must assume. What if they have plans of the property, tunnels and all?"

Terry smiled, teeth white behind the beard. "Then we revert to Plan B."

"Which is?"

"You remember we used to talk about the final scene from Butch and Sundance?"

"Of course. And in my opinion, they shot their way out and escaped."

"There you go then. Plan B."

***

While Terry was up in the roof space, preparing the firing positions, I gathered together weapons and munitions from the substantial subterranean armoury my friend had earlier shown me. I placed sniper rifles, close-contact automatic rifles, handguns, knives, flash-bang grenades and the real things in strategic positions around the house. If someone broke through our meagre defences, we were not going to be found short of firepower.

Preparations did not take long. Now it was all about waiting, and if Terry was correct about the probable timing of an attack, there were still an awful lot of hours yet to kill.

Hanging around for something to happen was not one of my remaining virtues. On Iraqi battlefields, I spent about ninety percent of the time kicking my heels, the remainder in a flurry of fevered activity. It was during those few moments where every sense became amplified.

Most people never have to see the remains of a person who has just been blown apart by an explosive. It was something you never forgot, I reflected. And never stop seeing, either. Not even when you are asleep.

Explosions and the sound of bullets being fired was just noise, promoting a visceral reaction. The sound that lingered most of all in warfare was the screams. I had discussed this often with my fellow commandos. To a man they agreed that those harrowing cries were more chilling than any other sound they had ever heard. Often your own colleagues, sometimes women and children caught up between warring factions. Like the mental image of body parts and physical carnage, the screams never left you.

Dry desert sands and infernal heat left a taste in the mouth that took an awful lot of booze to eradicate. At times, it had felt to me as if there could never be enough to wash it away completely. And I had tried. Not that it was only the baked sand and heat. At times, there was enough blood in the air that you were simply tainted by it in every conceivable way.

As for smells, that was a toss-up between burning human flesh and the foul stench of decomposing bodies. Every member of the armed forces knew that these two conditions caused particles to become wedged inside the nose, and no matter how many times you tried to clear it out afterwards, it felt permanently lodged up each nostril somehow. I had always found the decomp to be the worst, the one that lingered most of all.

I had felt the heat of the sand right through to the soles of my feet, mountainside rocks sharp and angry, baked dirt and sweat like cement coating my exposed flesh, skin tightening beneath the inflamed sun, eyes stung by grit from harsh winds, flares of intense heat from explosive devices going off. And then the bone-penetrating pain of the bullet that ended my career.

Yet, as a Marine, I had lived for those moments. That ten percent.

Today was different, I decided. Today I would rather have avoided the action altogether. The short burst in the early hours of the morning, during which four men had lost their lives, was enough for one day. Enough for the remainder of my lifetime. Yet what lay ahead was unavoidable; my friend had seen to that by not destroying Melissa's mobile phone. I hoped we all survived to remind Terry of that when it was all over. Whatever "over" entailed.

THIRTY-THREE

With Terry still busy, I wandered into the living room, where Melissa was keeping Charlie entertained.

"Hi, Mike," Charlie said. She smiled and waggled her fingers at me.

I returned the gesture. Matched it with a smile of my own. "Hey, kiddo. How are you doing?"

Charlie rolled her eyes. "Ugh. I'm so bo-ored."

Mel flashed her a look of mock disgust. "Hey, I'm doing my best here. It's not easy with you, you little horror." She reached out and tickled Charlie under her arms and down her sides. The little girl's laughter rang out around the room. An infectious sound.

Once again, I was struck by the bond between the two. At first, I had considered it respectful and protective, somewhat sisterly. Now I saw that I was wrong. Melissa's relationship with the girl was closer to maternal. And Charlie seemed to respond in kind. After all, any instinctive tie she might have had with her mother would be long forgotten. Melissa was the only woman in her life.

As I watched them together, I gave that some real thought. With her father dead, Charlie would almost certainly be raised by Chris Dawson. The very idea left a bad taste in my mouth. Where Ray had remained in the shadows to a large degree, his brother celebrated their infamy. He considered himself some sort of wiseguy of old, had been known to liken himself to Tony Soprano, from the TV show. He wore his criminal enterprise with as much pride as his ugly gold jewellery.

Is that what you have in store for you now, Charlie? I wondered. *You poor kid.*

"Hey, Charlie," I called out. "Do you have any money on you?"

She turned her head and shook it.

"Are you sure?"

A nod this time.

"You know what, I think you have. Just behind your left ear."

Charlie raised a hand to feel behind her ear.

"No, your left ear," I prompted, chuckling.

This time she felt behind the correct ear. "Nothing," she said. "I told you, silly."

"Come over here, let me see."

Charlie scrambled over to me, squatted by my legs. I leaned forward, reached a hand behind her left ear, and when I moved it back in front of her face, her eyes widened. Between my thumb and forefinger I held a shiny pound coin. "See, I told you," I said.

The girl squealed in delight. Her mouth formed a wide O. "More!" she cried. "More."

I laughed. "You think your ears are made of money?" I handed her the coin. "Here you go. Spend it wisely." She thanked me and ran back to Melissa, who sat there smiling at us both.

I wondered when Charlie would get to buy anything again. The simplest of pleasures such as purchasing an ice-cream was no longer an option for her. I had to change that. Myself and Terry. Anything else was unthinkable.

***

When Terry reappeared, he took Mel and me aside and made it apparent to us that we were all now to steer clear of any windows. "I don't think they would try to pick us off one by one at long range, but I've learned to rule nothing out."

"I'll have a job on my hands with Charlie," Melissa said. "She keeps begging to go outside as it is."

"We can't take any chances," Terry insisted. "Just do your best. I've pulled the curtains and blinds in many of the rooms, so you can move around a little. Right now, we need to eat and stock up on fuel. It could be a long night."

"I'm a dab hand at a fry-up," I said. "Well, grill-up more like."

"I have stuff in the freezer," Terry said. "Use the microwave to thaw things out if you need to."

Terry and I prepared it together. Thirty minutes later the four of us sat at the dining room table and devoured the lot. It was only then that I realised how hungry I had been, nerves and stress having taken my mind off food for so long. As a group we chatted amiably enough, although judging by the strain in their eyes, neither Terry nor Melissa were in the mood for social pleasantries. Charlie was engaging and funny, in complete contrast to her more sullen moods.

The remainder of the afternoon and early evening passed uneventfully. We all watched a little TV, Terry and I played several hands of friendly poker, and Melissa managed to persuade Charlie to take a nap for an hour. During that time, Terry made it clear to her the challenge we were about to face.

"This has all gone too far now," Melissa said at one point, shaking her head. "Why don't we call the police and take what's coming. It has to be better than risking our lives further."

"I wish we had that option, Mel," I said. "Believe me. But you're right, it has gone too far; too far to retreat. Those men out there cannot allow us to be taken in by the police. Terry and I checked the mobiles a short while ago, and we have no signal. Which means we're being jammed."

"These chaps are taking no chances," Terry said. "By cutting our mobile access they leave only the landline. Now they will be screening the number. At the moment, they are waiting for the tactical advantage of dusk. All of which provides us with the actual advantage of pre-empting their first move. But if we press that alarm bell, they will move in and damage us. We can fend them off for a while, but I doubt it will be long enough."

Nodding, I continued, "They could do it now if they chose to, but they won't want to announce themselves to local villages by staging a massive gun battle here. A clean strike by dusk, not quiet but not exactly loud, that's their aim. At least, it would be mine in their shoes."

"There speaks the real Mike Lynch," Terry said.

I flashed a grin, though my stomach complained. I understood how Melissa felt. If it were possible, I too would now happily give myself up to the police rather than take on the forces assembling outside. The time to do so had come and gone, however. There was no longer an easy way out of this mess.

I sat there for a while, reflecting on the past forty hours or so. From the first sight of what was then an unknown gunman, to the chase, discovering Mel and Charlie in the car, the claustrophobic fear of exposure in Chippenham, Sue's terrible murder, the relief at being delivered to a safe house by Terry, only to see that relative safety shattered, shooting and killing armed intruders, escape to another place of safety, and now the knowledge that myself and my friend were going to war again. Not a bit of it felt real. And yet, conversely, it also felt as real as it gets.

When I looked up, I noticed Terry peering across the room at me. The two of us nodded, and something passed between us. An understanding. I felt it bite deep into my chest. There was a recognition that this could all have been avoided, that mistakes had been made. But also that, now we were here, neither of us would back down. We were in this together, and only death would decide otherwise.

***

I was just about done with a final check of our weapons when Terry called me into a long and narrow galley-style office. This was another surveillance room, even better equipped than the last. "Take a look," he said.

On the screens were feeds from eight cameras. He explained that the system was wireless, and that the control panel allowed us to rotate each of the cameras pretty much as we liked. Terry had spent the previous twenty minutes looking at every nook and cranny surrounding us. In that time, he had spotted two snipers, one to the front, one to the rear on the other side of the river.

"Not a great deal of cover for them out there, but an unobstructed view of the house makes up for that," I commented.

"Precisely. Both are at around the limit of their range I suspect. In all, I think I picked up the locations of ten operatives, split into five pairs. That includes the snipers, who have range-finders with them. They will move in once the word is given. We have to assume there are more. Once I go, Mike, your job is to watch these screens like a hawk. They will give you ample warning of where the attack points are coming from. If they break through me, or if they spring a surprise attack, you head up to the roof space and start hammering them."

I nodded. "I'll keep them busy until you get back."

Terry's eyes met mine. "We need to talk about that. The lives of Melissa and Charlie can't hang on a wing and a prayer. I have no doubt that you will fight these men until your last breath, but if I get removed from the picture, they can regroup and wait you out. So, we need to establish a time limit. You give me thirty minutes. After that point, if you're coming under fire or are being surrounded and squeezed, then you have to get your baggage out of here."

"Through another tunnel?"

"Yes. This one is hidden at both ends. It starts off east, then dog-legs right, taking it alongside and parallel to the river. It opens up inside an old shed by a small bridge on the edge of the woods. On the other side of the bridge is a Land Rover. It doesn't look much, but it's deceptive. Keys are underneath the driver's seat."

I clicked my teeth. Looked down at my feet. "I don't know how much I can be trusted to walk away from you, Terry."

"You won't be walking away. If I'm not back, there's a good reason."

"And what about the whole never leave a man behind thing?"

"Different situations call for different measures. Better to leave one person than three."

I regarded my friend warmly. Nodded. "I guess that's how it has to be," I said."

Terry patted me on the shoulder. "You got it. Now, let's take a look at your escape route."

***

We needed Melissa to be part of it, should neither of us be around when the time came. Terry was calm but firm as he went over the instructions, speaking in clipped, precise terms as we made our way through the house. In what had once been a scullery, but had long since been converted into a utility room containing a washer, dryer and sink, he moved across to the far wall which was shelved from top to bottom. Terry made sure both myself and Melissa could see what he was doing, then hooked a finger underneath the third shelf from the top and pulled back. There was a loud click, and the entire shelf moved a couple of inches back, hinged along the left-hand side. He pushed it further open to reveal a small recess leading to some stone steps going downwards.

Terry looked at Melissa. "Repeat it back to me," he said.

"It's okay. I've got it." Melissa's voice was tight.

"Humour me. Repeat it back one more time."

She took a deep breath. "Okay. First thing, I remember to move the shelf unit back into place one we're through. The tunnel will take us beneath the back garden, opening up inside an old wooden shed – the flap we open can then be bolted from the top should anyone find the route afterwards."

"Good. And when you exit the shed?"

"We move right. Fifty paces or so along a dirt path we come to a bridge across the river. Once over the bridge we get the Land Rover running, take the left fork in the road. We follow that road for seven miles, and then come to a T-junction. We go right. The first field we come to on our right again has a red barn."

"Excellent." Terry nodded quickly. "And the combination to the padlock is?"

"9182."

"Good. You're a quick study, Mel. So once there you sit and you wait. Give it two hours. You'll be perfectly safe. But you can't stay there forever, so if neither of us shows, you get out of there. At that point, you will be on your own, though my advice is to go to the police and tell them everything."

He slipped a mobile phone out of his pocket. "This is a burner. Your phone and the one given to Mike by Susan will remain here. This new phone can't be traced back to anyone. If we make it out but are later than expected, I will call you. And that's it."

Terry looked at Melissa. "Any questions?"

She shook her head.

He looked at me. "How about you?"

"No. I've got it."

"I'm scared," Melissa said.

I reached out a hand and touched her arm. "It's okay, Mel. You won't need to go down that tunnel. We won't let it get that far."

Terry agreed. "You'll do fine. Both of you, keep your wits about you at all times, and expect almost anything to happen."

Melissa smiled. Nodded. "I don't know what to say."

"So, say nothing."

"Not even thank you? You don't know me or Charlie. What are we to you?"

"You're important to Mike. You and Charlie both. I can see that. Anyone could if they looked hard enough. And if you're important to him, you're equally as important to me."

"I'll never forget this." She turned her gaze from him to me. "Never."

No one said a word for a second or two. Then Terry glanced down at his watch. "It's just about time," he said. "Mel, you go get Charlie and you bring her here. Mike, back to the surveillance room. The attic is ready for you, weapons on each side. Be lucky."

With the slightest of nods, my friend stepped silently out of the scullery and was gone.

I turned to Melissa. "You'll do fine," I told her. "Whatever the outcome for me and Terry."

Melissa slipped an arm around me and pulled me into a hug. We stood that way for a few seconds. Then she pecked me on the cheek and pulled her head back, gazing into my eyes. "Come back," she said. "Just come back to us."

I had no idea what to tell her. Now wasn't the time for brutal honesty, however, so I simply gave her one final hug and said, "Yes, boss."

I was all set to turn away when the power went off.

THIRTY-FOUR

Parts of the tunnel network forced Terry Cochran to crawl on his stomach, using knees and elbows to propel himself forward. As he moved, fear lay on his chest like a lead weight. Not just because of likely encounters with the enemy, who might easily be lying in wait in the thick, black darkness ahead. But being underground also brought back memories he would rather forget.

***

The Afghani Taliban fighters were a mixture of talents, yet even the worst of them were warriors. Only they didn't send the worst of them down tunnels to fight. Even so, Terry could handle them; he was trained to, experienced in doing so. There were other tunnel rats down there, though. Real rats, some as big as small dogs. Then there were the real nightmares, the camel spiders, scorpions and snakes, many of which were venomous. Those fuckers came out of nowhere and could be truly silent and deadly.

The humidity was so intense that sweat fell from him like rain. At points it blinded him. Every few yards he followed the same routine: pause, listen, reassess. He could use no light, as it would make him an easy target for the Talibs. The very act of movement would give them warning of his approach, because they were waiting in absolute silence. These narrow tunnels were uniquely difficult places in which to stage combat. The main routes supplying cave systems were huge, and certain sections could be driven through. These minor shafts were created in order to provide drainage, but despite the danger they posed it was imperative for them to be cleared. It was a lesson learned the hard way, when a large unit of US troops were trapped in a major channel by Talibs emerging from the almost insignificant passageways behind them. Not a single US soldier emerged from the ensuing slaughter.

Terry's team had gained a reputation for the way in which they maintained safe passage for others. It was a hellish task, but also critical to specific outcomes. As he made his way forward, he reminded himself constantly of this. Ultimately, even his dead body would plug the hole long enough for others to make successful raids. Not that he intended to lose any fight.

Whether it was the inky blackness, the intensified senses, squirts of adrenaline, or simply the primal will to live, Terry relied on his instincts to tell him when the time was right to act. He did not believe in a sixth sense, so he told himself that this was merely experience and using one specific sense – hearing – so well that he could pick up the merest exhalation of an enemy combatant. This was, he had discovered an hour before entering the tunnel, his final such mission. It was no time to die, so he listened harder than ever before.

Nothing.

Not even the soft scuttle of a sand spider.

As he raised his shoulder to begin the next crawl, he heard it. A single breath.

It was all he needed.

In his hands he clasped an M4A1 assault rifle. It was suppressed, not because the operation especially required silence, but in order to spare his ears. It was not easy to shift the weapon in order to fire it, given he'd had to grip it in a certain way as he crawled. But Terry was well-practised in the tight conditions, and the movement was slick and silent. *Don't doubt your instincts*, he told himself. *You heard it. He's out there.*

There was no finesse in what followed. The weapon was switched to fully automatic – a setting seldom used in close quarters – and all it required was for him to pull on the trigger and spread the deadly spray of bullets around. The narrow channel and the close presence of a target which virtually filled it, meant it was impossible to miss his intended victim. A single burst was enough, and the biggest danger to him that day ended up being the hot cartridges being expelled by the rifle.

***

Seven years had passed since that operation; the last of that particular tour in Afghanistan. Now, as then, he wondered why he, with the more severe injuries, had been able to continue with his career, when Mike had been invalided out. Luck of the draw, he supposed. Mike's wounds affected his ability to run, his own were upper body and had healed well.

Enough to find himself in a tunnel once more.

This time, however, Terry's passage was sanguine by comparison. The final stage was on an incline, and he leaned into it. At the mouth he paused, the carefully placed foliage and branches providing natural camouflage to complement that which he had smeared across his face. He listened hard. If the two armed men he had seen on the CCTV system had not moved, they were no more than twenty yards away. Between him and the house. Hearing nothing to suggest a trap had been set for him, Terry moved.

The exit was shielded by woodland and heavy undergrowth, on the northern edge of the property. Terry emerged dripping soil and twigs, did a full 360-degree turn, took a knee. He looked down at a smart phone, which was streaming camera footage now that he was above ground again. The cutting of power to the house had not entirely taken him by surprise. That he had a generator backup system set to automatically trigger, had probably not figured in his opponent's calculations, however. He had also relied on the fact that the signal jamming system was limited to the property itself, and not its land. The screen revealed a full fifteen yards of cover between him and them, maybe a foot or so more. Their attention was focussed on the house. His on them.

Terry read the way ahead. No tripwires that he could see. These men were not expecting opposition from anywhere other than the house itself. The gathering gloom made it difficult to see clearly, but not impossible. Next, he checked the woodland floor, searching for a more natural giveaway, such as thorns or dry twigs. What he could see he could avoid.

He gradually made his way across to the two men, one careful tread at a time; little back-lift, little effort in the steps forward. The M4A1 – still his weapon of choice – he held in readiness; resting against his chest, angled forward, left hand supporting, fingers of the right brushing against the trigger.

Now Terry stood directly behind them. If either man turned, even a fraction, they would see him. Neither was prepared, so two shots each would do the trick. Supressed or not, the sound was different to any other being heard in or around the property at that moment, and whoever was running the show at their end would have used men capable of recognising the unusual. Which is why he did not intend using his assault rifle.

When he felt secure in his position, Terry silently unclipped his weapon and laid it on the mossy grass. From a leather sheath on his belt he took out his thirty-year-old Fairburn-Sykes, a double-edged knife that looked like a miniature sword. Its seven-inch carbon steel blade could be deadly in the wrong hands. Which is where it was now. Terry took a deep breath and, crouching low, coiled in readiness to spring, he inched forward.

The two men stood a yard apart, side by side. Not speaking, but not attentive, either. Certainly not making life difficult for him as he approached. As he moved to within a few feet, he assessed the two men more closely. The taller one on the right stood straight-backed, feet planted wide apart. The smaller one took up a more slouched posture, legs together. It was this difference that told Terry who to kill first, and how to begin the attack.

Blade in his right hand, he used his left to violently shove Smaller in the back. Taken completely by surprise, the man pitched forward and fell to the ground. In the same movement, and rising as he swivelled to his right, Terry cupped the taller man's mouth with one of his big mitts, yanking back as he did so, whilst he used the other hand to drag the blade swiftly across the man's throat in one unhesitating movement. As his hand drew back he arced it down in a single powerful motion and slashed the femoral artery in the thigh.

Without pausing to check, instinctively knowing the target now gargling on his own blood would be dead in seconds, Terry planted a boot into the soil for purchase and leapt onto the back of the fallen second target. Smaller's stance had made him vulnerable to the shove, and Terry had been certain that the way the man cradled his weapon would cause him to fall awkwardly. Though the fallen opponent struggled and heaved, his cry for either help or mercy was stifled by a big gloved hand, whilst the other did its work a second time.

And just like that it was over.

Less than ten seconds. No warning to others given. Two men down.

Terry had no time to congratulate himself. He had to dash back down beneath the earth and work his way around to the southern exit. Even if that went well, the three most daunting tasks lay ahead. As he made his way back into the tunnel, he wondered how well Mike was coping.

***

"Try not to shoot at all. But if you have to, do. Just try not to shoot too early, either."

Those had been my instructions from Terry. As good as, anyway. I had listened attentively whilst my friend described the ideal scenario.

"I need to take down half of their team before they start concentrating on the house. I should have little opposition around the wooded exits. The others lack cover, and that's where the shooting will start for certain. If I can make it back here without you having taken a shot, that will be terrific. If you have to shoot after I kick things off, then so be it. But Mike, please try your damnedest not to fire until either I or they take the first shot. Think of that as your starting pistol."

Easier said than done.

Now that Terry was gone, I thought of my friend's words and they irritated me every bit as much as they had when he uttered them. Sure, I was rusty. But I was no rookie. Terry and I had shared many a battlefield together. And hadn't I been the one to carry him across one of those bloodied fields?

I didn't like being the one left behind. I wanted to be out there taking the more proactive role. Not reacting to events, not with the added pressure of being Melissa and Charlie's last-hope guardian. But Terry had forgotten more about this type of warfare than I had ever known. If the shooting started – when the shooting started – I would stand up and do the job expected of me.

Terry had left to suit up, get equipped and make his way down the first tunnel. The two of us had comms, but radio-silence was to be maintained unless the men outside launched a pre-emptive assault before Terry had managed to claim his first few victims. While I waited, I sipped strong, hot coffee. I stood in the surveillance office, monitoring cameras affixed not just to the house and outbuildings, but also high in trees and on several other structures well away from the buildings. Each was motion-activated. Not that there was much of that going on.

I was so absorbed in the screens that I completely failed to hear the soft, pad of feet behind me until it was too late.

"What game are you playing?" Charlie asked.

I whirled. No way could I cover all of the screens at once, and I needed to keep them switched on. But Charlie had given me a way out. "It's a new one," I said. "I'm testing it for a friend. Well, me and Terry are testing it. We're playing it together. It's for adults only, though, sweetheart, so you need to go back to Mel."

"So, I can't play?" The smile she had worn was now gone, a bright sun masked by dark clouds.

I squatted down, so that we were the same height. "Charlie, there's nothing more I would love to do right now than to play a video game with you. I'm sure you'd win, because I'm useless. But you see, some games are too violent for children. It would be wrong of me to let you play this one. Mel would be very angry with me if I did. You don't want that, do you?"

Charlie shook her head. She didn't look happy about it, but she appeared to be accepting the decision. "Okay, Mike. I don't want you to get into trouble with Mel. Can we play a different game?"

"Later on for sure. Right now, I have to help out Terry or he'll be in all kinds of trouble as well. I have to save him. And hey, if you hear noises, like battle sounds and lots of action, that's just us playing the game. Now, off you scoot and tell Mel all about it."

The smile reappeared. She had a task, and it seemed to please her. She dashed off, and I watched her go, her little pipe-cleaner legs pumping. Some guardian I was. A little kid had just managed to take me by surprise and she wasn't even trying. Earlier we had agreed that Melissa would attempt to act as if nothing untoward was happening, and to keep Charlie engrossed in something noisy, or possibly have her wear her headphone buds. Somehow Charlie had slipped away, and I wondered how that had happened. Turning back to the screens, I let go of the thought and started to manipulate the cameras in order to locate the men who had come for us.

I had no joy with the flatlands out front. The only cameras pointing in that direction were either fixed to the house or hidden away inside a stone pillar into, which part of the bridge had been built. That meant the view was neither high enough nor close enough to any positions they might have taken up. If they had. I was out of practice, but I could not identify a single hiding place out there.

I fared no better with those to the rear of the house, either. Beyond the river, more flatlands. A few patches of scrub, some tall grass, so they were possibilities. Nothing came up when I briefly switched to thermal imaging, but if these men were as good as Terry believed them to be, they might well have wrapped themselves in thermal cloaking sheets.

Altogether, I picked up only six of the eight targets previously located by Terry. No matter how I manipulated the cameras I could no longer find two of them. That was a worry. About to make further changes, I noticed a lone figure appear as if from nowhere. I zoomed in and recognised Terry. Enthralled, I stood and watched as the figure moved with great caution towards two of the targets. I felt myself grow tense, my stomach stirring. Then the figure moved swiftly, and with devastating effect. One went down following a shove, the other reacted too slowly to save himself. Moments later, Terry made his way back to the tunnel and disappeared into its mouth and off the screen.

Two down.

At least eight to go. Probably more.

And only four now visible.

I checked my Glock. As I had already done on several occasions. It went completely against all that I believed in to stand there and watch as my friend made his way through the targets. But then my thoughts turned to Melissa and Charlie and I remembered my own role. Charlie's innocence and Melissa's naïveté were prizes worth fighting for.

***

The second pair was dispatched less easily, but relatively swiftly and efficiently nonetheless. The exit manoeuvres had been far more difficult this time. Rather than appear from behind the two operatives, Terry emerged ahead of them. This was perilous, but the one advantage he had was that the mouth of the tunnel was thirty yards off to the right of the pair, so he hadn't popped up directly in their line of vision.

He paused as long as he could at the mouth. Waiting. Listening. Terry's original plan was to navigate his way behind them, but he recognised it would take so long that he might jeopardise everything. Instead, he worked out a new path in his head. More dangerous, but far less time-consuming.

Terry traversed the wood, skirting undergrowth, hedgerow, side-stepping tree roots and overhanging branches. It was slow going, as he had to ensure that each step was silent. His own heartbeat grew loud in his ears. In retrospect, he reckoned this was where he made a misstep. Something, at least, had given him away.

Before he was within ten paces, both men turned in his direction. Terry reacted immediately. Stealth no longer an issue, he ran at the duo and launched himself through the air, both feet forward, legs spread slightly. He hit both men boots first, the impact driving him backwards onto his elbows. Both of his opponents let out gasps of pain and surprise. They were unprepared. He wasn't. That was the only reason for his success.

Springing forward and straight back to his feet (almost before he had hit the ground), Terry stepped into the man on his right who was the first to rise, and drove an elbow into his nose. This had the desired effect of both temporarily disabling his opponent, and causing him to sink to his knees. The man's partner was quicker than Terry had anticipated, however. An MP4 came out of the hazy greyness, sweeping up towards his head. He ducked and raised an arm. The weapon deflected heavily, but continued on its arc. He felt a molten pain sprint through the meat of his upper arm, and although the rifle only clipped his scalp, Terry felt his flesh open up and spew blood.

Scalp bleeds are rapid and copious. He had only seconds, or it would be in his eyes, blinding him. If that happened, he was done.

Terry used his opponent's momentum, guessing he would be unbalanced by the rapid strike and glancing blow. He sank down on his hips and pushed forward. The heel of his right hand caught the other man beneath the chin, slamming his head back like a boxer's speedball. The man staggered, swaying like a broken reed. In one practised movement, Terry pulled his dagger from its scabbard and thrust it deep into the man's throat.

His hand came back still gripping the blade's handle. He switched grips, and drove it sideways. This time the knife took his second opponent in the right ear and bit deep.

Sucking in air, chest aflame, Terry used up a few moments to take stock. Four down. There was a chance that the second skirmish may have been overheard, so Terry waited a few moments. No radio crackled, no shouts went up. He thought he was fine. His arm would stiffen, and his movement would suffer, but not for a while yet. The wound right at his hairline was bleeding freely, warm rivulets slipping down his face like wet paint.

It was time to weigh options.

He needed to keep moving. Yet it would ill-serve him to become blinded by the crimson tide. Experience told him the flow would only increase if he put himself under duress and exertion. Nodding to himself, Terry knelt and reached behind him into his small backpack. From within one of its many zipped pockets he withdrew a medical kit. First, he used a cotton swab to mop the blood away from around his eyes and across his forehead. Then he split a sealed packet, unfolded a moist towelette coated with an anti-septic and used it to dab at the wound itself. Terry cursed silently at the liquid's sting. Another swab to dry the area was followed by a small bandage, which he expertly wound around his head. It wouldn't hold, but it would get him one stage further.

And that was all he would need.

THIRTY-FIVE

I had watched in horror as the fight at the second point looked like going the wrong way. I had enormous faith in Terry, but I was fully aware that anyone can lose in a close combat situation, especially when outnumbered. It was over in seconds, but it felt a lot longer while it was occurring. I leaned forward with both hands on the table on which the monitors stood, and gave a relieved sigh when Terry finally started making his way back through the woods. So far so good, but we had both known going into this that the hardest part was to come.

The plan had been for Terry to strike first north, then south. To the west lay the wide expanse of flat fields, to the east the river. Instinct told us both that we ought to leave the area with a natural defence – the river – until last; which left venturing into open land as the third point of attack. Terry and I had debated this critical third stage for several minutes. Eventually, both of us agreed that the lack of cover out front made tackling that area too risky for a man working alone. Terry would head east and hunt down whoever waited for him there.

I had openly questioned my friend's decision-making from the beginning, yet I allowed the superior tactician to develop and carry out this plan virtually unchallenged. Even so, the pair of us had been nervous about this aspect. It was a plan, and even the best-laid of them can unravel almost before they have begun. However, this was a situation neither of us had been comfortable with.

Time and again I asked myself whether leading these armed men here was a good idea after all. On the surface, it seemed rash. One might argue worse than that. For once, I had not been able to see an end game. Still could not find my way past being so outnumbered; if not outgunned. It's every warrior's instinct to take the fight to the enemy, but a great soldier also had to know when to employ caution; to ensure he lives to fight another day. Terry had been right about one thing, though: things were as they were, not as I might prefer them to be. You played the hand you were dealt, and you did not blame the dealer.

The pivotal time period was now upon us. Terry was out of sight. One of the cameras facing the river was down, and that felt ominous to me. Not for the first time my urge was to follow Terry out there. Now, though, more than ever, it was vital for me to maintain discipline and keep both eyes on the front of the house. That was where our enemies would launch their final strike. Terry and I had agreed on that, at least.

And right at the point at which I felt that much would hold true, I saw the movement.

It was not discreet.

I knew then that Terry and I had been wrong. Terribly wrong.

No one had made their way covertly down into the flatlands as we had predicted. Instead they had remained behind the hill, irrespective of its lack of height. Our enemy had calculated – rightly so – that there was sufficient cover. Now they came, hard and fast. Not in the predicted attack order, not from the forecast location, and not according to logic.

Two armoured jeeps.

Heading our way rapidly.

My mind was working frantically. I could only assume that the men Terry had taken down were supposed to report in, and that the green light had been given when they failed to do so. It had always been a possibility. Their reaction to it, sadly, had not been considered. Terry and I had planned to have more time.

I reached for the two-way radio.

"We're blown from the west," I said, maintaining the illusion of calm. "Two jeeps. Numbers on-board unknown. I have no eyes on you. Sit-rep?"

Static.

"I say again, sit-rep please."

The radio crackled and hissed. "…feels like I'm alone out here… not right… have to give it a few more minutes."

"And the western offence?"

"You know what to do? I'll be there for you, but start the party without me…"

Static again.

I switched my attention back to the screens. The two jeeps had at first seemed close to each other, but now I noticed the gap between them. Another problem. They were on the flatlands now and they were pitching up dirt and dust into the air as they bumped their way across the scorched fields. All the while, I tried to think two steps ahead of them. Would they stop short of the ditch? Would one cross the bridge, whilst the other remained on the far side patrolling the perimeter? Or would they throw it all into a single blitz attack? I took a deep breath. Had to be the latter. I was counting on it.

No further word from Terry. Nothing from the other east-facing camera, but the one that had gone dark was the one that had been focussed on the most likely hiding area close to the riverside.

I swallowed hard. Everything in my mouth tasted thick and dry. The jeeps were close now. The one to the rear was maintaining its distance from the other. Just a little more speed, I whispered to myself. Get yourself on the arse of your brothers in arms. If you're going to support them, do it properly. You're in the second vehicle, but in your head, you arrive at exactly the same time. Don't lag behind, you fucker!

Two hundred yards.

A few seconds.

Faster, damn you!

It didn't happen. The first jeep slammed onto the bridge and kept on coming, foot down. It was almost over the ditch, practically at the end of the bridge. The second jeep was not going to make it on there in time.

I cursed and flicked a switch I had been holding.

The sight of forty pounds of TNT explosive, an armoured jeep, a wooden bridge and four stone pillars detonating was an incredible sight. The concussive soundwave came moments later, rattling the house itself and blowing out a couple of single-pane windows. The pall of flame and dust and smoke reached up and out and I suddenly realised I was now blind. I blinked rapidly, willing my vision to adjust. One jeep was definitely toast. The other looked as if it would have been close enough for its momentum to hit the spot where the bridge had once been. Not devastating, but hopefully a deep wound.

From which there would be survivors.

At least, that's what I had to allow for.

As I waited for my eyesight to improve and for the dust cloud to disperse, I kept watch to see if someone managed to crawl from the wreckage. I guessed three or four men in each vehicle. It was possible that someone could have survived in the lead jeep, but I would bet on at least two or three making it out of the second.

A minute ticked by.

Another, and another.

Something wasn't right. Not only was there no movement from the bridge, but no other cameras showed encroachment from the remaining members of the team. I ran a hand across my forehead and tried to think what this might mean. Could they have all been inside the two jeeps? If so, were they all now lying either dead or dying amidst the smoke and debris? Having your entire unit attacking from a single compass point made little sense to me, but then neither I nor Terry had conceived of them lying behind the rise of the hill out front. It was too far away. Anyone watching would see them coming for…

That was exactly it.

I realised then how badly I had misjudged the situation. An approach from that direction would obviously be seen. Long enough to prepare for it, too. Which would mean you would not commit all of your men at all. Instead, you would send the fewest.

I had just started using the zoom feature on the camera now pointing at the bridge when I heard the shots from the rear of the property.

THIRTY-SIX

Something had been nagging at Terry from the moment he had returned from the second tunnel. It wasn't so much that his strikes had been easy; but there should have been more personnel out there. Clearly these men had no idea about the tunnels, but he was certain that between ten and twelve enemy combatants would have been used. Positioning only two at each location implied fewer forces had been deployed, and he wasn't buying that.

At the back of the house, he kept shaking his head and cursing beneath his breath. There had to be men out there, and they had to be across the river. So why the hell could he not locate them? Terry was now convinced that a trap of sorts had been set, only he was unable to grasp any of its complexities. It made no sense to overload the front, where secreting themselves would be difficult enough for even a couple of men.

The chatter with Mike had not clarified matters, because Terry did not believe they would focus their main force from the west. He believed the jeeps were a diversion, that their intention was to draw fire and stop short of the ditch. The only reason for deploying the jeeps in this fashion was to conceal their real intentions: to storm from the other side of the river; buying time to do so.

The blast from the other side of the house came as a shock. The dynamite had been set many months before; a precaution he had decided upon in the wake of a veiled threat he had received from one of the Boko Haram leaders in Nigeria. His instructions to Mike had been to blow the bridge if any combatants or their vehicles tried to use it. Terry had been convinced they would have no need of the explosives. Since it had gone up now he could only assume they were in trouble.

With a shake of his head, followed by more muttered swearing, Terry started making his way back to the house. He remained above ground, suspecting he had been entirely wrong, and that the strike team had massed to the front and were now attempting to overwhelm Mike. If they did, Melissa and Charlie would be exposed. No way was he going to allow that to happen. He cursed his own ineptitude in not spotting the deception earlier.

Terry was out in full view, and if whoever was hunting them had posted a sniper anywhere within half a mile on this side of the house, he would be dead long before the sound of the shot scattered birds from the trees. He alternated between crouching and running, tracing zig-zag patterns across the uneven lawns. A good rifleman would still have him, and he was making so much noise that if anyone was lying in wait, they would be more than prepared for him.

Still he ran on, panting now, worried about what might be happening on the far side of the house. He could see the cloud of smoke and dust billowing over the rooftop. He had to get around there. Had to intervene before they breached Mike's defensive shield.

And then he stopped.

So suddenly he almost tripped over his own boots.

Mike had said two jeeps. A full-frontal attack, utilising all available men made no sense at all. But the one thing it was bound to achieve was to draw attention.

Everyone's attention.

Terry turned to look behind him. He was certain now that the attack team had discovered their fallen comrades. Possibly even the tunnels. There was only one reason to draw fire out front in such an obvious way: the real attack was coming from the point he had just vacated.

Terry sensed movement. Low and fast. He crouched down, hoisting his weapon. The muffled sounds he heard suggested that those coming his way were splintered. Moving across to his left, towards the tunnel entrance. As well as straight on towards him. There was no time to form even the most basic plan. He had to stop them accessing that tunnel. He rose swiftly, headed across to find some cover beside a rickety garden shed, most of its boards either missing or hanging askew. It was no hiding place, but it had the advantage of not being out in the open. Terry slid in whilst still on the run, throwing up dry dirt. He took position on one knee.

Movement again.

Followed by encroaching figures.

This time he opened fire.

***

The time for inaction was over. We had been duped. I was certain of it. The jeeps had been little more than decoys. I had no doubt now that the only occupant in each had been the drivers. Not exactly a suicide mission, but close enough. They could not have known about the TNT, but some form of hardcore defence had to have been anticipated. I understood my mission now was to ignore the wreckage at the bridge and concentrate on both protecting Melissa and Charlie, and helping Terry if at all possible.

The original plan would have had me sprinting upstairs into the roof space and using the weapons stored by each dormer window. But there was no tactical advantage to be had from the high ground now. It was either here, on the ground floor, or below the property. I turned it over inside my head as fast as I was able to process the variables.

Rusty, but not a newbie.

First job was to secure my baggage. Terry's instruction. My responsibility. I had to get Mel and Charlie headed down the tunnel that ran at a level lower than the others, away at an angle towards the river and safe passage via the Land Rover.

For them.

The intention was that I accompany them, but I had known all along that I would not do that. Instead I would help them on their way, close the door behind them and reposition the shelf. Then I would seek out Terry and discover for myself what had been started. I owed him that. He would not see things the same way, but he would have to deal with that afterwards.

I still had no idea why all of this had been set in motion. Not that it mattered now. My task was to ensure Mel and Charlie made good their escape. I would then stand with my friend. And I would put my faith in myself and Terry Cochran, safe in the knowledge that my baggage was secure.

Melissa and Charlie had been positioned strategically within the house. Central to all entrances and exits, yards from the scullery, which led to the basement, which in turn led to the subterranean channel out of this hellish mess, and on to safety. I made my way quickly but cautiously to the room I had left them in, threw open the door and started to speak.

My mouth flapped open uselessly.

The room was empty.

I made a rapid calculation. Melissa would have heard the explosion, and soon afterwards the gunfire from the rear of the property would have claimed her attention. Charlie would have been terrified at that point. Mel had been instructed to run if things so much as looked as if they had become unglued. The fact that she had moved was a good thing, I decided. A positive step.

I turned and headed for the scullery. Then stopped dead.

A figure in a camouflage style Operational Combat Uniform was making its way along the passage, moving silently from the kitchen where only hours before, myself and Terry had made our plans. I recognised the multi-terrain pattern as that chosen by UK forces. And even on a sweltering summer's day, the figure wore a ski mask to hide their features.

These men are no amateurs, I thought.

I had the drop on the intruder. Out of practice or not, my short-stock automatic rifle came up as one with my hands and I fired a suppressed two-burst round at the masked head. Only one bullet found its target, but the jet of blood and grey matter that erupted from the other side and coated the wall behind told me it was enough.

Heart clamouring, chest tight and heaving, I continued towards the scullery. This time I stayed in tune with my surroundings. Where there was one adversary, there would be another. These guys hunted in pairs. I felt pain behind my eyes, recognising the tension that had built up. I had killed two men today, and there was no coming back from that. Worse, I knew that in order for me to live, others would have to die.

Slowly, blood pounding in my temples, I sidled along the passageway. Darted my head back and forth when I reached the corner, snatching a glimpse around it. I wondered if I ought to take time to clear the kitchen. It was the smart thing to do; the move my training insisted upon. I inched my way forward, repeating the swift head movements. I saw no one inside, so I stepped in, rifle raised, red laser dot hitting the surfaces ahead of me.

Clear.

Back along the passage to the next door. I tried the handle and pushed, but it did not give. Locked. That had not been part of the plan. I glanced both ways, then removed my right hand from the weapon and rapped my knuckles on the door. Twice more when there was no reply.

I breathed out a sigh of relief. The locked scullery door told me one thing: Mel had taken Charlie to the waiting Land Rover. My baggage was on its own now. But it was safe.

A sharp snick of a noise to my left. A red dot on the wall, headed my way fast. I ducked and turned in the same blur of movement. Rapid fire came in my direction, shattering the wall just above my head, slamming into the heavy oak door to the scullery. I got off my own rounds in response, two at a time. Missed my target. I took a step to my left, then darted right, bullets zipping past my body and into the wall at the far end of the passage this time, destroying a painting, which fell and smashed to the tiled floor. My stance by this time was too awkward, and

I fell onto my backside. Fortunately, the slip gave me a better grip on the rifle. I flipped to automatic and let rip until my clip shunted on empty. Frantically now, gunfire echoing in my ears, I pulled another clip from my breast pocket, dumped the useless one, rammed home its fresh replacement and held the sight to my squinting eye.

Panting, partly from fatigue but mostly due to fear, I waited for the sound of my own shots to dissipate. The stench of gunpowder filled the passage, as did swirling dust stirred up by the concussion and dozens of strikes on plastered walls. There, just beyond the kitchen, at the far end of the corridor, lay my third victim of the day.

I'm officially a serial killer, was the absurd thought than ran through my head.

Rather them dead than me.

I let go a long sigh of relief.

That was when the screaming began.

***

Automatic fire in his direction came in short, disciplined bursts. Terry realised he would be pinned down unless he could take out at least two of these aggressors. He had selected an M16 carbine for one specific reason – a grenade launcher could easily be fitted beneath. Its 40mm shell had been highly effective for him in the past, and although it was a pump action device, like any effective soldier he kept one up the spout. The range was closer than he would have liked, at approximately forty-five metres, but he saw no alternative.

Terry raised the rifle a little higher and fired the grenade. Although the launcher's chamber was capable of handling a number of different 40mm shells, he only ever kept explosives in his. He struck his target with precision, the blast angry and decisive. No return fire followed the echo of the detonation.

Cautiously, he slipped out of the wooden shed and crept towards the devastation of hollowed-out earth, smoke and flame.

Two down amongst it all, brutally torn apart. Cochran glanced towards the area where the tunnel lay. Ran a quick check on himself. A little light-headed, despite having stemmed the flow of blood from his scalp wound. Fatigue, but a way to go before exhaustion took a grip. He was good to go. But needed to end it soon.

No time for caution, Cochran entered the tunnel as fast as he was able to move in the cramped conditions. Made his way along to the central spoke, took the steps up towards the house two at a time. In the narrow confines of the shaft the gunfire had sounded like bombs going off. As he emerged from the trapdoor into the house once more, the sound died away.

The loudest silence filled his ears.

Followed by the loudest of screams.

THIRTY-SEVEN

Her shrieks having subsided, Melissa was now sobbing uncontrollably. Mucus hung from her nose in thin ribbons, her eyes were bloodshot and puffy. Both hands were clasped around her cheeks as if holding her head in place. "They've taken her!" she cried. "They took Charlie!"

I put my arms around her to stop her falling, while Terry headed back underground. This time towards the river bridge. I pulled the inconsolable young woman close into my chest, whispering soothing words, knowing they were futile. I stroked Mel's hair understanding that it could never comfort her.

"We'll get her back," I said. I closed my eyes, unable to tear my mind away from the thought of Charlie being dragged off, terrified, unable to even call for help. I gulped down some air, fearing I might also start to weep along with her. A shudder ripped through Mel's body, starting in her stomach and moving swiftly to her chest. I felt it work its way up through her muscles.

"We'll get her back," I said again. This time I meant it. Felt it in every fibre of my being. Her convulsions, I knew, were caused by shock and fear. The same sense of overwhelming loss I was also beginning to feel.

Terry reappeared twenty minutes later. Shook his head. He fixed Melissa with a piercing stare. "What happened here?" he demanded to know. "How were you two separated?"

I hadn't thought to ask. Retaining the protective embrace, I pulled back and repeated my friend's question.

Melissa slowly shook her head, silent at first. Then her voice came in stuttering gasps. "I… I thought she would be safe.

I locked her in an… and came looking for you two. I grabbed a g… un. I wanted to help. I'm sorry. I'm so sorry."

Her knees buckled and she sank to her haunches. I moved with her. Looked up at Terry and shook my head. Pulled Melissa tighter and stroked her hair again. I felt I had to guard against her becoming catatonic with grief and remorse. That's what it was, in my mind. No question. She blamed herself completely. Always would, no matter what the outcome.

The thought gave steel to my earlier resolve. We would rescue Charlie. No matter what the cost.

I brought Mel to her feet. "Come on," I whispered. "Let's get you to a sofa and lie you down. I'll make you a hot, sweet drink."

"No! We have to go after them. We have to get Charlie back."

"And we will. We will. I promise you. But we can't go charging off half-cocked, Mel. Terry and I need to talk about how we're going to handle this now. You need to calm yourself, rest up. We need you with us, Mel. We need you there for Charlie when we find her. And she'll need you at your best."

But Terry was shaking his head. He stepped closer to intervene. "We have no time for that, Mike. Much of the gunfire was suppressed, but some of it wasn't and the explosions certainly weren't. Out here, the sound would have carried miles. Someone will have reported it. We need to be out of this place when the police eventually show up."

Nodding, I realised Terry was seeing things much more clearly than I was. I pictured only Mel's grief and Charlie's absence. He saw the larger picture. "Okay," I said to Melissa, hands laid on her shoulders as I stared into her eyes. "Terry's right. We need to go, and go now."

"Like this? The state we're in?"

"Hit the bathroom. Wash your face, fix your hair. We'll do the same." I turned to Terry. "Mate, grab a first-aid box and we'll see to your head wound once we're on the road. You and I will also scrub up and we could both do with a change of clothes. You must have something here to fit me. Let's get to it. Out of here in five minutes, right?"

I had taken charge, but it didn't seem to faze Terry at all.

I led Melissa – with some reluctance on her part – into the bathroom, where I helped her wash her face with hot water. While she scrubbed with a flannel, I used my fingers to comb through her hair as best I could. None of it would make her feel better, but we all needed to look as normal as possible once outside of the house. When I was done with her hair, I used my thumb to tenderly caress the curve of her cheek.

"Don't blame yourself, Mel," I told her. "I know you will, but it's not your fault. If it hadn't happened this way, it would have still gone down. The truth is we were outnumbered and out-thought. Terry and I are the only ones at fault for that. We didn't stand a chance. Know that. And when the time comes to grab Charlie back and we're all set to act, you stand by our side. Stronger. Wiser. Ready."

I took my chance to wash up. I had meant every word. Terry and I were to blame. The better plan would have been to place Mel and Charlie elsewhere before taking on these men. Have them sneak away in the gathering dusk. The two men Melissa relied on for her security had got it badly wrong. I blamed myself as much for not questioning the plan as I did my friend for coming up with it in the first place. Terry had been both over-optimistic and over-confident. I'd got caught up in all the machismo and relied too heavily on his judgement. It happened. And when it did there were always casualties. On this occasion, that victim was a child.

My baggage.

Seconds later, I shepherded Mel back out into the passageway. It still reeked of gunpowder, blood and bodily fluids. Unmistakable to anyone who had ever smelled the combination before. Both of my victims lay where they had fallen. Gaping holes decorated the walls. I kept Mel's head down, told her not to look at the bodies. Headshots had made their faces unrecognisable as such, their gaping, ugly wounds so much more disturbing than TV or movies could ever portray.

Terry found us and handed me a crew-neck T-shirt. "You'll never fit into the trousers so let's not even attempt it," he said. "Brush yours down, sponge off any blood if you have to."

I went to change and finish making myself presentable. I caught sight of myself in the mirror and was shocked by the ravages just a couple of days had wrought upon me. When I was done I collected Mel's shoulder bag and Charlie's little pink backpack, scooping up her various devices. There was no doubt in my mind that she would need them again.

Outside the house, I paused. The Range Rover was shot to pieces, the breach unit having disabled it in case anyone tried to make good their escape. The same treatment had been dealt out to the Land Rover on the other side of the river. I heard Terry jogging up behind me. I turned, noting that my friend had rubbed away the grime, blood and facial camouflage.

"The motor's fucked," I said. I hoped I had held back my rising swell of panic.

Terry brushed by me without a word, jerking his head towards the stone and wood barn to our left. Mel and I followed him across the uneven gravel, through the long grass. He heaved the barn doors open, stepped inside. A hoist allowed a set of chains to be attached to a large expanse of tarpaulin which covered a bulky shape. A few tugs on the hoist's handle and an old Toyota 4x4 Hilux flatbed truck was revealed. It was dark green, dappled with rust, but its front bull bars gave it a sturdy feel.

"The man is always prepared for any eventuality," I said, smiling and hoping to lighten the mood a little.

"I hope so," Melissa said, looking at me. "We're going to need him to be."

"Doors are unlocked," Terry said. "Jump in the back and buckle up, Mel. Lie down across the seat. It's best if you're not seen. Mike, you're riding shotgun."

I read his face. It looked drawn, pale. He had made mistakes. More than usual, and they had been costly. He was hurting in more ways than one. "You okay to drive? You left some blood back there, mate."

"I'm good to go," Terry insisted. "Let's get out of here."

***

"You think she was in on it after all?" Terry asked. We had escaped unobserved from the farmhouse as far as any of us could tell. Had travelled hardly any distance at all before he pulled off the winding road and found a spot to conceal the truck behind a grove of mature silver birch. The three of us sat for some time in silence, quietly absorbing all that we had experienced. We were alone when he asked the question, Melissa having remained draped out across the backseat of the Toyota whilst Terry and I exited the vehicle. The early hour still held some warmth from the day's sunshine.

I shook my head at the question. It needed asking, and I had considered it on several occasions since first suggesting her culpability. But I was now convinced that Melissa had not been acting back in the house. She had not betrayed Charlie. The poor woman was utterly devastated.

"She made a mistake is all," I said. "For the best of reasons, even if they were naïve. She picked up a gun with the intention of using it, and my guess is she's never so much as held one before. She left Charlie on her own, which must have been an agonising decision to make. Mel came looking to help us, Terry. It just went to shit."

He spent some time chewing that over. Finally, he nodded. "Agreed. Fact is, if she'd stayed put she'd probably be dead right now. I fucked up. That's the bottom line. This is on me. I misjudged these people, Mike. Underestimated them. I knew they were professional, knew they had to be a unit to respect. Despite that I thought I could take them down – sorry, that *we* could take them down. I was over-confident in the successful outcome of the plan. A plan that never once made allowances for one of their own. My fault. Not yours, and certainly not hers."

"We agreed the plan together, Terry."

"No. You agreed to agree. There's a difference. You deferred to my greater experience. You weren't happy with it, you told me so, but I didn't listen. You've been out of the game for a long time, I'm still up to my neck in it. I thought I knew best. Clearly I didn't."

I raised both hands. "There will be plenty of time for blame and self-recrimination later. Right now, we need to focus on getting that kid back."

He hung his head; the first time I had seen him looking defeated. "This fuck-up will perhaps have cost me your trust. Certainly, Melissa's trust. I now even doubt myself."

"Well snap the hell out of it." I met his gaze with a stern one of my own. "This is not the time for self-pity, mate. You're still the best bet we've got. We can all work together, but you're our go-to stormtrooper, Terry. Make no mistake about that."

This brought a vague smile to his face. "Okay. I hear you. So, let's make those plans."

I nodded. "Beginning with, how do we even begin to get Charlie back?"

I could not recall the last time I had felt so emotionally drained. Today I had killed men, watched others fall to my friend. A child – our child at the time, under our protection – had been abducted right from beneath our noses. I did not know what to do with that information and the emotions it brought with it, in which direction to turn. I looked to my friend for answers.

"Right now, I don't honestly know," Terry replied. "But we'll figure it out. I think we may just need to take a step back for a moment, wipe the slate clean in our minds. I suspect we're both sort of numb, and we need to be sharp."

"Yeah, no shit. We don't know where to look, we don't know who to look for."

"I'm beginning to get a feeling for these people, Mike. We can forget about it being related to the police, NCA, whoever. This Hendricks character was probably always intended to be the fall-guy. A pawn. As for the sniper back in Chippenham, what we went through this morning and now tonight, we're looking at them being the genuine article. No weekend warriors, Mike. Pros. Ex-forces, perhaps even current, looking for some moonlighting paydays no questions asked."

I regarded him closely. "Men like you," I said. To me this day had been a nightmare, death and destruction playing a looped spool of film in my mind. To Terry, this was just another day at the office.

Nodding, he said, "Yes. Men like me." I wasn't sure, but I thought I detected a note of regret in his voice.

I asked Terry who might pay for something like this, who could possibly want this bad enough. He had worked for private security forces. This was his killing field.

Terry arched his eyebrows. "In my experience, there's only one client I can think of in this particular situation, here in the UK, who could arrange such a hit and then have the determination to clean up after themselves with a skilled and deadly response."

I let out a soft whistle. "You mean government."

"I mean a part of it, yes. Home Office. MI5. SIS. Perhaps a combination of two or even all three. Not directly, I'm sure. Within those groups there is an awful lot of wriggle-room for the indirect, if you follow my meaning."

"For a gangster like Dawson?" I shook my head. "Why? What could he have over them? What sort of threat could he ever have been?"

"I don't know, Mike. Like you, I have far more questions than answers right now. It's clear to me that we need to regroup. We have no trail to follow, so we need to make use of the hours before daybreak to rest and to feed ourselves. The backpack I brought with me has some bread, jam and fruit in it. Bottled water, too. We need to eat, if only for fuel. We won't recover properly otherwise. Then we sleep. No point chasing our tails in the dead of night."

Although I could not imagine getting any rest, let alone the luxury and solitude of sleep, I saw the wisdom in my friend's words. Exhaustion would overwhelm us otherwise, leaving neither of us fit to tackle the problem of getting back our baggage. I nodded. Gently slapped Terry on the back. Then the two of us made our way back to the truck.

The next few hours were the longest I had known up until that point in my life. Terry closed his eyes often, yet I don't believe he slept at all. Knowing the man as I did, I imagined he would be beating himself up for his role in the events that had led us here. He was not a man to dwell on mistakes, but I got the impression those he had made today would scar him. Mel slept fitfully, starting awake as if from nightmares on several occasions, only to find worse waiting for her there in the dark. I felt so helpless. All I could think about was poor Charlie, trying to imagine how terrified she must be, and coming up short. It was impossible for me to fully comprehend how vulnerable a childlike Charlie must be in such dreadful circumstances.

I must have dozed, however fitfully, because the next time I opened my eyes a faint glow was emanating from the east.

THIRTY-EIGHT

We waited until dawn was in our rear-view mirror before we left that sheltered spot deep in the woods. Once again we did not travel far. A few miles was all we needed between us and the body-strewn battlefield we had left behind.

"I come here when I need to think," Terry told us. "At times when I need to clear my head."

"I would never have put you down as a religious man," I said.

"You don't need to be in order to have this place work its magic. Spend half an hour here and you start to feel insignificant. And if you are, then so are your worries."

I felt as if the history of Thetford Priory carried huge weight in the space it filled and the air around it, a presence that was almost palpable. Standing there in the early morning air, enveloped by the Priory's shadow, I understood exactly what Terry meant. I was not a man for wandering around admiring ancient architecture, but it was hard not to be drawn back in time when all around you stood the husks of buildings dating back as far as the twelfth century. It was an impressive sensation. An intimidating one, too.

Terry swept a hand out as he continued. "This place ceased being what it was built to be almost five hundred years ago, having been a functioning and thriving religious foundation for more than four hundred years before the Reformation killed it off. Can you imagine that, either of you? Can you even begin to wrap your heads around it? Remnants of a time some nine hundred years ago, still upright. Right here in front of us now. It takes my breath away every time I come here."

"To be perfectly honest with you, Terry," Melissa said dolefully, "I can't focus on anything but Charlie right now."

He turned. Nodded. Did not appear to be offended. "I feel the same, Melissa. Which is precisely why I came here. To have my mind choked with the sights and sounds and smells of the warfare we experienced yesterday is no help to either of you. Or to Charlie, for that matter. I need this to… reboot myself, if you like. I value it as a form of cleansing."

I had to agree. "Believe me, Mel, it takes something out of the ordinary to rid your thoughts of everything you experience during a firefight like that. For me it's anything to do with water: lakes, streams, rivers, waves. Even rain. But I can see why this place does the trick for Terry."

Its stone walled perimeter, ancient structures and the formidable gatehouse standing three storeys high, revealed a glimpse of the past in the way no history book can. Its status as a religious symbol was almost irrelevant to anyone who sought serenity not of the spirit, but of the mind. I never ceased to be amazed by my friend's little foibles. I regarded this as a noble one, however.

"I'm sorry," Melissa said. She dug her hands deep into the pockets of her denim jacket. "I didn't mean to belittle what you both went through back there. But I still believe I am to blame for Charlie being taken. My only job was to protect her, and now those people have exactly what they want."

Terry was about to answer when he froze. A ringtone was singing out. He pulled a phone from his jacket pocket. Melissa's mobile. I glanced at him, astonished that he had left it on and in one piece rather than strip it down so that we could not be followed. He merely shrugged at the unexpected intervention, put a finger to his mouth, pressed both the receive and speaker keys at the same time.

"Am I speaking to Mike Lynch?" the caller asked. His voice was deep, calm, London accent.

"No," Terry replied.

"Ah, I see. So then, you must be the man responsible for taking out so many of my men."

"Must I?"

"I think so, yes. Should I assume you left behind no wounded? Only, I was in a bit of a hurry when I got out of there, didn't have time to stop and check what with Ray Dawson's child wriggling and screaming in my arms."

"You can assume whatever you like."

"I see. A man of few words, eh? In that case, I will assume you are ex-forces. I will assume you spent time in the same commando unit as Lynch. And I will assume you know the score; where things stand now."

"Actually," Terry said, "why don't you explain it to me. Just so as there are no misunderstandings."

"Very well. The situation couldn't be clearer really. I have the child. I want to suggest an exchange. We want Miss Anderson and Mr Lynch. Your involvement is unnecessary. However, you could earn out of it and handle Lynch yourself for us. If not, then he must remain part of the exchange deal."

"I'll be the judge of what role I play."

"Then do that. Why not come and work for me? You're clearly a capable man."

"Yet you treat me like a child," Terry said, his tone remaining equable. "Your mission is to clean up after the botched murder of Ray Dawson. The child, her nanny, the man your cop let get away. But I'm part of that equation now. Therefore, I have to go as well. Those will have been your orders."

The line was silent for a few moments. Terry let it stretch out. I looked on, fascinated by the exchange I was witnessing.

Finally, the caller spoke once more. "I have a list here of everyone who served with Mike Lynch. I could work my way through that list until I find you."

Terry chuckled. "The only way you found me the first time was due to an outsider, and the only way you found me the second time was because I allowed you to."

"Yeah, and look at how well that turned out for you. Leaving the child alone was not such a good idea, was it." It was not a question.

"I admit, I screwed up. I won't make that same mistake again."

"All right. Enough posturing. We both have big sweaty balls. Let's go back to the exchange –"

"There is no exchange. You will kill us all."

"It doesn't have to be that way. I recognise the fact that I need some leverage here, so I maintain a degree of flexibility. Persuade them to give themselves up to me. What does one more victim of collateral damage matter?"

"Sorry. I simply don't believe you."

The man at the other end of the line sighed. "Well, I tried. I could still let the girl go. So, yes, maybe I don't intend letting any of you three adults walk away. It'll be your lives in exchange for hers. She's no threat."

"So, we hand ourselves over to you. Charlie goes free. We die."

"Quickly. You'll never feel it. None of you. What do you say?"

Shaking his head, Terry said, "I say call me back in sixty."

He killed the call.

I let go a long, deep breath. "He was blunt, I'll say that for him," I said.

"Once he knew I wasn't buying his bullshit."

There was something I could not let go of, however. I asked Terry why he had left the phone in one piece, allowing them to use the GPS all over again. He explained that it had been sitting in his jacket with the battery removed until moments before we left our canopy of birch trees earlier.

"After a night of stewing on it, I realised there was no chance of us finding these people as rapidly as we needed to," he said. "Our only hope was to draw them to us once again."

"Yeah, because that went so well for us before," I snapped. "And once again, Terry, you made a decision without consulting either of us."

Terry ran a hand through his beard. "Do you agree that the quickest way to re-establish contact was to have the phone live and available?"

"Yes, but –"

"Then why would we waste time debating it? I apologise to both of you for taking matters into my own hands yet again. I know I screwed up before, so you doubt me now. But this really was the only way to move us forward this time. We were all out of options."

"I agree," Melissa said, providing Terry with an unexpected ally.

I had to admit that, even had we discussed it at length, we would have ended up making the same decision. It pissed me off that Mel and I had been excluded from the process, yet it had been the most expedient course of action to take.

I hiked my shoulder and said, "I suppose now at least we know what we're up against."

Terry continued to run a hand over his chin. "Still it doesn't feel right, Mike. Again. That appears to be a constant thread. Something about this whole business keeps nagging at me, and I can't put my finger on why."

My friend did not operate on a physical level based on being reactive. He was reflective, intelligent, proactive. If something was still bothering him, then there was probably a good reason.

"Go on," I said. "We discussed this before – your concerns. Things have moved on since, though. Let's see if we can jar something loose."

Melissa took a step forward. The morning air was crisp, and she had both arms wrapped around herself in a hug. She had long since run out of cigarettes, and was probably feeling some withdrawal. "For what it's worth, if you think they will release Charlie, I'll give myself up to them."

"I know you would, Mel," I said. A thin smile stretched a line across my face. "I've seen the way you are with Charlie. If I didn't know otherwise I'd swear you were her mother. But Terry was right: they will never do that. So let's not go there again, because we need to figure out a whole different approach."

She shrugged. "I'm in your hands. If I were on my own, I would take the deal. But you know these sort of men better than I do. So, if you say it's a lie, then it's a lie."

"I'm not happy about any of this," Terry reminded us. "I get why they want you, Mike. You saw the cop shooting Dawson. In their minds, you have to go. But why Mel? That has never sat right with me. It made sense initially, but as soon as she told them in her texts that she had seen nothing they should have abandoned her as a target."

"Clearly they didn't believe her."

"I thought they did at the time," Melissa said. "They really tried to make me think Mike was dangerous. A danger to me and Charlie."

Terry nodded. "I think we can all agree that was a ploy. As for the rest of it, I'm not so sure. Okay, so they are paranoid. No chances. Take us all out. That's where we are now. Where you were before you contacted me, though – that's where I'm a little hazy. They had you, Mike. Both of you if they'd wanted. A concocted story about how you and Melissa were in it together. Hendricks had the entire police force and NCA behind him. He could easily have buried you both, had the pair of you in the frame. It wouldn't have mattered what you said in your defence. There was no need for the escalation."

"You mean killing Susan."

"Yes. It still makes no sense to me, Mike."

I shifted uneasily. Loose gravel crunched beneath the boots Terry had given me. "I don't disagree. I'm just not sure what you're trying to say. Or where turning this over and over takes us. Not any closer to Charlie, that's for sure."

Terry fixed his gaze on the hexagonal towers of the gatehouse for a few moments. I imagined his sanctuary was now ruined every bit as much as the ancient building itself. When he turned back, I saw his brow creased into a deep V.

"That may not be the case, actually. Not exactly. They still want you two. But I'm more intrigued by something that bastard said just now. He asked me what did one more victim of collateral damage matter."

"I assumed that was Charlie he was talking about," I said.

"No. No, I don't think it was. The conversation had moved on to you two throwing yourselves to the wolves in exchange for her life. So, if only one of you would be collateral damage, what does that make the other?"

Melissa threw both hands to her head, loosely wrapping around her ears as if words were somehow blows to ward off. "Will you stop saying 'collateral damage'! You make it sound so cold and detached. It's murder, plain and simple."

"Okay, Mel, take it easy." I spoke to her softly. I stepped forward and placed my hands on her upper arms, peering directly into her eyes. "We want Charlie back every bit as much as you do. And we'll get her back. I promise you."

"But it isn't your fault she's gone," she replied, tears streaming down her face

"It isn't? We were both there with you. It was our plan that failed, exposing you. It was my job to protect you. Both of you. My baggage, remember. I failed, too. But you can't carry that with you into the next fight, Mel. It's a distraction, and that can get you killed."

Silence followed. And in that moment of silence, Terry suddenly jerked backwards, and a bloom of red spread across his pale blue shirt. Only then did I hear the report of the shot that had caused it.

THIRTY-NINE

It was almost a day since they had returned from Wiltshire. Rhino was now sitting with Chris Dawson inside one of the family-owned casinos. This one was in Romford, Essex, the first ever purchased by the Dawson empire. The two occupied a sleek and elegant office on the floor above the space devoted to gambling and drinking. Dawson was on his second scotch of the day, whilst Rhino stuck to coffee before noon.

"I'm getting angry now," Dawson confessed, spite evident in his eyes. "It might be time to hold feet to the fire, Rhino."

The big man sat back in his chair. "Whose feet?" he asked. "Which fire?"

Dawson picked up the closest thing to hand – his crystal tumbler – and hurled it against the wall just behind Rhino's head. The glass shattered, its broken shards and the golden alcohol it had contained spattered across the carpet below.

"I don't pay you to ask me dumb fucking questions, I pay you to resolve situations for me!"

Rhino sat unmoved. "But it's not a stupid question," he argued reasonably. "This is way out of our league, Chris. If this was business I'd know who to see, I'd know who to squeeze. I'd also know why I was doing the squeezing and what I hoped to achieve. In this case, I have nothing to go on. Not a thing. Are you not getting anything from your insider?"

Dawson pointed a stiff finger in his direction. "There you go. There's one useless fucker whose feet can go into the fucking fire for all I care."

"If that's what you really want. Will that get us any further, or is the real problem the fact that he's no longer involved in the investigation and so can't tell us anything no matter what I threaten to do to him?"

"He says that's the case. Perhaps losing a finger or a toe or a tooth will make him think again."

"Seems like a long shot to me, boss. What exactly has he said?"

Dawson shook his head, clearly frustrated. "That the victim in the hotel was this Hendricks character from the NCA. He actually thought we might be responsible for that. He was surprised when I told him otherwise. Now he's thinking there must be some sort of connection with that shooting and the one in the car park."

"And nothing since? That does gel with what we're hearing from other areas. That the trail has gone cold. No sightings, no more bodies, nothing."

"Which can't be fucking right."

"Unless Lynch has gone to ground. And if he has, he could have done so anywhere."

Rhino could tell his boss was still seething, but he had calmed sufficiently that he could at least be reasoned with. There were times when he would have liked nothing more than to crush Chris like a bug and just walk away from it all. But it was a passing phase, and he'd get over it. He thought about a potential next move, and something stirred.

"Boss, did you hear on the radio this morning about some sort of commotion in East Anglia? Police were making no comment, and media had no confirmation of what actually went on, but there was some mention of gunfire and possible explosions."

Dawson was nodding. "Saw something about it on the news earlier. What're you thinking, Rhino?"

"I'm thinking that we go weeks, even months in this country without hearing about shootings. Now we have Ray, the woman in the car park and the NCA geezer. I'm wondering if it's just pure coincidence that twenty-four hours later there's potentially more shootings elsewhere. I said this Lynch bloke could have gone to ground anywhere. Why not East Anglia?"

Chris leaned forward, his hands clasped together on the desk he sat behind. "So, if Hendricks shot Ray, and we didn't shoot Hendricks, who did shoot him? Who shot Lynch's friend, and who the hell is doing the shooting now?"

"All good questions. Maybe I could drive up there and snout around."

"But explosions?"

Rhino shrugged. "Who knows, boss? Something iffy is going on. Wouldn't take me long to head up there."

"Not as if you've got any other fucking leads to follow up on. Go. Take Haystacks with you."

Rhino groaned. "Do I have to, boss?"

"Did I just give you a direct order, Rhino?"

"Yes."

Dawson nodded. "Then yes, you do."

FORTY

A second round came in before I had a chance to react. It struck Terry on the thigh and flipped him around, sending him sprawling to the ground. I grabbed hold of Melissa with both arms and dove to the floor, the young woman sandwiched beneath me and the hard gravel. Shuffling around to ensure I was side-on to the shooter, I put a hard edge into my voice and said, "You stay still until I tell you otherwise. When I say go, get up into a low crouch and scurry as fast as you can. I'll be dragging you along so just go with me."

Terry was cursing, but as another bullet narrowly missed him and chipped off a chunk of five-hundred-year-old masonry, he managed to pull himself up and scramble over the waist-high wall. Myself and Melissa were only yards away, but I knew the sniper would have switched his focus by now. The Kevlar was in the truck so we were exposed to the full force of the munitions. I could only hope it would not tear through me and on into Mel.

"I'm going to the truck," Terry called out.

I glanced back. "No. I'm bringing Mel to you. I'll get the weapons and body armour from the truck."

After that, I didn't hesitate. Heaving Melissa to her feet, I set off for the ancient stone wall. A round clipped my forearm, sending an electric jolt of pain right through to the wrist. I yelped, but continuing to crouch and run I towed Melissa behind me at speed. Another high-velocity bullet somehow missed me; I heard it scream by my right ear but it seemed to strike nothing. A yard from the wall I pitched Melissa forward beyond me and somehow hurled us both over the wall in a flurry of arms and legs.

The landing was heavy, and it drove the air from my lungs. My arm was stinging like a bastard as well. Nausea took hold, and bile rose up into my throat. I managed to keep it down, but it was a close-run thing. Gasping for air I looked up at Melissa, saw pain etched upon her face.

"You hit?" I asked. I heard the urgency in my own voice.

She shook her head, eyes wide and tearful. "Just… just winded," she said through clenched teeth.

Nodding, I looked across at Terry, who was keeping low and tight to the base of the wall. "Tell me what we have?" I asked.

"In the back, under the canvas. Three green bags: one small arms, one M4s, one ammo. Explosives and Kevlar in the maroon bag."

"Got it. You okay, Terry? How bad are you hit?"

"Thigh is not terrible, but a bleeder. The one in my side might be worse."

"What about you?" Melissa asked me. "Your arm looks in a bad way."

I looked down. Thick red blood glutted from the groove that formed the wound. I shook my head and waggled my fingers. "Somehow it missed the bone. I can move it. It's superficial and looks worse than it is. It needs attention, but that will have to wait."

I told her to edge in towards the stone base like Terry.

"Back in five," I said.

Scrambling along behind the wall on my hands and knees, I realised five minutes was a pipe dream. I had to clear the wall at the far end, then navigate my way behind whatever structures were available, all the way back to the parking area where the Toyota sat. Then return, only this time laden with weapons. And all whilst being shot at. Behind the wall I had no way of looking out for the sniper's position. I figured the gunman would relocate, shifting position as well as moving closer to us. By the time I reached the cache of arms, our unseen assailant could be a couple of hundred yards away from where he had taken his first series of shots.

I reached the end of the wall and peered around the corner. The Priory was a tourist trap, but fortunately at this time of morning it was relatively empty. The gunfire had been suppressed, so there was less chance of anyone else being drawn into what was going on. A couple of people on the far side by what had once been the monks' sleeping quarters seemed not to have noticed anything amiss. A few others stood and watched us, clearly bemused by our actions.

Uncertainty froze me to the spot. The most natural thing would be to grab up some weapons, spare clips and scurry back to Terry and Melissa. On the other hand, perhaps the best way to protect them was to eradicate the enemy. This rattled through my head while I worked out the easiest route over to the truck. I would be out in the open, but if the sniper still had a fix on the wall behind which all three of us had taken shelter, his focus might not take in the wider surroundings.

I looked back at the way I had come. The inelegantly constructed grey-stone wall had a curve which I now noticed only by looking down its length. Terry was still visible, and I waved my hand in a jerky motion in order to attract his attention. He lifted his head, raised a hand. I signalled back, using a special form of sign language: Show movement. Draw attention.

Terry did so immediately. From his prone position, he slipped off his jacket and raised it so that it could be seen above the wall. He moved it slowly from left to right, making it appear as if someone were crawling around back there.

Any sniper worth his salt would have been scouring the area with his scope, and would keep dropping back to the last visual contact. I hoped the movement had been seen, and that it would induce the rifleman to focus on that specific location. I did wonder whether they had a spotter, but dismissed the notion. It was unlikely that whoever was in charge would have risked two men, given the losses they had already suffered. However, if the sniper had reported back that he had us pinned down, support might well be on its way.

I had to move. It was a risk, and I had to resist the urge to hurry. Sudden movements were easy to spot peripherally, and I had no intention of becoming an easy target for the man out there now hunting us down like animals.

I moved.

I made sure that I was not out in the open and in plain sight for longer than ten seconds at any one time. Did not pause behind a sheltered spot for longer than five. In this manner, I created a jagged pattern in a dog-leg scramble across to the car park, which was becoming increasingly more active with vehicles and visitors. I slid around to the back of the Toyota, pulled open the canopy and started rummaging through the bags. I was so lost in thought that I never heard the scuffling movement close by until it was almost upon me.

I whirled, Glock in my right hand, finger paused but locked on the trigger. It was Terry, supported by an exhausted Melissa, who was bowed by both his weight and lack of mobility.

"Couldn't wait," Terry explained, grimacing and favouring his left leg. "I'm losing too much blood."

Melissa helped lean him against the side of the truck. Her breathing was ragged, and she bent forward at the waist, hands on her knees. "Terry thought… the man who shot at us… would back… back off… too many people now." She sucked in a lungful of air.

I glanced at my friend's wounds. Though by far the bloodier, the shot to the thigh would be the less troublesome. I had seen far more bullet wounds than I cared to remember, so I understood what I was looking at. And although the blood flow appeared to have decreased from Terry's abdomen, I was certain that was the one he could die from.

"You made the right choice," I said. "We have to get you out of here. No time for a fight."

"Won't they – he – just follow us?" Melissa asked, standing upright now, hands fixed on her hips.

"Probably. We don't have a Plan B, though."

"I thought they were negotiating," Terry said. "Instead, they were just buying time."

"Give me the phone," I said. Terry frowned, but dug his hand into his pocket, took out the mobile and handed it over. I snapped the cover off, slid out the battery and pulled the SIM card from its slot. I jammed the separate pieces into my own pocket. "Right. Let's get out of here."

"I have somewhere you can take me," Terry said through his pain. A film of sweat lay across his forehead. He looked as weak as I had ever seen him. "A quack I use for… emergencies."

Nodding, I said, "Okay. Mel, your job during the drive is to fix your gaze on the back and tell me if you spot the same vehicle on more than a couple of occasions. Just focus on three things: colour, shape and some part of the number plate. Just two or three characters."

"Got it."

Between us, Melissa and I helped Terry up and into the truck. We gently laid him across the back seat, taking the place Mel had occupied on our drive to the Priory. I couldn't stand to see my friend in such a bad way. I was now consumed by guilt, and that hurt more than my own aches and pains.

"Where to?" I called out, the Toyota roaring into life.

"Barton Mills," Terry replied. "Just the other side of Mildenhall. Straight run down the A11."

"Know it well," I said. "Taken many a flight out of the airbase."

"Yeah. I was with you on a couple of occasions."

I smiled to myself. I had been so raw back then, and Terry had taken me under his wing, despite being only a few years older. Even then I knew the man who would become my closest friend was a lifer. Only death or serious injury was going to prevent Terry Cochran from spending his entire career in the forces. As it transpired, I was wrong. The British Armed Forces decided that he could no longer be put into certain conflict areas. The price on his head drew too much attention and put those around him in harm's way. Rather than feel like a spare appendage, Terry had resigned his commission and entered the private security arena. One thing I could be sure of: he would be a fighter until the bitter end, however that might come.

"Keep your eyes on the road," I told Mel. "You see anything suspicious, have Terry take a look as well."

"I will. How's your arm? You're still bleeding."

"Not enough to be serious. I'll get us there."

As I sped away from the Priory, I couldn't shake the feeling that everything I had witnessed since Susan's murder had escalated far beyond the logical reaction to a botched strike. Whoever these people were, they were now operating in the open with apparently no thought of public awareness. It was wrong. I just couldn't pin down why.

FORTY-ONE

O ur thirty-minute drive to Barton Mills was uneventful. I had to trust in Mel and my own many rear-view mirror observations. Neither of us spotted a tail – which did not mean there wasn't one. I remained guarded as I followed Terry's directions through the village, but could not allow that to distract me. When we pulled off the road and onto a block-paved driveway outside a sizeable bungalow, its facing wall draped with ivy, we surprised an elderly man watering the front lawn.

The tall, angular figure, looked on with no apparent alarm as Melissa and I clambered out of the truck's cab. When we started to help Terry from the rear, the man sprang into action. He ushered us through into what he told us was his back bedroom, opening doors and clearing away the usual hallway clutter ahead of us. He helped us to settle Terry onto a sturdy hospital-style bed.

"Nice to see you again, old chap," the man said. It was as if the two had run into one another whilst out for a stroll.

"You too, Howard." Terry regarded myself and Melissa. "This is Howard Smith. Doctor, surgeon, friend of wounded servicemen and women everywhere."

The man turned. Smiled warmly and affected a mock bow. "I'm just an old sawbones who stitches mad bastards like Terry here back together again."

We exchanged greetings, before the doctor turned his attention back to his new patient. Howard Smith was a sixty-eight-year-old widower whose last decade had been devoted to helping ex-servicemen recover from various wounds. He explained this to us as he carried out a preliminary examination, after which he pronounced Terry unfit for further service.

"I can fix you up well enough," he told him. "There's no damage to anything vital, and no immediate potential for increased trauma. Blood loss is a concern, however. You'll require a minimum seventy-two hours recovery. Possibly a further twenty-four if we can't control the inevitable infection."

The complaints were loud and defiant as expected, but Terry was eventually convinced by all three of us that he would be a liability if he continued in his current condition. We could not afford any passengers if we were going to confront these people. Melissa left the room whilst the surgeon and I prepped Terry. I tuned out my friend's moaning dirge of a voice, and turned my thoughts instead to what lay ahead. With Terry out of the game, it was just me and Mel on the road together now. But perhaps not for long.

The idea had come to me at the point where I had begun to despair. My friend down, Charlie gone, there did not seem to be a way back. My thoughts turned to how the nightmare had started: Ray Dawson murdered, with his brother out for revenge and unseen forces hunting us down.

Chris Dawson was now the key. The throw of the dice we had not wanted to take.

Who would want Charlie back more? I asked myself. Family was family. Previously we had ruled out going to Dawson for help on two counts: first, the possibility that he had paid for the hit on his own brother. Second, he might have a shoot first ask questions later approach to negotiations.

"There is no way all of this is being controlled by a medium-size gangster like Chris Dawson," I reasoned back in the doctor's spare bedroom, once Terry was ready for surgery. "I am confident of that much. As for the fact that he may overreact when it comes to me, the man who supposedly murdered his brother, well I think now we have little choice but to put that theory to the test."

"That's a crazy chance to take," Terry said, shaking his head. "No, there has to be another way, Mike."

"Tell me what it is, Terry. It's just me and Mel now. We have to get some help."

"But Chris Dawson? How much help can he and his thugs provide?"

"Numbers. Men to hold and shoot guns. Plenty of them."

"But they're not trained," Terry argued.

"With the right plan, maybe they won't have to be."

"And you have a plan?"

"I do."

"You want to share that with me and Mel?"

I looked between them. Took a beat. "It's simple really," I said. "We use me as bait."

***

I pushed the Toyota as hard as I dared. Melissa sat by my side, her chin set as firm as my own. We consumed the miles in silence.

After more discussion following my suggestion, both Mel and Terry had given in. In the absence of any other strategy, mine would have to do. I didn't like it any more than they did. The risks were enormous, but Charlie was out there somewhere and she needed us to do the right thing.

Once we were all agreed and fed, I swiftly fitted Melissa's mobile back together again. Called the last number to have dialled in.

"That you, Cochran?"

I glanced over at Terry. Another layer of guilt to add to the skins I was already wearing. My actions had now led to his identity being discovered. I wondered in how many ways that might come back to haunt my friend.

"It's Mike Lynch," I said. "I think we need to talk."

"I think you could be right, Mike. Or, should I do the talking and you do the listening?"

I bit down on my bottom lip. The arrogance of the man oozed down the connection. I wanted to bury this bastard. Deep and forever.

"Actually, it's you who needs to listen," I said. "I have a trade to suggest. Me for Charlie Dawson."

"I'm afraid that won't do, Mike. I told your mate, it has to be you and Melissa for the girl, or no deal."

"It's a different game now. Your sniper took one of us off the board. If me and Mel hand ourselves over, there's no one to take Charlie off your hands."

After a brief pause: "We'll drop her off outside a police station. How's that?"

"Not good enough."

Another pause, shorter this time. "No. I don't like it."

"Why not? Mel saw nothing, so she can't hurt you. It's me you really want."

"Don't flatter yourself, Lynch."

"You know what I mean. Melissa can never hurt you."

"And you think you can? Without your wounded comrade?"

I paused for thought. "You know what I'm saying. You don't need us both. It's a fair exchange. I'm the one who saw everything that happened in that lay-by."

This time there was a momentary silence at the other end. "I'll consider the deal. What exactly do you have in mind?"

"Good. So now listen closely."

I outlined the exchange agreement. After a few minor quibbles, the time and place were agreed upon.

Terry had meanwhile postponed his treatment whilst he made a couple of phone calls of his own on the burner phone given to me by Susan Healey. While we waited, the ex-doctor patched up my arm and gave me a jab of penicillin. My wound was deep enough that it would hurt for a while, but had caused no muscle damage. Ten minutes later Terry received a call-back. I wasted no time taking the phone off him afterwards and punching in the number provided.

When I revealed my identity to Chris Dawson, the man began ranting and screaming at me down the phone. At least a dozen threats to my life were made in less than a minute. I allowed the man to tire of his own voice before speaking again. In a calm, authoritative manner, I told my side of the story. Dawson listened.

When the moment came to tell him about Charlie's abduction, the inevitable reaction was heated and loud. But I sensed it was half-hearted by this time.

"Do you want your niece back, Mr Dawson?" I had asked.

"Of course I fucking want her back."

"Then listen to me."

That was forty minutes ago. It had been a huge wrench leaving Terry behind, but he was in good hands. And safe, I believed. I would not have left my friend there and driven away otherwise. As I drove I went over the plan time and again, seeing it from all different angles, from many different perspectives. Like all plans it was about as steadfast as a paper towel in a monsoon, but experience had taught me that you had to start somewhere. After that, all you could reasonably do was react and adapt to changing circumstances.

Ultimately it had been easier to persuade Charlie's captors than I had imagined it would be. Sure, the man had argued. But he had also been persuaded without too much of a fight. I guessed that in our opponent's head, having me in the bag was a positive step. And given he was never going to let Charlie go, the deal meant they would have two of their three targets, with the third close by and exposed. I was banking on that being their line of thinking.

Still it bothered me.

To continue with their conspiracy, they only needed Melissa and me. They did not need Charlie; she was too young to influence anything. So why had they not held out for a swap that would hand them both me and Mel. That arrangement had been requested, but not fought hard for.

I badly wanted to know why.

FORTY-TWO

From what I knew of the Otterburn Ranges, in the Northumberland National Park, some of the hills that comprise the territory were Bronze Age burial mounds. There was also evidence to suggest that Roman soldiers used the area as a training ground during their occupation of Britain. These days it is owned by the military, and is still used as a training area for warriors. Much is freely open to the public, particularly hikers. Others visit the area because of the graveyard.

Instead of human skeletons, the land is littered with the remains of tanks from different eras. Some still have their tracks and appear to be undamaged, if stained by rust and naturally camouflaged by moss. Others are in ruins, innards stripped out, guns and cannons missing, treads long gone. Rusting hulks, inviting the interest of enthusiasts and ghouls alike. There was a time when the tanks were joined by the husks of old airplanes, but they had been either removed or destroyed.

In nearby Holystone stood another of Terry Cochran's safe houses.

He had told me and Melissa where to find the spare key, and gave me the six-digit combinations to both an underground arms cache and a safe hidden away inside the house. As soon as he mentioned its location, the idea for a meeting place where the exchange could take place took root inside my head. It was about a five-hour drive north from Barton Mills, much of it at speed in good conditions on the A1. I kept the dial at just on the 70mph limit, my mind wandering all the time from the road to the situation we were about to confront.

"You all right, Mike?" Melissa asked at some point. From the look of concern she gave me, I guessed she had read my body language.

"About as right as I can be," I said. "Given the circumstances."

"You look… crushed."

I nodded. "I feel it. I think it's the sheer weight of responsibility."

"For what?"

For what? For her, for Charlie, for Susan's death, Terry's injuries, and the discovery of his identity by those who wished us harm. I thought about each pull on my guilt, my conscience. Ultimately it would do no good to burden Mel with my problems. We had plenty to confront together.

"For what comes next," I said instead.

Melissa nodded. I hoped she understood the magnitude of our situation. The awful consequences should it all go to shit. There were a hundred and one things I had probably not thought of. A hundred and one things that could go wrong. A hundred and one ways for us not to get out of this alive.

I smiled to myself. A hundred and fucking one glances in the rear-view mirror, hoping like hell I was half as good as Terry at this sort of thing.

As we continued to leave miles of road behind us, the landscape changed dramatically. From the flatlands of the Fens and Lincolnshire, to the industrialised outskirts of Sheffield, Doncaster and Leeds, past the Yorkshire hills and dales, back into northern industry represented by Newcastle Upon Tyne, before bursting into the bleak and hostile, yet glorious and beautiful sweeping Northumberland countryside. Thousands of sheep spread across acres of land, penned in by low wooden fences. We came off the main drag and immediately encountered winding, narrow roads. After a sharp bend, the River Cocquet lay to our left. It was fast running but shallow, white foam smashing into rocks and boulders squatting on the bed.

"Here we are," I said, spotting the gate on my right-hand side. Terry had told me to look out for one painted blue and white. I nosed the Toyota off the road and onto a small plot of dirt barely able to take a single vehicle. I jumped out of the truck and strode across to a stone wall to which the wooden gatepost was affixed. I studied the grey, mossy rocks. Terry had said that one of them would appear out of place, but to me they all looked alike. I brushed a couple with my hands, and finally saw what my friend had meant. One of the stones was clearly darker, cut from a seam containing iron I thought. I wriggled it, pulling it back towards me at the same time. After a few seconds, it gave and came away in my hand.

The key to the gate's padlock was my prize. I popped the stone back into place, unlocked the gate and pushed it open as far as it would go. After shifting the truck past the opening, I closed the gate behind us and snapped the padlock into place once more. The route up to the farmhouse, which I could see lying further up the hill and half tucked away behind a small cluster of sycamore trees, was no more than a dirt track ground out by years of pressure from various sets of tyres. I followed it all the way, the house becoming more impressive as we grew near.

"Your friend Terry must be raking it in if he has all these properties," Melissa remarked. "Why isn't he sunning himself in the Bahamas instead of lying on that bloody bed with bullet wounds in him?"

"Because I called him," I replied, stepping out of the truck's cab once more.

She looked at me. Shook her head. "If it hadn't been you it would have been someone else. Think of the security and weapons we've seen. What we'll undoubtedly find here, too. Your pal is hiding from something, Mike. Or someone. Maybe even lots of someone's. He's clearly financially able to go anywhere, but he chooses to remain. It's his life."

I let that sink in. Melissa was right. No matter what came his way, and irrespective of the personal price, Terry lived for the action. He used to refer to it as the "juice". Leaving the forces could never have meant retiring to a country estate, turning to farming, or basking on a yacht anchored in the Med. To Terry, retirement might just as well mean death. And if he had to go out, he would do so on his own terms.

"I only wish he was with us now," I said, turning towards the house.

"Well, he's not. But from all we've been through together these past couple of days, Mike, you may be all we need."

I felt my forehead crease. Flat-handed my chest. "Me? And whose army?"

Melissa stepped towards me. Peered up at me. "I mean it, Mike. Something changed in you after… after your friend got shot and killed. It was in there, had to always have been inside you all along, but it came out strongly after that. You took charge. You stepped up. You did what needed doing."

"Mel, I took charge and stepped up by calling for help. By running to my old friend and fellow marine, tail between my legs."

"Don't say that!" Her cheeks flushed, and anger flickered in her eyes.

"Hey," I said, reaching for her arm. "It's okay. I'm sorry."

"No, it's not. How do you think I feel when you talk yourself down like that? You're in charge now, Mike. You are the one who will get Charlie back for us, no matter who helps. You think calling Terry was a sign of weakness. I call it a show of strength. You weighed up the situation and you recognised the fact that we needed help. There's no shame in that. Just the opposite. And I need that same strength from you now, Mike. I need it if I'm going to get through this."

Tears spilled from her eyes. I pulled her close. Rested my cheek against her head. Said nothing at all. Just held her until she didn't need holding anymore.

***

By the time we left the farm, at six-thirty that evening, we had both fed and armed ourselves. The rendezvous point was on the B6341 road to Elsdon, in a lay-by on the left-hand side. The irony of that arrangement was not lost on either of us. This was the first stage, and the point at which it could all go badly wrong. I realised that if I had misjudged Chris Dawson, if the brother had been responsible for Ray's death and subsequent hunting down of those who survived the shooting, then myself and Melissa were almost certainly not going to survive this initial contact.

During the time we had spent at the safe house, I showed Melissa how to fire a handgun. In a storage area beneath one of the property's three outhouses, I located a Glock 26; a sub-compact semi-automatic weapon that was small and light. Its polymer grip had subtle grooves that would guide the fingers into forming a perfect grip, and the weapon would fire whether it was dirty, wet or had just been dropped in mud. It used 9mm rounds, and I forced Melissa to fire off a dozen at the trees which stood by the house as if protecting it.

"Weapon out," I said to her now. Knowing the Glock had no external safety lever, I added, "Rest it in your lap, and make sure you point the damned thing away from me."

My own SIG P226, chosen from the range offered by Terry's stash, was within easy reach. It was the tactical version, suppressed on the end of an extra length barrel, and equipped with a night sight. Its magazine held twenty 9mm rounds, and I had a whole stack of magazines available in a bag just behind the driver's seat. Resting on top of the bag I had placed a H&K assault rifle, complete with a 40mm under-barrel grenade launcher. It was both a brutal attack weapon and, using its red dot laser sighting, a precision execution tool.

I grinned at the thought and shook my head. Terry was doing nicely for farmhouses, but even better with his caches of weapons. He must have bought half the small arms in Afghanistan back home with him, and none of the old Russian shit. And right now, I was glad of it. If I harboured any doubts about my own abilities, I was at least confident in the equipment available to me.

To us.

It wouldn't do to forget the role Melissa might yet play.

The lay-by swept into view, and already parked up were two silver Jeep Grand Cherokees. Up to five men in each, I thought immediately. I slid the truck in behind the Jeeps, keeping my distance.

The plan was for Chris Dawson and one other man to join us at the truck. Keeping the engine running, I flashed the lights twice. Then I took the Sig in my left hand and nudged the suppressor up against the door. If I pulled the trigger, the shells would pass right through it and anyone who happened to be standing on the other side.

Ahead, two doors opened on the second Jeep. I did not recognise the first to exit; a massive black man with no discernible neck. I had heard of some muscle within the organisation who went by the name of Rhino, and this guy certainly fit the bill. The second, however, was a slightly older version of the man shot dead by the NCA cop in that other lay-by. Arms spread wide as instructed, the two moved slowly across to the truck. Dawson came my way, the other man stepped over to the passenger side.

"Watch him closely," I told Melissa. "I'll keep tabs on the Jeeps as well as Chris, so you just focus all of your attention on your guy. If he so much as reaches a hand inside a pocket, you treat him the same way you treated those trees earlier. You hear me?"

Melissa nodded. Her hands shook, I noticed. I could hardly blame her. I recalled my first ever firefight, and the worst part was the anticipation that unravelled slowly beforehand. "Hey," I said. "Look at me for a second."

She turned her head.

"You'll do great," I told her. "Think of Charlie. Think of what it means to get her back. I have confidence in you. You'll do what it takes, right?"

Melissa nodded.

"Good. Now, you don't look at anything but your man until he's back inside that Jeep."

Chris Dawson walked up alongside the Toyota's cab. He and I were at eye level. The window was already powered down. I nodded once. Dawson nodded back.

"I see you've brought friends," I said without preamble. "Are there others in position as arranged?"

"There are. Plus, I have another four Jeeps parked up at different locations both in and outside of Otterburn."

"I have arms and ammunition in the back for them."

"They have weapons."

"Not like these they don't. I have grenades and explosives, too. Claymore mines if we need them."

Dawson raised his eyebrows. A single sign that he was impressed.

"So, let's get right into it and deal with the elephant in the room," I said. "Like I told you on the phone, Mel here was not involved in your brother's murder. I just happened to be in the wrong place at the wrong time. I had no option but to take your brother's BMW in order to escape, and when I did so I had no idea whatsoever that Mel and your niece were lying in the footwell in the back."

Dawson narrowed his gaze, which until now had not been entirely neutral. "Say I believe you," he said. He growled like a bear when he spoke. "Why didn't Mel call me?"

I flashed a glance ahead. No movement. "I don't want to make you any more hostile than you already are, but when Mel and I discussed what we should do, I did raise the theory that you might be involved. Mel wasn't having any of that, and she did want to contact you. It was me who put thoughts inside her head. I don't know you, but it's not unknown for brothers to murder brothers."

The silence that followed caused me to shift a little in my seat. My hands regripped my weapon, finger now resting against the trigger guard. Around twenty-four hours earlier, I had faced men of war, men trained in battle, hardened by conflict. They were my enemies, and they were disciplined, their reactions logical. Dawson was unpredictable, and therefore far more dangerous.

The man braced his shoulders a little. Met my even gaze. "And how do you know that's not the case?" Dawson asked.

"I didn't. Not until just then. Had no option but to take a chance on you. But I see it now. In your eyes."

Another pause. Longer this time. I risked another check of the vehicles in front. Back to Dawson. Who sniffed the night air and reached up a hand. "I'm indebted to you, Mr Lynch. I'm Chris. I believe we've got a bit of business to get into."

FORTY-THREE

The wild and overgrown mounds of grass and heather at Otterburn Ranges are easily capable of hiding vast numbers of men. To make it harder still to spot a potential adversary, the undulating hillsides were now grainy and grey as the day leaked away to the west. Amidst it all lay those rotting shells of decommissioned tanks.

Yet I surveyed the meeting place with grim satisfaction.

A couple of hours earlier a van had pulled up to our rendezvous point. A nondescript black Ford Transit, it carried a far from commonplace cargo. It, and the two men who stepped out of the vehicle, were a surprise to everyone but me.

Melissa's eyes were wide. "Who are these men, Mike?"

"Terry sent them," I replied.

"So, you arranged this hours ago?"

"I did. And before you bollock me, I was using Terry's tactics. The less you knew the less you could tell."

Melissa did not argue.

Both men were of average height, but solidly built. Dressed all in black. Ready for action should it become warranted. The driver sought me out, introduced himself as Rufus, and shook my hand. "Any friend of Terry's and all that," he said.

I made sure my grip was firm. "I can't tell you how grateful I am. I know you could get into real trouble for doing this."

He dismissed my words as if they were unnecessary. We walked around to the back of the van and the passenger who had shared the cab with him threw open the door. Along both sides was an array of electronics equipment and monitors. At a swivel seat bolted to the van's floor was a third man, also dressed in black combat gear. In the centre of the floor stood a squat, dark grey object that looked like an enormous metallic bug.

"Let's get her up in the air, shall we," Rufus said. Just like Terry, he was all business.

The drone was ready to go, and as soon as it had been carried out of the back of the van and set on the floor, its fan-like propulsion system kicked into life.

"You know what I need to see?" I asked, climbing into the spot where the drone had been sitting.

The drone pilot nodded and gave me a thumbs-up. I squatted by his side as he took it up in the air. I turned my attention to one of the monitors. The drone was guided around the area I had previously discussed with Terry, offering me a perfect panoramic view of the battleground we were set to encounter. Reading the screen, I saw what I had hoped to see there. I tapped the pilot on the shoulder and winked at him. Then I placed a call to Chris Dawson, who had moved on moments before the arrival of the Transit.

When we were done, the drone came back in. Seconds later it replaced me inside the van. Rufus checked his watch and confirmed with me the time I wanted it back up in the air again. I felt good about things. We were all set.

"The two of us are volunteering to accompany the mission," the driver said, indicating the passenger as well. "This is Gary."

I raised a hand at the other man, then abruptly shook my head. "No. Thank you, both of you, but no. This is not your battle, and I've already got Terry hurt. These past couple of days have cost me dearly so far. I don't want anyone else on my conscience."

The two black-clothed men swapped glances. Then Rufus said, "I misspoke. When I said we were volunteering, I actually meant we were insisting. Terry led all three of us through so many shite encounters, I can't even begin to describe to you. This is just another of those, and I think you could do with our help."

I closed my eyes for a moment, overcome with relief. I had meant every word I'd said, and it was great that Dawson's men were available to us, but I was also immensely relived to have these professionals working alongside us.

Now, having watched with interest the movement on the hillside with the aid of the drone cameras, I could not have been more pleased to have three warfare experts on my side. As expected, our adversaries had arrived early, checking out the tanks as potential hiding positions, before fading back into the shadows. I would not have been so obvious as to position Dawson's men inside the ruined machines, but I respected the fact that our opponents were thorough. I left the black Transit and made my way back to the truck before thumbing in the phone number on the burner.

The call was answered on the third ring. Through my binoculars I studied the black-clad men I was still able to spot further up the hillside, looking to see if any of them put a phone to their ear. They didn't.

"Are you ready to do this?" the man I had spoken to earlier in the day asked.

"Not exactly," I replied.

"Don't fuck me about, Mike. You want the child or not?"

"Of course. Charlie is with you now, yes?"

"She is."

"So, I can speak to her, then."

"No, you cannot. When are we going to get the ball rolling? The child is tired and scared. It's time you settled this."

"You seem to be in one hell of a hurry. Look, you're a professional, man. Act like one. See the big picture. We don't need to make this more complicated than it already is."

"I don't have time for this, Mike. Let's just get this over and done with."

I didn't like it one little bit. I was expecting to get double-crossed. Was counting on it, in fact. There was something so out of kilter here, though. I felt it clearly. It could be something as simple as the man being supremely confident, giving off an arrogance I could not abide. But the thing that had been nagging me all along now came sharply into focus. Something the man had said when our arrangements were first made. Something I could not ignore.

"I'll get back to you," I said, and killed the call.

Melissa was looking at me, mouth gaping wide. "What the hell, Mike? I thought this was it. I thought you were calling to give the go-ahead."

I nodded. "Yeah, that's what I thought I was doing, too. Thing is, Mel, I told you before that something didn't feel right. Well, it still doesn't. I need to think hard about something he said to me earlier. I need to try and understand what he meant by it."

"So, what was it? What did he say?"

There was a time and place to share information. I did not think this was such a time. I had an idea. Before giving myself the opportunity to question it, I acted. "I'll just be a couple of minutes," I told her. Then without giving Melissa any time to react, I climbed out of the truck and walked away from it. After twenty paces I dialled the same number again.

"I really hope you're ready to go this time, Lynch."

"What happened to calling me Mike? We're not friends anymore?"

"Just… just get on with it. You are really trying my patience."

I lowered my voice. "You said something when we first spoke. I thought you were insulting me. Now I'm asking myself if it was something more than that."

"Okay… such as?"

"When I mentioned the change in plans, that all you really needed was me, you told me not to flatter myself. The more I thought about it the more I asked myself if that wasn't an insult, what did it mean."

"Go on. I'm listening."

I bet you are, I thought. *Playing me all along.* "I also recall you talking about one more piece of collateral damage. Thing is, if I am that collateral damage, then what is Melissa? Why wasn't she being viewed as such? Both of those statements got me thinking. I asked myself if you needed me at all. Whether what I saw or did not see in that lay-by was irrelevant to you. And if so, then perhaps it's Melissa you really want. That in reality you've wanted her all along."

"And why would I or anyone else be interested in Miss Andrews?"

There was something in his voice that spurred me on. "I don't have the answer to that. But, if there is a good enough reason for you to want Melissa, and you can convince me of that, then I may be in a position to offer her up to you."

"Why would you do something like that, Lynch?"

Now there was interest. Genuine interest.

"Because I'm a prick. Frankly, I want nothing to do with this anymore. I've done my bit, gone as far as I'm willing to go. I'd want Charlie in return, of course. But if it's Melissa you want, I can give her to you."

"Okay. That sounds like a plan."

"Like I say, I would need to know why."

The line was silent for a few seconds. Then the man said, "Ian Ringrose. The name is familiar to you, yes?"

I scoured my memory. "The arms dealer?" I asked.

"That's the one. A man with a growing reputation. Now looking for a peerage and expected to be in the next honours list. Being groomed to go far in the political sphere."

"So, what the hell has Melissa got to do with an arms dealer?"

"She was his secretary for a short while."

The big shot Melissa had mentioned working for. The employer who wanted her to be more than an employee. "Okay," I said, still not seeing the problem.

"And his lover."

"Ah." I could scarcely breathe. I had guessed right after all. The shooting in the lay-by was never about Ray Dawson. The hit had been on Melissa. I glanced back at the truck. This nightmare had nothing to do with my stumbling upon and then fleeing the murder scene. I had been hunted down because of the person I had inadvertently driven away from the scene.

"How does all that lead to her being on a hit list," I asked.

The man paused. But he was too far along to stop now.

"During a recent in-depth vetting process, the security services discovered that someone had, during their time with Mr Ringrose, access to confidential data. Specifically, data linking Ringrose and a couple of high-powered men from Whitehall, with arms sales to the Taliban. In turn, those sales can be directly linked to the deaths of British troops in Afghanistan and now to ISIS."

"Fuck!" I breathed.

"Fuck indeed. After an exhaustive search, the identity of that person was eventually discovered in a safety deposit box belonging to Ringrose. Apparently, he retained it to use as leverage if necessary. Unfortunately, it revealed Miss Andrews to be that employee with access to the data."

"You say she had access to it, but you don't know if she actually knows anything about it?"

"That's correct. But you understand what it's like with these people – they don't like to take chances. And they certainly do not leave behind any loose ends."

I felt my stomach clench. My free hand balled into a fist, and my lower jaw started to ache with pressure. "And you're happy with this?" I demanded. "You're ex-military, you must be. You're happy covering up for what these people did? Selling arms to people who used them against us."

"I'm paid to do a job, Lynch. I don't work for the forces anymore. My private security company has premises and salaries to pay for. I can't pick and choose the work I like. It comes my way, I carry it out."

"So, you're just another bloody mercenary."

"If you like. I'm not going to debate morals with a man who is about to give up the women he's with so as he can get the hell out of Dodge."

"Like I said before, you're a professional. You won't let me go just like that."

There was a moment's pause before a response came. "I won't pretend. It's likely that once we've secured Miss Andrews, the next target will be you. On the other hand, by the time that happens, you could be long gone. Over the hill and far away. I'm sure you can live off the grid, one step ahead. I may even be able to persuade the higher powers that it serves no useful purpose hunting you down when you have no intention of telling your story."

"No way they will take that chance." I knew I was right. Someone wanted Melissa dead because of what she might know. Whatever happened, my name would remain on a kill list for as long as I lived.

"I suspect that's so. Whatever. As you figured out, Lynch, it is Miss Andrews that they want. Let's get that bit of business squared away first."

I ran it through my head one last time. "So, I hand her in to you, you hand Charlie to me. You get what you want. I get time to make sure Charlie is safe."

"And a head start for you, too. Don't forget that bit."

"I'm not forgetting anything."

"Then that's a deal I can make. And this conversation never happened, Mr Lynch."

"Give me ten minutes," I said.

Back at the Toyota, as I climbed into the cab and took my seat behind the wheel, I felt all of Melissa's scrutiny bearing down on me. "Well?" she demanded, arms crossed.

"There's been a change of plan," I told her.

FORTY-FOUR

High up on the moors stood a line of three FV4201 Chieftain tanks, each built around the mid-seventies. They were placed as if in convoy, though none of them had moved an inch in over a decade. Primarily now used for fake bombing runs and range target practice on live round days, the once-renowned military weapons still managed to look mighty despite their garlands of rust and veils of moss.

Having trained several times on these very moors, I was familiar with the monuments to what was once the most formidable battle tank in the world, with by far the most effective armour and largest main gun of any tank ever designed up until that point. Older statesmen around the base invariably mentioned hero worship when drink-fuelled discussions inevitably turned to these incredible machines. They spoke of times, not so long ago, when the British led the way with innovative design and military might.

Now they were simply a focal point for a clandestine meeting.

Breaking into the Otterburn Ranges had presented no problem at all for me. There were the official methods of entry, and then there were those I had come to know well when returning from nights out at local pubs. A padlocked gate into an open field was the sum of the barrier we had to overcome. Melissa and I sat in the Toyota truck, silent, contemplative. Shortly into the incline I had found it necessary to engage the 4x4 drive, and after that the truck managed the climb easily. I was grateful for the hard ground. In the depths of winter or even a wet spring, our passage would have proven impossible.

Fifty yards away from the trio of abandoned tanks, I switched from sidelights to headlights. I glanced across at Melissa.

"How are you doing?" I asked.

She nodded, but said nothing. Her eyes scoured the hillsides, and the metal giants standing waiting for us. I understood: this was the point we had been leading up to, the final stage where it could all go wrong. With renewed guilt, I wondered how Mel would feel if she knew the whole truth.

At the furthest reach of the truck's headlights, a man dressed all in dark camouflage stepped out from behind the tank taking up the centre position of the three. He held up a hand, palm outwards. I stood on the brake and brought the Toyota to a standstill.

"Wait here," I told Melissa, then climbed down from the vehicle.

I walked forwards until the man and I were just five yards apart. Despite the warmth of the day seeping into the night hours, the wind blew hard up here on these exposed hillsides, and the fierce gusts caused me to draw in a sharp intake of breath. Both of us were buffeted by the squalls.

"Do we still have our deal?" I called out.

"It's why I'm here."

"I want to know who I'm dealing with. What's your name?"

"Why does that matter?"

"Exactly."

The man smiled and spread his hands. "Faulkener. Now can we please move this on."

"Let me see Charlie."

"She's fine where she is."

"I don't doubt it. A health update is not what I asked for, though."

"Don't push your luck, Lynch. The girl is in my vehicle on the other side of the rise."

"Then I suggest you go and fetch her. I'm not allowing Melissa to get out of that truck unless Charlie is right by your side. You know the deal." I lowered my voice. "You let Charlie start walking over to my truck. I'll make sure Mel comes the other way."

Faulkener's face changed in an instant. Gone was the false bonhomie. In its place, an implacable stare. And a SIG Sauer appeared as if from nowhere in his hand.

"You really are a bloody fool, Lynch," he said. "Did you actually believe that if I had the girl here, and Miss Andrews here, that I wasn't also going to take advantage of having you here at the same time?"

"No," I replied. "I didn't."

As I said the words, two sets of headlights, one on each side of the hillside, sprang to life. Two large engines, also. Gears whined as two vehicles encroached at speed. Before leaving the Toyota's cab I had dialled Dawson's number on my phone, then pocketed the device as I climbed out. Dawson and his men had listened in on every word. At the pre-arranged phrase, they had entered their part of the plan.

The man looked from side to side, then back at me. "Company, Lynch? You're just one surprise after another."

He ought to have been more wary, but his tone was mocking. I caught it immediately. The two silver SUVs drew closer. When they were fifty yards away, Faulkener said: "Take them!"

From the other side of the tanks, fierce, powerful engines could now be heard. Four quad-bikes slipped swiftly into view, two encircling each Jeep. Eight dark-clothed men appeared, also from behind the line of tanks. Their weapons were evident, but they held their fire as they took up their positions. The quad riders also held semi-automatic rifles. I took it all in with one sweep of my gaze. Outnumbered and outgunned. In an ordinary battle, the disparity in numbers might not matter. But there was a world of difference between well-trained and experienced mercenaries and a bunch of hoodlums.

Unless, that is, you turned things to your advantage.

"We're good to go," I said. This time into a two-way radio device.

The earth around us erupted. Or at least, that's what it looked like to me. From deep within the dunes of grass and heather where they had been concealed for hours, further armed men appeared. Dozens of them, forming a tight circle. And two of the men were the real deal.

"Lay down your weapons!" cried Rufus, his voice now amplified by electronic equipment. "You men are surrounded. If you fire upon us, you will be fired upon. If you attempt to leave, you will be fired upon. If you do anything other than follow my instructions, you will be fired upon. This is the Special Air Services."

Even I felt intimidated by that, and they were on our side. They were security colleagues of Terry Cochran's these days, but they had once served in the regiment with him. Their drone had helped us form a mental grid, its on-board instruments locating deep ridges ideal for creating camouflaged areas beneath which more of Dawson's men could shelter until the time was right. My initial plan had been honed by Terry's brothers in arms, and it had made all the difference. Seeing Rhino there towering over the others, a huge shotgun in his meaty hands, also made me feel hugely confident of the outcome here. I'd been told that the smaller, bearded man by his side was every bit as brutal, vicious and determined. I felt euphoric at the thought of what we were about to achieve.

By now the SUVs had stopped. As had the bikes. Then one of the riders acted irrationally. Turned the quad and started speeding further up and to the left of the hillside they were on. As it sped past one of the SUVs, someone inside the vehicle tossed a few rounds in its direction. As if part of a devastating automatic chain reaction, gunfire echoed and flashed around the moorlands. I dashed back down to the truck, around to the passenger side and threw myself inside, spreading myself across Melissa. I hit her hard, and she cried out in pain. My only thought was that even if I had cracked one of her ribs, my bulk and the pain it had caused was better to endure than a bullet. It was getting to be a regular event.

To my relief the exchange of fire lasted only seconds.

I raised myself up and turned to look over my shoulder and out of the windscreen. Terry's colleagues, Rufus and Gary, were busy securing their targets. But then I heard another engine, and from behind the middle tank a Humvee burst out into the open, flashing by the two circles of men, and narrowly avoiding a heavy collision with the Toyota. I watched it rattle by, and as I caught site of its interior I saw Charlie's hands and face pressed up against the side window, mouth wide open in a scream I could not hear.

"Get out!" I immediately yelled at Melissa, climbing over her now and sliding into the driver's seat. "Go and find help!"

She stared at me. Mute. I leaned across, threw open the passenger door and told her to go. With my other hand, I pushed at her side, causing flares of pain in her eyes.

"He wants you!" I cried. "You were the target, Mel. It's you they wanted all along."

"What are you talking about?" she screamed at me.

The Hummer was getting away, Charlie inside it.

"I don't have time to explain. Mel, they have Charlie. I have to go and you can't be with me."

Whether it was the urgency in my voice, the words themselves, or the fear in my eyes, I had no clue. All I knew was that it worked. Melissa jumped out of the cab.

Dismissing the memory of when, just a few days ago, I had acted with similar recklessness, I started the engine, spun the vehicle around and hammered the bouncing, jolting truck in chase just as fast as I could push it. The Toyota bucked and jerked, metal groaned as if at any moment it might all give way. The massive 3.0 litre V6 petrol engine screamed. My world was a blur of excruciating sound and jarring movement, but I had eyes only for the Humvee fast approaching the foot of the hillside some 200 yards ahead of me.

Seemingly only moments later it disappeared from view as it rounded a copse of trees away to my left. I wondered whether Faulkener knew these moors as well as I did. Chances were he did, having probably trained here as well at some point. If the Hummer kept on going the way it was headed, it would emerge at the bottom of the gully with just a wire fence to smash through on its way to firm tarmac.

I realised I had no chance of catching the all-terrain vehicle before that happened, but once on the road if I could keep it in sight I would have the advantage. Just stay alive that long, I silently implored the truck. I can't let Charlie down now.

FORTY-FIVE

Three minutes later as I pushed the Toyota around a curve behind the trees, its headlights picked out a gap in the mangled fence, whose posts splayed and splintered, its wire twisted outward. There was no sign of the Humvee.

I reached the road and brought the truck to a halt. My window was down. I listened hard. Behind me from back up the hillside I heard raised voices, men shouting at one another. Somewhere there was also the low growl of a heavy-duty vehicle. But I couldn't tell from which direction. Thinking quickly, I backed up a few yards and stared through the beam of bright headlights on the dark road.

There.

Trails of dirt and residues of tyre rubber.

Headed east.

I put my foot to the floor and pounded the truck in that direction.

The road was now ideal for my vision, running straight and true, the terrain flat and unobstructed. I flew by a turning to my left which I saw was a T-junction. For a moment, I wondered if the Hummer had turned off there, but took a chance that the mercenary would not have wanted to decrease his options.

I looked for lights, but reasoned that they might well have been extinguished. It was a hard call, because with the night now set in, moving swiftly without even sidelights on these roads could prove fatal. There again, when all around were dark moorlands, any sort of illumination made life a hell of a lot harder to lose a tail.

As if to prove a point, I hit a right-hand bend too fast and the truck failed to hold its line. The Toyota slewed off the road onto the wide verge, and it was only then that I noticed the single lane track running off to my left, almost parallel to the way I had just come. As I corrected the steering, the truck narrowly avoided ploughing into another sign. A T-junction yet again. I took a gamble and chose to ignore it for precisely the same reason as the previous one.

A minute or so later two circles of stone wall, one either side of the road, swam into view from the murk beyond my headlights. I recalled having seen them before. I had driven this route many years ago, and now started thinking ahead, searching my memory. I remembered just a split second before I saw it: a turn to my left. I looked ahead. Saw nothing. Looked across to the left. Nothing. Had to make a choice as the road was coming up quick.

Then it was there.

I slowed, having trouble deciding.

I figured Faulkener would want to deviate eventually. And if he hadn't already done so, onto one of the roads behind me, then this was perhaps the ideal moment.

Hitting the brake hard, I threw the truck left. Ignored a dirt track that almost immediately branched off further to my left. It looked as if it led nowhere that might offer the chance for evasion. I could tell we were headed deeper into the moorlands again, the Toyota's main beam picking out distant gorges and crests nestling side by side on an undulating landscape. Coming up ahead were three more choices. A left turn first, but I was also aware of another on the right-hand side shortly afterwards. Or I could press straight on.

I tried to imagine what Faulkener might do. Opted for another left. Slowed, tapped the brake and started the turn. My mind was still courting the idea of the other turning, when, on the far-right periphery of my vision I caught a flash of two red orbs twinkling in the distance.

Tail lights.

I slowed, but did not stop as I manoeuvred away from the turn, back onto the road and headed for the next turning now coming up fast on my right. Grateful for grassy verges, I briefly wondered if I might now be following a different vehicle altogether. I felt I had to take the chance.

Still pushing the Toyota as much as it would take, I reasoned that if I could now see the Humvee then I could also be seen. If it were me being chased down, I would stop somewhere and seek to put an end to this chase. One way or another. Had I considered the same scenario a couple of days ago, the decision would have been very different. I wondered if I had ever changed so much as a person in such a short space of time.

I decided it didn't matter.

I had one goal, and one goal only: rescue Charlie.

What I *was* certain of was that if the Hummer driver wanted to stage an end game, then I was now prepared for it.

Edging closer, I exhaled a huge sigh of relief as the distinct desert camouflage colours of the Hummer were now clearly visible. I followed as the fleeing vehicle took a left. Up ahead, away on the offside of our vehicles, I saw a dark mass. As we drew closer I could make out two lines of long huts, separated by about fifty yards, and a two-storey building at the far end that linked to the huts to form an elongated U-shape. Something sparked in my memory. I thought back to my training in this area, and realised we had come upon a temporary barracks which had long since been allowed to become every bit as derelict as the tanks back on the plains.

"Now," I said, as if able to control the thoughts of the man ahead. "Do it now."

With a shimmy from its rear end, the Humvee left the tarmac without braking, hit a dirt road to its right. There was a two-man security hut about eighty yards in. Between it and a narrow wooden post on the other side of the track was a chain stretched out as a barrier, the steel glinting in the pale moonlight. It had no chance as the Humvee smashed through it and carried on towards the crop of buildings.

I followed it without pause. My guess was that my adversary would bolt into one of the buildings with Charlie, and then set himself up in a prime position to attack. I hoped Faulkener would choose one of the long accommodation huts. The two-storey had been an administration building, but since falling into disrepair it had been stripped out and used solely for training purposes. It was set up as a defence post, and the higher ground was crucial.

For a moment, I considered holding back, calling for reinforcements. Tactically it was the right call. On the other hand, it could promote a siege mentality. And whilst I doubted Faulkener would harm Charlie deliberately, any firefight from multiple weapons could prove fatal. As could a unit breach. No, I was convinced that the only way to resolve this was for me to face this man one-on-one. You had to live – and sometimes die – by such decisions. Right now, I felt like a man capable of making those sort of decisions again. A man adept enough to achieve a successful outcome. The only outcome that mattered.

Getting Charlie back.

As I had feared, my quarry headed straight for the larger building at the far end of the small complex. I looked on as the man exited the Humvee with a wriggling and screaming Charlie tucked under one arm, an M4 clipped to the webbing of his black combat jacket. He sped towards the twin doors to the centre of the building, aimed a kick at the narrow divide between them, a third of the way up. They exploded inward and the two figures were swiftly consumed by the building's dark core.

Cursing, I drew up alongside the long hut to my right. My opponent now held the physical upper hand having entered the administration building. There was one advantage I hoped to maintain, however: I had trained here.

I knew this complex well.

Using the truck as a shield, I wrestled my backpack into place and leapt from the Toyota towards one of three doors on this side of the hut. I had noticed it was leaning askew, hanging off its hinges. I had no need to pause before I was inside.

The long hut was empty save for debris. At the far end to my left, tucked away in the corner, there was a door. This, I recalled,

led to a short passageway, at the end of which was another door that opened inwards. Beyond, a set of double doors leading into the ground floor of the main building itself. Further on, a stairway running up to the second level. I pulled out a torch, switched it to a red beam and followed the path my memory had created for me.

At the door which pulled inward, I paused. Took a couple of deep breaths. If the man I was hunting knew about this method of entry, then he could easily be waiting for the door to move. I was an impossible target to miss from short range. I hefted my H&K, set the laser sight to on. The red dot was reassuring, but only if I managed to get through this entry unscathed.

I yanked it back, allowing less time for hinge-squeal. The cry it gave out was loud, but short. I was not met by a shit-storm of bullets, so I crept beyond the door and reassessed. Faulkener was good, and could only have chosen this building to make a stand because of its height advantage. There were two stairways. The central staircase opened up towards the far wall. I knew that it went up to an area of open floor where original rooms remained and office partitions had been torn down.

I licked my lips, again asking myself if it would be better to have support here for this. I came up with the same answer. Charlie's safety was now my prime concern, and whilst the regiment troopers were the best in the business and with the help of Dawson's men had easily handled the situation back on the moors, I felt time was against me. People had died, and who really knew what this man Faulkener was capable of? Perhaps he was the calibre of man who could easily and without conscience conceive of using Charlie as a human shield.

Taking the stairs slowly, I ascended in darkness. I opted not to use the torch at this point, wanting to avoid detection for as long as possible. Each step took an age, as litter and debris was strewn across the stairs and I needed to avoid kicking anything down them that would alert the mercenary to my presence. I hoped the man was focussed on the central stairway and not this one. I was counting on him not even being aware of it.

With one foot raised to take the next step up, the other firmly planted, I heard a scuffing sound. Not me. Couldn't be. Close, though. My heart raced even faster. This was going to get lively any time soo–

Right then the staircase filled with the sound of several double rounds being fired off. I didn't know how many, the noise echoing off the walls around me. All I knew was that none of them had struck me. I had seen the muzzle flash, chunks of wall plaster vanishing in a puff of dust, and as soon as I'd recovered from the volley of shots aimed in my direction, I fired off several of my own.

I ducked as more projectiles came my way, slamming into the walls and cement stairs, sending further clouds of dust and spurts of concrete shrapnel into the air. I fired back, raking across the stairwell opening above me. I switched to full auto and sprayed the remainder of the magazine. The reload took only seconds. When I was ready to go again I stood and listened, holding my breath. Heard only my own frenetic heartbeat and panting.

Remaining in place, still listening intently, I thought about what to do next. One more flight and I would have only a narrow shield of corner wall to hide behind, before being fully exposed to Faulkener.

I asked myself what choice I had.

There was none.

I took the seven treads of the staircase flight as carefully as the previous ones. Edged back against the sliver of wall standing between me and open space. I checked the walls and floor for the tell-tale red dot of a laser sight, but there was nothing. Every breath was proving more difficult than the last. I could only imagine what my pulse rate was, adrenaline flooding my system.

I heard rather than saw the object as it first cut through the air and then hit the end wall to my right. It bounced back and skittered along the floor towards me. I kicked out, and more in luck than judgement managed to send the device hurtling down the stairwell. I crouched low and closed my eyes in anticipation, thinking it likely to be a flash-bang.

It wasn't.

The sound of the full explosive detonation was immense. I missed the initial white flash, but my eyes automatically sprang open in time to see flame punching up the chute formed by the stairwell, followed by thick smoke. My ears were now screaming. I sank down further, getting as low as I could whilst still remaining mobile. As the sound of the explosion ebbed away, the smoke hung thick against the ceiling but thankfully began dispersing into the wide-open expanse of the first floor.

"You still with me, Lynch?" a voice called out.

For a moment or two I considered not responding. It was the oldest trick in the book. The surprise was that the man had opened a dialogue at all. I knew I needed to take this opportunity and expand upon it.

"Yeah," I said. "Why wouldn't I be?"

Faulkener laughed. "You immortal, Lynch? Or just immune to bullets and bombs?"

"Neither. Just better at this than you give me credit for. So, listen up, why go through this bullshit anymore? There's no point now. Let me take the kid. You go one way, we'll go the other. You forget me, I'll forget you."

"You know something, Lynch, I wish I could. I really do. It's not your fault you fell into this tub of crap. That idiot Hendricks was only supposed to hit the woman. I guess he saw an opportunity to get a two-fer – the target and his gangster nemesis. This was all so fucking avoidable."

"So then let us go. What stake do you have in it now?"

"You've seen me now, Lynch. You know my name."

"As do others by now. You gain nothing from continuing this."

"Like your friend Cochran, I can go dark any time I please," Faulkener said. "But I can't go all the way and leave you to identify me. Cochran, I can't leave alive because I know he'll stop at nothing in coming after me when we're done here today. So, when I'm done with you, it's his turn."

I took a breath. I was only buying time, knowing Faulkener was never going to let me walk away from this. I took one last shot. "Hey, I understand your target was Melissa. I understand you need me and Terry gone as well. But there's no need for you to hold on to Charlie, is there? You only took her in the first place to lure us into a meet, knowing you didn't have time to continue the firefight before the police arrived. So, do the decent thing and let her go."

"The decent thing? Did you really just say that? I can't believe you were ever one of us. As it happens, Lynch, I do have a role for the child to play still. Currently she is tied up and gagged in one of the far offices. I've attached a small explosive to her, which is on a timer. I'm not going to tell you how much time she has, just that every second you delay stepping out gives her less on the countdown."

"You're bluffing!" I called out. I thought I was right, but had no baseline by which to judge this man.

"Easy to say when it's not your life about to end."

"Not even you would do that to a little kid, Faulkener."

"Wrong. Especially me, Lynch."

Hanging my head, I spat out a wad of phlegm: smoke from the grenade explosion had dipped inside my throat. It didn't matter if Faulkener was bluffing or not, I thought. There was no way I could risk finding out I was wrong.

I stood and stepped out from behind the wall.

The red dot that I had searched for earlier came almost instantly, wavering over my neck and face. Faulkener was taking the possibility of body armour out of the equation.

I dropped my weapon, allowing it to clatter to the floor amongst the rubble. Raised both hands. In the dark recesses beyond I saw nothing other than the laser source. "Tell me," I said. "Were you bluffing?"

"You'll never know," Faulkener said. He took a step forward and prepared to fire.

The explosion that occurred next had to have been unscripted, for if his reaction was anything to go by, it took Faulkener by surprise every bit as much as it did me. The rooms at the far end spouted flame and smoke, throwing out debris in a vast, billowing cloud. I was shocked, but whilst he ducked and turned his head in the direction of the blast, I ducked and swept up my weapon.

The gunfire we exchanged next was copious but inexact. As we moved around one another, our trigger fingers remained depressed. Each of us hid behind whatever we could find. The gunfire was continuous, but it stopped coming my way seconds before my weapon clicked on empty. I peered around a filing cabinet, and saw Faulkener turned sideways on, his weapon pointed in the opposite direction from me.

Only then did my fragmented mind allow me to dwell on what the explosion had meant.

Charlie.

Enraged by the man's inhumanity that had caused the loss of such an innocent life, I reloaded, sprang out from my shelter and fired at him once more. The same sort of blind defiance that had overtaken me back in the car park in Chippenham rose up again. Faulkener turned, but too late. He took several rounds that twisted his body and threw it backwards. They put him down, but not out. His body armour would see to that. I walked towards him, still firing. He tried to wriggle away, but I gained on him and eventually stood over him.

Faulkener stared up at me, blood bubbling from his mouth. His lips and teeth were smeared with it as he laughed. "Take me in," he said. "My people will have me out again within an hour."

My hearing was still unclear. Chest heaving, I said to him, "What did you say?"

His laughter continued. My eyes flickered to the devastating scene behind him, the area in which he said Charlie had been secreted now alive with flame and dense smoke.

"What did you say?" I asked him again, this time shouting the words.

"I said, take me in. My people–"

He never got a chance to complete the sentence.

FORTY-SIX

fter firing the two shots that ended his life, I gave Faulkener no more attention than I would a dead rat. I dashed past him and made my away across to the far end of the upper floor, where splintered wood and shattered walls spoke of the devastation that had occurred there. The flames were everywhere, forming a barrier I simply could not cross. With all my heart, I wanted to get in there, to search for Charlie, but I knew there was nothing I could do for her now. She could not have survived the explosion.

I heard a sound then, and guessed it had to be my hearing playing tricks on me.

It came again. I knew it could only be my imagination, because it sounded so much like–

Melissa.

I ran across to the front of the building, stared out and down through one of the many windows shattered by the blast.

There, leaning up against the truck, was Melissa.

In her arms she carried Charlie.

And Charlie was very much still alive.

I got out of there as quickly as I could, taking the stairs two at a time, overcome with unadulterated joy and complete bemusement. I sped across to the pair of them, listening rapturously to the joyous sound of Charlie complaining.

"What the... how the..?" I started to say, uncertain as to whether this was a dream or that I had not survived after all.

"I jumped into the back of the truck before you pulled away," Melissa explained. "I saw and heard from down here what was happening. I knew that you were keeping him busy, so I crept up the stairs, worked my way behind him and found Charlie in one of the rooms. The grenade was only taped to her, so I unwrapped it and then as we ran for it. I pulled the pin and tossed it behind me. After firing at you first, that guy got off a few shots in our direction as well, but I knew you'd finish him off for us, Mike. I believed it with all my heart. You did finish him off, right?"

I nodded. Thought about those final two shots directly into Faulkener's unprotected head.

"Yes, I finished him off."

Melissa nodded. She held Charlie out towards me. "Good," she said. "Take her for me would you. I have a terrible pain in my chest. I think you broke my rib earlier."

I took the squealing Charlie from her. The kid looked absurdly pleased to see me, and wrapped her arms around my neck and started weeping. Then I looked at Melissa more closely and saw the blood on her clothes.

"Mel?" I said.

"I don't feel at all well," she said. Then her eyes flickered and rolled back, her body swayed and she slumped in a heap on the floor.

***

For twenty-four hours we were all kept apart. The investigation was broad and carried out by multiple agencies. Moving only between a holding cell to an interview room at the grand old red-brick Newcastle City Centre Police Station during that entire time, I bitched about my treatment to all who grilled me. It was only after I requested a solicitor that the police – at least – relented.

The spooks were a different matter.

I took each different agency – police, NCA, the counter-terrorism unit, MI5 – through everything that had happened to me, Melissa and Charlie, since the shooting and killing of Ray Dawson. The only issue I refused to discuss was Terry Cochran's involvement. It didn't matter to me that they insisted Terry had himself detailed his every step from the initial point of contact from me to the point where Mel and I drove off leaving him about to undergo surgery. If his name came up I declined to comment.

The two men from the security services – neither of whom identified themselves – were particularly interested in that one thing I refused to talk about. All manner of charges and threats were mentioned, but the solicitor provided to me by Chris Dawson batted them away each time. Twenty hours in, I was told that the police had cleared me of any involvement in the murder of either Ray Dawson or Susan Healey, Terry having confirmed his understanding of events relating to Dawson. Charges were being considered still at that point for what had happened at both safe houses, but the feeling was that the argument for self-defence was almost certain to be upheld.

The spooks kept at it for another two hours. Finally, they walked away, though they insisted they were unsatisfied with my lack of cooperation and would be questioning me further about the time Terry and I had spent together, as well as the events at the abandoned barracks. Two hours after that, I was released.

My solicitor, Carl Ingham, informed me that Terry was likely to be detained further. I met up with Chris Dawson in his suite at a nearby hotel, where we waited together for further news. The enormous black muscle sat at a table at the far end of the suite, chatting softly with the smaller, wiry man with scarring on his bearded face.

"You are going to look after Terry as well, aren't you?" I asked of the gangster.

"Absolutely. You and your mate only ever have to pick up the phone for help even after today is long over. My brief was going between the two of you, which is why things were delayed. Those MI5 bods really have a beef with your pal, though."

I nodded. "I suspect he worked, or may even still work for them at times. Off book, of course."

"Yeah. That was my understanding from Carl. The problem being that this Faulkener character may have been one of their own as well."

"It's a murky old world out there," I said.

"Yeah. I'm familiar with murk."

I nodded. "I think I'm pretty much in the clear. For the time being. There's a lot to unravel still. I worry about Terry, though. He gave up three safe houses to us, two of which are now definitely blown and which he cannot ever use again. His three colleagues melted away into the background before the police arrived on the scene, so they are out of the picture at least. Terry is very much the opposite. I don't want to tell you your business, Mr Dawson, but you owe him big time."

"Please, call me Chris. And for what it's worth, I agree with you. We'll cover any losses he has. Yourself as well. Whatever is necessary after you put yourselves at risk to get our Charlie back."

"How's she bearing up?" I asked.

Dawson shrugged. "Kids are resilient. We haven't told her about Ray yet, but she's been asking for him every ten minutes, so that's something we'll be dealing with a bit later on."

"But she knows Melissa is dead?"

"Mel collapsed in front of her, blood everywhere. It was not something we could hide."

One of Faulkener's final stray shots had not been so stray after all.

I nodded. "By the time paramedics arrived on the scene, Mel was already gone. I kept Charlie away from the worst of it, but the poor little mite was devastated at seeing Mel in such a bad way. I've had a long time to think about it now, I've questioned myself harshly. I just don't know if there was anything I could have done differently."

"Mr Cochran gave a pretty full account to Carl," Dawson said. "Everything he learned from both you and Mel whilst you were all together, plus what he got from his colleagues who were out there with you on the moors. Plus what I saw and heard myself. You did your best. You tried to prevent Mel from chasing that bastard down. You couldn't have known it would end that way, Mike."

"Maybe. Charlie is unharmed though?" I asked him. "Physically, I mean."

"She is. Fortunately, the men who had her treated her okay."

"I'm very glad to hear it."

"And yourself? How's your injury?"

"Fine." I reflexively glanced down at the bandage now covering what had amounted to little more than a flesh wound received during the firefight. It was as minor as the one from back in Thetford. "Could have been much worse."

It felt strange sitting there listening to this gangster ask about my welfare. A man who not so long ago was after my blood. He sat forward, meeting my gaze. "You name it and it's yours," he told me. "What you did was fucking heroic. I know a bloke like you won't want to have anything to do with a bloke like me, but you need to know that whatever you need and whenever you need it, all you have to do is ask."

"I appreciate it. I really do. I don't personally want or need anything above having Carl involved on my behalf if either the police or the security services come back at me. Other than that, if you take care of Terry, then you and I are quits."

Nodding, Dawson said, "That I can do. Happily. The offer holds. Indefinitely."

He then looked up and beyond me. I turned to see Carl Ingham making his way towards us. "Mr Cochran is keeping his cool," he told me, taking a seat alongside Chris. "There are several stories here, and several points of conflict and death. He has admitted his role, assuming responsibility for every man down at the safe houses. Neither the police nor MI5 have enough to compel us to veer from the self-defence plea. In every case, Terry claims the mercenaries shot first."

I thought back to the house in Peterborough. Terry had fired off the first rounds, but it was nonetheless an act of self-defence because the four men were not there delivering flowers. Same goes for Thetford, and those initial kills in the wooded areas either side of the house. No point in splitting hairs, though. Them shooting first worked for me. I could live with that.

"The problem for the authorities," Carl went on, "is that whilst your story, Mike, is fine when it comes to your time together before Terry was drawn into the chain of events, all of your comments relating to what happened afterwards are anything but fine. There's Terry claiming it was all down to him, you claiming it was all down to you, and as for Mel… well, sadly nothing now can ever be corroborated."

Chris Dawson turned to face me. "You told them it was all you?"

I spread my hands. "Hey, I dragged my friend into this shit-storm, I wasn't about to bury him in it up to his neck."

"I don't think there's any danger of that," Carl said.

"And why is that?" I asked.

"Because his friends in intelligence will make it all disappear. The security services are putting on a show. Terry Cochran knows where the bodies are buried. Literally. He's done too much work for them over the years not to. Plus, I get the impression they are rather fond of him and his… particular talents."

I nodded. "Well, that's good to hear. So he'll be joining us?"

"You know him better than I do, Mr Lynch. I get the impression he may walk out of that police station and disappear as if he had never existed."

"So how about this shit with Melissa?" Chris asked. "Those pricks in Whitehall ordered the hit on her. It was their decision that led to all of this, my brother, the whole fucking deal. I know none of them will pay, because their involvement will be something else the security services bury. But how can we turn that around?"

Here, I shook my head and said, "I don't see that happening. I think Terry and I are safe from harm. Cards have been marked, though. Careers will spiral downwards. Knighthoods will no longer be bestowed. More importantly, those involved will know that I am now pretty much untouchable, or they will also become something the security services make disappear. As for the original hit, what happened to your brother and then to Mel, you'll find these people are Teflon-coated."

I was about to comment further, when Charlie entered the lounge clasping the hand of a woman I had not seen before. The moment the girl laid eyes on us she broke away and came running. Her first hug was for Dawson, whom she held tight, squeezing for all she was worth. Charlie giggled as she was hugged right back. But then she broke away from that embrace and fell into my arms.

"How are you doing, kiddo?" I asked, delighting at her exuberance. "You feeling all right?"

Charlie nodded, giving me a huge wide smile. "I spoke to Roger, and I told him I like you as well now. He said that was okay. So, I'm happy again."

I laughed. Since my release I had avoided finding out a way to contact my own daughter. I needed to give myself some time to start thinking straight again, the events of the past few days having swarmed all over me, leaving me feeling almost broken with emotion. But seeing Charlie again, feeling the girl in my arms, I realised that there was only one way my day could improve.

"Carl," I said. "Is there any way you can make a few calls for me?"

He nodded. "Of course. What do you need?"

"My mobile must be in evidence somewhere. I need a number off it. I have someone I need to call."

"Are you going to speak to Mel?" Charlie asked. Her innocent face was so sincere.

"Mel?" I frowned, hoping I did not have to explain the circumstances of Melissa's death to her.

Charlie nodded. "In heaven. Are you calling her in heaven?"

I stroked the girl's hair, and pulled her in close for another squeeze. "Not right now, Charlie," I said. "But maybe one day. You want to do that with me?"

She nodded. Tears formed in the corners of her eyes. I used my thumb to wipe them away. "It's going to be okay," I told her.

And for once, I genuinely thought it would be.

FORTY-SEVEN

Malta's northern coastline seemed like the ideal place to get away from it all, although Qawra felt a little too commercial for my taste. It was a scorching hot day and the town positively baked in the sunshine. You could not stare at the cloudless azure sky for long. To hide my bandaged wounds I wore a lightweight cotton shirt, which hung outside my knee-length cargo shorts. Still it felt like I was wearing three things too many. I had joined a group of fellow tourists in taking a small cruiser out to St Paul's island, and was now dragging my feet up the rocky, dirt-encrusted steep incline towards the island's peak, feeling the heat burn through the rubber soles of my flip-flops as they slapped against my heels. I carried a chilled bottle of water, purchased from the boat's skipper, from which I sipped a little every dozen paces or so. It was just two weeks after the events that had turned my whole world upside down, and I was still feeling the cumulative effects of those few days.

At the crest of the hill stood the statue of St Paul, which rose high above the remains of an old stone tower that had once provided a lookout over the sea. I continued to labour towards it for a few more paces, but it was getting the better of me. A couple of young kids, brother and sister by the look of it, sped past me on their way up. I both admired and cursed their youthful vigour. The sight of them making the climb with such ease was the final straw for me.

I stopped walking, resting my hands on my knees. As I gathered my breath, a shadow fell over me.

"Enjoying the view?" someone asked me.

I turned my head, squinting in the sunlight. Nodded. "Yeah. Looks great from here. Close enough for me I think. I guess this is far as I'll be going." I sat down on a nearby boulder, its surface heat almost causing me to cry out.

Melissa sat down beside me, setting her own bottle on the rock, letting out a long sigh as she stretched out her tanned legs. "I could get used to this," she said.

I smiled at her. "Well, you can. This is your home now."

"So it is. And it's beautiful. Please tell Terry how grateful I am," she said. "The couple he recommended me to have been great, and their daughter is so sweet."

An old army buddy of ours, now retired and living on the mainland further south, had the ideal family to help Melissa heal. Not all of her scars were visible, however.

"No lifting duties yet though," I said, nodding at her arm which was held in place across her midriff by a protective sling. Beneath her lemon-coloured T-shirt I could also make out the slight swell of padding held in place by her own bandages.

"Could have been worse, Mike. A whole lot worse."

"That's for sure."

We were both quiet for a few minutes, sitting there as a sudden breeze took the edge off the heat for a few precious moments.

"You think we can ever tell Charlie?" Melissa asked me. She took a swig of water from her bottle.

"Maybe. When she's old enough. Perhaps it's better not to, though."

"Perhaps."

I had conceived the idea of faking Melissa's death as she lay on the floor beside the truck that night she was shot, Charlie sobbing and wailing beside us. Faulkener lay defeated inside the old barracks, his men by then rounded up, I imagined. But the orders had come from a lofty position. It did not matter how many of them paid for their mistakes, nor in what manner. If Melissa had been seen as a threat for what she might know, then that was not going to go away. Others would undoubtedly come for her. The only way she would be safe was if they believed her to be dead.

Once again it was Terry who had known who to speak with and how to perpetrate the fiction. He had lived on the edge and in the shadows for so long that such things were second nature to him. He also arranged for the ambulance to arrive on scene, one that would whisk Mel away to a place of his choosing rather than to a hospital. Terry pointed us in the direction of a man who could quickly come up with the fake documentation Mel required, both to explain away her demise and to begin anew. Then he and I worked together on providing Mel with a place to run to, a new hope in a brand new life. I had spun the web of deceit told to everyone, and Terry had arranged for the right officials to be in the right place at the right time to allow the lie to stick. Between us we made certain that everyone believed precisely what we wanted them to believe.

It might last, it might not. But for now, it would have to be enough.

"Jesus, it's bloody hot," I said, wiping sweat from my hairline and glancing sidelong at Mel. She already looked so much healthier with good colour in her cheeks.

She smiled and shook her head. "You still complaining, Mike Lynch?"

I laughed. "Nothing changes, eh?"

Mel put her head back, allowing the sun to beat down on her exposed face. "Everything changes, Mike," she said. "Everything, all the time."

"Except me, then."

This time she raised her sunglasses and peered over at me. "No. Especially you. And that's no bad thing."

I nodded. It really was no bad thing at all.

THE END

ACKNOWLEDGEMENTS

It may come across as a little trite, but I really do want to thank Bloodhound Books once again for having faith in me. This is the book I was writing when they first signed me to their wonderful kennel of authors, and I was determined to finish it. Scream Blue Murder represents a departure for me, as I set myself a challenge with this one. The story came to me and I had to tell it. It was a fast-paced action thriller inside my head, and no matter how many ways I tried writing it, ultimately, I decided Mike Lynch simply had to be written in first person POV – something I had never done before. I hope you enjoyed the ride.

Printed in Great Britain
by Amazon